"Listen," Paul said.

Slow footsteps echoed, a soft crunch in the dark. At first Jack thought Ronnie turned the flashlight off and snuck into the tunnel in order to scare them, but the footsteps were too heavy. They belonged to someone bigger.

"Reach out your hand, Paul."

"Okay."

They started to go but something found Paul first.

It jerked Paul back, and purely out of reflex, Jack clamped on to Paul's hand, this alone preventing him from being torn back into the tunnel by whatever was down there.

"It's got me hooked! Its arm is around me!"

Jack felt Paul leave his feet as his attacker hoisted him into the air, intent on dragging Paul back into the tunnel.

It pulled again, like a shark dragging a swimmer down, and it was too strong. Paul's hand slipped from Jack's, and Paul shrieked.

"Let me go! Bastard! Let me go! God, it smells bad!"

Jack charged ahead and slammed into someone as solid as a muscle man in a magazine. He wrapped his arms around the waist and pulled, but it was like trying to drag down a redwood tree. He was being dragged behind the guy like tin cans on a weddng car. It stank like old leaves or hair that's clogged in a drain, wet and dead.

What is it and why did we have to run into it?

BOOK YOUR PLACE ON OUR WEBSITE AND MAKE THE READING CONNECTION!

We've created a customized website just for our very special readers, where you can get the inside scoop on everything that's going on with Zebra, Pinnacle and Kensington books.

When you come online, you'll have the exciting opportunity to:

- View covers of upcoming books

- Read sample chapters

- Learn about our future publishing schedule (listed by publication month *and author*)

- Find out when your favorite authors will be visiting a city near you

- Search for and order backlist books from our online catalog

- Check out author bios and background information

- Send e-mail to your favorite authors

- Meet the Kensington staff online

- Join us in weekly chats with authors, readers and other guests

- Get writing guidelines

- AND MUCH MORE!

Visit our website at
http://www.kensingtonbooks.com

CRUEL WINTER

ANTHONY IZZO

PINNACLE BOOKS
Kensington Publishing Corp.
http://www.kensingtonbooks.com

PINNACLE BOOKS are published by

Kensington Publishing Corp.
850 Third Avenue
New York, NY 10022

All Kensington Titles, Imprints, and Distributed Lines are
available at special quantity discounts for bulk purchases for
sales promotions, premiums, fund-raising, and educational
or institutional use. Special book excerpts or customized
printings can also be created to fit specific needs. For details,
write or phone the office of the Kensington special sales
manager: Kensington Publishing Corp., 850 Third Avenue,
New York, NY 10022, attn: Special Sales Department, Phone:
1-800-221-2647.

Pinnacle and the P logo Reg. U.S. Pat. & TM Off.

ISBN: 0-7860-1732-5

First Pinnacle Books Printing: September 2005

10 9 8 7 6 5 4 3 2 1

Printed in the United States of America

To Jenn, for your constant love and support. I couldn't have come this far without you.

CHAPTER 1

As Jack Harding walked down Main Street in Brampton, a snowblower hummed in the distance and an orange snowplow cruised past, spraying slush against the curb. The snow hills piled at the curbs stood as high as elephants and the flurries blew in sideways. But the snow didn't bother him. Not now. Christmas break was a week away. He was with Chris and Paul, the three of them ready to bash out a game of king of the mountain. Life couldn't be better.

"Hey, check it out," Chris said. He tapped Jack on the shoulder and pointed across the street. A kid in a red jacket and blue snow pants charged down Main Street. His head was lowered and he skidded every few feet.

"Who lit his ass on fire?" Jack said.

"Looks like he's on the run from someone," Chris said.

The kid looked up, waved to them. They kept walking and rounded the corner of the police station. In the lot, three snow mounds as high as the second-floor windows stood beyond the police cruisers. God bless the plow drivers.

"King of the mountain, baby!" Chris charged up the hill and stood at the top with hands on hips, his blond hair poking out from underneath the front of his cap. "Check out these hills."

"They must be ten feet high," Paul said.

"Which one of you is going to try and knock me off?" Chris said.

"You're a dead man," Jack said, plowing up the hill. Paul followed him.

Life stayed good, or at least normal, until fifteen minutes into the game, footsteps trod up the hill, the snow going crunch-crunch underneath. Jack heard them, turned his head, and saw someone reach the top, slip, and roll down the other side.

The kid stopped at the bottom and rolled onto his back and lay in a crucifixion pose. He had a moon-shaped face, pink cheeks, and narrow eyes, blue as the winter sky. He might have taken a men's small in that jacket, and his jeans seemed to bulge at the seams. Jack took him for about a hundred and fifty pounds, a baby moose.

"You guys gotta help me," he said, breathing hard.

They stood staring at the chubby kid. Chris with his arms folded as if he owned the whole hill and Paul wringing his hands and already looking over his shoulder for an escape route.

The new kid stood up. Jack climbed to the bottom of the hill, and his friends followed.

"Hi. I'm Ronnie Winter," he said, extending a gloved hand toward Jack.

Jack looked at Chris, then shrugged. Why not? Kids his age usually didn't shake hands upon meeting, but he didn't suppose it would hurt anything. "Jack Harding." Jack shook the gloved hand.

Ronnie approached Chris with an outstretched hand, but Chris kept his arms folded. This didn't seem to faze Ronnie and he walked right up to Paul and thrust his hand out. Paul looked at the hand as if it might grow teeth and bite him. He shook it quickly and jerked his hand back.

Ronnie's breath plumed out like exhaust from a tailpipe. "You guys have got to help me." He sucked in another deep breath. "They chased me all the way down Main."

"Who did?" Jack asked.

"Some greasy-looking kid with a big nose."

Jack's stomach fluttered, for he knew right away who had chased Ronnie down Main Street. None other than Vinnie Palermo. An invasion of flesh-eating aliens would be preferable to having Vinnie show up.

"Oh, shit. Vinnie?" Paul did a nervous little dance in the snow, as if he couldn't decide which way to run first. "I have to go."

Jack didn't blame Paul for being jittery, and if Vinnie had busted Jack's nose at one time, he might want to run, too.

"Relax, Fussel. He won't do anything while I'm here," Chris said.

"That's easy for you to say, too-tall," Paul said.

"Yeah, you could bench-press him if you wanted to," Jack said.

"Twenty-four-inch pythons," Chris said, flexing his biceps.

"I got your twenty-four inches right here," Jack said.

"So will you guys help me?" Ronnie said.

Before Jack could answer, Vinnie Palermo stormed over the top of the bank.

Vinnie stood at the crest of the hill, wearing a jean jacket with a black T-shirt underneath, despite the twenty-degree temperature. His slicked-back hair exposed a pimple-ridden forehead, and one bushy black eyebrow loomed over his eyes like a storm cloud. Vinnie kicked the toe of his black work boots into the snow and started down the hill.

Jack noticed Vinnie didn't take his eyes off Chris the whole time, and with good reason, because Chris might pound him into the snow like a railroad stake if given the chance.

"Come here, you fat faggot," Vinnie said.

As many times as Jack had seen Vinnie, he never got over the freakish nose that occupied a good portion of Vinnie's face. It was hooked, with a small lump in the bridge, and looked as if some practical joker of a sculptor slapped a triangular piece of flesh in the center of his face. The nostrils were large and little nose hairs jutted from them. The kids all called him "the beak" or "the schnoz," but never when he was in earshot. Doing so might result in early death.

Vinnie stepped toward Ronnie, who backpedaled.

"Come here." Vinnie beckoned him with a finger. "I'm not going to tell you again."

"What's your beef with him?" Chris asked.

"Stay out of this," Vinnie said.

Vinnie advanced on Ronnie, and Joe Leary climbed over the hill. He was stocky and dark-haired, with a face full of brown freckles. Leary wore a dirty leather jacket and black jeans, now caked with salt around the ankles. They had to deal with Vinnie and one of his flunkies. Not good.

"There's fat boy," Leary said.

"Just what did he do to you?" Jack said.

"Threw a snowball at me," Vinnie said.

"You started it," Ronnie said.

"I don't like getting hit with snowballs."

"Didn't hit you," Ronnie muttered.

"Did too. And if I said you did, you did."

Vinnie's coat was dry as dust, which led Jack to believe Ronnie's snowball had missed its target.

He took another step toward Ronnie. Paul flinched as Vinnie approached, and the shark smelled blood. With a wicked grin on his face, he shoved Paul, and Paul tumbled backward, landing on his ass and scrambling backward like a crab. Leary laughed, a dirty heh-heh-heh.

"You're coming with me, fat ass." Vinnie clenched his teeth as if he might bite Ronnie's nose off. It wasn't out of the question.

"Take a walk before I decide to beat on you," Chris said.

"Bite me, Francis."

Vinnie lunged for Ronnie, but Chris intercepted and grabbed him by the jacket and spun him around. Vinnie swung at Chris, but Chris threw his arm up and blocked the punch.

Jack spotted Leary chugging down the hill to help out

Vinnie. No way Chris could handle both of them, so Jack decided to help, even if it cost him later.

Vinnie rose to his feet, and Jack snuck up behind him, hooked his foot around Vinnie's ankle, and shoved. Vinnie sprawled and landed face-first in the snow.

God, that felt good, Jack thought.

Chris turned toward Leary, who lowered his head and slammed into him. Grabbing Leary's coat by the shoulders, he turned and flung him aside. Now Vinnie was on his feet, a thin line of snow coating his eyebrows and the front of his hair. He looked like an evil snowman coming to get revenge on someone for stealing his top hat.

"You're dead, Harding," he said, pointing at Jack. He reached into his jacket pocket, flicked his wrist, and pulled out a gold butterfly knife.

Paul muttered, "Oh no."

What would it feel like to get stabbed? Would the blade feel hot or cold as it pierced him?

Ronnie stood with his mouth open, as if surprised one snowball caused all this commotion. It was his fault, damn it. Even if you were new to town, you didn't go around throwing snowballs at people like Vinnie Palermo.

Vinnie started forward, the blade looking as big as a cutlass. Even Chris looked worried.

"I'm gonna cut you in half, Harding."

"No, you won't."

The voice came from the top of the snowbank. It was Officer Stavros, his thick black mustache coated with snow. A blue knit cap was jammed on his head, and he carried a blue duffel bag with the word *Police* written on the side. He was either leaving or coming to work.

"What's this all about?"

"We were playing king of the mountain when these two idiots showed up," Jack said.

"That fat fuck threw a snowball at me," Vinnie said, then added, "Officer."

"Watch your mouth, Palermo. And give me the knife," Stavros said.

"Why don't you come and get it?"

"Maybe I should throw your butt in one of our cells."

"Fine," he said, giving Stavros a look that said: *I would like to see you eat a shit sandwich.*

Vinnie lunged at Jack, feigning attack. Jack flinched, expecting Vinnie to drive the knife into his belly.

"This isn't over." Vinnie pointed at Jack. "Not by a mile."

Officer Stavros took the knife from Vinnie, folded it, and slid it into his coat pocket. "I want all of you to go home. Palermo, you and your friend leave first. And don't get any ideas about an ambush. I'll be watching you," he said.

Vinnie and Joe Leary trudged over the snowbank and disappeared into the swirling flurries.

"Stay away from those two. I really think he would have stabbed you," Stavros said.

"Me too," Jack agreed.

They walked out of the lot, Jack expecting Vinnie and Joe Leary to be waiting for them, but they were gone. The snow whipped around them and Jack had hoped for at least one day home from school, but the superintendent was a stubborn son of a bitch and kept it open. He didn't have to walk in it.

The four boys turned right onto Main Street, Chris and Jack in front, Ronnie and Paul behind them.

"You guys saved me back there," Ronnie said.

"You almost got us killed," Chris said.

"Sorry," Ronnie said, hanging his head.

"I think Chris is exaggerating," Jack said.

"Just what is Vinnie's problem, anyway?" Ronnie said.

"Terminal case of asshole fever," Jack said, and the others laughed.

"He's a Neanderthal," Paul said.

"What the hell is that, Fussel?" Chris asked.

"It's a caveman," Paul said.

"Who told you that?"

"I read it in *National Geographic*." Paul rolled his eyes. "You might know that if you ever read a book."

"I read," Chris said.

"*Sports Illustrated*," Paul said.

"Knock it off, you guys," Jack said. "So, Ronnie, what happened with you and Vinnie?"

"Him and that other kid were coming down the street. When they passed by me, Vinnie called me a fat pig. So I made up a little snow missile and fired it at him."

"Did you score a hit?" Paul asked.

"Naw. It went over his head and plopped on the sidewalk. But it pissed him off pretty good."

"You got balls, kid. I'll give you that," Chris said.

Jack wasn't sure if that was a compliment or if it meant Ronnie was really stupid.

"You think so?" Ronnie said. He had a big grin on his face, as if Chris had bestowed on him the ultimate compliment.

"Yeah. Vinnie doesn't screw around," Chris said. "A couple years ago he slashed Frankie Coldgrass across the arm with a razor blade. Kid had ten stitches."

"Wow," Ronnie said.

"I'd stay away from him," Paul said. "Broke my nose two years ago."

"You'd stay away from a kitty cat, you pansy," Chris said.

Jack burst into laughter at Chris's use of the words "kitty cat," and was still laughing thirty seconds later when they reached Argon Street.

"What's so funny?" Paul said.

"Nothing," he said. Sometimes certain phrases just got to you and ignited a big old belly laugh. It was usually during a test or in church, where you would get into the most trouble, and it was always uncontrollable.

"Well, boys, this is my stop," Chris said. "You'd better watch your back, kid. Vinnie doesn't forget easy." Chris turned down Argon Street, giving them a wave, and the three boys continued down Main. The wind gusted and Jack tucked his chin to his chest for protection.

"How long have you been here, Ronnie?" Paul asked.

"We moved onto the Steadman place a week ago."

Jack stopped. The kid was full of crap. The Steadman property was over eight hundred acres and had a selling price of three million dollars. There was a thirty-thousand-square-foot mansion, houses for groundskeepers, stables, and barns. Harold Steadman III had died of a heart attack five years ago and the property sat vacant. Nobody wanted it because of its history, and the state of New York was ready to snatch it up and make it a park. Apparently they found a buyer.

"You live in the Steadman place?" Jack said.

"Yep."

"And I'm the king of France," Paul said.

"Then we'll go there and I'll prove it to you guys."

Jack would give his left nut to see even the grounds of the estate, and to see the mansion he might cheerfully give them both up. "Let's go then."

"Not me. My dad will kill me if I'm late for dinner," Paul said.

"Later, Paul."

"Later."

Paul ran across Main, dodging a Metro bus, whose driver blasted the horn at him.

The wind rippled Jack's scarf like a piece of ribbon.

"Let's get out of this cold and see this house of yours."

CHAPTER 2

Emma Greer's head throbbed and her throat felt raw. Cold sweat enveloped her body, and no matter how tightly she wrapped herself in a comforter, the fever made her shiver.

Strep throat was a pisser, as Mom might say. The last week of school before Christmas break was starting tomorrow, and she was going to miss it. The teachers served punch and cookies and let the last few days of class slip by with no homework assignments. And Emma was missing it because of lousy strep throat. She thought Christmas was a little silly, keeping a tree in your living room, but the parties were fun.

Her mother entered the bedroom carrying a tray with a navy blue bowl and a matching coffee cup on it. Myra Greer had the same rich olive skin as her daughter, and her black hair showed strands of gray at the temples. The first signs of crow's-feet appeared around her eyes, and she had a few more wrinkles around the mouth every year. They weren't from smiling.

"Hello, dear." She set the tray on Emma's lap. "Brought you some tomato soup and tea."

"Thanks."

She placed the back of her hand on Emma's cheek.

"You're still warm," she said, caressing Emma's hair.

"Cold, too."

"Those antibiotics we got from Dr. Spears should start kicking in soon."

"I hope so. I want to go out and play."

"We'll see about that when the fever goes away."

"You don't want me playing with them, do you?"

"Emma, you know how I feel," her mom said.

"They're my friends." She picked up the spoon and dabbed at the soup.

"They're also boys. Twelve-year-old girls are supposed to play with girls. Not dirty, grubby boys. Now if one of those boys asked you on a date, it might be different, but I don't like you playing football and street hockey with them."

"All the girls talk about is Duran Duran and how cute Simon LeBon is and all that other crap."

"Watch your mouth."

Why couldn't her mother understand that? The girls at Brampton Middle were dipsticks, always talking about the latest copy of *Tiger Beat* or bragging that their mothers let them wear eye shadow. Big deal. Makeup was for clowns and mimes. Give her a baggy sweatshirt and a pair of faded jeans and she was happy.

"Have you thought about the school dance?" Her mother wrung her hands and looked down at them, something she did a lot lately.

"Are you kidding?"

"Just asking."

She would never tell her mother, but she secretly hoped Jack Harding might ask her to the dance. Lately she found herself wanting to spend time with Jack and not the other boys, but she really could not say why. Chris and Paul were nice guys, but Jack was the one she thought about. About the two of them walking home from school together and him slipping his hand into hers. That was her secret, and thumb-screws couldn't get her to tell it to anyone.

"I don't want to go to any stupid dance," she said.

Emma slipped her hand from under the blanket, picked up the teacup.

"Most girls your age want to do those things."

"Well, I don't."

"I wish you would, Emma. You're such a pretty girl."

"No way."

"I'll buy you a dress."

"You asked me that before and I think I said no."

Her mother wrung her hands again. She had purplish bags under her eyes and she always slumped a bit when she walked, the sixty hours a week of work as a seamstress taking its toll on her. All day long she ran cloth through a sewing machine at the M. Wile Factory, making suits for junior executives.

"At least think about it."

Emma lifted her spoon and slurped soup.

Mom stood up and stopped when she reached the doorway.

"You're too pretty a girl to be hanging around with a group of dirty boys all the time."

"I like them."

"And that music you listen to."

"It's cool."

"I don't approve of some of it. Men with long hair."

The Motley Crue tape in her storage crate would blow Mom's mind. "Are we done? I'd like to finish my soup."

"It's those violent games you play."

"King of the mountain isn't violent."

"Paul sprained his wrist last year playing on the snow mounds."

"He's a wussy."

"Emma . . ."

"Well, he is."

"There's no talking to you anymore. I just don't know," she said, shaking her head and leaving the room.

Let her be mad. The only reason she did not want Emma

hanging out with boys was that Myra Greer had issues with
men in general. Emma'a father, Frederick, had gone out for
a newspaper when Emma was four and never come back.
That had stuck in her mother's craw for years, Mom blaming
herself for him leaving. So when she criticized Emma for
hanging out with boys, Emma knew her father's leaving was
at the root of it. But Mom wanted Emma to take one to the
school dance, which made no sense. Maybe she was afraid
her little girl might turn into one of the dirty boys.

If only she knew about cousin Jacob.

That was one dirty boy.

Jacob was seventeen years old, five years Emma's senior.

Emma had developed breasts last spring, and by summer
she needed a regular bra, having gone well beyond the training stage. For most of the summer she had worn baggy
T-shirts, but there was a week in August when the temperature spiked to ninety and only a tank top would suffice. That
Monday in August, she put on a yellow tank top and a pair of
cutoff Levi's, not caring if her new boobs looked as big as
zeppelins. At least she felt cool.

Aunt Samantha invited them for a cookout that evening,
and as always, Jacob was home. Jacob was always home,
practicing his violin, which Aunt Sam claimed was his ticket
to Carnegie Hall. Emma imagined him up there picking
boogers out of his nostrils and eating them. It suited him better than Carnegie Hall.

They had been at her aunt's an hour, sitting by the in-
ground pool and drinking lemonade. Uncle Rex fired up the
grill and tossed on chicken breasts marinated in Italian dress-
ing, along with potatoes wrapped in foil. Emma drained the
last of her lemonade and got up to get herself a refill.

She entered the kitchen, opened the door on the Amana,
and took out the pitcher of lemonade. Aunt Sam had not put
ice in the pitcher and Emma wanted a few cubes to chill the
drink even more. She opened the freezer and mist rose from
inside. As she gripped the ice cube tray, it slid from her hand
and crashed on the floor. But the cubes stayed in the tray.

She shut the freezer door and bent over to pick up the tray. Jacob stood in the doorway, his eyes fixed on Emma's chest. She made eye contact with him, expecting him to look away in embarrassment, but he kept right on looking. She hopped to her feet, leaving the ice cube tray on the floor.

"Hey, Emma."

"What do you want?"

Why were boys so interested in boobs?

"Looking good."

"Whatever."

He stepped forward, so close she smelled the body odor that followed him like a cloud of poisonous gas. She noticed rings of damp sweat around his armpits and wondered why he didn't just invest in some deodorant.

"Looks like things are blossoming," he said.

"Excuse me?"

"I mean the cherry blossoms in the yard."

"I have to pick up these ice cubes."

"Go right ahead. Hope nothing falls out."

God, he was a booger.

Squatting down, she clasped her top closed as best she could. Then she scooped up the tray and stood up to prevent him from peering down her shirt.

When she tried squeezing past him, the trouble started.

"Where you going?"

"Going to put these back in the freezer, where you think?"

She slid past him and to her utter shock, his hand shot out and pinched her hard on the left cheek. Emma spun around and he gripped her by the shoulders, pinning her to the fridge. The metal felt cool against her shoulders and the little vegetable-shaped magnets dug into the middle of her back.

He looked down at her chest.

"Things really are blossoming," he said. Jacob's breath smelled like rancid salami.

Then he slid a hand up her top and squeezed her right breast. A small choking noise escaped her lips, and she wanted to scream, but all she managed was a gurgle.

He pulled his hand out and backed away.

"You're a real shit, Jacob."

"You liked it."

She tore out of the kitchen and darted out the screen door to the patio, slamming into her mother on the way out.

"Emma! Slow down."

She looked up at her mother, positive her face was the color of strawberry jam. Tears ran down her cheeks and she wiped them away.

"What's wrong, honey?"

"Nothing."

"Don't tell me nothing."

Come up with a lie, and quick.

"Um. There was a wasp in the kitchen and it landed on my hand. It scared me."

"Did it sting you?"

"No," she said, sniffing.

"I'll have Uncle Rex see if he can find the little pest, okay?"

"You might want to look in Jacob's room," she said.

Mom gave her a puzzled look but said nothing and they returned to the patio. Emma crossed her arms over her breasts just in case the booger was around, hoping to get another peek at her. She remained by the side of the pool for the rest of the evening, not daring to enter the house for fear of running into Jacob.

That had effectively ruined the rest of her summer.

If only her mom knew what had happened, she would never accuse Jack of being a dirty boy again. He wasn't the kind of guy who would grab a girl like that.

But unfortunately, Jacob took pleasure in things like that, and with the holiday coming up, she would be seeing a lot more of him.

She had to find a way to stay away from him.

*   *   *

They walked up to spiked iron gates. A cobblestone wall ran from the gates and along the road, surrounding the edge of the property. A rectangular speaker stood mounted on a pole with a white button labeled TALK.

"I'll call for our driver," Ronnie said.

"A driver?"

"Yeah. You didn't think we were going to walk all the way to the house, did you?"

Jack supposed it was a pretty long walk.

He hoped the driver would hurry, because his lungs ached from the cold.

Ronnie pressed the white button and a moment later a deep voice came over the intercom.

"May I help you?"

"It's me, John."

"Who's me?"

"Ronnie."

"And?"

"Can you come get me? I'm at the main gate."

"Be right out."

The intercom buzzed and crackled.

Five minutes later, a boat of a limo pulled up to the gates, its windows a shiny onyx.

"Watch out," Ronnie said, stepping back.

Jack did the same.

A motor hummed, and the gates swung open.

Ronnie and Jack approached the car and a bald black man stepped out of the limo, wisps of steam rising from his head. He looked big enough to play linebacker for the Giants and his wool overcoat strained at the shoulders.

"Hi, John," Ronnie said.

"Master Ronnie." His voice reminded Jack of Lurch on *The Addams Family*.

"This is Jack," Ronnie said.

John approached them and offered a leather-gloved hand to Jack. Jack took it, and the big man pumped his hand.

"Jack's gonna come up and see the house," Ronnie said.

"Outstanding." John let go of his hand. "Maybe have some cocoa and cookies?"

"Yeah," Jack said.

"Great," John said, clapping Jack on the shoulder.

John opened the passenger door for them and once they piled into the limo, he closed it behind them.

The interior of the limo was dark gray with walnut paneling on the doors. Crystal tumblers rested in a bar next to a decanter of honey-colored liquor.

"That's scotch," Ronnie said.

"You think I didn't know that?"

John ducked into the driver's seat and a moment later they rolled toward the estate.

"I bet Vinnie wouldn't bother you if John was around," Jack said.

"Hell yeah," Ronnie said.

They drove the rest of the way in silence, an endless sheet of snow dancing across the windows. As they drove uphill, the limo's motor hummed. They passed a crisp white barn and stables surrounded by a split rail fence. Jack saw no horses, but they were probably inside to protect them from the cold.

Farther up were three red houses, all with firewood stacked on the porches. The front doors all had an S in the center. Did the Steadmans forget their last name started with S?

"Those are the groundskeepers' houses. John lives in one of them."

Jack gasped when he saw the mansion, four stories of gray stone with long, narrow windows. Ivy spiraled down the walls like a brown waterfall and twin turrets stood at either end of the mansion, giving the appearance of a medieval fortress. The roof jutted out in points and gables, and a dozen chimneys rose from it. Jack had never seen anything like it.

They pulled around a circular driveway in front of the steps, which led to two doors made of heavy wood. An iron knocker was secured in the center of each. Twin lions flanked the steps, each caught in midroar and challenging any would-be intruders to the mansion.

John opened the door and the two boys climbed out of the limo and into the lengthening shadows. A statue of an arm-less, bare-breasted woman stood in the center of the circle, like something out of a museum.

"This way. And watch your step going up the stairs." John pointed to the steps. "They're a little slick from the ice."

They ascended the steps, rock salt crunching under their boots.

"What do you think?" Ronnie said.

"Amazing."

CHAPTER 3

Paul reached the side door, wheezing and puffing from the run home.

As daylight had faded, he broke into a run, hoping to get home and avoid an appointment with the belt or extension cord. In the process of sprinting home, he had hit an icy patch and skidded sideways into a snowbank. Dark, wet patches covered his pants, and he felt as if he had stuck his rear end in the freezer for an hour. He couldn't let his father see his pants like this.

Paul opened the door and to his relief it didn't squeak. Once inside he slipped off his moon boots and placed them on the welcome mat next to the cases of Molson Canadian. The General was never without a constant supply of the stuff, and Paul didn't know how much beer cost, but he guessed it wasn't cheap. When he had asked for a new Huffy over the summer, his father replied: "Not enough money around." But there always seemed to be enough money for beer.

He padded up the stairs, opened the side door, and stepped into the gloom. The house had a stale, sour smell that his mother never failed to remove despite repeated cleanings with ammonia. The smell made him ill, and he felt somehow cheated because you weren't supposed to hate the way your house smelled. It reminded him of a hospital or funeral home, one of the places where the smell was supposed to turn you off. Jack's house always smelled like baking cookies or the fresh flowers his mother kept on the table. Why couldn't his house smell like that?

He snuck across the kitchen, listening every step of the way for heavy footsteps to approach from behind. "Ride of the Valkyries" blared from the living room, his father watching *Apocalypse Now* for the umpteenth time. Paul could almost see the Hueys whizzing overhead with guns and rockets blazing. His father had seen it forty or so times, and other war movies were close seconds, most notably *Patton* and *The Longest Day*.

Paul crept down the hallway to his bedroom and eased the door shut. The hum of his aquarium pump filled the room and it felt soothing. This was the only place in the whole house he felt comfortable. He had his goldfish (Frodo, Sam, and Gollum), a stack of *Dungeons and Dragons* books, and his *Lord of the Rings* trilogy, purchased at a garage sale for seventy-five cents. That was the best money he ever spent.

A poster of Darth Vader hung on the wall. The Dark Lord of the Sith was shrouded in fog and his light-saber cut through the mist, and Paul often imagined himself as Vader, all-powerful. Vader choked enemies without even touching them, and the Dark Lord would not be afraid of his father.

Ever mindful of his father's presence, Paul stripped off his pants, socks, and shirt before the General saw him like this. He took out an A-Team T-shirt and other dry clothes. After changing into them, he balled up the wet ones, crept into the bathroom, and shoved them into the hamper, careful to bury them under the other items.

As he returned to his room, his mother's snores came from her bedroom. She would wake up soon, cook something of the frozen variety, and stay up until eleven o'clock reading Harlequin novels. Then it was back to bed for more sleep. That was all she did, sleep and eat. Maybe it was her way of avoiding the asshole.

He opened the lid to his aquarium and picked up the box of fish food. It was slick on the sides and he jerked to catch it, but it hit the floor and spilled the brown flakes all over the rug. The lid rolled like a runaway quarter and hit the bed before stopping.

He bent down and brushed the flakes into his cupped hand.

"What are you doing?"

Paul looked up at his father, who looked nine feet tall in the doorway. Five o'clock shadow filled in around his jaw and his eyes were bloodshot and glassy.

His father stepped forward, his striped tie askew and the dress shirt untucked. "So?"

"I dropped the fish food." Paul continued scraping up the flakes.

"I can see that, genius."

"Sorry." The fishy scent of the flakes was all he smelled, but it beat his father's sour beer breath.

"Clean this up. You're always doing stuff like this, Paul, and I don't know why."

Paul wanted to crawl under the bed and live with the dust bunnies. That was cowardly, and he knew if Darth Vader or Strider were here, either would lop off the General's ugly head. Paul wished he could be that brave, but his father's gaze usually turned his legs to pudding.

"Paul. There you go daydreaming again. How do you expect to get anywhere with your head in the clouds? You're so unfocused."

Paul looked down at the carpet and let the flakes fall off his hand and into the container.

"And I thought you were going to take these posters down. They're babyish."

"I like them."

"Are you being a smart-ass?"

Paul shook his head.

"Better not be." He scratched his belly and yawned. "I want these posters taken down. You're almost a teenager."

His father turned to leave and Paul could have left things at that, but he loved the posters and wanted them on the walls.

"I'm not taking them down."

His father stopped and rubbed his chin, the stubble making sandpaper noises. "Knock it off, okay?"

"I'm not taking them down. I like them," Paul said, folding his arms.

The General strode forward and hoisted Paul up by the arm, scattering fish flakes across the rug and sending the container rolling. He got up close to Paul's face. The smell of old beer and sweat filled Paul's nostrils.

"I'll take the damn things down myself."

He shoved Paul to the floor and tore the Darth Vader poster, ripping the Dark Lord's head off. The remaining part of the poster sagged like a dying flower. He crumpled the poster in his hand and tossed it at Paul.

"Take the rest of it down," he said.

He stalked off, leaving Paul with a sore arm and a ruined poster. And damn that son of a bitch, Paul burst into tears.

Jack felt as if he had stepped into something resembling a basilica. The floor in the entrance was white marble and he had to crane his neck to view the vaulted ceiling. Paintings that looked like they belonged in museums hung on the walls and a gold-framed mirror near the doorway appeared to be worth more than his father's car. To top it off, a white baby grand piano waited for someone to come over and tickle it.

"Take your coat off," Ronnie said.

Jack unzipped his coat and felt it pulled from his arms. He turned around to find John smiling down on him and neatly tucking a hanger into the coat. John then took Ronnie's coat and hung it on a coatrack inside the doorway.

"Would you gentlemen like some cocoa and cookies?"

"Sure, but I have to be home by six," Jack said.

"John will drive you home, right, John?"

"Certainly," John said.

John motioned for them to follow and they did, strolling down a crème-colored hallway and arriving in a kitchen that rivaled Jack's house in size. Silver pots and pans hung on a rack over stainless steel counters. Everything was stainless, the counters, the commercial-size ovens, and even the door to a walk-in freezer.

The burner on the stove hissed to life as John turned the knob. He reached up and took down a pan, then sidestepped to the fridge and got out a gallon of milk. It lapped into the pan as he poured.

John headed for a wooden door at the far end of the kitchen.

"That's the pantry," Ronnie said.

John returned with two packets of cocoa and a sleeve of chocolate chip cookies. Jack heard the milk start to bubble in the pan and John took two white mugs from under the counter and poured the hot milk into them. Then he tore open the packets and stirred in the powdered mix. After fixing the cocoa, he left down the hallway from which they had come.

"Have a seat," Ronnie said.

Ronnie hoisted himself up onto one of the stools and grabbed the counter for balance. His rear end half slid off the stool and he had a panicked look as if he knew he was going to hit the floor. He lost his grip on the counter and plopped onto the floor. Jack stifled a laugh.

"You're not too swift on your feet, are you?" Jack said.

"Shut up." Ronnie stood up, rubbing his hip.

They managed to get on the stools without further incident, and Jack ripped open the wax paper wrapper that enclosed the cookies.

"You guys saved my butt at the police station."

"I wouldn't go pissing off Vinnie again. He's probably going to get you back."

Jack took a cookie from the package and flipped it so it landed in his palm.

"I'm used to bullies," he said.

Ronnie looked down at his cocoa with a weariness Jack had never seen in someone his own age. He studied the kid for a second, the fleshy face, the broad nose, and the freckles covering his cheeks. Ronnie's hair came down straight across his forehead in a bowl cut that would have made Moe Howard proud. Kids like Ronnie were like chum to sharks, and it was a shame, because he probably deserved better.

Ronnie took his third cookie from the sleeve.

"Make sure you steer clear of Vinnie. At least for a few weeks."

"He'd better steer clear of me. Hey, wanna see the pool?"

"Sure."

"Ronnie." It was a woman's voice.

"That's my mom. Let's go see what she wants."

Ronnie slid off the stool and rumbled down the hallway. Jack looked around, thinking you could host a cooking show in a kitchen like this. In his entrancement with the kitchen, he did not notice John slipping up behind him.

"How's those cookies?"

"Not homemade, but they'll do."

"I heard Ronnie say you saved him. What happened?" John pulled up the stool vacated by Ronnie and sat down.

"Just some bullies."

"Tell me about it."

Jack told him what had happened outside the police station.

"Ronnie's always had trouble. Sometimes he starts it and sometimes he doesn't, but that boy's a magnet for bullies."

"He told me that, too."

"Couple years ago some kids beat him into a coma," John said.

"That sucks. Why'd they do it?"

"Didn't like the look of him. Or maybe because he's overweight. People don't need a reason to be mean to one another."

"What happened to the kids that beat him?"

"They were punished."

"Like sent to the Father Baker Home?" Jack asked.

"Not a boys' home, but they got theirs."

Jack desperately wanted to know what had happened to these kids. "Did they go to a regular prison?"

"Another time. You think Ronnie can be your friend?"

"Sure."

"Good. He needs someone to look out for him."

John leaned in close again, showing bloodshot webs running through the whites of his eyes. His bald head seemed enormous.

He lowered his voice to a whisper. "If you're gonna be Ronnie's friend, there is two things you have to know. Always be good to him in front of his mother. You'll meet her shortly. And if you're coming to the estate . . ." He looked over Jack's head to make sure no one was coming. Then he looked Jack in the eye and placed his hands on Jack's shoulders. "Never stray away from the house. Stay in the house proper."

"Sure, John."

"Promise me."

"Promise."

He patted Jack on the shoulder and said, "You listen to those two things and you'll be just fine."

Something about John's words chilled him to the core.

CHAPTER 4

Ronnie poked his head into the kitchen. "Come on and meet my mom."

Jack slid off the stool and wiped his mouth with the back of his hand. He followed Ronnie out of the kitchen and down the crème hallway until they wound up in a study.

The room had bookshelves on all sides, stacked to the ceiling and filled with leather-bound volumes that looked like they belonged at Oxford. The fire warmed Jack's skin as he entered the room, and a log hissed from inside the firebox. Jack looked around, taking the room in, and glanced out the window to see the silhouette of the woods in the distance. It made him think of John's warning to stay in the house, and there was no likelihood of him going into those dark woods.

He had been so enamored with the room he didn't notice the woman sitting in the leather wingback chair.

"Like the room?"

Jack nodded.

She was the opposite of Ronnie. Where Ronnie was short and squat, the woman was tall and the bell-bottom jeans she wore clung to her long legs. She stood up and seemed to glide toward Jack, a smile on her face.

Up close she was a knockout. Flowing red hair and eyes as blue as the Caribbean. A generous mouth with full lips that nearly matched the color of her hair. If he saw her on the street, she would warrant a second or third look, no question.

"You're quite a handsome boy. If you haven't figured it out, I'm Ronnie's mother. Cassie Winter." She held out her hand and he shook it. Cassie watched him, smiling, and he thought his knees might turn to Jell-O pudding. She seemed to enjoy watching him.

"What are you thinking right now? Be honest."

"About Christmas break."

"Are not."

"Really—"

"You think I'm pretty, don't you?"

Jack looked away, examined the books on the shelves. "Yes."

"That's okay. Come here."

Cassie held out her hand and he took it. She led him to another wingback opposite hers and sat down, crossing those long legs and letting her foot dangle. "Who are those boys that bothered Ronnie?"

"Vinnie Palermo and Joe Leary. Couple of goons."

Ronnie sauntered in and plopped down on the floor next to Cassie's chair.

"Had to take a leak," he said.

"Ronald," Cassie said.

"So you chased these boys away?" she asked Jack.

"Not exactly."

"Ronnie could use a good friend like you."

Jack shrugged.

"Why not?" he said.

The mantel clock dinged six times.

"Crap. I have to be home at six." He tried to stand up, but Cassie placed a hand on his arm, and he immediately felt a sense of calm. It was like lying on a warm beach, the sun pleasantly browning his skin, and sinking into the throes of an afternoon nap. He exhaled, relaxing but still thinking about Mom grounding him. And being grounded during Christmas break would suck the big one.

"I can see the worry in your face, Jack. I'll take care of your mother. And, Ronnie, what did I tell you about antagonizing bullies?"

"They started it," he said.

"Ronnie," she said.

"Okay. No more."

"John, will you drive Jack home?"

Jack turned to see John leaning against the doorjamb, arms folded in front of him.

"Of course."

"Don't worry about your parents, just tell them where you were and it will be fine," Cassie said.

She smiled and Jack felt his knees go to syrup again. Any man who saw that smile must have fallen in love with her, whether he wanted to or not.

"Are you okay?"

"Just a little dizzy," he said.

Ronnie poked him in the arm. "I hope we're in the same class," he said.

"That'd be pretty cool."

It occurred to Jack he hadn't seen Ronnie at school yet.

"You're just starting a week before Christmas break. Man, are you a lucky dog!"

"Two weeks off right away. Not bad for the new kid," Ronnie said.

If the new kid kept pissing off Vinnie and his gang, he might wind up with a broken nose, or worse. At Brampton Middle (and other schools, he was sure), the fat kids, the speech-impeded, and the science geeks were fodder for the cannons. Ronnie's being fat put him behind a very large eight ball right from the start.

"Ronnie, go wash up for dinner."

Jack turned to follow his new friend.

"Jack, can I talk to you before you go?"

What was this all about?

* * *

Alan Quinn kicked his '73 Buick in the rust patch that occupied the driver's-side door. Little flakes of rust crumbled off, landed in the freshly fallen snow, and were covered as quickly as they hit. He should have kicked his own ass for forgetting to stop at the Sunoco, for the needle had been just above E when he left the house, and now he was stuck.

Now he stood beside the car on Big Fork Road, next to the pines that marked the edge of the old Steadman property. He kicked the car again, this time muttering "bitch" under his breath as if the car were at fault.

Clear mucus trickled from his nose and he wiped it with the back of his glove. Five minutes in this Antarctica and his nose ran. The pine trees rocked back and forth, swishing and shaking with the wind. Every few minutes, headlights passed him, but no one stopped to offer help.

He opened the door, pulled the keys from the ignition, and proceeded to open the trunk. He shoved aside a wool blanket and jumper cables until he found the five-gallon gas can he kept for times such as these. A shake of the can confirmed it was dry.

Not only was the weather rotten and his chances of flagging down a car slim, but he was missing out on an early Christmas present. Carrie's parents were in Orlando for two weeks and she had promised him a gift that involved whipped cream and her naked body. If he made it to her house and collected his present, the ensuing story would make him a legend in the dorms.

He checked his watch, and it read ten after six. He'd promised Carrie he'd be there between six-thirty and seven, and she told him not to be late. After closing the trunk and zipping his parka, he started down the road, head down to minimize the effects of the wind.

He followed Big Fork Road, walking parallel to the wrought-iron fence that protected the Steadman property from the common folk on the road. Five minutes later, he passed a set of gates and the driveway leading to the mansion. Upon second glance, he noticed the gates were opened and thought it strange. He shrugged and trudged through the snow.

A minute later, he heard something under the wind, a low crunching sound that moved along in a steady beat.

He stopped and turned, shielding his brow, hoping to see through the flurries of snow, but blinded by the darkness. He heard it again. Swish-crunch, swish-crunch.

"Anybody there?"

Don't get freaked out, just keep walking.

He turned around again to find someone standing three feet from him.

"Hey."

Something struck him in the chest, feeling like a piston, and knocked him backward. He hit the ground and the freezing snow stung his cheek and filled his ears, making him feel as if he were listening through cotton. As he tried to rise, the someone pinned him down, a cold hand closing on his throat.

CHAPTER 5

"See you tomorrow at school," Ronnie said. He tromped out of the room.

"I'll bring the limo up," John said.

Cassie thanked him.

"Have a seat, Jack," she said, opening her hand, palm up, to indicate the wingback chair.

Jack sat back down, and Cassie sat opposite him, tucking her legs underneath her.

"Ronnie's different," she said.

"How do you mean?"

"Come on, Jack."

"Maybe a little."

"Then we agree. I'd like you to watch out for him."

Jack shifted in his seat and the leather squeaked underneath him.

"I know you just met him, but he needs help. His mouth has a habit of acting before his brain can stop it. Understand?"

Jack nodded.

"It's difficult for him. His father died when he was young, and this is his third school in the past four years. Plus, there's the weight. I know kids aren't kind to heavy kids."

There was no disputing that fact.

Jack glanced at the clock and it read ten minutes after six.

"Don't worry about the time, dear. I might worry too much about Ronnie, but he's all I've got."

"We could be friends, I guess."

He wasn't sure he liked being pressured by someone's mom to befriend a kid, but he couldn't say no with her facing him like this.

"Thank you, Jack."

Cassie leaned forward and clasped his hand in hers, and he felt as if his blood had mixed with warm syrup.

John entered the room, his overcoat dusted with snowflakes and drops of water on his head. "All set, Jack?"

"Uh-huh."

He stood and Cassie did the same.

"We'll be seeing you around. Remember to take care of my Ronnie."

He felt as if he'd been recruited for something, but for what he had no idea.

The limo pulled up to 47 Church Street and John got out. The door handle clicked and Jack's door swung open, a flurry of swirling flakes pelting him in the face. He stepped out, thanked John for the ride, and hurried up the driveway. At the door, a wreath with a red ribbon and silver bells swayed in the wind. His mother watched out the front window and let the curtain go, no doubt on her way to let Jack inside.

Jack picked up his saucer sled off the driveway. The wind would toss it like a Frisbee if he left it outside. His mother opened the door, a frown stamped on her face. That frown that said he was in trouble and about to face the wrath.

"You're twenty minutes late," she said.

"I was at a friend's house."

"Who?"

"A new kid in town. I met him today."

"Does this person own a clock?"

"They have a sundial. They're antitechnology."

"You're in enough trouble already."

She tugged on the front of his jacket and pulled him into the hallway, where he kicked his boots onto a rug, tipping Mom's duck boots over. He leaned the sled against the wall.

"Pick that up, Jack."

He stooped down and arranged the boots in a row.

"So what's your excuse?"

For a mom, she was pretty cool, letting him go to the Shriver Mall with the guys or allowing him to blast Def Leppard tapes on the stereo. Paul wasn't allowed this luxury—his father thought heavy metal signaled the decline of Western civilization. She always had cookies or brownies for him and the guys, too. Not a bad mom at all.

But come home late and she assumed you had been kidnapped by a serial killer or flattened by a Metro bus. In Mary Harding's world, tardiness meant the police were scraping your carcass off the street.

"Are you going to answer me? And why the limo?"

"That's a new taxi service. They've thrown out the yellow cabs."

"You're pushing it."

"It's Ronnie's," he said.

"Ronnie?"

"He lives up at the Steadman place."

She placed her hand under his chin and tilted it so he was looking up at her. "Jack, please."

"Honest, they're loaded."

"The Steadman place as in the fabulously wealthy Steadmans?"

"Yep."

She held his chin for another moment, then let go, apparently satisfied. "We'll see what your father thinks."

The case is going to trial, ladies and gentlemen.

He proceeded to the kitchen to find his father reading the *Buffalo Evening News*, the paper draped across the table. He bunched his nose and squinted, trying to make out the small print.

"Little late, sport."

"Lost track of the time," Jack said.

Jack Harding Sr. crossed his legs, his wool dress pants hiking up and revealing his hairless calf just above the dress sock. Tall and rangy, he had played high school basketball, but the once trim athletic body had given way to a saggy paunch in the middle.

Dad smoothed his remaining hair. "You were supposed to be in by six."

"I told Mom I lost track of time."

"Maybe we should get you a watch for Christmas."

"Maybe not," Jack said.

His mother entered, slid on oven mitts, and removed a blue roaster from the stove.

"He said he was up at the Steadman place with a new kid in town. Imagine our son hanging out with the rich and famous," she said.

Jack rolled his eyes.

"The Steadman Estate. Come on, Jack," his father said.

"I'm not kidding."

Dad folded his paper and placed it on the table. "I did hear someone bought the place," he said.

"You don't believe that cockamamie story, do you?"

Leave it to Mom to come up with a word like *cockamamie*.

"Let's hear what our boy has to say."

Jack pulled out a kitchen chair and sat down, while his mother hovered around like an angry hornet in a holding pattern. He told them the afternoon's events, starting with Ronnie's near demise at Vinnie's hands and ending with the limo ride home.

Dad leaned back in his chair and looked at Jack, sniffing for lies.

Jack added, "His mom pulled me aside and asked if I would look out for Ronnie. She said to apologize for missing my curfew but she needed to talk to me. And that I had great parents because of my good manners." He was amazed how easy the lies slipped off his tongue.

"Don't let it happen again," his dad said.

"I suppose being a few minutes late didn't hurt anything. But next time call," his mom said.

He wanted to ask them who had abducted his real parents and replaced them with aliens. Ordinarily, he was looking at a minimum of a day's grounding for being late, but for some reason the governor had dialed in a pardon at the last moment.

"Go wash up. The chicken's about done," Mom said.

Jack left the kitchen and proceeded to the bathroom, where he washed his hands with a blocky bar of Dial. As he scrubbed, he thought of the nice warm rush Cassie Winter's touch had given him, that it was a little scary. And the way she told him not to worry about being in trouble. Did she have anything to do with Mom and Dad's demeanor when he came home?

Drying his hands, he dismissed the thought and looked forward to digging into some chicken and stuffing.

CHAPTER 6

At seven-fifty, ten minutes before homeroom, Chris appeared at Jack's locker, knocking on the open door. Jack was stuffing his boots and coat into the locker and looked up to see Chris grinning down at him.

"When are you going to get rid of these pictures?" Chris asked.

The inside of Jack's locker was adorned with a Spider Man poster, a shot of Ricky Henderson sliding into second, and a photo of Christie Brinkley in a white bikini. He had swiped that one from his mother's *Cosmo*, and so far it had gone unnoticed by the Brampton faculty.

"Baseball's a fairy sport, you know," Chris said.

"Fuck you, Watson." That retort was usually reserved for when someone said, "No shit, Sherlock," but somehow it fit the moment.

"You hear about the body they found?"

"Who's they?"

"The cops, you doof."

"Where?"

"By the Steadman Estate. My dad's got a police scanner." Chris switched his stack of books from one arm to the other. "How was the mansion?"

"Huge. Amazing."

"That's it?"

"His mom was pretty hot."

Chris snickered, a low conspiratorial chuckle. "Really?"

"Seriously."

"I might have to go up there myself."

"So what about this murder?"

Jack pulled out his math book, two spiral notebooks, and a Bic pen. He tucked the books against his side and slid the pen into his back pocket. Anyone who was remotely cool stopped carrying a book bag back in fifth grade. Instead, guys carried books with one arm, against the hip. Girls carried them across the chest, perhaps hoping for some eighth grader to come along and offer to carry them. The only kid holding on to the book bag was Paul, who took daily ribbings for his Dungeons and Dragons backpack.

"Some guy's car ran out of gas. They found him down the road from his car, all torn up. It was on *Wake Up, Western New York* this morning, too."

"Man."

It gave him a serious shiver because he had just been at the Steadman place, and John's warning echoed in his mind. The one to stay in the mansion proper, as he had put it. Jack hadn't given it much thought at the time, but with someone getting killed, it made him want to stay away from Ronnie Winter and his massive home.

"So his mom's hot?"

"Get off it already," Jack said.

Paul hurried down the hall, his backpack slung over one shoulder. He was breathing in short gasps when he arrived at Chris's side, his hair still wet and frozen just above his forehead.

"Hear about the murder?" Paul asked.

"No, we live under a rock like your mom."

"Up yours," Paul said. "We'll talk about it more at lunch." He glanced at his watch. "I've got to get to homeroom."

"You've still got five minutes, Paul. Relax," Jack said.

"You guys should get moving, too," Paul said.

"Yes, Mother," Chris said.

Paul flipped him the bird and jogged down the hall.

Jack closed his locker and clicked the Masterlock shut. He and Chris walked down the hall, parting and saying they'd see each other at lunch. Chris and Paul had Mrs. Jason, while Jack and Emma had Mrs. Eckerd. Jack also got stuck with Vinnie in his homeroom, but having Emma made up for it, and it was even better than having Chris or Paul. He had Emma all to himself and Chris and Paul didn't care, but it was hot shit to him.

Jack entered the classroom, passing the wooden sign marked SHALOM that Mrs. Eckerd kept on the door. He slid into his desk, fifth row near the blackboard where the smell of chalk dust hung in the air. He looked over to Emma's desk, still empty. She had been out on Friday, and whatever sickness had struck her, she was still busy fighting it off.

The class filtered in and took their seats, Sue Sneed sitting her melon head in front of Jack and blocking out the board. She didn't get the name Six-Foot Sue for nothing. Steven Padowski sat next to Jack, his frizzy red hair sticking up like weeds in a garden. The kid always smelled vaguely of Swiss cheese, earning him the nickname Cheesy Stevie.

"Hey, Jack."

"Hi, Stevie."

"What are you doing?"

"Sitting here. What's it look like?"

"Want to come over and play little cars?"

"I've got to help my mom with some chores."

"Maybe tomorrow."

"We'll see."

Dodged that bullet for another day, he thought.

Vinnie Palermo strolled in, dressed in a black T-shirt and steel-toe work boots that he called his "ass kickers." He liked to kick kids in the shins when they weren't looking,

usually between change of classes. Jack slid lower in his
seat, as if Vinnie might not see him, but it had the opposite
effect, as Vinnie strutted over to the desk.

"I owe you for tripping me yesterday. If that cop didn't
show up I would've cut you."

Cheesy Stevie leaned across his desk, watching Vinnie
and Jack.

"What are you looking at, Cheesy?" Vinnie said. Stevie
took out his math book and started flipping pages.

"I'll see you after school," Vinnie said, poking Jack in the
chest. He strutted away.

The rest of the class filtered in, and the bell rang, signal-
ing the start of homeroom. The old radiators hissed and the
room heated up, making sweat trickle down Jack's sides.
Mrs. Eckerd walked in, stopped at her desk, and pumped lo-
tion from the dispenser. Rubbing it into her hands, she turned
to the class and reminded them that the Christmas dance was
next Friday. Jack didn't hear much of the details because he
was figuring out a way to avoid Vinnie after school. It would
eat at him all day.

The classroom door opened and Ronnie Winter stumbled
in, dropping his books on the floor with a clatter. The class
burst into laughter and despite his black mood, Jack joined
in.

Ronnie stooped to pick up his books and Vinnie chimed
in, "Oh, great. The fat faggot is in our class." Mrs. Eckerd
frowned but said nothing. It was the general consensus of
Brampton Middle's students that Vinnie scared even the
teachers.

"Why are you late? You're Ronald, right?"

"Ronnie, and I have a note."

Ronnie straightened up, his books clasped against his
chest. With his free hand, he reached around and dug in his
back pocket until he pulled out a folded piece of paper. Mrs.
Eckerd read it over, clucked her tongue in disapproval, and
tossed the note in the trash can.

"I'll excuse you because it's your first day, but don't be late again. Sit down."

"Okay," he said.

Ronnie approached, the jumble of books in his arms, and sat in the desk to Jack's right.

"The two fags are sitting next to each other," Vinnie said.

"Vincent."

"My name's Vinnie, got it?"

"Settle down," Mrs. Eckerd said.

"Never."

Ronnie slid into his seat, but not before dropping his social studies book again.

"This is cool. You and me next to each other," Ronnie said.

A purple smear dotted the corner of his mouth.

"Something on your mouth." Jack pointed to his own mouth to indicate the location of the stain.

Ronnie licked his finger and scrubbed the jelly off with his fingertip. "You're always looking out for me. I would have looked like a real ass with that on my face all day. Right next to each other, I can't believe it."

"This is sure turning into a wonderful day," Jack said.

It was about to get even better.

CHAPTER 7

Lunchtime started out quietly enough.

Jack, Paul, and Chris took their seats at the round table, joined by Rick Lopez and Donny Bannon. Rick and Donny were okay to join in a pickup football game, but they weren't regulars in the group, and they never would be. They were fringe kids, and no matter how hard they tried, they would not be part of the inner circle. Jack ignored them.

Chatter echoed through the cafeteria, rising to a low roar as the room filled to capacity. Jack looked out the courtyard windows to see the snow still blowing hard. The paintings of Jefferson, Edison, and King that hung near the windows were oblivious of it all, but Jack watched the snow, imagining monster snow hills and snowball fights.

"What do you have good?" Chris asked.

Jack opened his brown bag and looked inside to find the same old Monday lunch: peanut butter sandwich, Fritos, two Oreos, and a juice box. Mom was nothing if not predictable. Chris opened his lunch and took out two foil-wrapped sandwiches and two bananas.

"What did Mommy pack for you?" Chris asked.

"I packed this myself," Paul said.

Paul unsnapped the latches on the lunch box and pulled out a bag of Lay's chips and a can of grape Faygo.

"That's real nutritious," Jack said.

"I can eat whatever I want. Pretty cool if you ask me," Paul said.

From the look on his face, Jack knew it wasn't very cool with him.

"Want half my sandwich?" Jack said.

"Yeah, you can have one of these if you want it." Chris held up one of the sandwiches and waved it back and forth.

"Nah, this is fine."

"Take it," said Chris. "It'll put some meat on your bones." Chris held out the sandwich, and this time Paul took it.

"Sometimes you're all right, too-tall." He unwrapped the sandwich, took a bite, and said, "Hear anything else about that murder?"

"Not since last period. You know what we should do," Chris said.

"Here we go," Jack said.

"I bet Ronnie would let us up to his place, and if he did, we could check out a real crime scene. I bet we'd see some leftover blood."

"Ding-dong, you're wrong, bub," Paul said.

Jack nearly inhaled his sandwich, sucking in a big breath to laugh at Paul's choice of words. He had a million goofy words, all left over from the 1950s, words like *bub*, *buster*, and *neat-o*.

"What's so funny?" Paul asked.

"Nothing, bub."

"Bub. I don't know where you come up with these, Paulie," Chris said.

"As I was saying. Last night's snow would have covered up any blood. It's long gone by now."

"He's right," Jack said.

"Yeah, but how often do you get to see something like that?" Chris said.

"Count me out," Paul said.

"It's a bad idea," Jack said.

"Don't tell me you're turning chicken like Paul," Chris said.

"No."

"Be a man, then," Chris said.

Jack didn't like the idea of going into the woods, but his fear didn't compare to the ragging he would take from Chris if he didn't go.

"Come on, Jack."

"Maybe I'll ask Ronnie about going out there," Jack said.

"Excellent." He punched Jack in the arm.

"Easy, you damn gorilla."

Vinnie appeared at the table, working a toothpick in his mouth, from one side to the other. Joe Leary stood next to him with his arms at his sides, the hands curled into fists. It worried Jack that Harry Cross was with them, because Harry was the type of kid who tied firecrackers to cats' tails. He had that blank look in his eyes, like a guy in a mug shot, where the wiring in his head was not exactly up to code. Harry was thumbing through a copy of *Hot Rod*, a leggy blonde in a red bikini sprawled across a Camaro on the cover.

"Hey, girls," Vinnie said. "We'll be waiting for you after school."

"Get lost, Palermo," Chris said.

"The Jolly Green Giant can't always protect you," Vinnie said, looking away from Chris.

"I'm not afraid of you," Jack said.

"You should be. I'll squash ya."

He curled up his fist, lifted his arm over his head, and swung it down, smashing Jack's sandwich. Peanut butter squirted from the sides like a dead beetle's guts. Harry Cross doubled over laughing, the patches of acne on his cheeks turning redder from laughter. Leary said, "He'll squash you all right!"

Paul sank lower in his chair, looking like he wanted to

pass through the seat by osmosis. Chris sat staring, his gaze fixed on Vinnie's hand, still planted in Jack's wounded sandwich.

"You didn't have to do that," Chris said.

"I'm gonna do that to him and that other fat ass after school."

Jack looked at his sandwich, at Vinnie's greasy paw stuck in the middle of the bread, and thought of his mother packing the lunch for him with the utmost care. His stomach had been growling since third period and now the king of the assholes had ruined his lunch. That angered him more than anything. He wanted to stuff the sandwich down Vinnie's throat, and that was his second choice of locations.

Vinnie took his hand from the sandwich, grinning as if he were lord of the cafeteria.

"You wrecked my fucking sandwich. That was my sandwich."

Jack balled up his fist, and pushing the chair away, he thrust upward, popping Vinnie right on the chin. Vinnie's head snapped back reflexively and a look of shock crossed his face. Apparently one did not do such things to the lord of the cafeteria.

Leary and Cross started toward Jack, and Vinnie reached out, grabbing a handful of Jack's shirt and twisting it. Chris sat staring, mouth open, his sandwich with a crescent bite taken out of it still in his hand.

By now the kids at other tables stopped talking, and the cafeteria was as silent as Grant's Tomb. Students turned in their seats to get a better look.

"Now you're really dead," Vinnie said.

Vinnie pulled back, ready to deliver a haymaker, but Jack saw Mrs. Williams coming at them, her breasts swinging back and forth under her turtleneck sweater. She got her arm between the two boys just as Jack closed his eyes, ready for the blow that would send him into the stratosphere. Mrs. Williams smelled like cheap perfume and cigarettes.

"Cut it out. Now," she said.

Vinnie took another halfhearted lunge at Jack, but Mrs. Williams had stepped between them, and he backed away.

"Get going," she told Vinnie. "I should give you both detention."

She turned her head and looked at Vinnie, no doubt giving him a menacing look. Vinnie rubbed his chin where Jack had tagged him.

"We'll see you after school," Vinnie said.

"You'll do no such thing. Get back to your table." She shooed him away.

With this crisis over, Mrs. Williams hurried to another table, where Ben Childs was preparing to launch a tinfoil ball at Theresa Gardner's head.

Jack returned to his seat, lamenting his beaten sandwich and the confrontation sure to come when the bell rang.

"I'm a dead man," he said.

"Sorry, man. I'd back you up but I have practice after school," Chris said.

"It's okay."

But it wasn't.

The last three periods went by faster than Jack would have liked. Mrs. Randolph's math class, which normally made eternal damnation seem appealing, breezed right on by. When he wanted the class to drag, it wouldn't.

After physical science, the last period of the day, Jack returned to his locker and drew out the process of putting on hats, gloves, and boots. The chatter in the hallway had died out as the bused kids hurried for the doors, and those who were anxious to get outside fled with visions of snowball fights in their heads. Jack shut the locker and Gene the Janitor pushed his wide broom down the hall, slumping over as if the broom were the only thing keeping him up. Jack guessed him to be at least eighty years old.

He nearly messed his shorts when a hand clapped him on the shoulder.

"Come on, slowpoke. You going to spend all day here?"

Jack turned and looked into Ronnie's grinning moon face.

"Don't scare me like that," Jack said.

"Why are you so jumpy?"

"I thought you were Vinnie."

"He's still after you?"

"Didn't you hear?"

Ronnie bunched up his face in a look of intense concentration. "Hear what?"

"I popped him one at lunch."

"Holy shit!"

Ronnie's voice echoed in the hallway, and he clapped his hand over his mouth, as if to contain the curse. Gene the Janitor turned and frowned. He resumed sweeping the hall.

"I went to the library during lunch," Ronnie said.

"Him and the ugly twins are gunning for me," Jack said.

Ronnie stared blankly.

"Leary and Cross. That was a joke, son."

"Oh, I get it."

"They're probably waiting for me, so I've been stalling."

"I'll walk with you," Ronnie said.

"No reason for us both to die. Vinnie wants to kick your ass as much as he does mine."

"He'll have to face both of us, then."

Ronnie tugged on Jack's arm, no doubt leading them to imminent disaster.

On their way out of the school, they found Paul leaning against the wall in the front foyer. He looked like a rabbit waiting for a hawk to swoop down on him. The thud of basketballs on hardwood and squealing sneakers came from the gym, confirming that Chris was in practice and could not help them.

"Let's go. Maybe we'll miss them," Jack said.

They stepped out the door and into a raw wind that swayed the skeletal trees on the school's front lawn. Icicles hung from the statue of Michelangelo, and the snow crunched beneath their feet, a true indicator of the bitter cold. Jack's cheeks and nose felt as if small pebbles had stung them.

"Colder than a witch's titty," Jack said. He was hoping for a laugh out of Paul, who almost always found that line amusing.

They forged ahead, awaiting an ambush.

CHAPTER 8

Vinnie Palermo shoved his hands in his pockets and danced from one foot to the other. He refused to wear a heavy coat, preferring a jean jacket and T-shirt to a dumb-ass winter getup.

"You cold, Vin?" Harry said.

"No. I ain't."

"Could've fooled me."

"Shut the hell up," Vinnie said.

If Harry didn't stop with his crap, Vinnie might smack him in the mouth. His chin still hurt from where Harding hit him (a sucker punch if ever there was one), he was shivering, and he wanted a smoke. Usually he swiped a pack of Kools from his mother's dresser drawer, but he had left before she did this morning. He felt mean enough to put out an eye.

"Where are they? I'm cold," Leary said.

"How the shit am I supposed to know? They have to come through here. Harding and Fussel both live this way," Vinnie said.

"Yeah, use your head, Leary," Harry said.

"Eat me. How do you know they didn't go around the block?" Leary said.

"They won't."

"How do you know?" Leary asked.

"Will you two shut up?" Vinnie snapped.

God, these two could get on his nerves. They were good at fighting, though. Especially Harry, who was crazier than shit. Last summer Harry caught Mrs. Endberg's cat and the three of them had taken it up on the Conrail tracks. Harry produced an M-80 from his pocket, tied it to the cat's neck, and lit it. That cat blew into a million pieces, and Vinnie nearly threw up from laughing so hard. Harry was good for some things, even if he pissed Vinnie off once in a while.

"What are we going to do with them?" Leary asked.

"Pound them into jelly. I'm not letting a turd like Harding make me look stupid," Vinnie said.

"He already did," Leary said.

"You want to join him?" Vinnie said, making a fist.

Leary shook his head.

"Then shut your hole. Here they come."

Vinnie, Harry, and Joe crouched in the alley between Jane's Pharmacy and the Yellow Submarine Pizza Shop. Vinnie periodically poked his head around the corner and he finally spotted Jack walking with Paul and Ronnie.

"This is even better than I thought. They've got the fat kid with them, too. The one who threw a snowball at me and Joe."

"Yeah," Joe said. "I want some payback."

"Me first," Vinnie said.

Once again, he peeked around the corner, but the three geeks didn't see him, for it was snowing hard and they were looking back, expecting Vinnie and his crew to ambush from the rear.

"Perfect," he said.

"Maybe they forgot about it," Paul said.

"I don't believe that and neither do you," Jack said.

"I guess you're right."

They waited at the light on Main and Pine Streets, at the

end of the school block and leaving the general protection the school gave. The light turned yellow and a red Pontiac screeched around the corner, trying to beat the light and spraying all three boys with slush.

Paul immediately went into panic mode.

"Oh, man. Oh, man. My pants are trashed," he said, brushing the icy slush off his jeans. Jack brushed himself off as best he could, and Ronnie seemed unfazed, only wiping a small bit of slush off his cheek.

"Why are you so upset? Won't your mom just wash them?" Ronnie said.

Paul didn't hear him.

"His dad's got a thing about dirty clothes. He'll give it good to Paul when he gets home."

"Bummer," Ronnie said.

"What am I going to do?"

"Come to my house. My mom'll throw those in the wash and dry 'em for you. You can put on a pair of my sweatpants until they dry. Call and tell your dad you stopped at my house."

"Yeah, yeah. That might work. Thanks, Jack."

"No problem."

"What's with your dad?" Ronnie asked.

"He's an asshole."

Jack laughed and so did Ronnie, although Jack had seen a lot of bruises on Paul over the past few years and knew no amount of laughter would change Paul's nutty father.

"I never had a dad. Died when I was young."

Jack didn't know what to say to that, but Paul chimed in, "I wish my dad would bite the big one."

Every second they stayed outside left them more vulnerable, so Jack urged them on by saying, "C'mon, ladies, before the light changes again."

They crossed Pine Avenue, passed the First Methodist Church, the Art Works shop, and a white house with a massive pillared front porch. They might almost make it home without taking a beating.

The three boys reached Jane's Pharmacy, whose picture window displays were filled with walkers, canes, a wheelchair, support hose, and a commode. The blue awning that normally hung over the front of the store was rolled up, no doubt to keep it out of the high winds.

"Hey, Paul, do you crap on one of those?" Jack said, pointing to the commode.

"Screw you, Harding. Your mom uses one when she pinches a loaf."

"Both your moms use that. Then I bet they ask the druggist for hemorrhoid cream when they're done."

Jack and Paul stopped, looked at Ronnie, and then both burst into laughter, Paul with his odd tee-hee laugh, and Jack clapping Ronnie on the shoulder. "That was pretty good," he said. *The new kid made a funny, what do you know?*

They got to the alley between Jane's and the Yellow Submarine and Jack knew they were in trouble. He saw them out of the corner of his eye, well aware who it was before his brain could actually register. His feet started to move, but they were on him too quickly. Vinnie grabbed him, and Leary and Cross pulled Paul and Ronnie into the alley along with Jack.

"Hey, boys."

CHAPTER 9

The Brampton Middle Wildcats had lost their last game to Saint Amelia's by the score of eighty-three to forty-two, and Coach MacGregor was making Chris and the others pay. Chris glanced over at him, standing on the bottom bleacher, the whistle clamped between his teeth like a cigar.

A stitch burned in Chris's side from the suicide drills MacGregor made them run as punishment for the horrendous loss to Saint Amelia's. A suicide meant starting at the baseline and running to touch the near foul line, half-court line, far foul line, and far base line. After touching each line, the players had to run back to the starting point before running back down the court. It was MacGregor's way of pounding a winning attitude into his team.

MacGregor blew the whistle after the last drill, and Craig Cummins sprinted for the garbage can. He leaned over it and wretched, emptying green vomit into the can.

"Layup drills!" MacGregor said.

Chris took his place in line and started forward to take the pass from Robbie Munch, but the stitch came back, forcing him to double over. The ball rapped him in the head and bounced out of bounds. The whistle shrieked.

"Francis. Suicide."

"Shit," Chris said.

"Nice catch, Francis," Munch said. He was the only guy on the team as tall as Chris, but he had cement hands. Dropped passes, got the ball stripped, and couldn't sink one if the coach hung a hula hoop from the backboard.

"Now, Francis."

Chris ran his suicide drill, holding his side the whole time.

"Scrimmage!" Tweet-shriek from the whistle. "Shirts and skins."

Chris stripped off his T-shirt, wiped his brow with it, and tossed it on the bleachers.

The scrimmage started with Scotty Dugal playing point, weaving up and down the court, doing a nifty crossover dribble to beat his man across half-court. Chris staked out a spot down low and posted up against Munch. His back to Munch, he raised his hand to call for the ball, and Scotty fired it over to Danny Popich, the small forward. Danny pump-faked, got his man to jump, and drove into the lane.

Munch shoved Chris, and Chris shoved back.

"You can't score on me," Munch said.

"Keep dreaming," Chris said.

Danny slung a bounce pass to Chris, who reeled it in. Munch slapped at the ball and missed. Chris spun away from him and hit a fadeaway jumper, the net going *thwap!*

"Nothing but net," Chris said.

"Don't come into Ewing's house again," Munch said.

"You're no Ewing."

Chris's squad got back on defense, and Munch positioned himself in the key, backing against Chris and ramming his rear end into Chris's groin.

"Hope you wore your jock," Munch said.

"You probably liked that," Chris said.

Lester Banks, the opposing guard, put up a shot and it clanged off the rim, over Chris's head. Munch grabbed the rebound and raised the ball over his head to shoot, elbows out. Chris moved in to block the shot, and seeing this, Munch swung his elbow and smacked Chris in the mouth.

The whistle again.

"Munch! Francis!"

Chris recoiled from the blow and Munch put the shot up and made it.

"Nice defense, Francis."

"You cheap prick."

Chris grabbed Munch's shirt, yanked on it, and spun him around. Munch stutter-stepped, looking like a crazy break-dancer trying out a new move. MacGregor jogged over from the bleachers and stepped between them.

"You two have been at it the whole scrimmage."

"He started it," Munch said.

"I don't care. The two of you just got six inches until practice is over."

Chris wiped his lip with the back of his hand, smearing blood on the side of his mouth. Not only did he have a sore lip, but the prospect of doing six inches loomed before him. The two boys took a spot between the bleachers and the gym door, lying on their backs. Chris raised his legs out in front of him, ankles six inches from the floor, and held them until the muscles in his thighs knotted in agony. MacGregor said, "Rest."

They were allowed to set their legs down for five seconds before holding them up again. After ten minutes of this, sweat dripped down his back and chest. Nothing made practice worse than having to do six inches.

"Hey, Francis, your dad just walked in."

Check that.

Vinnie gripped his jacket, and Jack jerked and bucked, but Vinnie was too strong. "This is for the cafeteria, jack-ass." He fired his knee into Jack's balls, and immediately Jack wanted to cry and puke at the same time. Vinnie let go and shoved Jack to the ground, Jack cupping his wounded crotch and landing on a pile of broken-down cardboard boxes. Ronnie and Paul weren't faring much better.

Leary wound up and blasted Ronnie right on the chin, staggering him back against the wall. He hit a patch of ice and slipped, landing on his side and letting out a grunt.

Harry Cross had Paul in a headlock, and Paul let loose with a string of curses. He swung his arms, trying to escape the headlock, but only succeeding in creating new and interesting curse words.

Vinnie stood over Jack, and he wanted to get up and run, but there was no moving as pain radiated through his crotch and lower back. "This is for the other day on the snow pile."

Vinnie wound up and slammed his fist into Jack's ear. Jack covered his head with his hands, and Vinnie switched tactics, bringing back his boot and kicking Jack in the ribs. It felt as if his side had caved in.

"C'mon, baby. You gonna hit me now?"

Another kick with the boot, this one not as hard, but still painful.

Leary moved in on Ronnie, who held his chin and staggered, uncertain of his surroundings.

Jack curled himself into a ball to protect himself from any further damage. Vinnie booted him in the ribs again. Jack muttered "asshole" to him, figuring that he was already getting stomped, so why not throw in a few last words?

"What did you say to me?" Vinnie said.

Jack looked up and expected to see Ronnie taking a whipping from Leary, but instead he stood against the alley wall, arms splayed, snorting like a bull ready to charge. He stopped his foot and yelled, "Toro! Toro!"

Ronnie continued his impression of a bull, stopping Leary in his tracks and even causing Vinnie to turn around and say, "What the hell is he doing?"

Ronnie charged forward at Leary, who looked like a pedestrian in the path of a Mack truck. Ronnie lowered his head and shoulders, making little bull's horns with his fingers, and plowed into Leary's midsection. Leary fell backward and sprawled over a garbage can.

Jack took the opportunity to rise to his knees and immediately regretted it as Vinnie turned around and saw him, then shoved him back into the wall, where he bumped his head.

"We're not finished yet," he said.

Jack put his hands up, prepared for more of a beating, but instead he heard a noise like Oooff! Ronnie the human bull slammed into Vinnie. Vinnie rocketed forward, landing on his belly. Ronnie stood over him, triumphantly wild-eyed, and at that moment Jack believed the new kid thought he was really a bull.

Harry Cross had Paul in a headlock, and Paul's arms had stopped flailing.

"Okay, you fat faggot. Why don't you try that with me?" Harry said.

"Gladly, señor." He snorted and chuffed.

"What in the name of Jesus is going on?"

Ronnie slowed, then stopped, lowering his hands, his bull's horns disappearing.

"Now, if I didn't know any better, I'd say this looks like a fight. Can I join in?"

John stood at the front of the alley. He had on a pair of wraparound sunglasses that made him look pretty darn cool.

"Who the hell are you?" Vinnie said.

"That's none of your business, boy."

"Don't call me boy."

"I'll call you whatever I please. Don't you think you should be running along? You all are bigger than these boys and that don't seem fair to me."

"Listen, spook—"

"Watch it."

John stepped toward Vinnie, who flinched and backed up. Even Vinnie Palermo wasn't stupid enough to mess with a two-hundred-fifty-pound man.

"All right. Let's go." He motioned for Leary and Cross to follow him.

The three of them left.

John turned to watch them go.

"Anything I hate it's a bully," John said. "You two all right?"

Ronnie nodded and Paul said, "That dumb ape ruined my hearing."

"I doubt he did. But those ears will be red for a while. Here, Ronnie."

John produced a clean blue handkerchief from his pocket and handed it to Ronnie, who wiped his nose, then blew it at foghorn level.

Jack lay crumpled against the alley wall, and he tried to stand but a burning stitch cut into his side and he slumped back down to the ground. His head ached almost as bad as his ribs.

John knelt down beside him and put a hand on his shoulder. "Don't move. I'll help you up."

In one fluid move, John scooped him up and the pain was so bad his head spun.

"You're not supposed to move an injured patient," Paul said.

"It's okay. He won't be hurting much longer."

What did that mean?

"Am I going to die?"

"Far from it. Matter of fact, you'll be feeling better in no time at all. She'll see to it."

They left the alley, John with the wounded Jack in his arms, Paul following, and Ronnie bringing up the rear.

CHAPTER 10

By late afternoon Emma's throat had settled down to a low burn and her fever was under a hundred for the first time in four days. She felt well enough to get out of bed and go downstairs, where her mother was spooning chocolate chip cookie dough onto greased sheets.

"Feeling better?"

"A little."

Emma made her way to the counter, dipped her finger in the bowl, and licked the batter.

"Don't eat that. It's got raw eggs in it."

"You worry too much, Mom."

"It's my job."

"If strep throat didn't kill me, raw eggs won't."

"You shouldn't be eating them."

Her mom spooned out the batter, snapping the spoon so the balls of dough landed on the sheet with a plop. Then she stirred it again, picking up the bowl and tucking it against her side while stirring with her other hand.

"I can't get this to mix, damn it."

"You okay, Mom?"

"Fine, dear. Yes."

She didn't look fine. She worked the batter hard, almost frantically, like a crazy person. Emma didn't like the way she was acting.

A black-and-white television sat on the counter, and *Eyewitness News* came on. The anchorman, dressed in a gold blazer and wide blue tie, reported the economy was bad, Reagan had angered the Russians, and there was a murder in Brampton. That got Emma's attention.

"Did you hear that, Mom? Someone got killed right outside the Steadman Estate."

"I wish you wouldn't watch the news."

"You want me to stay informed, don't you?"

"You just wanted to hear the gory details."

She finished stirring and went to set the bowl down, but only half on the counter, and it slipped and clattered on the floor, dumping a glob of cookie dough on the tile.

"Nothing is going right today."

Mom slammed the spoon down, bent down, and picked up the bowl. Then she took a paper towel from the rack over the sink, wet it, and wiped up the floor.

"Nothing is ever easy. Remember that, Emma."

"Sure, Mom."

She looked into her mother's eyes and saw weariness. Purple and puffy, the eyes of someone who had too much on her plate and not enough time or resources to deal with it. Mom had called in sick at M. Wile today, the first time in years that Emma could remember. Her mother had been employee of the month twice for her hard work, cranking out more garments than anyone else in the plant.

"No, nothing's ever easy," she said, with a sigh.

"We need more paper towels."

Emma stood up and unraveled three paper towels from the roll, then tore them off and resumed wiping cookie dough off the floor.

"Thank you, honey."

"No problemo. Mom?"

"What?"

"Are you okay?"

"Fine, why?"

"Was Mr. Miller mad when you called in sick?"

"Not really."

"You sure?"

"Well, maybe a little."

"I hope I didn't get you in trouble."

"Nonsense. You're more important than any job."

She knew from the stacks of bills that Mom left on the kitchen table, and from the ones marked FINAL NOTICE, that the job was at least as important as Emma. Her mother wouldn't say it, but Emma figured they were just getting by.

"Mr. Miller was a jerk, wasn't he?"

Mom paused for a moment and looked at Emma, as if pondering the response. "He wasn't exactly friendly on the phone."

"What did he say?"

"First he wanted to know if I thought I could make it in and I said no, my daughter is very sick. Then he asked if I could get a sitter. I told him no. Then he said he couldn't afford to have people out sick and he hoped it wouldn't be a habit. Then he said he hoped I felt better and he supposed there was nothing he could do if you were sick."

"That doesn't sound so bad," Emma said. She finished wiping up the cookie dough, took the lid off the beige garbage can, and tossed in the towels.

Mom stood up, took some Dawn from under the sink, and squirted it on her hands. She scrubbed them together, worked the soap into a lather.

"I've worked a lot of places, Emma. Most bosses won't come right out with their disapproval when you call in sick, but you can always tell. They wish you well, but the underlying tone is you should come to work. And Mr. Miller will make me pay for this in subtle ways. Maybe putting me on the ironer for a few shifts. More info into my personnel file. Lord, I hate that ironer."

"You always come home sore when you have to use the ironer. I hate seeing you like that."

"You're sweet, dear. Stay that way. And don't let men like Mr. Miller ever put you down."

Here it goes. Speech number 862 on the evils of men. Frederick Greer had left when Emma was four, flying away to Las Vegas intent on building the next Dunes or Tropicana.

"I won't."

"That's why I don't want you hanging around with those boys. Boys become men and instead of throwing rocks at you and lifting up your skirt, they dump you, or give you black eyes. Be your own woman, Emma."

"But I'm only twelve."

"That doesn't matter, dear. Build a strong foundation now and you'll never have to rely on a man. Look at that murder on the news. Probably done by a man."

"I get the point, Mom."

"I'm just trying to help you."

"I know."

"Come here."

Her mother held out her arms and Emma went to her. She pressed the side of her face against Mom's chest, and the wool sweater scratched. Mom hugged her and let go. "Feeling better?"

Emma nodded.

"Good. I think you could go back to school tomorrow."

"If I have to."

Good time to talk to her about Jacob.

"Mom? Can I ask you something?"

"Sure, hon. Did I tell you Aunt Sam and Jacob are coming for dinner?"

Emma felt her heart sink down into her guts. "No, actually, that's what I wanted—"

"Why don't you run upstairs now, okay? And you be careful when you're outside. There's no telling who's running around after that boy got killed the other night."

"I was thinking—"

"Go on and get changed. Our company will be here soon."

"Okay."

Emma went upstairs, knowing she only had a little over an hour before Jacob arrived.

CHAPTER 11

Jack awoke on a bed in a cool, dark room. He touched his side and felt bare skin. His ribs ached and he flinched.

What happened to me? he wondered.

He had a vague notion of what had happened, but his head felt fuzzy, the same way it did after the surgery to remove his tonsils.

The last thing he remembered was John scooping him up and setting him on the seat of the limousine. The limo had climbed the hill going up Main Street and then he had fallen asleep. Right about now his mother was probably on her third stroke and wondering what happened to her little boy.

He sat up and a voice said, "Rest, Jack."

Ronnie's mother appeared at the bedside, smiling at him. She stroked his hair and he felt nice and warm.

"What happened to me?"

"Some boys hurt you."

"My mom's really going to be ticked," Jack said.

"Don't worry about that."

"Where's Paul?"

"Out in the kitchen having cookies. You boys are very brave."

If getting the snot beat out of you meant you were brave,

then he deserved the Medal of Honor. The pain in his ribs flared again, and he winced. She put her hand, palm down, on his ribs and pressed, Jack drawing a sharp breath as she did this.

"Relax," she said.

The hot spot in his side turned cold, and Cassie closed her eyes and muttered words he did not understand, words that sounded like an old language.

She removed her hand and exhaled slowly.

"You should be feeling better," she said.

He propped himself up on his elbows, going slow to avoid another sharp pain. There was a small twinge, but nowhere near the pain he felt before she had touched him. The ache in his head was gone, too.

"What did you do to me?"

"I helped you because you helped Ronnie. Here." She held out his black T-shirt and he took it. After pulling on his shirt, he swung his legs over the side of the bed and stood up.

Shadows filled the room, and a crème-colored candle on a wrought-iron stand provided the only light. A log tumbled off of the iron holder in the fireplace, and the fire glowed orange blue. Purple velvet drapes hung on the far wall, the window beyond them dark. Cassie sat on a mauve love seat and took her teacup from a carved table that looked somehow French to Jack.

She sipped the tea and set the gold-rimmed cup down.

"Come here," she said.

He stepped forward, head spinning, and held his arms out to keep his balance.

"Whoa," he said.

"The dizziness will go away soon," she said. "Ronnie needs someone, Jack. A protector. We talked a little about that before."

"Or to keep his mouth shut. No offense."

"Will you do it?"

"I don't know what you mean."

"Be his friend. He's all I have, Jack."

"I said before I'd hang out with him."

"You have to do more than that." She sipped her tea. "Promise me something."

What was he getting into? Ronnie was a loose cannon, and Jack didn't want to be around when Ronnie fired cannon-balls at Vinnie Palermo.

"Give me your hand."

He hesitated.

"It's okay," she said.

Cassie extended her hand and leaned forward. Jack didn't want to take it, because he somehow knew it would bind him to her. But she looked him in the eyes, the soft blue swirling. His limbs felt as if they were coated in concrete, but his arm extended in front of him, as if pulled by an invisible pup-peteer. The fire glowed behind Cassie, and suddenly the room was as warm and comfortable as a sleeping bag on a cool fall night.

"Promise me," she said.

"I promise," he said.

His voice seemed muffled, as if he were speaking with his ears plugged.

"Good."

She released his hand and the fire snapped, bringing him back into focus. He jumped backward, knocking one of the teacups off the table. It hit the floor and cracked into three pieces.

"Sorry about that."

"Don't worry about it."

She knelt down and plucked the pieces from the rug. Then she set them on the table and brushed her hands to-gether.

"Your promise means the world to me," she said.

"Okay."

What had he promised her? His head hurt again, and the last few minutes had been replaced by black space in his mind.

"You and your friends are welcome here any time. I only have two rules, though. Stay out of the woods and don't break your promise to me. You don't want to break the rules."

"I really need to get home."

His stomach felt hot, and his skin burned. Again, there was mention of the woods, and her warning to stay out gave him the creeps. And Mom would feed him to the wolves for being late. He wanted to go home, climb into bed, and forget the whole day.

"You're worried about your mother. What's your phone number?"

He told it to her.

"What's Paul's phone number?"

Jack recited Paul's number.

"Go down to the kitchen and I'll call both your parents. Can you find the kitchen?"

"I think so," he said.

"This is a secret, all right?" she said.

"If you say so," he said, and turned to leave the room before she talked him into anything else.

Cassie picked up the receiver and dialed the Hardings' phone number. As it rang, she turned and observed the room, noting the brown spot on the carpet where Jack had spilled the tea. A woman picked up on the other end.

"Hello."

"Mrs. Harding?"

"Yes."

"I'm a friend of Jack's."

"Do you know where he is? Because I'm about to call the police."

"He's fine, trust me."

"Who is this?"

Cassie closed her eyes and cleared her mind, blocking out sound, thought, and light. Solid, encompassing darkness filled her head. Slowly a picture formed, blurry at first and becoming clearer. A woman in a brown turtleneck and matching wool slacks appeared, heavy in the bosom and rear end.

There was an apron tied around her waist, its front adorned with embroidered tomatoes and carrots. She tapped her fingers on a white rotary phone. The polish was clear, the tip on the middle finger chipped.

"Are you still there?" Mrs. Harding asked.

"He'll be home soon."

"Why won't you tell me who you are?"

"Cassie Winter. Ronnie and Jack are best friends."

A pause on the other end.

"Isn't he the boy Jack met the other day?"

"They've been friends since they were little. They went to kindergarten, remember? He came over for cocoa and cookies."

You won't remember this. He'll be home soon. Safe and warm.

"I'm sure Jack is fine," Mrs. Harding said. "I don't know why I worry so much."

"I understand, believe me. He'll be home in a bit," Cassie said.

"You're right."

"Good-bye. We'll talk again," Cassie said.

"Okay."

Cassie saw the woman hang up and put her hand on her chest, sighing in relief, as if she was just told a suspicious lump wasn't cancer. A bookish man with thinning hair entered the kitchen, a paisley tie dangling from his neck.

"Find out where Jack is?" the man asked.

"Yes. It was Ronnie's mother. He'll be home any minute."

"That kid better have a good reason for being late," he said.

The image of the Harding kitchen began to dissolve, Jack's parents smudging to colors, their faces losing features until they resembled blank mannequins. The colors faded, and the blackness returned to Cassie's head, a clean slate. She opened her eyes, and after using the Reach, her head ached.

The Harding woman cracked easily, swallowing the thoughts Cassie planted in her head. When Jack returned home, his mother would think he had been at his childhood friend's house, sipping hot chocolate with his mother's permission.

That was the power of the Reach, the one given to her as a girl by the Gypsy woman Hartha. That was two hundred years ago, Hartha, the dark-skinned woman who smelled of spices and sweets, telling her she had something for Cassandra. A drink that would change her, give her powers created thousands of years ago.

They had sat in the hovel with the thatched roof, and Hartha handed her a wooden cup with thick black fluid in it. It smelled of burned wood and berries, and it tasted bitter.

She drank it, the liquid clenching her stomach into spasms as soon as it hit. She rolled on the ground, the image of the dark-skinned woman blurring until young Cassandra passed out. When she awoke, the woman was gone.

She went home and took a whipping from her mother for returning late from market. But she felt different after drinking the fluid, and scarcely felt the leather strap on her back.

She knew her mother's words before they came out of her mouth (Brat of a child, I'll whip you till there's no skin on your back), and she knew how many pups their dog Molly would have (it was nine). And when one of the pups died, she took it out in a field and put her hands on it, and its chest pumped and it wobbled to its feet and growled at her. It had charged at her, snapping its teeth and biting down on her wrist. She ran away from it, and it followed, but she outran the pup, and still heard it growling low at her.

That pup grew, and it killed twelve sheep and a calf before the men of the village hunted it down and stabbed it with a pitchfork. It came back to life, but it came back mean and full of hate. Just like Ronnie's father.

Nearly two hundred years since her transformation, since the thing under her skin grew and took life, pulsing and beating like a second heart. Two hundred years of living as a woman and a beast created from a single drink from a cup.

Two hundred years and twenty-two children, all of them

dead and lost. Edward to cholera, Simon crushed by a horse cart, Lucinda and Laura dead from the plague that followed the Great War. John in the Second World War, shot as he stormed Omaha Beach and now buried in a cemetery adorned with white crosses. So many children, and now she had another to look after, and it nearly broke her when she thought of him in pain.

I must not lose Ronnie.

And though she guarded Ronnie as dragons guard gold, she couldn't follow him to school or go around punishing bullies. That was Jack Harding's role, helping Ronnie, and helping her avoid another heartbreak.

The kitchen was bigger than Paul's house, the silver appliances gleaming so sharp he saw his reflection in them. Paul jiggled his leg up and down in a nervous patter, the stool underneath him shaking. He anticipated another slap or punch from the old man for being late, and that meant another line to feed the teachers. *I fell down*, he would tell them. They never believed him. Mrs. Avino, the eighth grade science teacher, threatened to call Child Protective Services, but she never did, and it continued.

Despite his nervous stomach, he had downed three Snowballs and a glass of milk. He wished he lived in a place as nice as this, some place nicer than his own house. How much money did they have? A hundred million? Five hundred million?

Ronnie brought out another pack of Snowballs from the pantry.

"I hope Jack's all right," he said, and stuffed a Snowball into his mouth.

"Good thing your friend John showed up," Paul said. "You know things at school are going to get worse for us."

"Relax. My mom will handle things. She always does." Chomping and talking. "She could call your dad so you don't get grounded for being late," Ronnie said.

"What good would that do?"

"Mom's good at talking people into things. I bet your dad wouldn't even be mad."

"You don't know him," Paul said.

"He hits you?"

"All the time."

"Son of a bitch," Ronnie said. A piece of coconut fell from his mouth.

"Watch your mouth. You don't want your mom to hear," Paul said.

"This place is so big she'll never hear me." He wiped his mouth. "You going to the Christmas dance?"

"Are you kidding?"

"No."

"I don't suppose you're going," Paul said.

"Sure. With Jessica."

"You're dreaming, bub."

Jessica was a goddess among girls. A full head taller than Paul, she had honey-colored curly hair and a chest that was the stuff of legend. Paul had lain awake many nights thinking of her, about how it would feel to touch one of her boobs, feel the nipple under his palm.

"I'm not dreaming."

"She's loaded, to boot. Her dad's the president of M and T Bank."

"Look around, jerky. What do you think bought all this?"

"Money won't buy you a date. I hear she likes freshmen," Paul said.

"I can still ask."

"You won't," Paul said.

"Dare me?"

"I dare you."

"Done deal. Spit shake on it." Ronnie hawked a glob of spit into his palm and held it out for Paul to shake hands. Paul recoiled, but Ronnie said, "We've got to make it official."

Paul reached out and shook Ronnie's hand, the warm spit

slimy against his palm. When they released hands, Paul wiped it on his jeans.

"I'll ask her tomorrow," Ronnie said.

"If you don't, you're a wussy."

"Hey, wanna see my room?"

"Sure."

Paul followed him down a hallway painted in soft yellows and blues. Gold-framed paintings hung every ten feet, depicting flowers or fruit or women on bicycles. They turned right at the end of the hall, where a white vase with pink roses stood on a table. After that, they reached a spiral staircase and took it to the second floor.

The corridor looked long enough to stretch across the New York State line, and at the end of the hall was a door, looking small as a mouse hole from here.

"Follow me."

Ronnie led him to the door at the end of the hallway. He gripped the knob and the door opened into the room.

"Check it out," Ronnie said.

Paul stepped through the door and expected his heart to stop.

"Wow," he said.

CHAPTER 12

George Kempf popped the lid off the Tums container, gave it a shake, and tilting his head back, popped three of the tablets into his mouth.

"Goddamn flavored chalk," he said, crunching the antacid.

Lately the ulcers had been gnawing full-time at his guts, and he started to wonder if he didn't have a piranha swimming around in his belly. His dad had had the big C in his stomach, and it killed him within a year of being diagnosed. *Should get that checked out, Big George.* He tried not to think about the volcano that was his stomach right now. Kempf had bigger problems to deal with.

There was a pile of papers, forms, envelopes, and crime scene photographs spread out on his desk, which faced a yellow wall. A frosted window leaked air, although with the near nuclear fusion heat the radiator gave off, the air wasn't that noticeable. The only thing that brightened the room was the photo of the sailboat he planned on buying. White and sleek, with a red stripe down the side and a rainbow-colored sail. It sailed a crystal sea with a big orange sunset bleeding in the background.

When he retired, that baby would be his.

But first there was a murder to solve, and a particularly

nasty one, to boot. He picked up the photo of Alan Quinn's face and looked it over. From the neck up, the kid looked as if he had stuck his face in a lawn mower. The face had been torn into bloody strips, the throat laid open, looking as if it had exploded from within. The M.E. listed the official cause of death as asphyxiation. Whoever killed him slashed through the trachea and cut off his air.

He set the picture aside.

The only other murder that had taken place on his watch was when Tiny Griffin came home and found his wife in an embrace with the Schwann deliveryman. He took his sixteen-gauge off the rack on his truck, chased the guy down the driveway, and blew nice neat holes in his back. Then he went into the house and finished off Linda Griffin. Tiny was doing life in Attica. Linda Griffin minus most of her head was gruesome, but this Quinn murder was ten times worse.

Who the hell would do such a thing?

He stood up, ready to refresh his coffee, when Chief Samuel Ramsey strolled in, inspecting his nails. The overpowering aroma of his cologne filled Kempf's office, making Kempf's nose itch. Ramsey sat down in the chair next to Kempf's desk and leaned his elbow on the desktop.

"How's it going, Tank?"

"Been better," Kempf said.

"Oh?"

"This thing is eating a hole in my gut," Kempf said, and nodded to indicate the crime scene photos.

"I can imagine, Tank." Ramsey crossed his legs and tugged at his slacks.

He always called Kempf "Tank," a reference to Kempf's nickname as center for the Brampton High Panthers football team. When Ramsey said it, Kempf always thought it sounded like "asshole."

"We can agree this has the potential to be one big mess, right?"

"That's a given," Kempf said.

"We can't let the condition of Quinn's body get out to the public, right?"

"You know I know that."

"The last thing we want is a panic," Ramsey said.

"Where are you going with this?" Kempf asked.

"Glad you understand all this."

Ramsey straightened his tie and smoothed out his shirt-sleeve. "You're the man I need for this."

"For what?"

"Got a reporter coming in from the *Gazette*. He wants an interview, but I'm just too busy right now. So that makes you the interviewee."

"I'm flattered."

"Great. Remember to keep things vanilla. The *Courier Sun* already started a rumor that a serial killer might have strolled into town. You need to deflect that, and give as few details as possible."

"I really don't need this right now, Chief."

"You'll do fine."

Ramsey patted him on the forearm, trying to be reassuring but only raising Kempf's blood pressure by a few notches. On his way out of the office he said, "Make us look good."

The fire kicked up in Kempf's belly again and he reached for another Tums.

CHAPTER 13

MacGregor's whistle cut through the air, and he yelled, "Showers!" This was the official end of practice, and as Chris rose to his feet, Munch said, "Good luck with your dad, Francis." He laughed as he walked away, his fleshy belly jiggling.

Dad shook hands with MacGregor, the two of them no doubt reliving past sports glories that existed only on the pages of yearbooks. Coach and Chris's dad were teammates on the Brampton High team that took the state finals in 1967.

Chris wiped his forehead with a towel and started for the locker room, hoping to avoid talking to his father.

"Chris. I want to talk to you," his dad said.

Chris stopped and turned around.

"Coach said you had some trouble in practice."

"Blame Munch," Chris said.

"You shouldn't have lost your cool."

MacGregor said, "They were both bumping pretty hard."

"But getting thrown out—"

"Water under the bridge," MacGregor said, thumbing his whistle. "At least it shows some fire in your belly. Just don't do it again."

"Sure, Coach," Chris said.

MacGregor could be an ass wipe, but he was a somewhat forgiving one.

"Hit the showers," Coach said.

"We'll talk about this later," Dad said.

Chris opened the locker room door, and the sound of showers streamed in the background. It smelled of old sweat and dirty clothes, with an undercurrent of deodorant and hair gel.

Chris showered, toweled off, and got dressed. Outside the locker room, his dad waited, standing like a cigar-store Indian, expressionless. Right now Chris would rather do six inches for a week than make the ride home with his dad.

They exited the gym through the red double doors, and the wind nipped at them, snatching the door from Chris's hand. He had to lean his shoulder into it in order to close it.

They made it to the Trans-Am, a late-seventies model, black with the gold firebird on the hood. Chris thought of it as the *Smoky and the Bandit* car, but he never said that to Dad, because his father hated Burt Reynolds's movies. The custom license plate read SPORT1 (his Jeep was SPORT2). Chris was amazed he brought his baby girl out in the snow.

"Looks good, doesn't it?" He ran his hand over the dashboard, the recipient of a recent Armor All job.

"Why'd you bring it out on a day like today? There's salt all over it."

"Just for the hell of it. We can go cruising," he said.

The pine tree dangling from the mirror swung back and forth.

"Reggie B kills me," Dad said.

"Is that all you listen to, sports talk shows?"

"No. There's more to life than just sports. You know that."

"Is that what you used to tell Mom?"

"That's not fair."

"Sure it is."

"Your mother had to have everything her own way. That's why she left me."

He flipped on the heater, and warm air whooshed from the vents.

"If you say so."

"Stop saying that. A guy's got to have hobbies, interests outside of just family and marriage. Some guys hunt, some play golf, and my hobby happens to be following sports."

"And betting on them."

"You'd better watch it, Chris."

Chris knew he'd hit a sore spot, the spot that eventually became a bleeding ulcer and ruined his parents' marriage. One Friday afternoon in March after leaving Francis Motors and feeling good because he had pawned off a beater of a Gremlin on an anxious seventeen-year-old, Peter Francis had stopped for a beer at Malone's. After five or six too many, he had gotten a nip from the betting bug and decided he felt lucky. He took two thousand dollars out of the account of Peter and Wendy Francis, met with his bookie, and placed numerous bets on the NCAA tournament. Lost the whole thing.

"I'm sorry. I shouldn't have said that."

"No. I had it coming. But I'm trying to make things better for you and me, right? Things are picking up at the lot. Hey, I sold four cars today without breaking a drop of sweat on my ass. How about that?"

"Yeah, that's something," Chris said.

"I'm working hard, Chris. That's why I don't need aggravation like what happened today in practice."

Here it comes, the big speech.

"MacGregor tells you to do something, you do it. I know that Munch kid is a pain in the ass, but he couldn't carry your jock. You know that, right?"

"Yeah."

"Getting punished like that is for guys like Munch. It's embarrassing when you do stuff like that."

"How do you think I felt?"

His dad paused for a moment, apparently rolling that one

over in his mind. He drummed his fingers on the steering wheel before responding.

"Of course you were embarrassed. Not just me. But it's over now, right? Let's go get some burgers. You want that scholarship to Saint Jerome's, don't you?"

"I suppose."

His legs ached and he felt as if he could curl up on the seat and go right to sleep. He still had homework to do after dinner, and the last thing he felt like doing was getting into a pissing match with his father. A pissing match he would lose.

"Good. Glad you agree. Let's hit the BK. I'm starved for a Whopper."

His father gunned the engine and the car fishtailed, the rear end dancing back and forth in the slush. "Pretty good in the snow, huh?"

If he had the energy, Chris would've just shaken his head.

CHAPTER 14

The booger would be here any minute. Emma slipped on a gray sweatshirt, the sleeves coming down past her finger-tips. The sweatshirt had a splotch of white paint across the front of it from when she helped Mom do the living room. It did the job, though, big enough to hide her chest. A pair of blue sweatpants completed the ensemble, baggy so they didn't cling to her butt. Cousin booger didn't need any eye candy to tempt him.

In the kitchen, Mom took a roaster from the oven, lug-ging the pan to the counter and setting it down. She slid off her oven mitts and licked her index finger.

"Damn mitts are wearing through," she said. "That's going to blister."

"Want me to get you an ice pack?" Emma asked.

Mom took a good look at her, ignoring the burned finger for the moment.

"What?" Emma said.

"You know what."

"My hair?"

"Emma."

"Not enough makeup?"

"Emma!"

"The clothes," Emma said.

"Change them."

Emma made small circles on the floor with the toe of her slipper.

"But I'm comfortable," she said.

"You know better to dress like that when we're having company."

"But—"

"Do you like looking like a boy? Because that's how you're dressed."

"Like a what?" Emma said.

"A boy."

"These clothes are fine, Mom."

"Those boys are rubbing off on you. Go on and change, and put that turtleneck Aunt Sam bought you on."

"It's too girly," she said.

"Exactly. Now march."

"I have to tell you something."

Mom pointed to the stairs and Emma desperately wanted to tell her the reason for not wanting to wear the turtleneck. It made her breasts look like overinflated water balloons, and would catch Jacob's attention. She started toward the stairs and then stopped at the first step. It was building in her like steam in a boiler, but the words got stuck in her throat. *Go ahead and say it. Jacob is a pervert.*

"Are you going? They'll be here soon. And put on that black skirt with the white tights."

"Mom."

"Go."

She climbed the stairs and from behind her, Mom muttered, "I don't know what gets into that girl."

In her room she changed into the white turtleneck with roses and vines embroidered onto the neck. She slipped on the ribbed tights and the black corduroy skirt, the tights making her legs itch. Emma almost tore the clothes off before she hit the bottom step. The turtleneck felt two sizes too small, clinging to her chest like plastic wrap. Wearing the prison uniform meant sitting the whole night with her arms folded over her chest to cover it. Jacob had always taken little peeks at her, his gaze going to her chest or butt. After the incident last summer, she became even more aware of it, and it scared her.

In the living room, Jacob and Aunt Sam sat together on the couch. Aunt Sam had her legs crossed and sipped a glass of red wine. Her auburn hair was done up in a bun and pink rouge dotted her cheeks. She sat forward, chatting, leaned back, and uncrossed her legs. The wineglass went from left hand to right, then down on the table, then in her hand again.

Jacob was busy shoving cheese and crackers from a platter into his face. He wore the same clothes as always: blue oxford shirt, gray wool pants, and scuffed loafers. As usual, his hair shone and flecks of dandruff clung to the strands of his oily mop.

"Hello, Emma. Is that the outfit I got you?"

"It is."

"Come here and let me see you."

Aunt Sam stood up and smacked a kiss on Emma's cheek. "You are turning into a beautiful young woman. Doesn't your cousin look nice, Jacob?"

The booger looked up from the plate and his gaze flashed across her chest, then back to the platter. "Yeah."

He sandwiched a piece of yellow cheese between two crackers and shoved the whole thing in his mouth. Emma wrinkled her nose. Aunt Sam hit her with a barrage of questions. How was school? Did she have a boyfriend? Was she going to the dance at school?

Mom fluttered in and out of the room, restocking the cheese platter and refilling Aunt Sam's glass from a bottle of merlot. Fifteen minutes to dinner, and Emma asked Mom about helping in the kitchen. Mom said no, and to Emma's horror she suggested the unthinkable.

"Why don't you show Jacob your room? You must have some tapes or albums he would be interested in."

"I only like classical," Jacob said, and Emma sighed in relief.

"I only have things like Bon Jovi and Motley Crue."

"I like Motley Crue," Jacob said.

"Why don't you listen to some music for a little while before dinner?"

"I still don't feel so hot, Mom." The turtleneck felt like an iron shackle around her neck, and the tights itched. It felt as if little tsunamis crashed against the walls of her stomach, and the smell of onion from the kitchen made it worse.

"I'm sure you'd rather listen to music than hang out with us boring adults," Mom said.

"We're no fun. Go on Jacob," Aunt Sam said.

"That might be fun," Jacob said.

"Mom, I really don't want to."

"Don't be rude to your cousin. I'll call you when dinner is ready."

Jacob rose, cracker crumbs falling from the front of his shirt. More crumbs were stuck in the corners of his mouth, and for one horrible second Emma imagined those lips on hers. Pressed against hers, the stale cheese breath filling her mouth. Gross.

"All right, but I really don't think you'll like any of my music," Emma said.

They entered the room and Jacob flopped on the bed, and the frame shook. "Why don't you show me something?"

Cassie led Jack to the spiral staircase and upstairs to the long hallway. "That's Ronnie's room. Why don't you join the other boys?"

"I really need to get going, Mrs. Winter."

"Just stay a few more minutes. John's warming up the limo right now."

He opened the door to Ronnie's room and said, "Whoa."

A *Raiders of the Lost Ark* pinball machine stood to the

right of the door. A basketball hoop was affixed to the wall, and Ronnie had a full-sized hockey goal with a mound of sticks, pads, and helmets piled in front of it. That was for starters. He had GI-Joes by the hundreds, a *Dragon's Lair* video game, and even his own computer on a desk near the window.

Ronnie pulled out a cardboard box full of comic books, and Paul joined him at the foot of the bed, looking like a kid on Christmas morning.

"The ceilings are high enough for you to shoot baskets in here. Amazing," Jack said.

"Check out this Spider Man," Paul said, holding up a comic with the web slinger adorning the front.

"That must be worth something," Jack said. "Awesome room."

"Yeah, real neato," Paul said.

Jack rolled his eyes.

"I can have anything I want," Ronnie said.

"No shit, Sherlock," Jack said. "This is all cool, but we should get going, Paul."

"I'm only through half the box." Paul slid the Spider Man back into the box and pulled out another comic with Green Lantern on the cover.

"Your dad is gonna kill you," Jack said.

"You're right," Paul said, and stuffed the comic books back in the box. "Let's hit it."

"You guys can't leave yet," Ronnie said. "I'll be bored."

"I'd never get bored if I had all this," Jack said.

"It happens." His face lit up. "Hey. I know something we could do. Really cool if you guys are up for it."

"Me and Paul have to go."

"Wait."

Ronnie scrambled to his feet, hiked up his pants, and hurried to the nightstand, where he opened the drawer. He produced a yellow flashlight with a black switch and turned it on.

"What's with that?" Paul asked.

"Tunnels."

"He's loony," Paul said.

"Under the estate. They run all the way out to the road. That old guy Steadman built a small rail system to run through the tunnels. Three workers died building it and they never finished it. What do you say?"

Jack mulled it over, thinking he was already in trouble enough and a little while longer wouldn't matter. A little jolt of anticipation washed over him, like the feeling you got before a fight or a big test. How many people ever got to see something like that?

"How do we get there?" Jack asked.

"I'll show you. You're not afraid of ghosts, are you?"

"Nah," Jack said.

"Me neither," Paul said, drumming his fingers on the box of comic books.

"Let's do some exploring." Ronnie thumped across the room, flung open the door, and took off down the hallway with flashlight in hand.

"Last one down's a loser!" he echoed from the hallway.

Jack raced Paul, nudging him out of the way as they reached the door. Paul's arm hit the jamb and he said, "Ow!" Ronnie ran ahead of them, the flashlight beam bobbing up and down.

He made a quick left and headed down a staircase flanked by a smooth wooden banister. The stairs ended in the second biggest room Jack had ever seen (next to Ronnie's kitchen), a great room. It had a bar lining the entire wall, a billiard table, and a dartboard. He whizzed past a big-screen television and a Foosball table before ending up in a small kitchen off the great room. Paul bumped him in the back.

"You're last, loser," Jack said.

"Stuff it, Harding."

"This is where Mom keeps the stuff for parties," Ronnie said. "You guys aren't afraid of ghosts, are you?"

"You already asked us that," Paul said.

"I know. But the workers who built the tunnel? Their ghosts walk down there."

"Bullshit," Jack said.

"Double bubble bullshit," Paul said.

"How do we get down there?" Jack asked.

"Help me move the fridge."

Ronnie set the flashlight on the counter, crouched down, and leaned his shoulder into the side of the refrigerator. Jack and Paul got next to him, pushing and grunting until it slid across the linoleum.

"There it is," Ronnie said.

A white door with a black doorknob stood chest high on Jack. The lock looked old, a skeleton keyhole underneath the doorknob. Ronnie pulled the door open, revealing an opening darker than the maw of a shark.

Ronnie scooped up the flashlight.

The smell of must, damp and heavy, permeated the room. Jack looked out the window to find the entire estate covered in darkness, and he imagined the blackness in the tunnels was five times worse. His heart sped up. If he chickened out now, the other two guys would brand him a pussy.

"What are you waiting for? Let's go," Jack said.

Ronnie shone the flashlight into the opening, revealing a flat concrete pad and three steps leading into the tunnels. The top step had a jagged crack in it, and cobwebs dangled from the top of the door frame.

"We're off to see the wizard," Ronnie said, ducking low under the door. He wasn't low enough, and he bumped his head on the frame. Jack and Paul chuckled.

"What if someone comes down and sees us?" Paul asked.

"You sound like an old lady. Quit worrying," Jack said.

In truth he wanted to get going down the stairs before his legs refused to move. Despite the flutter in his guts, he felt good. The headache was down to a low throb, and the pain in his ribs felt no worse than after a game of tackle football. Whatever Cassie did to him, it worked.

He started through the door with Paul in tow.

CHAPTER 15

Emma squatted down, tugging the back of her skirt to make sure it covered her legs. Behind her, the bed creaked, sounding as if a baby elephant sat on it instead of her weirdo cousin. Her tapes were stored in a white plastic crate, and Motley Crue rested on top of the pile. Mick, Nikki, Vince, and Tommy graced the cover, hair teased, clad in leather and spandex. They snarled for the camera, fists clenched as if they would slug you with no provocation. Every parent's nightmare. The music made Emma's neck hairs stand up, and she considered Tommy Lee a babe, even though she would never admit that. They sang about sex, drugs, and the devil. Jacob was sure to hate it, and she hoped it might actually drive him from the room.

She was about to stand up when he leaned over her shoulder, the cheese breath strong in her face.

"What a bunch of freaks. They look like girls," he said.

"They could kick your fat butt."

"Those guys probably can't even spell butt."

He took a step back, but she didn't have room to stand up, so it left her kneeling in front of him. Looking down, he smiled a yellow-tooth smile at her, and she was aware that something about this position was dirty. She backed up and stood quickly, fumbling the tape and then catching it.

"You going to play that tape or juggle it?"

"I don't know why you wanted to come up here."

"You know why."

Jacob wandered over to her dresser and looked in the mirror. There was a Boston Celtics pennant tucked into the corner and he pulled it out.

"Girls aren't supposed to like sports," Jacob said.

He dangled the banner in front of him, swinging it like a pendulum.

"Put it back."

"Maybe you're a little dyke."

Jacob dropped the pennant on the rug.

"Pick it up."

"Get it yourself, dyke."

"Stop calling me that," she said.

"You don't even know what it is."

"It holds water in place," she said.

"Ha!" he snorted, sounding like a hog.

"What's so funny?"

"You're a dumb one, so I'll tell you. It's a girl who likes other girls."

"I like girls, so what?"

"Like girlfriends. They have sex with each other," he said.

Emma's face went hot and prickly.

"Tell you what. You made me laugh so I'll pick up your pennant."

"You're disgusting. That's gross, having sex with other girls."

He bent down and his belly spilled over the beaten belt.

"Whatever," he said, tossing the pennant on the desk. "What's this?"

He picked up her stick of Tussy deodorant and popped off the cap. Then he sniffed it. "You wear this so you smell good for your girlfriends?"

"Get out of my room, Jacob."

"Nah," he said, setting the deodorant on the dresser. "Let's check out your drawers." He opened the top drawer, pulled out a pink training bra, and stretched it like a slingshot. "Lookie, lookie. Emma's got boobies. But we already know that, don't we?"

She cocked her arm and whipped the tape at him, but he sidestepped it, and the tape clattered off the mirror.

"Can I keep this?" He waved the bra like a matador waiting for the bull to charge.

"Give it back!"

She charged forward, smacking into him, reaching for the bra, but he was too tall and held it over her head, just out of reach. Up close she got a whiff of his body odor and saw the pus-filled pimples dotting his forehead. It would be ten thousand years before a girl ever gave him a second look.

"Glad you came over," he said.

She realized too late that she had done exactly what he wanted. While she reached for the bra, Jacob lowered his free hand and reached around, gripping the back of Emma's thigh. He slid his hand up her skirt and squeezed her right cheek. She yelped in surprise.

"How's that feel?"

"Not so good. How's this feel?"

She slammed her knee into his crotch. He let out a gasp and, still holding the bra, doubled over, cupping his nuts, the bra swishing against his knees.

Emma looked at him, a little shocked at her actions. Seeing him bent over with the bra dangling was surreal. It was the first time she ever hit a boy there, and one thing came to mind: laughter. It burst out of her, and she covered her mouth with one hand while pointing with the other. It was too darn funny seeing the booger like that.

Jacob moaned and looked down at his crotch as if expecting to see blood on his trousers. He looked at the bra and threw it to the floor. Fresh tears welled up in his eyes and whether they were from physical pain or some deeper hurt, she didn't know; it made her feel as if she had kicked a dumb animal.

He charged her, pinning Emma against the wall. The thick glasses made his eyes as big as golf balls. "You little bitch. Are you laughing at me? You won't laugh the next time I get you alone."

He squeezed Emma's shoulders, the nails pinching her skin through the fabric of the turtleneck.

"What's going on up there? You sound like a herd of elephants," Mom said from the foot of the stairs.

"Tell her I tripped, Emma. Don't piss me off more."

She considered screaming, but that might make him angry enough to crack her skull against the wall.

"Jacob tripped, Mom. It's nothing."

"Come down for dinner."

Saved by the dinner bell.

Jacob let go, breathing hard, spittle dripping from his lower lip. He flipped her the bird as he headed down the stairs.

"Gonna be sick," she said.

The three boys ducked through the opening and started onto the concrete pad. Ronnie trained the beam on the steps and it lit up the walls, showing smooth stone on either side. At the bottom of the stairs, they ended up in a small chamber facing a cracked, rotted door.

Goose bumps broke out on Jack's arms and he figured the temperature had dropped twenty degrees since leaving the mansion. He wished for a coat.

"You came down here by yourself?" Jack said.

"Yep."

"You're nutty," Paul said.

"Come on," Ronnie said.

Ronnie moved ahead of them, unfazed by the darkness and general creepiness of the place. Maybe the kid had a screw loose in the old noggin. Normal people didn't go around angering Vinnie Palermo or cheerfully running into underground tunnels.

Jack turned and saw light the color of platinum-blond hair streaming through the open door. It looked warm and inviting, a place where the cookies were warm and the milk was cold. But if he backed out now he would look like a pussy, and that was the worst crime possible among twelve-year-old boys, one he didn't want to commit.

Ronnie had already disappeared through the door, and in the absence of light, the darkness covered them like dirt on a coffin lid.

"Jack, you still there?" Paul said.

"Right behind you."

"What do we do?"

"Follow him. He's got the light."

He wanted more than anything to turn and hightail it up the stairs, but number one, he would look like king chickenshit and number two, he didn't think he could even find the first step without sprawling over and cracking his teeth. Instead he nudged Paul's arm with his elbow.

"I'll hold on to you so we don't get separated," Jack said.

"You're not a homo, are you?"

"Shut up and keep moving. If we lose him we're screwed."

Paul moved ahead, feeling his way toward the door until his fingertips touched the splintered wood.

"In here! C'mon!" Ronnie's voice echoed.

"Bring the light back here," Jack said.

"What?"

"We can't see squat!"

He heard Ronnie mutter, "Oh."

The beam bobbed in the doorway, and Ronnie followed, a stringy cobweb stuck in his hair. "Sorry, guys. I just got excited."

"Don't do it again," Paul said.

"Watch your step."

He shone the light down, and they saw a rail running

along the floor. There were timbers in between, most of them black with rot, and the rails were coated with rust.

"Old man Steadman was a little weird, huh? Started this rail and never finished it," Ronnie said.

"What was he trying to do? Couldn't his servants just walk around, or use a car?" Jack asked.

"Nah. John said the guy crapped money and he got bored so he decided to build this thing."

"He must've been pretty eccentric," Paul said.

"How'd you find out about these tunnels, anyway?" Jack said.

"When we moved into the mansion, John brought me down here and told me all about them. He said if he ever caught me down here he would hang me up by my toes. I think he wanted to show me how dangerous it is."

"It really worked, too. We shouldn't be down here," Paul said.

"Why, are you chicken?"

"Of course not," Paul said, puffing his chest out.

"Let's prove it then. Jack, you're not a clucker, are you?"

"No way."

"Follow me."

Their fearless leader started ahead, and the two other boys followed him, stepping over rotted timbers and almost tiptoeing to avoid tripping.

"John said these tunnels were here already. This was a hospital before Steadman bought the place, and these were used by the staff to get around."

"What happened to the hospital?"

"It burned to the ground. Huge buildings. All wood. Whoosh! John said a hundred people died. They tore the rest of it down and sold the land to Steadman after that."

"That's creepy. All this bad stuff happening here. The hospital burns down; then the workers die in the tunnel," Jack said.

"John said legend has it there's a nurse who burned to

death in the fire whose burned body still walks around down here from time to time."

"All right, that's enough, bub. No more ghost stories."

"We might see one, you know. Maybe the nurse, all black and crispy and shit," Ronnie said.

"Yeah, like a hot dog that's been on the grill too long," Jack said.

"Shut up," Paul said.

"I'm kidding, Fussel. Do you really think there's ghosts down here?"

"Anything's possible," Paul said.

They reached a fork in the tunnel, and Ronnie stopped and shone the light on the right side. "Let's see, was it the right or the left side?" he said, a man in deep thought with himself.

"Oh yeah. The left."

He barreled ahead, Jack and Paul with no choice but to follow him, for he was their only source of light, and without the Duracell, they wouldn't be able to see the tips of their noses. Jack didn't know what he liked less: following Ronnie deeper into the tunnels or being left in the dark to fend for himself. It was like being on *Let's Make a Deal* and having man-eating tigers behind all three doors. Some choices.

They entered the left tunnel and the rail ended. They wove to the left, Jack feeling his way along the tunnel, the stone smooth and cold under his palm. The tunnel felt like the belly of a gigantic serpent that had devoured them, and the mouth was back at the doorway, the only way out. Icy air prickled the back of his neck, and when he exhaled he saw his breath.

"Okay. Stop."

"Now what?" Paul said.

"Time to see who's a clucker and who's got a pair," Ronnie said.

"Let's just get the hell out of here. My mom's probably called out the National Guard by now," Jack said.

"And I'm gonna need them to protect me from my father. Maybe the marines, too," Paul said.

"Dares are on. You guys do the dare and we leave. You don't do it and I smash the flashlight and we're all in the dark," Ronnie said.

He shone the light on his moon face, the way you did when telling a ghost story, holding it under your chin so as to look creepy.

"You won't do it," Jack said.

"Don't tempt me."

"Knock it off. You wreck that light and we're screwed," Jack said.

Ronnie leaned in close to Jack, still shining the light on his face, and said, "I'll do it, Jack. I'm crazy like a loonie bird."

Ordinarily, Jack would have been on the ground trying not to let his bladder burst from laughing, but something in Ronnie's eyes chilled him. They got wide, and his eyebrows twitched. For a second, there was a blank stare, as if Ronnie were looking right through him, trying to read something tattooed on the inside of Jack's skull. He'd seen footage of Charles Manson as he was led into court, and it was that same type of stare. But Ronnie wasn't a homicidal maniac. At least Jack hoped not. He really didn't know the kid all that well, but he didn't doubt after seeing that stare that Ronnie Winter would turn that flashlight into plastic shards if provoked.

It was starting to look like they had made a horrible decision. The kid had popped a spring in his clock.

The tunnel wound left until they came to two archways, both darker than deep space.

"This is where it happened. The tunnel on the left," Ronnie said.

He shone the beam on the archway but the darkness resisted, as if it were solid and capable of breaking the light in half.

"One of us has to go in there," Ronnie said.

"I'm not going in there, bucko."

"I need to hold the flashlight, so that leaves Jack to go by himself," Ronnie said.

"Why would I do that?"

"To prove our friendship. It's like blood brothers. A real friend would do it."

"What if I don't do it?"

Ronnie waggled the flashlight back and forth. "Then it's bye-bye, Mr. Flashlight."

It was either listen to crazy Ronnie or deal with his mother. He didn't forget the warning, the admonition to be nice to Ronnie and the underlying tone that something bad might happen. Jack had no choice.

"I'll do the dare," Jack said.

"That's more like it, Jackie."

CHAPTER 16

The dare sounded simple enough. Go into the tunnel and sit on a rubble heap for one minute. No flashlight and Ronnie would count out the time.

"How will I know when to stop if I can't see?"

"Guess. Try not to trip over any bricks. It's back a ways."

"All right. But I do this and we get the hell out of here. Or I'll take that light from you and leave you with your thumb in your ass," Jack said.

He saw the sting on Ronnie's face, as if Jack had spit on him.

"You going or not?" Ronnie asked.

"Don't rush me."

Jack started forward, and Paul grabbed his arm, nearly stopping Jack's heart cold.

"Don't scare me like that."

"You can't go alone. You'll get killed," Paul said.

"Nothing's gonna happen," Jack said.

"I'm not telling your mother you got killed. I'm going with you." He jerked his thumb in Ronnie's direction. "Flashlight boy can wait here by himself."

"But Jack needs to go alone," Ronnie said, stomping his foot like a kid used to getting his way.

"It's a test of loyalty, right?" Paul said.

Ronnie nodded.

"Then we're both loyal, two blood brothers."

Ronnie's face lit up and Jack half expected him to shout Eureka!

"I never thought of it that way. Okay, I'll count to sixty and yell when it's time to come out."

"I'll go first," Jack said. "Hold on to the back of my shirt and don't let go." He started forward and Paul fell in behind, wadding up Jack's T-shirt in his fist.

"Leave the shirt on my back."

"Sorry. Nervous," Paul said.

The two boys reached the archway, a piece of stone crumbling and bouncing off Jack's shoulder. Jack ran his hand over the stones, feeling cracks running through most of them. That made the prospect of a cave-in more frightening than any ghost.

"Is it safe?" Paul asked.

"Not really, but I think he'll bust that flashlight if we don't go along."

They moved ahead, Jack the engine and Paul the caboose. Jack hoped for a sliver of light, but the darkness was complete. He reached out in front of him, feeling for the brick pile or anything else that might be in his way. Paul's tattered breathing echoed behind him.

They had walked about a hundred feet when Jack stubbed his toe on something hard. A brick or rock rolled ahead of them, clanking on the concrete.

"I think we're here," Jack said.

"How can you tell?"

"I've kicked a couple bricks or stones. We have to be near the stone pile."

"Just be careful."

Jack caught his foot on a pile of something hard and stumbled forward, for a moment visualizing his skull cracking open on a rock. He put his hands out to break the fall, and they hit cold, hard stone. His knees hit harder and Paul landed on Jack's back. The weight of Paul drove him into a pile of rubble and he groaned.

"You all right?" Paul asked.

"Not really, but we found the cave-in site."

"You sure you're okay?"

"I'd be better without a fairy on my back."

Paul pushed off and rolled to one side, stones scraping as he moved.

Jack got to his feet, palms stinging and knees aching. Cold air kissed his knee where the concrete had torn his jeans open.

"Where did you go, Paul?"

"Right here."

His voice came from Jack's left.

"Reach your hand out and feel around," Jack said.

Paul's hand brushed Jack's pants, and he was grateful to feel his friend's touch. It would be a nightmare being trapped in here alone.

Jack turned around and lowered himself like a ship slipping beneath the waves. His rear end found hard stone. Cupping his hands over his mouth he yelled, "All right! We're on the pile, so start counting!"

No response from Ronnie.

He hollered again and once again, no response came. The only noise was the drip-drip of water coming from an unseen source. It hadn't occurred to him that the fucker might abandon them in the tunnel, but that's exactly what had happened.

"This sucks. You try and help the guy—"

"Jack."

"What?"

"Someone's in here with us."

"Bull crap."

"Really. Listen."

Under the drip-drop of water and the occasional hollow clank in the tunnel came a low shifting noise. Jack pricked his ears, trying to determine the location of the noise. It came from his right, although how far he couldn't tell.

"Hear it?" Paul said.

"It's nothing."

The stone shifted, clicking, rolling, a sound like two bowling balls tapping together.

"Are you moving?" Jack asked.

"No."

"Put out your hand. We're getting out of here."

"I got a porterhouse and a Budweiser waiting for me." John turned his hand, checked his watch. "Where are those two fools?"

He had been sitting in the limo for half an hour, the heat blasting out of the vents. He had stripped off the ski vest and gloves, nearly on the verge of passing out. Gave them five more minutes, then turned the motor off. John exited the limo and climbed the steps, the two stone lions now coated with snow.

Once inside he glanced at the baby grand piano, thinking it would be nice to take an ax and chop the bastard into firewood. Most folks would do somersaults at the thought of living here, but the estate made him want to puke. He put on a good face in front of the bitch, playing little Mr. Sambo. That was only because she had him by the marbles and would never let go.

The thought of Maureen and Ray kept him going, but as time went on, it became apparent he might never see them again. But Cassie dangled his family in front of him like a steak before a wild dog. She told him they would all be together again someday, and part of him wanted to believe that.

For now he had Ronnie, and although he liked the kid, keeping up with him was a full-time job. The kid insulted bullies twice his size, egged houses, and made prank phone calls by the dozen. John was the one to clean up Ronnie's messes, soothing angry home owners with raw egg on their windows. Without John, Ronnie would not make twenty-five without going to Sing Sing or sleeping on a morgue slab.

He searched Ronnie's room and the kitchen with no luck. Next stop was the great room, where Cassie kept all the goodies. John expected to find the boys lounging on the furniture, or staging a mock wrestling match, but they weren't there.

"I find that kid and he's getting a size fourteen up his rear end."

He stuck his head into the butler's pantry and what he saw made him want to punch a hole in the wall. The fridge was moved back from the wall and cans of soda littered the floor.

"That fool."

At least now he knew where they had gone. John pulled open a drawer and he flipped aside silverware and a bottle opener, but found no flashlight.

"Have to find them in the dark," he said, and ducked into the entranceway. He dreaded the descent into the bowels of the estate and realized it was too damn dark to be without a flashlight. He would have to go back and get one.

He was halfway through the kitchen when Ronnie stumbled out of the doorway. His face was smudged with dirt, and he gave John a lopsided grin.

"What did I tell you about going down there?"

He stomped across the floor and pulled Ronnie up, brushing cobwebs from the boy's hair.

"Ow."

"Don't give me no 'ow,' " John said. "Where's your friends?"

"Still down there. Jack made me do it."

"And I'm Ronald Reagan. Where are they?"

"Near the cave-in site."

"And they don't have a flashlight."

Ronnie nodded.

He snatched the flashlight from Ronnie and warned him to stay put.

CHAPTER 17

Stone shifted and rocks clattered like marbles in a sack.

"Listen," Paul said.

Slow footsteps echoed, a soft crunch-crunch in the dark. At first Jack thought Ronnie turned the flashlight off and snuck into the tunnel in order to scare them, but the footsteps were too heavy. They belonged to someone bigger.

"Reach out your hand, Paul."

"Okay."

"Snap your fingers."

Paul snapped his fingers and Jack reached out, gripping his cold hand. Jack tugged his own shirt and placed it in Paul's hand.

"Hold on to me. Stand up."

Paul tugged on the shirt and pulled himself up. They wouldn't be able to go fast, but it was more important to stick together in the dark. If they were lucky, they wouldn't trip and wind up a tangle of legs and arms on the ground.

Jack took Paul's hand and put it in his own.

"What are you doing?"

"We're going to hold hands and run side by side."

"I'm not holding any guy's hand."

"See you later, bater."

"All right." Shallow breathing from Paul. "It's getting closer."

"Don't hyperventilate on me."

"Give me a break. I'm nervous."

They linked hands as more rock tumbled in the darkness, and the stone shifter came closer.

"Here it comes!" Paul jerked forward, nearly taking Jack's arm with him. Jack held tight and got his legs moving.

"Slow down."

"It's coming."

Jack's worst fear came true as he got too close to Paul, his right foot tangling with Paul's left. Both of them whacked the cement, Jack flipping over on top of Paul.

Jack got up, totally disoriented, feeling as if he had a dark sack over his head, yelling for Paul to get up.

"Jack! Where are you? I can hear it!"

"Keep yelling."

"Over here."

He felt around like a blind man, sure that he would smack into a wall and knock his teeth out, or worse, run into whatever was down here with them.

"Again!" Jack said.

"Over here."

Paul was smart and stayed put. Luckily Jack had only fallen seven or eight feet from Paul, but down in the darkness it may have been as bad as seven or eight miles. He continued ahead until he felt hair, Paul's hair. Paul let out an involuntary yelp.

"It's me. Reach your hand out again and snap your fingers."

Paul did, and Jack gripped his hand.

They started to go but something found Paul first.

It jerked Paul back, and purely out of reflex, Jack clamped on to Paul's hand, this alone preventing him from being torn back into the tunnel by whatever was down there.

"It's got my shirt!"

Jack dug his heels in and held on to Paul's hand tight,

fearing that Mr. Skin-and-Bones-Fussel's arm would snap like a chicken wing. He couldn't see who had Paul.

"Oh, Christ! It's got me hooked. Its arm is around me!"

Jack felt Paul leave his feet as the attacker hoisted him in the air, intent on dragging Paul back into the tunnel.

It pulled again, like a shark dragging a swimmer down, and it was too strong. Paul's hand slipped from Jack's, and Paul shrieked.

"Let me go! Bastard! Let me go! God, it smells bad!"

Dull thuds came from yards away as Paul pounded on his captor.

Jack charged ahead and slammed into someone as solid as a muscle man in a magazine. He wrapped his arms around the waist and pulled, but it was like trying to drag down a redwood tree. He was being dragged behind the guy like tin cans on a wedding car. It stank like old leaves or hair that's clogged in a drain, wet and dead.

What is it and why did we have to run into it?

The vomit came up, hot and sour. Emma puked into the garbage can, trying not to be too loud, but sure Mom heard her downstairs. She felt like crying, and the thought of Jacob's hands squeezing her rear end made her stomach lurch again, and she dry-heaved.

"Oh God." She pulled a tissue from the box and dabbed her lips.

What was she going to do? Go down and tell Mom that Jacob had groped her? Mom would never believe her, because even though he was a total turd in Emma's eyes, Jacob never got into trouble for anything. He was usually pretty quiet and no one would ever suspect him of doing something like this. Aunt Sam would get defensive and say that her little Jacob wasn't capable of something like that; Emma was surely making it up.

She wished Jack were with her right now. He was a good listener and usually pretty smart about things. Maybe he would even be chivalrous and offer to punch booger Jacob right in the mouth for her.

Somehow she knew she could tell Jack about what happened even if she couldn't tell her mom. But not in front of the other two, Chris and Paul. They were okay guys, but not like Jack. He wouldn't laugh or go running to school the next day and tell all the boys in the locker room.

Right now she had the issue of dinner and a garbage can full of barf to deal with. She stood up and threw the dirty tissue into the trash can. Looking in the mirror, she saw there were no chunks on her shirt, but her face was the color of pea soup. Mom would know something was wrong.

"Emma, dinner."

"Coming. Just have to use the bathroom."

"Hurry up."

She picked up the garbage can and went downstairs, peeking around the corner to make sure no one would see her. The chattering and the clinking of silverware from the dining room told her they were seated at the dinner table. Good. She ducked across the hall and into the bathroom. Once inside, she turned on the hot water and let the vomit sluice off the sides of the can (luckily Mom had emptied it before she threw up). Then she dumped the pukey water in the toilet and flushed.

She rinsed out her mouth with water, then grabbed Listerine off the vanity, swished, and spat a gob of blue into the sink. Satisfied that her breath didn't resemble rotting cabbage, she set the trash can on the stairs and went to the dining room.

Jacob sat next to Aunt Sam, head down, gnawing on a dinner roll. Aunt Sam sipped her wine, and Mom spooned mashed potatoes onto her plate in globs.

"Do you feel all right?" Aunt Sam asked.

"Just a little nauseated."

"Your color's off, Emma. Are you sure you're okay?" Mom said, pausing in midspoon.

"Something made me sick. Can I be excused?"

"You don't have to eat, but stay at the table, okay? Your cousin and aunt are anxious to spend some time with you."

"I'm sure they are . . . especially Jacob."

"Of course," Mom said.

Mom went back to spooning out potatoes, completely unaware that her only daughter had been in danger of being raped.

It became clear to Emma that Jacob was her problem and she would have to solve him on her own.

CHAPTER 18

Jack's hold on the guy slipped and he fell, arms still wrapped tightly, but now around the ankles. The guy tore his foot away, and Jack hung on to a single ankle. It dragged him across the cement.

"Jack, where are you?"

"I'm still here."

His arms throbbed, his knees ached from banging on the concrete, and the stink of the thing made him gag. When he didn't think he could hold on any longer, he heard footsteps smacking the pavement.

Please, God, let that be help.

He was running out of options, for the hulk in the darkness was too strong, but he couldn't let it take Paul without a fight. He followed his nose to where the rotting smell was strongest, about six inches in front of his face. He opened his mouth and clamped his teeth onto the ankle, biting through fabric, and then flesh. The man grunted, and Jack bit harder. Fluid dribbled from the wound, and it trickled into the corner of his mouth. It tasted like rancid cough syrup and he half expected his tongue to curl up and turn black.

He jerked his head back, feeling like he had tasted poison.

It was enough to get the guy to stop, and he kicked at Jack, flinging him off to the side.

The heavy footsteps got closer, and Jack turned in their direction.

"A light."

"Jack! Paul!"

It was John.

Jack wasn't entirely sure what happened next. Paul let out a yelp as he hit the ground, and his captor either dropped or threw him to the ground. Something whooshed past him, a purple shadow in the beam from John's flashlight. It ran past the beam and down the tunnel, blowing past John.

"Jack?" It was Paul's voice, up ahead.

"Over here."

Jack stood up, intent on locating Paul and flying the coop, but a big hand came down on his shoulder.

"C'mon, Jack. Let's get out of here."

It was John, praise be the Lord.

"Paul! Come over here. Toward the light."

Paul staggered out of the darkness, his skin bleached, his lips blue.

"You boys have had quite a scare. Let me take you home."

They left the tunnel, John with his arms around their shoulders.

Emma lay on the bed with her hands across her belly, as if compressing it would somehow make the nausea disappear. She was waiting for her mother to come up and ask her if she was okay, and she dreaded it almost as much as another encounter with Jacob. To say discussing the Jacob situation with her mother was uncomfortable could be the understatement of the century.

She had showered and dressed in a blue sweatsuit. Downstairs, the water ran and dishes chimed as Mom finished cleaning up after supper. Two hours she spent down there, scrubbing grease and caked-on food, refusing to let Emma help her because she didn't feel good tonight. Whenever Emma suggested Mom get a dishwasher, she resorted to the parental standard: we don't have a money tree in the back-yard.

The water shut off, and Emma pictured Mom folding the dish towel in thirds and placing it over the dish drainer.

Emma shut her eyes for a moment, and when she opened them her mother was in the doorway with a bottle of Pepto Bismol in her hand.

"How are you?"

"All right, I guess."

"Touch of the flu. Maybe you should stay home another day."

God, she would go batty if cooped up for another day.

"Just a little upset belly."

"If you think you're okay."

"Yep."

"Did you enjoy seeing Aunt Sam and Jacob?"

No. And double no.

"Sure."

"Honey, are you sure you're okay?"

"Can I just be alone please?"

"Is there anything you want to tell me?"

Here was her chance. Mom had opened the door and all she had to do was walk through it to get cousin creepo off her back. She started to open her mouth but then closed it.

"What is it?" Mom said.

"Nothing."

"Are you sure?"

"Positive."

"All right, but if you change your mind you can tell me."

"Okay."

She kissed Emma on the cheek and wished her good night.

"Remember, you can talk to me."

I wish I could, Mom. I wish I could, but you just don't know.

CHAPTER 19

They climbed the stairs and ducked through the small door leading to the kitchen. Ronnie stood there giggling and pointing at Jack as he came through the entranceway.

"Haw, haw! Have trouble down there, Jack? Did you make fudge in your drawers?" More laughing.

"You're about as funny as a brain tumor."

"I would've given my left arm to see the look on your face. Haw, haw!"

He was nearly doubled over laughing, obviously very pleased with himself, and for one moment Jack saw him as a fat, slow moron who deserved whatever beating he got from guys like Vinnie Palermo.

"Did you see any ghost?"

That was it. As a certain spinach-eating sailor used to say, "That's all I can stands."

He stepped forward and shoved Ronnie, his palms slapping against Ronnie's chest.

Ronnie didn't budge. "Hey! Blood brothers don't do that kind of stuff."

"Blood brothers don't ditch each other either."

"Why you so bent out of shape? I was just playing a joke."

Paul came through the door and stood behind Jack.

"It wasn't funny at all," Paul said.

"No, it wasn't." *It was awful. It was scary. It couldn't be real . . .*

The rich voice came from behind him, and he could feel John behind him, towering like the Empire State Building.

"You boys gather round me."

John crouched down, and even then he still seemed like a giant.

"John, he pushed me!" Ronnie stuck out a fat finger, pointing at Jack, as if John would have trouble seeing him otherwise.

"Did you push him?"

"Yeah, but—"

"Don't do it again. Some people might get upset about that, Jack."

John looked at Ronnie, then Paul, then Jack, staring each boy in the eye and pausing for a moment for effect.

"You all listen to me. What you did today was stupid. Damn stupid. You could've gotten lost or hurt down there. And you, young Mr. Winter, I told you to keep your butt out of there in the first place. Leaving these two down there with no light was a rotten trick. I catch any of you fools down there again and I'll kick your little white butts."

"Aw, John," Ronnie said.

"Don't give me that. You know better. And you should apologize."

Ronnie lowered his head and muttered, "I'm sorry." He sniffled, and although Jack couldn't see his face he was pretty sure there were tears in his eyes.

"You guys won't stop being friends with me, will you?"

"No," Jack said. "Unless you pull another stunt like that."

"Good. What about you, Paul?"

Paul pursed his lips and frowned. He looked at Jack and Jack gave him a nod.

"All right. But do that again and no more friends."

"Now that we have that settled, I need to get you two home," John said.

So far no one had brought up what happened in the tunnel, and Jack had been so angry at Ronnie that he forgot about biting the guy on the leg. His lips and tongue felt as if they had been packed in ice, and the bitter taste permeated his mouth. Hopefully that thing didn't poison him.

Maybe John would have an explanation for what happened. Although he didn't know who would frequent an underground tunnel built by an eccentric millionaire. Whoever it was made bad company.

"Let's hit it, boys."

John motioned for them to follow and they left the kitchen.

The limo pulled away and Jack waved as it disappeared into the curtain of snow.

Jack trudged up the driveway, his legs feeling like two iron posts that took monumental effort to drag behind him. Shivers pulsed through his body, and nothing sounded better than sliding underneath his flannel sheets. John had dropped Paul off first, then Jack. Before he had gotten out of the car, John warned him again about staying out of the tunnels, and that bad things could happen to little boys down there. He didn't have to tell Jack twice.

He swung the chain-link gate open and tugged on the doorknob. A pine wreath hung on the door and Jack inhaled, sucking in that smell and thinking of Christmas morning and the stack of silver-and-red-wrapped presents under the tree. He rang the doorbell and Mom padded down the stairs and opened the door.

"Did you have fun at Ronnie's house?"

"You knew I was at Ronnie's?"

"Of course."

"How did you know?"

"His mother called me. Nice young lady. Must've been pretty young when he was born from the sound of her voice."

He could tell that Mom didn't approve of *that*.

"Are you going to stand there all night?"

"Invite me in."

Jack came in and after a quick cup of cocoa, he showered. He stayed in the shower a good twenty minutes, letting the hot water take the chill out of his bones. He got out, dried off, and slipped into his flannel pajamas.

He suddenly wished Ronnie hadn't come tumbling over that snowbank yesterday with Vinnie and his boys in hot pursuit. Now he was Jack's problem, and as he remembered the cold stare Ronnie gave him, he thought Ronnie Winter might be a little crazy. And why did his mom have to choose Jack to babysit the kid anyway? Anyone who provoked guys like Vinnie Palermo deserved what they got. *Why should I take responsibility for him?*

He slipped under the covers and twined his hands behind his head, staring at the ceiling. It was in moments like this he did his best thinking. He tried to avoid thinking about what Ronnie's mom had done to him. Mended his ribs and soothed his aching head, but how? What the hell was Cassie Winter?

Ronnie lay on his bed, knees up and covered, a miniature Everest. A gust of wind rattled the window, throwing snow like a child tossing jacks, and he pulled the covers up to his chin. *Don't like the wind*, he thought. *Sounds like people in pain.*

Mom would be up soon to talk to him about the trip into the tunnels. He had disobeyed John, but grown-ups didn't know how much fun, how radical pranks were.

They made his motor hum. Leaving flaming dog crap on steps, putting M-80s in mailboxes, and throwing mud balls at windows were the king. Almost as good as calling big kids names and seeing if they chased after you. It got the heart racing and the adrenaline flowing. The other guys were going to love pranks, and once he got to know them better, Jack and Paul would be egging houses right alongside him. The prank in the tunnel was a good one, and he really didn't know what had happened, but Paul and Jack looked like they wanted to piss their pants. Pranks were a pisser, all right.

The doorknob turned and Mom entered, her hair in a ponytail. He sat up on the bed and folded his legs Indian-style.

She sat on the edge of the bed, the shadows outside growing longer. Ronnie didn't like the estate at night. The snow looked bleaker, as if they were dropped in the middle of an arctic landscape with no hope of rescue.

"What's the matter?"

"It's spooky around here when it's dark," Ronnie said.

"Nothing to be afraid of."

"We're safe in here."

"Right. What happened in the tunnels today?"

"I don't know."

"John told me but I want to hear your version."

He was in deep this time.

"Well?" Mom said.

"We went down there. I dared the other guys."

"That's better."

He told her the whole story, including how Jack got mad and pushed him.

"I don't like him pushing you."

"It wasn't that bad," Ronnie said.

"He's supposed to be your friend."

"I deserved it."

"Don't ever say that."

She clamped on to his wrist and he flinched.

"Mom, that hurts."

"Never let anyone treat you like that. You don't deserve anything like that."

"It was just a push."

"First it's a push; then they're calling you fat, and then they're chasing you home from school."

She let go of his wrist. He pulled it back, scared of her when she got like this.

"They're cool guys, Mom. Don't worry so much."

"We'll see. Look at me and not out the window. You are never to go into those tunnels again. Bad things can happen."

"Like what?"

"Like being drowned, crushed, lost, freezing to death, or other things."

"Pretty scary. Why would someone build them?"

"The Steadmans had too much money. He was one of the richest men in the country. The tunnels were already here. He tried to build the rail system but abandoned it when the workers died. You're not thinking of going back into those tunnels, are you?"

"No Mom." He swore that woman read minds.

"Good."

"Tell me about Dad again," he said.

"Don't change the subject."

"Please?"

"Your father was very rich, like the Steadmans. He owned over a hundred and fifty manufacturing plants. They made car parts, brake pads, drums, air-conditioning units. WINCO was worth twenty billion dollars when he sold it."

"He got all that money?"

"All that money. Enough to never have to work for a thousand lifetimes."

"How did he die?"

"I've told you this a thousand times."

"Tell me again."

"His plane crashed on the way back from a ski trip to Aspen. It hit a bad storm and went down."

"Whoa."

"Enough about that. Remember what I told you about the tunnels."

"What was he like?"

"That's enough," she said.

"Why won't you—"

"Enough!"

She clapped her hands together inches from his face, and Ronnie flinched.

"Sorry," he said.

He felt as if he'd been punched in the chest.

"I'm sorry, honey," she said, stroking his hair. "I just get a little tired of telling the same story over and over."

"If you love someone you shouldn't get tired of talking about them."

"I have to go downstairs." She stood up and strode out of the room.

CHAPTER 20

Paul made the point of taking his boots off and tiptoeing into the house, hoping that the General wouldn't hear him. He was out of luck, for when he walked in the door, there he was, standing with a bottle of Molson in his hand, oxford unbuttoned, his belly hanging out.

" 'Bout time you came home."

"Uh, sorry, Dad."

"You're lucky that Rocky kid's mother called me and told me where you were."

"Ronnie."

"Don't correct me!" He raised his hand and then lowered it, as if hitting Paul right now would be too much effort.

Paul lifted his hand to shield his face. "Sorry."

"Get your ass to bed. It's getting late."

He took a swig of his beer, scratched his belly, and headed for the living room.

Paul expected a cuff across the cheek at the very least. One time his watch had stopped and he came home a half hour late. The General had beat him across the back with an extension cord, and he expected the same this time. Ronnie's mother must have been a miracle worker to soothe the savage beast inside his father.

He hurried to his room for fear his father would change his mind about a beating. While stripping off his clothes he looked up at the *Star Wars* poster the General had trashed, and decided it needed to be fixed. He rummaged in his top dresser drawer, found an old roll of Scotch tape, and taped the poster together, smoothing it with his hand. You could still see a jagged tear in it, but it was a pretty good tape job.

Ruin my posters, will you?

He threw on a T-shirt and hopped into bed, and like Jack Harding a block away, he pulled the covers up high, remembering the incident in the tunnel. That fat porker Winter had left them down there to rot, and he didn't know why he agreed to remain friends with him. The smell of the guy that dragged him away permeated his nostrils, the smells of decay and rot. And then there were the hands, freezing cold, as if the guy were already dead.

Maybe they should ditch the Winter kid. Bad news, he was.

He would talk to Jack about it tomorrow because Jack always knew what to do.

Paul whipped off the covers and emerged into the cold air. Winter mornings were the worst; it was cold, dark, and the bare floors almost stung your feet. Despite the cold, he was glad to be awake and alive. The room was nowhere near as cold as whatever had grabbed him in the tunnel. He had never felt cold that pure, as if no amount of heat could thaw it. And it had smelled like a dead horse rotting in the sun.

He had dreamt of it, the hands clasping around his throat. In the tunnel, dim light grew brighter until a maw of razor teeth appeared before him, snapping at his face just as he woke up. The same dream came every time he fell back to sleep.

He dressed and grabbed his backpack, realizing he had never done his homework last night. Ordinarily this would have thrown him into a panic, but after the events in the tunnel, missed homework was nothing. He carried a ninety-eight average, and the teachers were bound to cut him some slack this one time.

He crept into the kitchen. Dishes caked with dried egg, spaghetti sauce, and sour milk were piled high in the sink. The sour smell of old beer wafted up from the empty bottles on the counter. Ever since Randy had left for the navy last year, things had gotten worse around here. Randy had done the housework and helped him with chores, keeping the General off Paul's back.

The General loved Randy, who was determined to go through BUD/S training and become a Navy SEAL. That was his father's wet dream: having a kid in the Navy SEALs. Paul was scrawny and liked to read sci-fi and fantasy, everything his father despised. He hated the bastard, but every night he went to sleep with a dull ache in his chest, hoping Dad would come in and kiss him good night. It never happened.

He threw a can of Coke, chips, and a Twinkie in his lunch box and snapped it shut. His stomach felt sour, so he skipped breakfast, washed up, and brushed his teeth.

With a last look of disgust at the mess in the kitchen, he walked out the door.

Mother Nature and Jack Frost continued to put a hurt on Brampton. Another eight inches of snow had fallen overnight, and the weathermen were calling for another six to twelve. The town's salt barn was down to a quarter capacity and one of the big yellow plows blew a hydraulic line, putting it out of commission. Already the remaining plows were putting in overtime, and the drivers were bitching up a storm. Dutch Finney threatened to quit if he couldn't go home and grab at least a couple of hours' sleep.

Traffic wasn't much better. A Toyota and a Bronco had met head-on in the middle of Main Street, and the Bronco's driver bought it on the way to Erie County Medical Center.

Max Browman's F-150 spun out, hitting a telephone pole, and Sylvia Platz's Camry skidded into the corner of Burger King, knocking concrete blocks in the foundation loose.

Although the weather was rotten, it occupied the back of everyone's mind. At Russ's Diner, the retirement set jawed over the topic of who killed the college kid. The rumors flew and the coffee flowed as the town tried to be brave. But everyone was scared. Parents drove kids to school, and residents who usually left their doors unlocked now clicked dead bolts into place. More than one handgun was pulled off the shelf and loaded.

School was done for the day. Barney Lillie, the weatherman at WKTO, was calling for six more inches of snow, adding to what had already been a blisteringly cold winter. The adults grumbled about it, but to Jack it didn't matter. It was three days to Christmas break, and even better, Emma had come back today. He had gotten to homeroom before her, and a pleasant little jolt coursed through him when he spotted her. She smiled and gave him a little wave, and the little rush came again, starting in his belly and fanning out.

Vinnie and his boys had even left Jack alone. Either his appetite for violence had been satisfied, or John had scared him so bad he decided to back off for a few days.

Before homeroom, Jack, Paul, Chris, and Emma had gathered at Jack's locker and agreed to meet in Paul's basement room. It was away from any adults and meetings could be conducted in secret. The perfect place for Jack and Paul to share the story about the encounter in the tunnel.

After seventh period, as Jack pulled his coat on he felt a tap on the shoulder. He turned around and found Emma standing there.

"Miss me?"

"Yeah, like I would miss diarrhea."

"Sit and spin, Harding."

"How you feeling?"

"Better. My throat still hurts, but there was no way I was staying home another day."

"Ready for our meeting?"

"I don't know what you and Paul could be up to that's so supersecret."

"It's big, trust me."

Vinnie Palermo and Harry Cross strolled by, the smaller kids parting like the Red Sea as they passed. "You and fruit-cake going steady?" Vinnie said.

Emma turned around and flipped Vinnie off.

"You wish," Vinnie said, and strutted down the hall.

"I hate that turd," Emma said.

"I hear you. I'll tell you all about him in our meeting."

"Okay. Can I talk to you in private after we meet?" Emma said.

"Huh?"

"Your hearing going? I need to talk to you about a couple of things. Things I don't want the other guys to hear."

"Uh, sure."

"Here they come."

Chris and Paul, looking like David and Goliath, walked side by side down the hall. They approached and the four friends said their hellos.

"No practice today, Chris?" Jack asked.

"I'm skipping out."

"Won't MacGregor be ticked off at you?" Emma said.

"He's already pissed at me. Besides, it'll serve him and my old man right. Let them stew in their own juices for a while."

"It's your hide, pal," Paul said.

"Don't worry, Mother."

"Your dad won't be home, right, Paul?" Jack said.

"Not until five-thirty or six."

"Good. No offense," Jack said.

"None taken."

That was a good thing. One time Paul hadn't come into the house fast enough when Mr. Fussel called him, so he took off his shoe and whipped it at Paul. Paul ducked, but it missed his head by inches. Jack thought Hitler might have made a better father than Mr. Fussel.

"Let's head out," Jack said.

They left the school for their big meeting.

CHAPTER 21

Kempf turned on his wipers as Dion played in the background, full of static on the unmarked car's factory radio.

He had found the Winters' number in the phone book and called this morning. They were listed under Cassie, but a man with a voice that started in his shoes had answered the phone. He agreed to let Kempf see Mrs. Winter after a five minute delay in which he set the phone down.

Kempf rolled up to the gate, lighting up a Camel to get the last smoke in before talking with the unseen Mrs. Winter. He cracked the window and blew smoke out. Official department policy prohibited smoking in patrol cars, but he was the only one who ever used it. Besides, it calmed his nerves. With a killer loose in his town and a reporter coming to see him about it, he needed all the help he could get.

He rolled the window down, reached out, and pressed the button on the intercom box.

"May I help you?" It was the same rich voice from the phone.

"Detective Kempf to see Mrs. Winter."

"I'll open the gates, Detective. Can you find the house okay?"

"It might be hard to miss."

"Fair enough. The property's large."

A motor whirred and the gates swung open. Kempf pulled the car through and crawled up the hill to the mansion. He took a last drag on the cigarette and flicked it out the window between his fingers. The damn things didn't even taste good, and he had quit a year ago, only to start up again two months ago. The habit grew from three smokes a day to a pack and a half, no doubt helped along by his illustrious boss. Ramsey would glide in and out of Kempf's office, asking him about retirement plans, or when he was going to buy that sailboat. Ramsey always mentioning his nephew Larry and how Kempf could show him the ropes, teach him how to be a detective. *Not giving in to you yet, Chief*, he thought.

The snow pelted the car harder, and through it he saw the silhouette of the mansion.

He pulled the car around the circular driveway and parked it at the foot of the steps. After rolling up the window, he got out and climbed the stairs. He rang the bell and it gonged from inside the mansion's depths.

The door opened and a young woman appeared. She had brilliant red hair, creamy skin, and wore bell-bottom jeans. Her toes, also painted red, poked out from the cuffs of the bell-bottoms. A real looker, maybe the daughter.

"Is Mrs. Winter home?"

"I'm Cassie Winter."

"Oh."

"You can pick your jaw up off the floor."

"I'm sorry. You look so young."

"What did you expect?" She smiled, looking at Kempf as if he were dressed in a clown suit.

"Someone about thirty years older."

"A wrinkled old widow."

"Something like that. Can I come in?"

"Certainly."

She stepped aside and he entered the hallway, stomping

his feet on a welcome mat depicting two cocker spaniels lying in the grass. He brushed the snow off his shoulders and out of his hair.

"Nice to meet you."

She held out her hand and he shook it. It might have been nerves (the pretty ones always turned him to putty), but he felt a surge of warmth in his arm when he shook Cassie's hand.

"Come in please."

He followed her, passing a baby grand piano, ducking under an archway, and proceeding down a hallway. They passed a ballroom with hardwood floors and a door marked POOL. He knew the Steadmans had money, but never imagined enough to build a place like this. It was a palace.

She stayed ahead of him, bottom twitching as she went. "See anything you like, Detective?" Cassie said. He blushed and reminded himself he was a married man and old enough to be her father.

They wound up in a study, something that looked like it came out of *Masterpiece Theatre*. He strolled over to the window and looked out, trying to gauge what you could see from in here. Like someone being killed or a murderer fleeing across the property.

"Care to sit down, Detective?"

"I'll stay on my feet."

He removed his overcoat and draped it over a chair. "You've heard about the murder that took place."

"It was right outside my doorstep."

"Did you see anything, Mrs. Winter? Anyone strange on your property? Strange noises?"

"It's a large property. And technically it wasn't even on the grounds, right?"

"That's right."

"I don't think I'll be much help."

"I was hoping you would be. The killer could have fled onto your property."

"Oh, my." She placed her hand palm down over her chest.

It looked calculated to Kempf. "You don't think I have something to do with this?"

"Not at all. But I suspect the killer fled across your property. He may even be hiding somewhere on it."

"Do you really think he's still around? That's frightening."

"Are you sure you didn't see anything?" Kempf asked.

"What time did the murder take place?"

"The coroner estimated the time of death between eight and nine P.M."

"I was probably asleep at the time."

"Probably or were?"

"I said I was. Is that so hard to believe?"

Had he hit a nerve? Did she know something? People quick to the defensive usually had something to hide.

"Fair enough. Nothing though, huh?"

She ignored him, staring out the window. Time to make nice with her.

"I'm sorry. Didn't mean to push."

"I suppose you're just doing your job."

The smile came again, one that said *I have a secret*. The same smile prom queens and cheerleaders flashed in high school, capable of cutting deep. It made his mouth go dry just thinking about it, and when he reached in his pocket for a business card, he fumbled. It dropped to the floor. *Still no good around the pretty girls, George*. He stooped over to pick it up and when he stood up, she was right in front of him.

"Are you married?"

"Is that a proposal?" she asked.

"No. Just wondering where all this money came from."

"He's deceased. Surely you've heard of Ronald Winter."

"The WINCO Ronald Winter?"

"Yes."

"I should have made that connection. Here's my card."

He handed her the business card. "Do you mind if I have a look around the property? It would be for your own safety."

"I'll give you a tour myself. And who knows? Maybe you'll stumble onto something."

I already did. Just not sure what.

Kempf turned on the wipers. The snow fluttered down in front of the car and he wondered if they would ever see spring after all this.

Someday I'll be on the Gulf of Mexico in that boat. Then the snow can pile up to the treetops for all I care.

"You mind if I smoke, Mrs. Winter?"

"They're your lungs."

He took out a fresh Camel, dug out his lighter, and lit up.

"You know that's bad for you."

"Tell me something I don't know," he said absently.

"Ronald smoked. Mostly cigars."

"Some snow, huh?"

"I like it," Cassie said.

"Oh?"

"I've got everything I need here. A wonderful home. More money than I know what to do with, and Ronnie."

"Ronnie?"

"My son. He means the world to me."

"How old is the boy?"

"Twelve."

He almost swallowed his cigarette. She didn't look old enough to have a kid that age. Kempf raised his eyebrows in surprise, and she picked up on it.

"I had Ronnie very young, if that's what you're wondering."

"It's just surprising, that's all. Do you think your boy might have seen anything?"

"He's not very observant."

"You never know. Do you think I might be able to talk to him?"

"I don't want to expose him to all this, Detective."

"You sure?"

"Don't press me on it."

A sharpness crept into her voice that hadn't been there before.

"It'd be nice if you cooperated."

"It would be nicer if you left my son out of this."

"Fair enough."

He decided not to press, for he didn't want to completely alienate her. Besides, the kid probably hadn't seen anything. It was just a possible angle to work.

Kempf had noticed a barn, a stable, and two red houses off in the distance. He assumed the houses were for grounds-keepers.

"Are the other buildings still in use?"

"One of the houses is occupied by our driver, John. The other is empty. I plan on purchasing some horses and some sheep."

"And the barn?"

"Full of tools and an old tractor."

"Do you mind if I have a look at it?"

"It's so full of junk you wouldn't be able to even get in the door."

"I think I'd like to have a look."

"No, you don't want to."

At that moment he couldn't describe what happened to him. It was like the start of a headache. His body twitched, almost like having a dream where you fall and catch yourself at the last second. The car jerked to the right and his whole body convulsed again before he pulled the sedan back onto the road.

"What the hell were we talking about?" Kempf said.

"How bad the weather was getting."

"We were?"

"Uh-huh."

What the hell had she done to him?

"Are you okay?"

"Just a little light-headed."

Two roads appeared before him and his vision went in

and out of focus. Nausea overtook him and he sincerely thought he might blow chow all over little Mrs. Winter's lap.

"Would you like to come back another time, Detective? You don't look well."

"I think I will."

For a horrible moment he thought he was having a stroke. Didn't your vision sometimes get messed up right before you blew a gasket in the old melon? He knew he should have quit smoking.

He slowed down and pulled the car over to the side of the road. Kempf put it in park and cranked the window down, hoping the fresh air would relieve his dizziness. Snow pushed into the car, a blast of flakes hitting him in the face.

It did nothing other than freeze his face, so he rolled the window back up. He leaned forward, resting his forehead on the steering wheel, eyes closed, reciting the drinker's prayer that was so familiar during his partying days: make it go away.

That prayer was usually said to the white porcelain god, and the same prayer would be repeated the next weekend after too many Genny beers. It never worked when he was praying not to puke up his liquor, but the nausea did subside after about thirty seconds. Likewise for the dizziness, though he still for the life of him couldn't remember most of the conversation from the last five minutes.

The Camel had burned down to the filter, but he couldn't remember smoking it. He took one last drag, rolled down the window, and tossed it.

"Would you like to come back up to the house?" Cassie asked.

"No, no. But let me drop you off. We covered everything, right?"

"I believe we did," she said.

He pulled away from the side of the road, did a three-point turn, and drove back to the mansion. He thanked her for her time and she said if she could be of more assistance to call her anytime.

He agreed he would.

Cassie Winter agreed they covered everything, and for the moment, Kempf believed that. But why did it feel like someone just blew fog into his brain? If he were a superstitious man, he would have believed she had done something to cloud his judgment.

But that was nonsense. He pulled around the circle in front of the mansion and drove off, wondering what he had said to her in the car.

The four friends removed their boots and padded downstairs to Paul's basement. The basement was dry and warm; the furnace whooshed as it kicked on. They walked around it, next to a stack of cardboard boxes. A pile of soiled white shirts sat on the floor in front of the washers, and next to the boxes was a stack of dusty books with titles like *Hitler's Generals* and *The Rise and Fall of the Third Reich*.

Beyond the boxes was a door that led to the playroom. Paul opened it and flicked on the lights. They all came in and sat in a small circle on the rust-colored rug. One wall was lined with cabinets, stocked with plastic army men, *Star Wars* figures, GI-Joe vehicles, and *Dungeons and Dragons* books. Paul's father had built the room not so much out of wanting a special place for his son to play, but as a way to keep him out from underfoot.

"So what's the big secret?" Emma asked.

"Where should we start?" Paul asked.

"With the Palermo situation," Jack said.

Jack recounted their first meeting with Ronnie Winter, the way he pissed Vinnie off, and Jack's shot to Vinnie's face after Vinnie flattened his PB and J.

"I already know all this," Chris said.

"We're just filling Emma in," Jack said.

"So Vinnie's gunning for us and Ronnie. We left school and halfway down Main they were waiting for us in the alley."

"Who's they?" Emma asked.

"The Three Stooges. Vinnie, Harry, and Leary," Paul said.

"I wish I could've been there to help you guys out," Chris said.

"Anyway, they jumped us," Jack said.

"Jack got it the worst," Paul said, then looked to Jack almost apologetically.

Jack gave him a look back that said *it's okay*. He was only telling the truth, for Vinnie *had* pounded the snot out of him.

"What did that shit do to you, Jack?" Emma asked.

"Basically used me as a punching bag. And kicking bag. Kicked me right in the ribs."

"You don't look like you're hurting too bad," Chris said.

"We'll get to that part," Jack said. "The only thing that saved me was Ronnie's driver. Big black guy. He could play for the Bills if he wanted to. Scared the three turds off."

From there Jack told them about John scooping him up and putting him in the limo. Then the ride up to the mansion and waking up in Mrs. Winter's room.

"You were in the hot mom's room? Did anything happen?" Chris said.

"Anyway I wake up and I'm not hurting anywhere near as bad as when I went in there. My ribs hurt, my head hurt, and my nuts—" He hesitated, remembering that Emma was in the room, and she smiled at him. He never noticed before, but she had a cute little crinkle in the corner of her mouth.

"So?" Chris said.

"I think she did something to me. I think she healed me somehow. My rib might even have been broken, and then there was almost no pain."

"Vinnie really gave it to him good. He was hurting. Scout's honor." Paul raised his hand, three fingers held up.

"What about you, Fussel? Didn't they hurt you, too?" Chris said.

"Harry got me in a headlock but the worst I got out of it was red ears," Paul said.

"What happened next?" Emma asked.

"She says she wants to talk to me, and then she goes into this whole thing about how Ronnie needs someone to look after him, and how I'm the one to do it. I didn't want to do it at first, but she made me take her hand and I felt all woozy. I agreed with her, I guess, but I really can't remember it. Things started swirling and when I looked into her eyes it was like being hypnotized," Jack said.

"Weird," Paul said.

"You guys are shitting us, right?" Chris said.

"No, Scout's honor," Paul said.

"C'mon," Chris said.

"Why would I make something like this up?" Jack said.

"For a goof."

"I think they're telling the truth," Emma said.

"Why?" Chris asked.

"Because Jack wouldn't lie. I know that for a fact," Emma said.

Chris was a good friend and a great guy to have around if the bullies were on your tail, but he had no imagination. They could never play guns or Dungeons and Dragons or tell ghost stories with him. He usually sneered and said, "There's no such thing." If it didn't involve playing a sport, he usually didn't want any part of it.

"I say they're setting us up," Chris said.

"Tell the rest of the story, Jack," Emma said.

"So I agreed to look after Ronnie for her, keep him out of trouble."

"Are you nuts?" Chris said.

"I'm telling you, it was like she put the answer in my mouth. I had no choice."

"That's creepy," Paul said. "What if she's a witch or something?"

At that Chris let out a belly laugh and slapped Paul on the back. "That's a good one, Fussel!"

"Believe what you want. I'm telling you what happened, you ass."

"We all met in the kitchen after that," Paul said.

"Then what, Frankestein and the Wolfman showed up?" Chris said.

"No, you cretin. I'll tell you what happened," Paul said.

Paul decided to tell the next part of the story, since he had experienced the tunnel thing more vividly than Jack. He had a bad moment when he thought he heard the back door open, but it was just the wind. If his father caught them down here, Paul would take a whipping for sure, because he wasn't supposed to have friends over when his mother was sleeping. Luckily, she slept like a hibernating bear and hadn't heard them.

"You had it wrong, Jack. You met us up in Ronnie's room. You should see the place, like a palace. Ronnie said he had something to show us and pulled out a flashlight. We all went down to the first floor and wound up in tunnels underneath the estate."

"There's tunnels under the place?" Emma said.

"Yeah. Steadman built them. We went down there with Ronnie and he dared Jack to go down one of the tunnels that caved in and killed some workers. He threatened to break the flashlight if Jack didn't do it."

"That kid's nuts," Chris said.

"I'm afraid what might happen if we ditch him completely," Jack said.

"What do you mean?" Paul said.

"I got the feeling bad things might happen to me if I don't stay friends with the kid. Don't ask me how I know, I just do. Tell them about what happened in the tunnel."

Paul recounted hearing the noise on the rock pile, then the thing coming closer and snatching him up. He couldn't help but shiver at the thought of the cold hands gripping his arms. They were so cold they felt like they would bond right to his skin, the way your tongue would if you stuck it to a metal fence in the winter. He recounted how Jack saved him.

"I bit the damn guy," Jack said. "My mouth still feels funny, but not as bad."

"John the limo driver showed up and scared the guy off," Paul said.

Emma said, "That's awful. Fussel, you're lucky Jack was there to slow the guy down."

"That's another thing," Jack said. "I don't think it was a guy."

"Now I've heard everything," Chris said, throwing his hands in the air.

"I bit into the leg and it was almost like biting a frozen piece of meat. My mouth got tingly and cold, and it tasted like crapola."

"Let me guess, the kid's mother is a witch and you two bozos ran into a zombie."

"Would you just keep an open mind?" Paul said.

"I'll tell you what else I think," Jack said. "I think whatever was in that tunnel killed that college guy."

"I can't believe I skipped basketball practice for this." Chris hoisted himself up and started for the door.

"Think about it," Paul said. "The murder took place just outside the grounds of the estate, and then we run into something in the tunnels. It obviously was something bad. What if it killed the guy and then hid down in the tunnels? What if it has a lair down there?" He was beginning to freak himself out.

Chris waved his hand, dismissing them.

What Emma said next caused all of them to freeze in their tracks.

"I say we go down and find out what it is. Unless you're chicken, Chris. That's the only way Paul and Jack can make you believe."

"You read my mind," Jack said.

"No way," Paul said.

Jack had lost him on that one. The chances of him going back down there were slim and none, and slim just took the last train out of the station.

"I'm not chicken. I ain't no girl."

"Then you'll go down there?" Emma said.

"Sure. I'll prove these two wrong anytime."

"Jack, why do you want to go back there?"

"To show Chris. And maybe we can help out the cops, stop someone else from getting killed."

"How do you know the tunnel guy committed the murder?"

"I don't know. It just makes sense. Think of it. We could be heroes. What if we cracked the case?"

"Yeah. I like that idea, Harding," Chris said, rejoining the circle. "We could get on television. Not that I think there's anything down there," he added.

"Jack's right. I'm sure he is," Emma said. "I'm in."

"You'll have to prove it to me but I'm in, too," Chris said.

"Paul?" Jack said.

Even as the tunnel thing had clutched him, he was sure someone would come down into the darkness and save him. And someone did. Besides, the tunnel guy was probably long gone by now, right?

"All right, I'm in," Paul said. "What about Ronnie?"

"He'll have to go with us. It's his house, after all."

"I hope you know what you're doing, Jack. I'll go with you, but I don't really like it," Paul said.

"Stick with me, kid, and we'll go far," he said, ruffling Paul's hair and drawing a grin from him.

"Then it's settled," Emma said. "Jack can call Ronnie tomorrow and we'll go. You think he'll go for it?"

"I don't think it'll be a problem. I'll dare him if I have to," Jack said.

"Now that that's done, would you two mind leaving us alone? Jack and I have to talk about something."

Paul looked at Emma, then at Jack, who nodded.

Standing up, he said to Chris, "C'mon, beanpole, let's leave them alone."

"No smooching, you two," Chris said.

Paul punched him on the arm, and they left the room.

CHAPTER 22

Kempf collapsed into his office chair, opened the top left drawer to his desk, and pulled out a bottle of Anacin. He popped two of the aspirins, chewing them and wincing at the bitter taste. He'd had a pounder of a headache since his meeting with Cassie Winter, but at least he didn't feel like he was going to pass out or puke. He remembered going up to the mansion, being let in, and getting into the car to tour the estate. The Winter woman had become prickly when he asked about her son, and that was about the last thing he remembered before the drive back to the station. It was as if someone had reached in and plucked out a slice of his memory, like a missing puzzle piece.

Head down, he massaged his temples, resting his elbows on the desk. It was cold against his skin. The manila envelope with the crime scene photos of the college kid's body caught the corner of his eye. Maybe having another look at it would jar something in his memory. Sometimes investigations could be like doing one of those word searches where the words were hidden forward and backward. Look at it too long and it would drive you buggy, but take a break, come back, and you might find something you missed.

He loosened his tie and took the photos from the envelope. He flipped through the first few, but nothing hit him. The third one he looked at was a shot of the kid's head and shoulders. His head was cocked to one side, revealing the jellied mess that was his throat. Arms splayed, he looked like he might be making a snow angel.

Kempf stared hard at the photo, knowing there was something waiting to jump out at him. The kid had been wearing a dark blue parka, and bits of the lining rested on him from where it had been slashed open. They looked like little downy balls of cotton. One piece in particular caught Kempf's eye, and he took a magnifying glass from his desk drawer. He couldn't say why it was unusual, but it warranted a further look.

He moved the picture closer to his face and peered through the magnifying glass

It was an inch by an inch, triangular, and ragged around the edges. Some type of cloth. He squinted hard and could make out crosshatching in the fiber, like mesh. Or gauze.

"Gauze," he said.

"What's that, Tank? Talking to yourself again? It's when you start answering that you're in trouble," Ramsey said. He was propped against the door frame, arms folded, which surprised Kempf because he might actually crease his precious uniform shirt that way.

"I may have found something. Piece of gauze on the victim's body. I'm going to check with the boys in the lab to see if they have anything on this."

"Good, Tank. Probably nothing, but you never know."

"It's probably something we missed the first time. Could be important."

"If you say so. Hey, don't forget that reporter's coming by today. Remember, give him the company line, that's it."

"Company line, right."

He barely heard Ramsey. Kempf was already dialing the number for the crime lab in his head. The report didn't mention anything about the gauze, but it wouldn't hurt to give the lab a call and see if maybe they had something else on it.

"Catch you later, Tank." Ramsey made a little shooting gesture at Kempf and left, strolling down the hall and whistling.

Kempf felt juiced for the first time in a long time. First he would call the lab and see if they had anything; then he would go to the scene and look for anything the crime lab might have missed.

He dialed the number for the Wingate County Crime Lab, hoping that they had a piece of gauze from the scene secured in a plastic baggie somewhere. On the night of the murder, the technician looked like he'd been doing his job, going over everything with a fine-tooth comb. How could they have missed the piece of gauze?

The report listed the kid's clothes, a condom found in his pocket, scrapings from his hair and nails, and a gas can, among other things. There had been no bandages on his body, and no gauze found on his person. It had to be from the killer. It was goddamn windy that night, and the only thing Kempf could think of was the evidence might have blown away before they could collect it.

He got the operator and asked for Jerry Spidel.

"Spidel."

"Jerry. George Kempf."

"Hey," Spidel said. His manner of speaking always reminded Kempf of Eeyore the donkey.

"I need some information on the Quinn case."

"Yuh."

"I didn't see anything on the report from the lab, but I was wondering if you had anything at all on gauze found at the scene."

"Gauze, huh?"

"Yeah."

"Hang on, let me pull the file."

He set the phone down and papers ruffled in the background.

"Uh, nope. Nothing on gauze."

"Nothing was collected from the victim's body?"

"Nope."

"And he wasn't wearing any gauze. No bandages on the body from the autopsy. Shit. Okay, thanks, Jerry."

"Sorry, George. If you find anything else we'll run it for you pronto."

"Thanks."

The reporter was due at four o'clock. A check of his watch told him it was three-fifteen, and that left him plenty of time to drive up to the scene and take one last look.

The fuzziness in his head subsided, and he chalked the whole thing up to exhaust or stuffy air in the car. He still couldn't remember what he had seen (if anything) on the Winter property, but another trip might refresh his memory.

He grabbed his coat and headed for the parking lot.

Emma knelt on the floor. She wrung her hands, then smoothed them on her jeans, hoping to dry the sweat. She licked her lips to moisten them.

Jack came over and sat on the floor cross-legged in front of Emma, and she knelt across from him. Outside the room, the furnace clicked on. Paul's and Chris's muffled voices echoed through the doorway, and Emma didn't think they could hear her, but still she decided to whisper.

"So what did you want to talk about?" Jack asked.

"Lower your voice."

"Sorry."

Here it went. She hoped the words would get around the lump fast forming in her throat. "The first thing's about my cousin Jacob."

"Jacob the nerd?"

"The one and only."

"What about him?"

"Something happened. Twice. Maybe I shouldn't tell you. Maybe we should go."

She had started to stand when Jack reached out and

placed his hand over hers. It shocked her so much that she almost lost her balance, teetering to one side for a moment.

"You can tell me, Emma. I promise I won't laugh or tell anyone."

If he touches my hand like that again, I might burst, she thought. "Not even Fussel or Chris?"

"Scout's honor." He imitated Paul's Scout salute and it made her laugh.

"He grabbed me. Once over the summer and once yesterday up in my room."

"Grabbed you where?"

She felt a blush for the ages crawling into her cheeks.

"My boobs. And my rear end."

Jack couldn't have looked more surprised if boobs sprouted from his own chest. The look of amazement quickly turned to that of someone who has just gotten a whiff of sour milk.

"That's disgusting."

"I know. It made me feel slimy and gross. . . . What am I going to do?"

The tears dribbled down her cheeks. Tears never had good timing.

"Did you tell your mom?"

"I can't." Emma lowered her face and covered it with her hands, the tears wet on her palms. "My aunt would just defend the creep and no one would believe me. They think Jacob doesn't even like girls."

She looked up to see Jack digging in his pockets for something. "What are you doing?"

"Trying to find you a Kleenex."

"That's sweet."

How lame, in the middle of a crying fit, telling a boy she had known since they were four how sweet he was. *Get it together, Emma*, she told herself. But it was sweet, and that was Jack. Chivalrous Jack.

"Uh, thanks. I don't have one though. Sorry." He looked away.

"He said he wasn't finished with me," she said, wiping the tears on her shirtsleeve.

"We'll see about that."

"I think he might try to do worse things. But I did slam him a good one right in the nuts."

"That's awesome. I mean, not the situation. The shot to the nuts. Wait till I tell—"

"Not anyone, Jack. Not yet. Please."

"Why did you tell me?"

"Because somehow I knew you would help me."

"I will. We all will if you want. I know Paul and Chris would. If you let me tell them."

"Not yet, okay?"

"Let me think about what we can do to him. When are you going to see the ass wipe again?"

"No time soon if I'm lucky."

"We'll get him good."

"Thank you, Jack."

She leaned forward and kissed his cheek. He immediately turned pink.

"And one more thing," she said. *Here goes the big question, and me with tears and snot running down my face.* "Will you go with me to the Christmas dance?"

"Sure." There was relief in his voice.

And she gave him a slick smile, much like the one Cassie Winter had used on George Kempf, only Emma's had much better intentions.

Kempf gave the sedan gas and it fishtailed, the rear end kicking out, the tires sliding on the icy road. He was trying to hurry but then saw an abandoned white station wagon in a ditch and slowed down.

Mother Nature wasn't helping any. He had the wipers going at full speed to clear away the snow as it rocketed into the windshield. Every so often a gust of wind rocked the car, so much so that he had to white-knuckle the steering wheel to keep the car from being shoved into the oncoming lane. A yellow county snowplow passed on the other side of the road, its blade throwing snow to the side of the road. Salt fell from its tail end, getting up into Kempf's wheel wells and making a rickety sound.

"They're never going my way."

As he neared the scene of the murder, he flipped on his blinker and eased over to the side of the road. He threw his hazards on, but in this weather it was doubtful anyone would see them before they were ten feet from his taillights. There was enough room to go around his car, but he would have to hope that they saw it first.

Better make this quick and then get that heap off the side of the road.

He checked the rearview and when he was confident no one would come along and make road pizza out of him, he stepped from the car. The wind came hard, flipping the back of his trench coat up over the back of his head. After a moment of struggling with the coat (and looking like a colossal asshole in the process) he managed to get it down and button it. He knew he should have worn the big eastern parka that was now sitting in his front closet, and if he could physically kick himself in the ass, he would have. It was damn cold. Too cold for a London Fog raincoat.

Head down, he slogged through the snow and saw the spiked fence separating the Steadman property from the road. He squatted down in the approximate area where the kid's body had been found, but all he saw was freshly fallen snow. This was futile. Anything on the ground was long gone by now.

He spent five more minutes looking around and was about to head for the car when something on the fence caught his eye. His ears burned from the cold and his nose felt as if it might break away like a glacier, but he had to check it out. Something flapping in the breeze, attached to the gate, perhaps only a stray plastic bag, but maybe not.

He got close and saw it was a scrap of fabric, navy blue and torn. Wispy threads hung from the edges. Bingo.

He took out a plastic evidence bag from his pocket and a pair of tweezers. Careful not to dislodge it before he could grip it with the tweezers, he pinched it and dropped it into the bag. Once sealed, he stuck it in his pocket.

When he turned to go back to his car, the hairs on his neck prickled. Someone watching. The estate had dense pines, firs, maples, and sycamores on the other side of the gate. The watcher was in those trees, of that he was sure. Squinting to see through the blowing snow, he scanned the trees from left to right, and he caught a glimpse of someone behind a tree, twenty yards away.

"Show yourself."

No answer.

He had drawn his gun exactly one time in the line of duty, when chasing a suspect who robbed the Lucky Goose mini-mart. Now was the second time and there was no question he should draw it. As if by reflex, he pulled out the .38 special and dropped into a shooter's stance.

"This is Detective Kempf of the Brampton police! Show me your hands and come out of there slow!"

The guy stepped out, but not slowly and not with his hands up like all bad guys were supposed to do when you had them covered. He strode ahead, and something in his guts told Kempf to run, a sensation that originated in his testicles and spread up through the belly. The guy moved quicker and Kempf yelled, "Stop or I'll let you have it!" It would occur to him later that it sounded like a bad line from a Jimmy Cagney gangster flick.

The guy kept coming, almost to the gate, a man dressed in blue coveralls obviously not afraid of the gun. As he approached, Kempf saw the bandages covering the man's face. They were black and dirty, full of pus below the mouth and nose. It looked like something a leper would put on to cover his affliction.

Something was off (besides the bandages) and he didn't notice it at first, but when he looked again he saw it and almost pissed down his leg.

The eyes were hollow sockets, black as an eight ball. The guy had no fucking eyes. "Oh, good Lord Jesus!"

The bandaged man stood across from him, silent as the dead.

Get gone, George. Now.

He backed away, nearly stumbling ass over tin cup into the snow. The bandaged man watched him go until he was into the car. He gripped the wheel hard to keep his hands from shaking and his heart thudded so hard it hurt. If he didn't have the big one right now, he never would.

"That'll give me enough fucking nightmares for a while."

When he looked in the rearview mirror, the man in the bandages was gone. Kempf radioed for backup, and in the ensuing sweep of the Steadman property, seven Brampton police officers found only snow and trees.

Jack and Emma emerged from the basement room to find Paul and Chris sitting on the steps.

Emma's tears had dried, and the only evidence of crying was her red-tinged eyes.

He looked at her. Emma, just one of the boys (until she had asked him to the Christmas dance, apparently), always one of the best at throwing a fastball, running a buttonhook, or whipping snowballs with sniperlike precision. Until recently he had thought of her only as a pal, someone to knock around with on a Saturday afternoon. But lately more and more he had noticed the way she smiled, the nice soapy smell when she walked by, even the curves that were sprouting under her sweatshirts. The invitation to the dance made his day, hell, his whole year.

They headed to the stairs, the dusty-dry smell of old books in the air.

"Everything okay?" Paul said.

"You two weren't making out in there, were you?" Chris asked.

"I save that for your mom," Jack said. "Everything's fine."

"Cool, Daddio. Let's split before my dad comes home."

They started up the stairs single file, Paul in front. The side door groaned and feet stamped on the throw rug in the hallway.

"Oh, shit," Paul said.

"What?" Chris said.

Jack could see up the stairs from under Paul's arm. Paul's father stood in the hallway, snow in his hair, a gray waist-length coat on, and a paper bag tucked under his right arm. If Jack had to guess, he would say it contained some type of alcohol.

"We were just—"

"You were just breaking the rules."

"I didn't mean to."

"What's so hard to remember, Paul? You're not supposed to have anyone in the house."

"It won't happen again."

"You're damn right it won't."

The snow on his forehead had begun to melt, and water dribbled down and ran off the tip of his nose.

"Get upstairs. And I want your friends out of here."

Paul slunk ahead, head bowed, moving quickly past his father as if he expected a swat. At first Jack thought he would go upstairs and that would be the end of it. It appeared Mr. Fussel didn't want to hurt Paul in front of his friends (too many witnesses for the bastard), and Paul would remain unscathed.

On the stairs, Paul said, "I live here too."

That was all Mr. Fussel needed to hear. He took a step forward and slammed his fist into Paul's back, and it landed with a wicked thud. Paul fell forward on the stairs, and Jack could hear him gasping for air.

Without hesitation, Jack brushed past Emma to the landing where Mr. Fussel stood.

"Mouthing off, too," Mr. Fussel said.

Jack got as close as he dared to Paul's father, who was built like a lumberjack.

"You didn't have to do that," Jack said.

"What?"

"You're a lot bigger than him," Jack said.

"This is none of your business, Jack. Get gone before I call your parents."

"My parents know all about you. They'll take my side."

Jack shot a look at Paul, who propped himself up and was sitting on the steps. His breath came in shallow rasps, and he crossed his arms, hugging his rib cage.

"Get out of my house, you smart-ass son of a bitch."

"Paul, come with me," Jack said.

"Yeah, Paul, come with us," Emma said.

"It's not safe here, Fussel," Chris said.

"I can't believe what I'm hearing. It'll be a cold day in hell when I let—"

Paul moved like a greased eel, darting to the left of his dad, who reacted almost as quick, trying to pin Paul to the wall with his hip. He lost his balance and started forward, bending over, his wide butt presenting a great target for Jack. Jack lifted his leg and nudged Paul's dad, sending him face-first onto the stairs. The bag fell to the stairs and glass broke. The aroma of beer filled the small hallway.

Paul was first out the door, followed by Chris, Jack, and Emma. They ran down the driveway, skidding on the ice, and Mr. Fussel came out roaring behind them. Jack looked back, and Mr. Fussel stumbled, windmilling his arms. He had a beer bottle in his hand and Jack realized with horror that he was winding up to throw it.

"Look out!" Jack shouted.

He whipped the bottle, but it skipped off the driveway and rose up before landing harmlessly in a snowbank.

"You better not come home, you little shit!"

The four of them turned the corner onto the sidewalk and didn't stop running until they were a block away.

CHAPTER 23

Kempf pulled the car into the lot of the Brampton Police Station, nearly spinning into a donut. He parked, got out, and started across the lot, lowering his head to avoid the wind. Stavros passed him, the snow collecting in his bushy mustache, and Kempf nodded a quick hello to him. He reached the door and wrestled it from the wind before finding refuge in the rear foyer.

After stamping the snow off his shoes, he removed his coat and headed to the combination locker/break room. He poured the remains of the coffee into a Styrofoam cup and swigged it down. It tasted about as good as paint thinner, but it was hot and warmed his insides.

He went back to his office and was settling in his chair when Mike Blessing, the dispatcher, stuck his head in the door.

"Someone out here for you, George. Reporter."

"Ah, shit. Tell him I'll be out in a minute."

He set his coat on the back of his chair and took out the evidence baggie with the cloth in it.

Who the hell are you, my friend?

Better yet, what are you? If somebody had no eyes, how the hell would he see?

And the bandages. The guy could have been a burn victim, or maybe he was deformed under there and wore the bandages to cover himself, much like John Merrick did with a sack. But the eyes, those damn eyes. He looked like something that crawled from the grave, one of those zombies out of that old Romero movie, only worse. Kempf thought back to his youth, going to Saturday matinees and watching movies like that, where zombies walked the night. Half the fun was being so scared you almost clawed the seats open.

But this wasn't a movie. That thing at the estate had stood in front of him and stared with those dead eyes. That was too real.

His ulcer flared in his gut like lava spewing from a volcano. He gave a little tap on his chest with his fist and belched.

He turned the baggie in his hands, working it around, hoping to get his mind going. Did anyone see them from the road? He didn't remember seeing any cars, but the snow was blinding and he was so scared he couldn't think straight, let alone notice passing traffic. It would be better if he had a witness, because he was going to have to tell Ramsey, and it was questionable whether the chief would believe him.

And the sweep of the grounds had turned up nothing.

He was anxious to get the sample to the lab and have it analyzed. Hopefully it would tell him more and present a sane and logical explanation for what he had just witnessed. Good old science would right things. He hoped.

Blessing appeared in the doorway. "That reporter, George. He's getting antsy."

"Let him. I need to talk to Ramsey first. Give me ten minutes."

"Whatever you say."

He picked up the receiver and rang Ramsey's office. The chief said he'd be right over.

Ramsey came in and sat on the chair beside Kempf's desk. His tanned skin seemed to glow, and Kempf wondered if that radiance couldn't power a small city.

"What's up, Tank?"

"I collected this from the scene out by the Steadman place." He handed Ramsey the evidence bag.

"Where was it?"

"Stuck to the fence."

"Hmm. Could be anything, couldn't it?"

"It's not just anything. It's from the killer's clothes."

"How do you know that?"

"Because I saw him."

Kempf explained how he went out to talk to the Winter woman and came back with nothing. He told Ramsey about the piece of gauze in the crime scene photo, and how it got him thinking to take another look out there.

"I found this, and then I felt like someone was watching me," Kempf said.

"Yeah, we didn't find whoever you thought it was."

"It was our guy," Kempf said.

"Don't know, George."

"Serial murderers often return to the scene of their crimes to relive the thrill of offing someone."

"So that proves it was our killer?"

"No. But the bandages on his face did. Remember how I said there is gauze on the victim's body? This guy's whole face was bandaged up, like a burn victim or something. He also had on blue coveralls, which I'm positive is the same fabric as the swatch I collected from the fence."

Ramsey crossed his legs and leaned on the desk. "This is good work, Tank, real good work. Get that sample over to the lab. I'm going to get on the horn with the sheriff and see if they can help us out. We'll step up patrols in the area by the Steadman Estate. A bandaged man is hard to miss."

The chief seemed almost giddy about the whole thing, but he hadn't seen the crazy-looking bastard. If he had, he might not sound so chipper.

They could find out for themselves when and if they found this guy that he didn't have any eyes in his head. If Kempf told Ramsey that, Ramsey would have him carted off to the booby hatch in no time.

"We'll hold a press conference, too. The civilians are shitting in their drawers over this. We need to give them confidence."

That was Ramsey, never missing an opportunity for some camera time.

"What about that reporter?"

"Tell him to go piss in the wind. You've got more important things to do."

Ramsey clapped him on the arm and said, "This is really nice work, Tank." He smoothed his hair, no doubt preparing for the press conference that would come. "Fill out a report. We'll consider this guy armed and dangerous. I'm a little concerned he got the drop on you, but it was because of the snow, right?"

"Yeah. I couldn't see shit out there."

"Okay, Tank. Just want to make sure you're not losing a step."

Ramsey strode out of the office, full of purpose.

John had just popped open a can of chunky beef stew when the phone rang.

"Damn it. Can't even get a meal around here."

It was Cassie on the phone, and she wanted him to come up to the main house as soon as possible. He said he'd be right up and hung up the phone. After rummaging in the kitchen drawer, he found a small plastic container and lid. He dumped the soup from the can into the container and set it in the fridge. The gourmet dinner would have to wait because the boss lady needed him, probably for something stupid like throwing more wood on the fire.

His house on the estate had a fireplace made of gray stone with a raised hearth. He jabbed it with the poker, then shut the glass doors so no sparks would fly onto the rug. He put on his wool coat and gloves and stepped out the door, amazed that the snow continued to fall. This was one time he wished he had hair, because his head felt like a chilled cue ball almost immediately.

He drove his pickup to the mansion, parked in front of the steps, and went inside. Cassie had said she'd be in the solarium (it always reminded him of playing Clue as a kid), and that's exactly where she was.

She was sitting on a padded bench running along the window. Outside, the back of the estate ran on in a seemingly endless blanket of snow, interrupted only by pines. A brown rabbit scampered in front of the window, sat up on its haunches, and darted off. Steadman's old groundskeeper had told him there used to be abundant wildlife on the estate. Deer, raccoon, woodchuck, and even the odd coyote were seen in the woods, but they had thinned out once Cassie brought It here.

She sat with one leg folded under her, a teacup grasped in her hands.

"I want to talk about some things that happened, John. I'm sure you can guess what they might be."

"I have a pretty good idea."

"The boys were in the tunnels."

"I know."

"They're not supposed to be. Ronnie told me the Fussel boy was almost taken away by Him."

"I gave them a talking-to."

"I don't want them down there again. Understood?"

"Yes."

Yeah, it's understood. Other things could be understood, too. Like you understanding my hands around your throat. It would be so easy if you were just a woman, so easy to wrap the hands around the throat and squeeze until it collapsed. Many a night he had thought about it, but he knew whatever lived under that skin would tear him to pieces in minutes. He had seen the end product when people had fucked with her, and it wasn't pretty.

"You're not thinking bad thoughts, are you?" she asked.

"Go on."

He turned and left, glad to be away from her. John knew what he had to do, which was call Jack Harding and tell him to be very careful. But how would he get in touch with the boy? He doubted Jack's parents would let their son talk to a grown man on the phone (especially a grown black man), and it would be even more suspicious if he showed up at the door. Cassie said she would only send a warning, but with the Wraith, you never knew. It lived to consume, to kill, to rend flesh and break bones.

He would have to go to the Harding house and watch over Jack. If Cassie found out, it might cost him his life, but he had to do it to protect the boy.

He strode down the mansion's never-ending hallways, plotting.

They moved single file on the sidewalk, each of them looking back every few moments to make sure the General wasn't chasing them. Paul felt as if he had a small roller coaster whirling around in his head. There was no possible way he could go home after this, for he would wind up buried in the backyard with his old dog, Scooter. That's where his father would put him for good.

They all slowed to a walk, trudging through the snow, seven inches deep and crunchy.

"You guys saved my bacon back there."

"No problem, Paul. You can stay at my house tonight if you want," Jack said.

"I don't think I can ever go home again," Paul said.

"We'll straighten things out, Fussel. Don't worry," Chris said, and patted him on the shoulder.

"You guys aren't half bad."

"Let's get to my house," Jack said.

"I've got to split," Chris said. "My old man's gonna be shitting bricks sideways when he finds out I cut practice."

"My dinner's ready by now. Gotta go. See you guys,"

Emma said, favoring Jack with a smile that left as soon as it came. Something was going on between the two of them, and Paul wasn't in on it. Yet.

Emma and Chris continued ahead toward Main Street, disappearing into the snow.

Jack and Paul made it to Jack's house, stepped in the side door, and took their coats off. They walked up the steps and into the kitchen where the most wonderful smells permeated the air. Frying hamburgers, sizzling in a pan, and raw onions in a bowl on the counter. Jack's stomach groaned.

His mom stood at the stove, flipping the hamburgers and making them hiss. "Hello, boys. How are you, Paul?"

"Okay, Mrs. Harding."

"Mom, can Paul stay for dinner?"

"Well, you should let me know ahead of time. But if it's ckay with his parents, it's okay with me."

"His dad said okay."

"I'll throw on a couple more burgers then."

Mrs. Harding always had enough food in the house to feed the First Army, and if you happened to drop in at dinner, you weren't leaving with an empty belly.

Ten minutes later they sat down to eat, and Paul devoured two burgers in record time, relishing the slight greasiness of them. Jack's dad asked him if he'd ever eaten before, but Paul barely heard him while tearing into the burgers. He washed them down with a can of Sunkist and let out a huge belch, which Jack followed with one of his own. Jack's mom frowned, but his dad chimed in, "Good one."

Jack's mom cleared the table, scraped the food off the plates into the garbage can, and rinsed the dishes. Paul and Jack sat at the table, Paul working on another Sunkist. That was the great thing about coming to Jack's house: you could eat as much as you wanted and on top of it, no one hit you.

"Can Paul stay over, Mom?" Jack asked.

"It's a school night."

"Please?"

"Not tonight, Jack. You've got homework and I'm sure Paul does too."

"Tonight's a little different," Jack said.

"How is it different?" she said, squirting dish soap into the sink. Tiny bubbles rose from the sink and popped.

"Paul's dad gave him some trouble. He got really mad because we were in the basement playing when he wasn't home."

"Who's we?"

"Me, Paul, Chris, and Emma."

"And I take it Paul's not supposed to have anyone around with no grown-ups."

"Yeah," Paul said.

"What happened when your father came home?"

"He shoved Paul on the stairs. Then we ran. He was like a crazy person," Jack said.

"Is that true, Paul?"

"Yes. I'm afraid to go home."

Jack's mom clucked her tongue and said, "That's rotten. A boy shouldn't be afraid to go home."

Jack's dad entered the kitchen, a copy of the *Buffalo News* tucked under his arm. "What's going on?"

"I need to talk to you," Mrs. Harding said.

She motioned for him to follow, and they went to the dining room. Paul could hear them whispering but not well enough to pick up exactly what they were saying.

Jack leaned over to him and said, "I think they're going to let you stay."

"I hope so."

A moment later they came back out, Jack's dad with his hands in his pockets, newspaper tucked under his arm. His mother pretended to straighten canisters on the counter, and Paul thought she looked nervous.

"You can stay here tonight, Paul. But I'm going to call your father and let him know where you are. It sounds like we've got a mess on our hands, huh?"

"Yes," Paul said.

"I'll see what I can find out. Do you have any other family in the area?"

"Just my aunt Helen."

"Okay."

He really didn't want to stay with his aunt Helen; her house always smelled like cabbage and she made him do jigsaw puzzles with her.

"When are you going to call him, hon?" Jack's mom said.

"Right now."

"Be careful."

"He can't hurt me through the phone, dear."

She scurried over to the sink, took a sponge out of the dishwasher, and rewiped the counter.

"You guys have homework to do?"

"Yeah," Jack said.

"Then get to it. We'll see if we can find some clothes for you to sleep in, Paul," Mrs. Harding said. "I'll wash those for you so they're clean for school tomorrow."

They were just so goddamn nice. It was alien to Paul, to have parents that actually gave a darn about you and didn't lie in wait for the next opportunity to lay a beating on you.

"Maybe you guys could adopt me," Paul said, half kidding.

"That's sweet of you, Paul," Jack's mom said.

"Then I'd have a midget for a brother," Jack said.

"Hey!" Paul said.

"Jack, that's terrible," his mom said.

"That's his middle name. Jack the Terrible," Jack's dad said.

They all laughed. Why couldn't Paul have a family like this?

Emma ran all the way home, her legs pumping up and down as she slammed through the snow. By the time she hit the door she was breathing hard, but it didn't matter because she was jubilant. She found Mom in the kitchen, stirring the contents of a stainless steel pot with a wooden spoon.

"What's for dinner?"

"Spaghetti and meatballs. Did you get into trouble with those boys?"

"Nope. I ran home. Just felt like it."

"Go wash up. Dinner's in five minutes."

She washed her face and hands, the hot water stinging her cold skin. She looked at herself in the mirror and she was grinning, a big idiot grin that only those in love possessed. Was she really in love with Jack? She didn't know what love felt like, but if this was it, it was pretty darn cool.

They sat at the kitchen table, tucked into one corner with two benches against the wall. The TV played a *Three's Company* rerun and Mom changed the channel to the Channel Four News. Emma picked up her fork and twirled the spaghetti. This was one of her favorite places in the whole house, tucked into the corner, the kitchen warm from the oven while the snow and wind did their worst outside.

"Why are you so happy? Did you get your period?"

"Mom!"

"Well, I was just wondering if Aunt Flo came to visit."

"Aunt Flo?"

"I'll explain it later. When you actually do get it."

Emma picked at her spaghetti, but she was so jazzed up that she couldn't really focus on eating. All that kept coming into her head was the dance. Should she wear a dress or pants? Hair in a ponytail or down? She was acting like a girly-girl, fretting over hair and dresses, but she couldn't help herself. Before, it was never important how she looked in front of Jack, but now she worried about every detail. Would she be pretty enough for him? Would she say something dumb or trip over her own feet? And why the heck did she care so much? It was just Jack after all.

"Are you going to eat that spaghetti or just stare at it?"

"Oh, sorry."

The top of the news started, and Stephen White, the lead

anchor, came on, his hair combed over a bald spot and the sides overgrown.

"When is he going to cut that thing off?" Mom said.

"You say that every night."

"It looks like a squirrel up and died on his head."

The story cut to Kevin Hall standing outside the gate at the Steadman Estate, the wind swaying him to one side. It was about the college kid they found dead, and he went on to say the Brampton police had no leads or suspects. The police were advising against going out at night unless you were with somebody.

"I want you home every night before dark," Mom said.

"I'm always home before the streetlights come on."

"Even before that. There's no telling who's doing such awful things."

Mom wiped her mouth with a napkin. "So is there something you want to tell me? You've been acting funny all week, especially when Jacob was here."

"There is something."

"You can tell me, honey. Anything."

"I got asked to the Christmas dance at school."

Her mom dropped her fork and it clinked against the plate.

"Emma, that's wonderful!"

"Really?"

"I can't believe it. Who are you going with?"

"Jack Harding."

Here it comes. She's going to go on about how Jack is one of her "dirty boys," boys who slog through the mud, throw snowballs at cars, and curse. But to Emma's total surprise, she didn't.

"Jack's a nice enough boy. A little rough around the edges, like all of them, but he seems polite. We'll need to get you a dress."

"You don't have to buy me a dress, Mom. I know we don't have much."

"That is the sweetest thing. Come here."

She got up and her mom slid over on the bench. Emma sat next to her and Mom put her arm around her shoulder and squeezed. Their heads touched.

"Why are you crying?" Emma asked.

"We just don't have many moments like this anymore. I guess I'm getting sentimental in my old age. I'm sorry, honey."

"Don't be."

If she could have stayed there for a month, she would have, Mom's arm around her while the rest of the world froze. Up until now, it was one of the happiest moments in her life, however small.

"Let's finish our dinner and talk about that dress," Mom said.

"That sounds great."

Chris stopped at Tops on the way home and bought a Reese's Cup just to avoid going to the house right away. He crammed it in his mouth and chewed without really tasting it, then crumpled the wrapper and tossed it on the sidewalk. It would be covered with snow in minutes, unearthed only in the spring like an ancient relic.

He reached the driveway and walked all the way back to the garage, where he peered in the window to find the Trans-Am wrapped in its tarp. While walking home, he actually had a moment of hope that his old man wasn't there yet, but that was shattered when he saw the car.

He went in, took off his winter gear, dropped his gym bag by the stairs, and entered the living room. His dad sat on the couch, poring over the sports section of the *Buffalo Evening News*. The headline read: BILLS' WOES CONTINUE.

"There's pizza on the counter. I stopped at Romano's. Pepsi's in the fridge."

"I'll grab a slice in a second."

"How was practice today?"

Here it was, the moment every child dreaded, when you

had to make a split-second decision. Did you lie and hope to get away with it, or did they already know what you did and were trying to catch you in one? It was like being in a bear trap and having to gnaw your own leg off. There was no possible happy ending.

"Did MacGregor call you?" Chris asked.

"So you didn't go?"

"You know I didn't."

"I stopped by, thinking maybe you'd want a lift, but you weren't there. Coach said you never showed."

"You're mad," Chris said.

"No, I'm not mad."

Great. He was so mad he wasn't mad. That was worse than all-out screaming and yelling mad.

"So what was more important than practice?"

"Nothing."

"It must have been something."

"Just hanging out with the guys. We had to talk."

"I see. Coach thought about suspending you for a game, but I talked him out of it."

"That was really great of you," Chris said.

"I wouldn't be smart right now," he said.

"Can I be excused to eat?"

"Fine."

His dad ruffled the paper and flipped the page, effectively dismissing Chris.

Why was basketball practice so important to the guy? One missed practice wouldn't hurt him, for he could out-shoot and out-rebound every one on the team. He had been groomed for sports ever since he could walk. Dad had him on ice skates at two, a hockey stick in his hand at three, and his first football at four. "Look at the legs on that kid. Those are fullback's legs," his father would exclaim.

His father's obsession for sports ran deep, like coal through a mine. It was the be all, end all, and if you didn't talk sports or know sports and you were male, then, buddy, something was wrong with you.

Chris found the pizza box on the counter, dug out three slices, and grabbed a can of Pepsi from the fridge. Then he sat at the table and dug into the pizza (after picking off the mushrooms and onions), wanting to finish it and get on to his homework.

Halfway through his second slice of pizza, his dad strolled in, pulled out a kitchen chair, and turned it so the back was facing forward. He sat down, resting his arms on the chair back.

Chris kept his head down and ate pizza. He knew what was coming next.

"MacGregor was pretty disappointed, you know. He expects that kind of stuff from guys like Munch, but not you."

"Why not me?" he said through a mouthful of pizza.

"Jeez, Chris, we've been over this a million times."

"I know, I've got a shot at the big time and the other guys don't. I've got talent and they don't."

"Do you really want to screw that up?"

"Sometimes I don't care."

"How can you say that? I'd give my left arm to have the skills you have. MacGregor says you're one of the best he's ever seen. You remind him of—"

"Larry Joseph. I know."

Larry Joseph had played for Brampton Middle and gone on to a scholarship at U.C.L.A. after high school. The Denver Nuggets took him in the first round, but he blew out his knee midway through his first season in the NBA. Now he worked on cars at Midas Muffler and hadn't touched a basketball in ten years.

"You're even better than Joseph. I saw him play and you're better."

"If you say so."

"It's a sin to waste talent, Chris. Yours is athletics. You were given that gift for a reason. Use it to your advantage."

This from a guy who hadn't seen the inside of a church since his wedding day.

"Do you really care about me or do you want me to do this because you didn't get anywhere in sports?"

"Of course I care about you. More than anything."

He looked away when he said that, and Chris knew it was hard for his dad to say stuff like that, because it didn't happen often.

"Sorry. I didn't mean that," Chris said.

"I know. Look, I know I put a lot of heat on you, but it's because I want you to excel. Look at me, Chris. Your mom left because I couldn't control my gambling. Every day I go down to that car lot and sell people cars I know are junk. And we do all right, but we're not exactly the Rockefellers."

"Who were they?"

"Extremely rich people. My point is you can do better and I want you to do better than me. Okay?"

"All right."

"Wipe your mouth. You've got some sauce on your cheek. I'll go down with you tomorrow and talk with MacGregor if you want. I have a feeling he'll keep you on the team, but you're probably going to run your butt off."

"Yeah." Chris dabbed at his chin with the napkin.

At this time tomorrow his legs would be one big throb from all the suicide drills.

"I'm going to catch the Blackhawks game. Get cracking on that homework."

"Hey, Dad?"

"Yeah, buddy?"

"I might be invited to sleep over somewhere this week. What do you think?"

"Where's somewhere?"

"A new kid's house. Ronnie Winter."

"I suppose."

"Thanks."

His dad disappeared into the living room and the TV knob clicked as he tuned into the Blackhawks-Sabres game.

He hadn't been invited to sleep over yet, because it was his own idea. That would get them into the tunnels and then he could prove Fussel and Harding were full of horseshit.

CHAPTER 24

Jack sat at the kitchen table staring at his math book, unable to concentrate on division and multiplication. His thoughts kept returning to two things: Emma's invitation and going back into the tunnels. The first thing made him feel alive, wired, as if he had a low current humming through his bones. He couldn't wait for the dance. The second had him worried. Had they really agreed to go back into the tunnels just to prove to Chris the story was true? He wanted to back out in the worst way, but if he did that now, he would be seen as a chickenshit and a liar. Chris would rag him about it until next Christmas if they didn't go down there again. His honor was at stake and there was only one way to defend it. Go underneath the estate.

"You thinking about the tunnels?" Paul asked.

"Yeah. Thinking we need to do it but that I don't want to."

"What if we run into him again?"

Jack set his pencil down and rubbed his eyes.

"We won't," he said.

"If you say so. Do we really have to prove Chris wrong?"

"If we don't he'll rib on us until there's no tomorrow."

"I suppose you're right. What do you think it was?"

"I don't know. It wasn't an ordinary man, though."

It was like one of those guys in the horror movies that got up no matter how many bullets you put in them. Hell, you could put Jason in a meat processor and he would still come after you as hamburger.

"What if it gets one of us?" Paul said.

"It won't because it's probably long gone by now."

"You don't really believe that, do you?"

"Let's finish this math. It's our last assignment, and then we can watch TV."

Jack looked at the octagon clock on the wall. It was eight-thirty, time enough for them to catch some of *Night Rider* if they hurried.

Jack's dad came in, opened the fridge, and poked his head around. He pulled out a Schmidt's and went to the cupboard, where he retrieved a can of Planter's peanuts.

"I've got a mission for you boys," he said, popping open a beer. "By the way, Paul, I called your house and there was no answer. Were your parents going anywhere?"

"The General's probably passed out by now and my mother's probably zonked out on the couch."

"The General?"

"He's into war movies. He thinks he's Patton."

"I see," Jack's dad said, peeling the lid off the nuts. "How's about you do an old man a favor and take the garbage out for me? I totally forgot it's garbage night. There's a beer in it for each of you."

Paul looked as if someone had poked him in the gut, causing his eyes and mouth to open wide at the same time.

"He's kidding, lame-o," Jack said.

"I knew that."

They pushed the chairs out, went to the hallway, and put on coats, gloves, hats, and boots. The snow outside the door was like a sheet, and Jack didn't really feel like going out in it, but parental authority ruled the world, so he was going to get wet and cold.

They marched up the driveway and the snow was almost

up to their knees, and Jack's lungs pumped harder with every step he took.

They each grabbed a can from behind the house, removed the lids, and dragged them back down the driveway. Halfway down, Jack's dad popped his head out the door and reminded them to get the newspapers out of the garage for recycling.

When they finished with the cans, they approached the garage. What a creepy building. One wall leaned in to the rest of the garage like a weary fighter pressing against his opponent. The shingles, once black, were going gray in spots (when you could see them), and a piece of gutter hung down in front to the sliding doors. They were having it torn down in the spring, and for Jack, it wasn't soon enough.

"Help me slide the door," he said.

The garage was a three-car, with two doors overlapping each other. They slid on tracks, allowing one carport to be open at a time. They both leaned on the door and pushed hard, forcing something out of the gutter as the door rattled. It was an old bird's nest, the grass in it dead brown.

Jack flicked the light switch. Dad's Buick took up the first space, and Mom's wagon the second. Peg Boards covered the walls, and on them hung shovels, hoes, a pitchfork, a Weed Eater, and dozens of other outdoor tools. The snow-blower and lawn mower sat in one corner, the lawn mower with a strand of cobweb across its handle.

"Gives me the creeps," Jack said.

The wind gusted and a flurry of snow pelted the rear window.

Jack found the papers in the empty carport, the one where the blower and mower were stored. They leaned up against a five-gallon gas can and were wrapped in a brown paper bag.

"All right, let's go."

Paul shrieked, startling Jack so bad he dropped the papers, scattering them all over the floor.

* * *

The chunky soup would have to wait. He stopped at his house, hurried in the door, and grabbed a blue watch cap to keep his dome from freezing over. Once back in the truck, he opened the glove compartment and made sure there was a clip in the .45.

He drove down the main road and out of the estate.

The roads were void of traffic, covered in a sea of powdery snow. He turned onto Jack's street, intent on driving by once or twice and if he saw anything, getting out of the car. He couldn't very well go snooping around the property (people were funny about having a large black man sneaking around their property—he didn't know why) unless he had reason. If Jack's parents caught him, he would need a damn good reason why he was on the property.

He passed by once, slowing the truck but not able to see anything through the blowing snow. So much for that idea. He would have to get out and look. Pulling the truck over, he rolled it half onto a snowbank and hoped the plows would see it (he put the flashers on but even then they might ram it). Slipping the .45 in his coat pocket, he got out and headed for the Harding driveway.

Hope I'm not too late.

Jack spun around to see Paul pointing at the window.

"What the hell is the matter with you?"

"I saw something in the window."

"What?"

"It was the tunnel guy."

"How do you know? You didn't even see him down there. It was too dark."

"It was him!"

The hand pointing to the window trembled, and his lower lip quivered.

"Paul, there's nothing. I'll show you."

He turned around to take a look at the window and there was a face wrapped in grimy bandages peering at them. Jack whimpered. His crotch suddenly felt hot, like he was going to empty his bladder right there. "Close the fucking door."

Jack ripped the pitchfork off the wall as they hurried to the door. Paul raced ahead of him and leaned into the door, sliding it on the track.

"Shut the light off so he can't see in here," Jack said.

Paul hit the switch and they were plunged into darkness.

They had stood listening for a moment when the first thump on the door came.

The wind pushed John off balance, and every step became a battle. He trudged past a pair of steel garbage cans, lit up by a streetlight on the front lawn at the curb.

Passing the front windows, he took a peek and saw the lights were on, but saw no one inside. Once he was closer to the house and out of immediate view of the street, he slipped the .45 from his pocket, and getting close to the house, he slid under the windows.

A dull thump came from the backyard, barely audible under the wind, but still there. Three times in slow succession.

He hustled toward the back.

CHAPTER 25

The thumping started at the far end of the garage door and came closer. Paul tapped his foot in a tattoo against the concrete. There was no doubt in his mind that the thing from the tunnels had come to finish them off. Somehow it had found them and intended to drag them back under the estate and slaughter them.

"Hold the door shut as hard as you can," Jack said. He held the pitchfork out in front of him like a soldier with a bayonet.

Paul leaned into the door, but he doubted he would have the strength to fight the tunnel man off and keep the door closed. Its grip on him had been like steel shackles, and he guessed it to be incredibly strong.

The thumps came closer. Ten feet, five feet, three feet.

"Jesus, Jack, oh, Jesus."

"Shhh."

As if the situation weren't bleak enough, Paul realized the wind would act as a natural sound barrier and they could scream their lungs out but Jack's parents would never hear them. They might as well be five miles from the house. The only hope was for one of his parents to look out the window, but even then with the thick snowfall they might not see the intruder. It was a good thirty feet from the house to the garage.

"Listen," Jack said.

It was quiet save for the wind. Paul listened hard, and so intent on listening was he that he relaxed his grip on the door handle and it was ripped from him, moving him back three feet.

"Shit!"

The hand shot in the door, catching Paul by the sleeve and yanking. Material ripped and Paul jerked backward, but the hand still had him good. Jack raised the pitchfork to chest height, lunged forward, and jabbed the hand. The tine plunged into the hand, and this allowed Paul to slip his arm free. It would occur to him later that there was no blood from the wound, and the attacker made no noise when the fork dug into his skin.

Paul backed away from the door, but still the hand waved around, searching for someone to reel in. Jack poked at it again, piercing the skin on top of the hand, but again there was no blood. The guy pushed through the crack, first the whole arm up to the shoulder. Jack dropped the fork and pushed on the door, hoping to keep their visitor out.

Paul joined him at the door, squeezing hard against it, but the two of them were not strong enough and it slammed the door back against them.

It was in the garage and it was awful.

Dirty bandages covered its face (they had no other choice but to think of the attacker as "it"), streaked with clots of brown mud, and the gauze flapped in the breeze like a battle-scarred flag.

Jack and Paul backed up in between the garage door and the bumper of the station wagon.

"Go around the front of the wagon. There's enough space so maybe we can beat him around and to the garage door," Jack said.

It lunged forward and the boys slipped around the side of the wagon on the passenger side. Paul was the first to the front of the car and he slid between the front bumper and the wall with ease. Jack wasn't as small or quick as Paul and he stumbled, the whole time feeling the thing bearing down on his back.

It swiped at him, ripping his jacket as he slid past the bumper, and he half turned to get a good look at it. It was three feet away and for the first time he looked into the face; there were no eyes. He hadn't noticed when it entered the garage, because it was too far away and too dark.

He sidestepped past the car, leaving his pursuer on the other side of the wagon for the moment. There was a thud as it climbed over the hood, still on his heels.

"Come on, Jack," Paul said.

Paul reached the door and gave it a shove, the big door clicking on the track. Snowflakes busted into the garage, a rude visitor pelting Paul. Jack hurried between the cars, his pursuer only five feet behind him, feet scraping on the oil-spotted floor.

He bolted past Dad's car, hitting the bumper with his hip and knocking him off stride. It was all the thing needed to catch up to him, and it did, wrapping an arm around him and lifting him off the floor as if he weighed no more than a sack of groceries. The other arm embraced him and now he was caught in a bear hug.

He thrashed his legs back and forth, trying to wiggle free, but it was like a condemned man trying to escape the electric chair. Once strapped in, you were riding the lightning whether you wanted to or not.

"Paul!"

But Paul was already charging, swinging his arms furiously as he slammed into the thing's side, punching hard.

John entered the yard, no longer protected by the house and at the complete mercy of the wind. It rocked him good, but he plowed on toward the garage, where he was certain Jack Harding was very close to being killed.

He entered the garage, relieved to be out of the wind, and found Jack in the clutches of the Wraith. It had him off the floor, clasped in its arms, and Paul was beating on its arms, throwing punches with no effect. They wouldn't have any effect because things that were dead felt no pain, but the boys didn't know that.

They stood at the rear bumper of a green station wagon with wood paneling on the sides. Jack kicked his feet as if madly pedaling a bicycle, but the Wraith's grip wouldn't give, and if it wanted to have him, it would.

John aimed the gun at it, knowing it would be useless. Crouching, he approached it, the barrel leveled at its head. "Set him down now," John said. "You don't want to hurt that boy."

John hoped his words would penetrate the Wraith like sunlight through barren, rocky soil.

Paul beat on the Wraith, and it tired of him, slapping him aside and smashing him into the garage door. It still had one arm clasped around Jack.

"Shoot him!" Paul said. "Shoot him, for fuck's sake!"

"You don't want to hurt a little boy, do you?"

The dark sockets fixed on him, and he didn't know how it saw, or what it saw, without any eyes, but he had its attention.

"He did nothing to you. Don't let her make you hurt Jack."

The grip loosened a bit, and Jack slid down closer to the floor.

"That's it. Let him loose."

"Yeah," Jack said.

The Wraith dropped its arm to the side, and Jack landed on the floor, quickly rolling away in between the parked cars.

It started toward him, one step, then another.

"Get going."

It came closer, nearly past John, who pressed himself against the garage door, giving it room to pass.

When it was in front of him, its hand shot out and clutched

John's neck, squeezing hard. He tried sucking air, but not much got through. This was what a hanging must feel like, and not the kind where they drop you and snap your neck, but where the condemned is allowed to strangle.

He sucked air only to hear a choked gasp come from his own throat. He tore at the hand, getting two fists around the wrist and trying to pry it loose, but it was as solid as a tree limb.

The Wraith turned its head and those eight balls looked right through his skull. Could Cassie see him right now? He wanted to spit right in its face, but he could not draw a breath, let alone work up a gob of saliva.

Its fingers relaxed and it pulled its hand back. He slumped to the floor, his throat raw, tears running down his cheeks because his eyes watered so badly. The Wraith took off through the garage door, and John knew it would be back on the estate in record time, faster than Carl Lewis ever dreamed of moving. He gulped air, and the cold breeze was the sweetest air he had ever tasted.

Paul and Jack came to his side, both of them asking if he was okay. He nodded and said in a raspy voice, "I'll walk you to the house."

"What was that?" Jack asked.

"We'll talk. Let's go before it decides to come back."

Rudy Campana wished he could take a flamethrower to all this godforsaken snow and melt it for good. Dressed in a yellow fleece sweatshirt, gloves, and duck boots, he wished now for a heavier coat.

Rudy Jr. was out of milk and Kathy had volunteered Rudy to trek to the minimart and get more of the white stuff. Not that he would have let her go out in the storm, and if it made the baby happy, then it made him happy.

But did it have to be so damn miserable out? He didn't mind getting milk for the kid; hell, he would have walked ten miles over broken glass for him. The little guy had the biggest set of brown eyes you ever wanted to see (much to the chagrin of Kathy's mother, who disapproved of "Mediterranean" features—the bitch). And he was going to be strong, almost straining Rudy's neck when he hugged.

That took some of the sting out of the cold.

He slogged through the parking lot, where a group of teenagers in a maroon Mustang ripped donuts in the snow, the car spinning like a globe.

"Kids," he said, shaking his head.

He entered the minimart, shook off the cold, and headed for the milk cooler, where he nearly slipped on a wet patch. He paid for the milk, stuffed his change in his wallet, and walked back into the cold.

The kids in the Mustang swung out onto Riley Avenue, driving like Satan's own chauffeur. No regard for the conditions. That's what caused accidents.

He tucked the gallon of milk under his arm and fought the wind all the way down the sidewalk in front of the plaza. He turned right onto Riley, and luckily he only had about another block and a half to go before he was in his house drinking hot tea. Kathy would have it ready for him, and he couldn't wait to heat up his insides with it.

He reached the bridge that ran over Fox Creek, and ahead to the right was a cluster of trees on the lawn of Dr. Peach's offices. There were fresh tracks leading from the office building to the cluster of trees, which was odd, because the office had been closed for hours.

He was nearly past the trees when he was jerked off his feet, yanked by the arm so hard he thought for a moment it was torn off. He landed on his side in the snow, muttering, "What the hell?"

He looked up and saw a man towering over him. The guy was dressed in blue coveralls and damn it all if he didn't have bandages wrapped all over his face. It took Rudy only seconds to realize he was in deep trouble.

As he rose to his knees, the guy grabbed him by the front of his jacket. His knees buckled underneath him, but the man jerked him back to his feet.

"Holy shit."

It hit him in the gut, feeling like a cannonball slamming into his abdomen. The air left his lungs and he gasped, too stunned to see that the guy's fist had exited his lower back, impaling him.

CHAPTER 26

John led them to the side door, coughing in fits every few seconds.

"Are you okay?" Paul said.

"Throat hurts," John said, and held his throat. "But I'll be okay."

"What was that?" Jack asked, and his voice came out higher than he would have liked.

"I'll explain everything to you boys. Wait at the corner of your street, both of you. About three-thirty tomorrow and I'll pick you up. I don't want to come to the house because I don't think you want to explain to your mom why you got a limo ride. In the meantime, stay inside. I mean that."

He put one arm on Paul's shoulder and one on Jack's, stopping them and looking hard at each boy. They both nodded in agreement, and Jack thought he would probably never set foot in that garage again, no matter how much his dad complained.

John left them at the door, ducking down the driveway. The boys went inside. Jack stomped his feet to break off the snow from his boots and Paul did the same. They took off their winter gear and hung the hats and coats on the rack in the hallway.

"What took you so long?" Jack's mom stood at the stove, stirring the contents of a pan with a wooden spoon.

"Paul dropped the papers all over the place," Jack said.

"Oh, sure, blame me."

"That's what happened, didn't it?" Jack said, elbowing him.

"Oh yeah. Made a big mess."

"Your father wants to talk to you before you have your cocoa. Paul, you can come and sit down; then you guys should get ready for bed."

Paul pulled out a chair and plopped down. Jack's mom set the cocoa in front of Paul.

"Paul, you're shivering. You want a blanket to put over your shoulders?"

"No, thanks. I'll be okay, Mrs. Harding."

Paul sipped his hot chocolate. From the living room, Jack's dad yelled, "In here, Jack!"

"Be right back."

Jack entered the living room. His dad sat in a lemon-yellow recliner. Duct tape crisscrossed the arms of the chair, and it looked as if someone had beaten it with a crowbar. But his father refused to get rid of it, and if Mom ever threw it out, Jack's dad might petition Congress to declare war.

He leaned forward, hands folded between his knees. "Pull up a seat," he said, pointing to the green ottoman.

Jack pulled out the footstool and sat down.

"Get the newspapers out?"

Shit. In the chaos that had ensued outside, they had forgotten about the papers. Hopefully Dad wouldn't check. "Yeah."

"How's Paul?"

"He's Paul."

"You know what happened with his dad is pretty serious stuff, right?"

"Yes."

"Your mother and I are going to call Child Protective Services."

"It won't help," Jack said. "He's a psycho."

His dad sat back and crossed his legs. His pant leg rode up, showing his nearly hairless calf.

"He can stay here as long as he wants. I'll buy him clothes if I have to, but I'm not letting that gorilla lay another hand on him. He's a good kid, and he'll need a good friend. It's a hard time for Paul, and he really looks up to you. You need to be a man." Dad winked at him. "You can do it."

That was the ultimate compliment to Jack. "Really?"

"Be his friend, Jack. I know you guys are already tight, but he'll need someone to support him."

"Got it."

His dad reached out and shook his hand, the way he did when his buddies came over to watch a Bills game. He pumped Jack's hand, then shook hard, making Jack's arm flop like spaghetti. "Whoa, that's some handshake you got there," he said.

Jack leaned over and kissed his dad on the cheek, the eight o'clock shadow rough on his lips. It would be the last time he kissed his father until Jack Harding Sr. lay dying from liver cancer in Buffalo General Hospital, thirty years later.

Dad smiled, perhaps knowing it would be the last kiss he received from his growing son.

"Go get some of that hot chocolate before it gets cold," he said, and clapped Jack on the back.

Jack bopped out of the living room, so pleased that he had forgotten about the incident in the garage. For the moment.

Cassie Winter slammed the fireplace poker down on a log and the fire spat sparks at her, the embers landing on the hearth. She ground them into the tile so hard the bottom of her foot ached. Instead of setting the poker back on the rack, she flung it against the brick, and it clanged to the floor.

"This wasn't supposed to happen."

She had sent the Wraith to frighten Jack Harding, and not only had John gotten involved, but someone had been killed. She should have known better than to set it loose, and she had less control of it once it was off the grounds. The images had come to her in flashes, like a slide show at a hundred miles per hour. The Wraith picking up Jack Harding, John entering the garage, then the Wraith choking him just to put John in his place. From then it stalked an unsuspecting man coming home from the store. Another victim.

I've made it too vicious, she thought.

"Damn it!" She pounded her fist against the mantel. The bone china rattled on its holders.

"What's the matter, Mom?"

Oh no. Ronnie.

The boy stood clad in Spider Man pajamas, the red and blue shirt strained by his stomach. Either she had to get him some new pajamas or put him on a diet. She would send John out tomorrow to buy him some new pajamas, then start rationing his intake of Ho-Hos and Ring Dings. Poor little fat boy. And all her fault, letting him stuff himself with cupcakes and pastries.

"Are you okay, Mom?"

"Sure I am, sweetheart." She crossed the room and knelt in front of him—although in another year he would probably be as tall as she—if not taller—and took his hand.

"I was down in the kitchen and I heard banging."

"You shouldn't be out of bed looking for snacks."

"But I was hungry."

"No more snacks today."

"But—"

"No buts," Cassie said. "I burned my hand on the hot poker, that's all."

"I really like my new friends."

He smiled, and it nearly broke her heart to see him happy. "Really?"

"Jack and Paul are neat guys. I feel bad about what happened in the tunnel, but I'll make it up to them somehow. Maybe a sleepover?"

"I don't like that he shoved you."

"It was just a little shove. I suppose I deserved it after what I did."

"Don't feel like you have to take that from him, even if you did play a prank on them. And I suppose a sleepover would be okay."

"Really?"

"Just remember mothers see and hear everything, even if you don't realize it. Especially this mom."

"Thanks."

He wrapped his arms around her waist. She kissed him on top of the head. His hair smelled of jojoba shampoo, sweet and clean. "You're welcome, hon. Now get to bed."

"Super!" he said, pumping his fist in the air and then barreling down the hallway yelling, "Party!"

It did her heart good to see him happy. So often it wasn't the case in recent years. Maybe he was finally breaking through with other kids, making real friends instead of having kids who hung around him because of all the toys and free food.

She sighed, picked up the poker, and set in the holder.

Kempf pulled up in the driveway, took the garage door opener off the visor, and pushed the button. The door opened and he pulled the car in, feeling like a caterpillar in a cocoon.

He tucked the late edition of the *Buffalo Evening News* under his arm, got out of the car, and went into the house.

He peeled off his London Fog coat and hung it on the coatrack. Tomorrow he would wear the big parka, a hat, and gloves. Damn the torpedoes and full speed ahead and who cared if he looked like a stuffed olive? Better to be warm than fashionable.

Jules sat at the table reading Sidney Sheldon's latest and sipping a cup of coffee. The mug was the one he got her for Valentine's Day in 1978 and it read TO MY WIFE—I LOVE YOU. The red letters were fading and it had a chip on the brim, but she refused to throw it out. Somewhere she had the dozens of letters Kempf had written on college-lined paper. Jules the pack rat, the sentimental romantic.

"Hi, hon," he said.

"Hey," she said, setting the book down.

He went over, bent down, and kissed her on the lips. She tasted like coffee.

"Dinner's warming in the oven. Hope you don't mind I went ahead and ate," she said.

"Naw." He grabbed a pair of oven mitts and took the roaster out of the oven. Pot roast, potatoes, and carrots. He spooned himself up a plate, grabbed a Schmidt's from the fridge, and joined her at the table. He loosened his tie and set it on the back of the chair.

"What happened, George?"

"Is it that obvious?"

"I can tell by the new wrinkles in that knotty old head."

He sipped the beer, relished the bitterness of it.

The woman had a knack for knowing when something was eating at him just by the look on his face. Twenty-seven years gave you almost-ESP.

"It was bad, Jules."

"How bad?"

"Never seen anything like it. I know who killed that kid over by the Steadman place."

She gripped his forearm and gave it a little shake. "That's great."

"He got away."

"I'm sorry."

"Don't be. I'm not sure I want to tangle with this one."

"What do you mean?"

She put her bookmark, a pink job with gray kittens on it, inside the book and set it aside. She leaned forward, elbows resting on the table, giving him her full attention. On days like this when his ulcer was boiling over and there were extra creases in his noggin, she let him talk. Didn't butt in and tell him all about how some biddy at the craft shop thought she was overcharged for candlestick holders. Never cut him off or tuned him out. Just listened. It was a skill that most people would never have.

"The guy had no eyes, Jules. And bandages all over his face."

"No eyes? I don't follow."

"I mean no eyes. Like someone plucked them out and left sockets."

"Are you sure?"

"He was three feet from me."

"My God. What happened?"

He told her how he went back up to the estate to search for the piece of gauze. Then about spotting the freak in the woods.

"We swept the property as best we could, but it's something like eight hundred acres. We're stepping up patrols in the area and Ramsey's holding a press conference to warn the good people of Brampton that they should stay locked up tight. Real good of him to spook the civilians even more."

"You always said he was a PR hog."

"Yep."

"You'll come out of this okay, George. You always do." She leaned over and kissed his cheek.

"Something else happened, too. I went out to the Steadman place to talk with the new owner."

"That doesn't seem strange."

"I got dizzy, nauseated. And if you would have asked me my name right then I don't think I could have told you. Scared the hell out of me. I thought I was having a stroke."

"I want you to make a doctor's appointment." The tone said it was nonnegotiable. "Pronto. I don't like your health lately, George."

He sliced off a piece of pot roast and put it in his mouth.

The phone rang. Kempf turned around and took the receiver off the wall.

"Hello," he said, still chewing.

"Tank. How are you?"

"Good, Chief. What's up?" He was trying his damnedest to sound upbeat, but he knew the news from Ramsey would not be good. Ramsey had called him at home twice, and both times involved someone dying in Brampton. The first was when Cynthia Parsons ran down her estranged husband with the family Buick and the second involved Tiny shooting the Schwann man.

"I need you to come down to the minimart by Riley Street. It happened again."

"I'll be right there."

"See you there," Ramsey said.

Kempf hung up the phone, the pot roast in his stomach feeling like razor blades.

"What is it?" Julie said.

"I gotta go out."

"Why can't they just leave you alone?"

"It's my job, dear."

"Dress warm."

She kissed him on the cheek and he headed for the hallway to put his parka on.

Jack lay in bed, hands folded on top of the comforter. He closed his eyes, opened them, and closed them again as he had done for the past half hour. He rolled onto his left side. Pillow was too lumpy. Rolled onto his right side and his neck ached. Beside him, the cot springs squeaked, suggesting that Paul wasn't asleep, either.

Outside, the wind continued its barrage and every so often the whole house shook. The window rattled. Jack pulled the covers up to his chin.

"Jack?"

"Yeah?"

"Still awake?"

Jack rolled his eyes. "No, I'm sleep-talking."

"You think it's still out there," Paul asked, "in the yard?"

"For some reason I don't. I think it's scared of John."

"It almost choked him to death," Paul said.

"It could have killed him if it wanted. You felt how strong it was and so did I. I think it's back under the estate in the tunnels."

"It killed that guy, didn't it?"

Jack rolled onto his side so he was facing Paul. Paul sat there with the pillow on his lap. He picked at the pink pillowcase.

Mom had dragged out the old cot, the one with purple flowers on the mattress, so Paul wouldn't have to sleep on the floor. It squealed a lot, and the springs had a tendency to poke you in the back, but it was better than sleeping on the hardwood.

"I think so."

"I'm not going back into the tunnel. I don't care what Chris thinks of us. If we're liars, then we're liars. At least we're alive, bucko."

"You're right. We're not going. We'd be nuts."

Paul let out a long rush of air, exaggerating a sigh.

"But we have to find out more about what that thing might be. Get closer to Ronnie and spend time on the estate," Jack said.

"Why would we do that?"

"I'm afraid not to." Jack looked to the window again, half expecting a pale fist with cracked nails to smash through and grab one of them. "Can I tell you something?"

"Yeah, no secrets, right?"

Paul was right. There were no secrets between them. They knew each other's worst. Like Paul running out of toilet paper in the second-floor bathroom and using his report on the Battle of Bull Run to wipe his ass. Or Jack sneezing in the library without a tissue and runners of snot shooting from his nose. And right in front of Laura Stein and Amy Grubny.

No keeping secrets, but wasn't that what Jack and Emma had done by asking Chris and Paul to leave the basement room? Jack felt a stab of guilt. "Emma asked me to the Christmas dance."

"Are you serious?"

"One hundred percent. That's why she wanted you guys to leave."

He didn't tell them the other reason. That would be like stepping on Emma's heart. When she wanted the other two boys to know about Jacob, she would tell them. Jack telling them would be a betrayal, and that was the last thing he wanted to do to her.

"And you said yes?"

"Of course."

"Major neato news. Congratulations. You're becoming a fine young man, Jack." Paul stuck out his hand to shake and Jack nearly fell off the bed laughing.

"I'm a fine young man? Where do you come up with this shit?"

Paul laughed too, stifling it at first with his hand, then breaking into a full-out belly laugh.

"Shh! You'll wake up my mom and dad!" Jack said.

"Sorry. That's cool, man. So what do we do about the tunnel thing?"

"Talk to Ronnie. Start hanging with him more. He's really not that bad, you know? A little out there, but he could be a fun guy to hang with," Jack said. In reality, he was afraid not to hang with Ronnie.

"What if we solved the murder? Do you think we'd get a medal?"

"Maybe," Jack said.

Paul rested his head down on the pillow and pulled up the red quilt. "You sure are lucky."

"How?"

"I wish I had your mom and dad," he said, in a tone that made Jack want to cry. "My dad's such a major asshole it's not even funny."

"You can come here any time you want."

His own father's admonition to help Paul out and be there for him echoed in Jack's head. He wanted to extend that feeling out to Paul without sounding like a total dork. As a rule, eleven-year-old boys did not share Hallmark moments.

"You're a good friend," Paul said.

"Did I really boot your dad in the ass?"

"Yeah, that was great."

"Good thing he was half smashed or he might have hit us with that beer bottle," Jack said.

"He has lousy aim when he's drunk. One time he tried chasing after me with Jiffy Pop, you know, the one you do on the stove?"

"Was it already popped?"

"Yeah. He's running after me with it, waving it and screaming. I ran in my room and slammed the door. He threw it and it whizzed over my head before I could shut the door. Bam. Popcorn everywhere, the drunken asshole."

"Pretty corny story," Jack said.

"Don't give up your day job to become a comedian."

"I don't have a day job."

"Jack?"

"Yeah?"

"What if it comes back?"

"It won't." He wished he could believe that.

"You sure?" Paul said. His voice sounded small in the dark room.

"No."

CHAPTER 27

Kempf pulled up on the scene, sweating under his red parka. He unzipped it and loosened the scarf scratching at his throat. Felt like barbed wire to him. He stepped out of the car.

Two prowl cars were parked on the side of the bridge, their lights reflected in the steel rails. A uniformed cop (it looked like Stavros from here) made his way up the embankment leading from the creek. Ramsey stood at the top of the embankment, hands on hips, lording over the whole scene. He had on brown duck boots, but Kempf couldn't figure out why, because there was no way the chief would get his feet dirty. That was Kempf's job.

Kempf approached Ramsey and tapped him on the shoulder. He turned, his normally tan skin turned pink from the cold. Tiny rose-welts covered his cheeks and nose from where the snow had pelted him.

Ramsey said, "Hell of a night, huh?"

"What have we got?"

"White male. Thirty-two years old. Gutted like a carp."

"Who found him?"

"Jogger. She's over in one of the cars keeping warm. Snow covered up the footprints. Pretty convenient, huh?"

Kempf's bandaged friend had been busy again, no doubt using the adverse weather to cloak his travel.

"We'll need to question people at the minimart. Stavros and Baer are checking behind the doctor's office to see what they can see." He crossed his arms, looked thoughtful. "I need to call a press conference first thing in the morning."

A white van with a circled number 7 in red pulled up.

"Better get down there and have a look," Kempf said. "Get someone up here to keep the jackals back."

"I'll have Stavros do it."

Kempf hurried away, wanting to avoid the news crew (they would most likely be all over Ramsey, anyway). He sidestepped down the embankment, arms out like a tightrope walker.

The creek wound right and back to the left before going under the bridge. The victim lay on his back at the edge of the creek. Head cocked to the left, eyes open. Snowflakes matted his eyebrows and the front of his hair. A blue knit cap rested on the ground next to his head, along with a paper bag, now soaked dark brown.

Poor son of a bitch was probably out picking up bread or milk and this happened. Probably had no idea what hit him.

In the dark, the bloodstains on the jacket looked violet. A section of intestine looped over the victim's side, and Kempf had a thought so awful it made him want to puke right there. The guts probably steamed when he was unzipped.

The Crime Scene boys came down the embankment, one of them with a big leather bag in his hand, and the other with a duffel. Kempf nodded to them.

"What do you think, Detective?"

"I think we've got a major fucking problem on our hands."

They went to work, photographing the victim, taking scrapings from under the nails, and collecting up evidence in bags and envelopes. The knit cap went into a plastic bag, something Kempf was sure its wearer never expected to happen.

Kempf made a sketch of the crime scene on his pad, some

notes and impressions of the site. No doubt, though, that the bandaged man killed the guy.

He slogged up the embankment while the Crime Scene Unit did their thing.

Ramsey stood at the top of the embankment in a wash of television camera lights. Baer, a big man with slumped shoulders, stood behind Ramsey with his arms out as if this would ward off curious photographers. He looked like an overgrown scarecrow.

Kempf scurried over to the squad car. He opened the door and crouched down. She was sallow-skinned, with a pinched nose and a smattering of freckles on her cheeks. Her forehead was covered by a blue Adidas headband, and over that, earmuffs.

"I'm Detective Kempf."

She offered him a mitten-covered hand. "Danielle Belmont."

He shook her hand and said, "Little cold to be out jogging."

"Not really. I do it in all kinds of weather. Keeps me in shape."

From the way the skin clung to her cheekbones, he would say she overdid it on the jogging and ate like a sparrow.

"I'd like you to come down to the station and make a statement. I have to go to the minimart first and talk to them. Are you okay to wait here for a few minutes?"

"The killer isn't still around, is he? I'll be safe?"

"As a baby in a cradle. There's plenty of officers around. Besides, whoever did this is long gone."

"Okay. I'll wait."

"Thank you. Watch your fingers."

He shut the door and scurried past the news hounds. Fighting the wind, he turned the corner at the plaza and ducked into the minimart.

It was brightly lit, and a band Kempf thought was called Culture Club was playing from the speakers. The rug in front of the doorway squished under his feet, and a yellow sign reading CAUTION—WET FLOOR stood propped at the end of the rug. Kempf stamped his feet, drawing more water from the rug.

He approached the counter where a longhaired kid sat slouched. He was reading a Spider Man comic and picking at a pimple on his cheek.

"Can I help you?" he said, looking up. The reddish hair covered his eyes.

"Detective Kempf," he said, flashing his badge.

"What happened?"

"A guy came in here a little while ago to buy milk. About five eight. Mustache. Sandy blond hair. You remember seeing him?"

The kid scratched his head. "Yeah. Yeah, I did. Came in about an hour ago. Why?"

"We found his body around the corner," Kempf said. "He's been murdered."

"No way." He brushed the hair out of his face and Kempf saw a silver cross dangling from his left ear.

"Did you see anyone follow him out of here? Or was there anyone waiting outside when he left?"

"I don't think there was."

"Did he seem nervous or scared? Like someone might be following him?"

"No. Just came in and paid for his milk. Bitched about the cold but that was it, dude."

"Are you sure there was nothing funny? Out of the ordinary?"

"Sorry, man. Hey, is it the same guy who offed the other dude by the estate?"

"Can't say. Can I get your name and phone number?"

"Brian Parker." He told Kempf his phone number as well. Kempf jotted it down on his pad and tucked it back into the coat pocket. "Thanks, Brian."

Kempf left Brian to his Spider Man comic, but as he was walking out the door he said, "How are you getting home, Brian?"

"My dad's picking me up."

"Good. Wait in here for him. I think you'll be safe, but you still shouldn't walk home alone."

"Thanks, dude."

Dude. When the hell did kids start talking like that?

Back at the station, the jogger was waiting for him in the office, legs tucked up on the chair, her arms wrapped around them, knees to the chest.

"Some coffee, Miss Belmont?"

"No, thanks. I'd just like to get home."

"We won't keep you long."

Kempf sat down, pulled open the desk drawer, and took out his Tums. He flipped the lid and popped two in his mouth. The entire content of his stomach felt as if it had been drained and replaced with high-powered battery acid. He had to get back to the doctor soon.

"Feeling sick?" she asked.

"Ulcer." He felt like he should be asking her the same question. She was probably a health nut who subsided on tofu and yogurt, then ran as if the devil were chasing her. Those types of people were usually always sick, straining their bodies with too little food and too much exercise.

"So you were jogging. And you looked over and saw the body?" Kempf took out a legal pad and a blue pen.

"Yeah. Just as I reached the bridge. It was pretty windy and the snow was blowing around, but I could make out a shape. I saw his jacket. That's when I climbed down the embankment."

"And you saw the damage, obviously."

"Who would do something like that to another person?"

"That's what I'm trying to find out. So what happened next?"

"I ran up the embankment and to the minimart. That's when I called the police."

Kempf nodded while writing. "Did you see anybody near the scene?"

"No. But I had the feeling someone was watching me. From a distance. It was creepy. That's not weird, is it?"

"Not at all," Kempf said. "You're sure you didn't see any-one?"

"I thought maybe I saw something move around the cor-ner of the doctor's office before I climbed the embankment, but I couldn't be sure."

"I think this is all we need. If I need any other info can I have your phone number?"

She recited it and he scratched it on the pad. "Officer Baer will give you a ride home."

"Thank you, Detective." She stood up and hurried out of the office. If she was like most civilians, she was nervous around cops even though she'd done nothing wrong.

The bandaged man had most likely watched Danielle Belmont from the woods, and perhaps she was lucky she had climbed the embankment when she did.

The whole thing was getting worse by the day. Kempf lowered his head and rubbed his eyes.

Ramsey walked in, surprising Kempf. He thought the chief would have been at home in bed by now.

"What do you think, Tank?" He sat in the chair and leaned back.

"It's obviously the same guy."

"I've got a press conference scheduled for tomorrow. People are going to be scared. We have to calm them down, reassure them of police presence."

"That's not going to be easy. And who knows who will be next?" Kempf said. "He used the storm to catch them off guard, you know."

"The county sheriff's giving us two prowl cars with two men each. I'm going to ask the town board to authorize over-time until we catch this guy. I want patrols going twenty-four-seven."

"I should get that fabric sample back from the lab soon."

"Make sure and do that. You might need it. Never know, do we?"

Kempf didn't care for the tone of his voice. "No, *we* don't."

"See you tomorrow. Try and get some sleep." Ramsey clapped him on the knee, got up, and left the office.

After a moment, Kempf followed him, shutting off the light on the way out.

After leaving the station, Kempf stopped at Dunkin Donuts for two crullers and two decaf coffees. The clerk tried making small talk with him, asking him if he heard about the guy that just got killed. Kempf told him yeah, and the clerk noticed the badge clipped to his belt. The kid said, "Yeah, I guess you would know." And then asked him if he was in any danger working this late. Kempf replied, "Not unless the guy has a bad donut fetish." He left the clerk puzzled.

He drove home, cursing the weather, the homicide, and Ramsey. The chief would get up on the podium tomorrow, hair sprayed to perfection, pearly whites all in a row, and do his best at making it look like they had everything under control. Kempf didn't think it would work and he knew they didn't have things under control.

His guts told him it was hiding out on the Steadman Estate, but for the life of him he couldn't remember much of his conversation with Cassie Winter. It was like having someone's name lodged in your brain and not being able to get your tongue to say it.

When he arrived at the house, Jules was waiting for him, coffee mug in hand and a glass of milk sitting on the counter.

"You'll probably be needing this with that ulcer," she said. She handed him the milk.

"You bet." He took a swig and wiped his mouth. "Brought some donuts." Kempf set them on the counter along with the coffees.

"Bad this time?"

"As bad as the first one. It was the guy I saw outside the estate that day. I know it. I told Ramsey about it and he agreed to step up patrols, but he doesn't want to go prowling on the estate." Kempf took another swallow of milk. "We need to do another sweep of the place. Every building, the woods, the whole shooting match."

"He never listens. You know that. He's a glory hound. Always has been," she said, fire coming to her eyes.

"The old glory hound will get his chance at the press conference tomorrow," Kempf said. "I think the son of a bitch is probably planning on running for sheriff next year."

"So what now?"

"Now I go to bed and don't really sleep. I have to think of something before someone else gets it. I'm hoping a sample I sent to the lab gets me something."

"If you want to call it quits, George, you can. With my income and what we've got saved, we'd be okay. Retirement isn't such a bad thing." She kissed him on the cheek and left the room, her bathrobe flowing behind her.

"Maybe not. But I can't let this go," he said.

CHAPTER 28

"Why did your mom drive us to school?" Paul asked.

"Nervous about the nut job running around town. You should be too. We saw him, after all," Jack said.

They strolled down the main hallway, past a bulletin board decorated with red and green construction paper. It proclaimed: DON'T FORGET THE CHRISTMAS DANCE. In ten years, it would become the holiday dance, and after that the December dance, in a nod to political correctness.

"How did you sleep?" Jack asked.

"Lousy. I had bad dreams all night."

"He killed someone else. After he left the garage," Jack said.

"Jeepers, not another one. How do you know?"

"I got up before you this morning. My dad had *Wake Up, Western New York* on. It's all over the news."

"What are we going to do?"

"Hope it doesn't come back again," Jack said.

"Bad dreams," Paul said.

"I didn't sleep good either," Jack said.

Paul had had the same dream three or four times. In the dream, he slept in his own bed, and when he woke up, the room was pitched with dirty gray light. Water dripped from a spot on the ceiling and pooled on the rug. The paint and plaster flaked from the walls, revealing the lath underneath. He climbed out of bed and the wind chilled him. The curtains flapped in front of a broken window.

He stepped onto the carpet, the water squishing under his bare feet. The hallway revealed more dilapidated conditions. A rat scurried in front of him and cockroaches scampered left and right. The hallway light hung with no fixture, the wires jutting out in all directions. It was as if he had stepped into a slum version of his house.

He turned right, into the bathroom. Mold flourished on the walls, black and spotty. The toilet had a jagged crack in it, and another rat sat on top of it, its red eyes watching Paul. He wanted out of here. The air in his lungs felt as if it had been replaced with liquid nitrogen.

He faced the shower curtain. It was shredded as if by claws. He pulled it aside and found a piece of gauze on the floor of the tub. It belonged to the tunnel thing, no doubt. When he turned to run, he found the creature standing in the doorway, a gnarled hand reaching for Paul and nearly grabbing him before he woke up.

"Paul, you still here?"

"Yeah. Just thinking about my dream."

Jack said, "I kept dreaming he was at the window. I would pull the curtains open and there he was, looking in at me."

Paul wrinkled his nose and said, "Let's stop talking about it for now."

Paul stopped at his locker while Jack went to his own. Paul dialed the combination, opened the door, and hung his jacket inside. A poster of a red dragon, its scales shimmering, hung on the locker door.

"Hey, it's the Dungeons and Dragons dork," Vinnie said from behind him. Paul turned to see him and Harry Cross standing behind him. Harry grinned.

"What do you want?"

"Just wondering how your pussy friends are. Is Harding out of the hospital yet?"

"Actually, he's at his locker," Paul said.

Vinnie glanced over to Jack's locker. He flinched a little in surprise. Jack Harding was alive and well, thank you.

"He's got to be hurting," Vinnie said.

"Looks okay to me," Harry said.

"Shut up," Vinnie said, giving him a look that could stop the devil in his tracks.

"After school," Vinnie said. He walked away, leaving Paul wondering what he had done to incur the wrath of Vinnie. It appeared their bully immunity was wearing off.

Vinnie stomped over to Jack's locker, and Paul followed him.

"What are you doing here?" Vinnie said.

"Going to school," Jack said.

"How's your ribs?" Vinnie jabbed him in the side, just below the armpit.

"Ow. Okay. Didn't you do enough already?" Jack said.

"No way. You're still here instead of the hospital." Something caught Vinnie's attention and he turned to look down the hallway. "Hey, look. Here comes the fat fuck."

Jack turned to see Ronnie strolling down the hallway, a powdered donut in his paw, sugar framing his lips.

"What's going on?" he asked through a mouthful of donut.

"Get lost, fat ass," Harry said.

Ronnie ignored him.

"Let's get to class," Paul said.

"Shut up," Harry said. He turned and shoved Paul. So far none of the teachers had noticed the little altercation, but he hoped one might come by.

"Leave us alone," Jack said.

"You're lucky you can still walk, Harding."

"Maybe we should kick his ass again," Harry said, punching his open palm and making a flat smacking noise.

"We don't want any more trouble," Jack said.

"Aw. Isn't that too bad? You're going to get it anyway, pussy."

At that point, Paul was sure Vinnie had all intentions of

leaving them alone, at least for now. If they were lucky, it was only Vinnie blowing off steam. Ronnie Winter managed to change all that.

The day had started out well enough, John warming up the limo and getting it nice and toasty for him. He had French toast for breakfast (with a little vanilla in the batter—his favorite), and he managed to sneak a powdered donut from the pantry. Now, as he stood in the hallway, he was determined not to let the moron brothers ruin his fine morning.

Vinnie and Harry stood with arms crossed. Trying too hard to look hard.

"We aren't pussies, hook nose," Ronnie said.

Jack turned around quick enough to cause whiplash. "Are you nuts?" he whispered.

"What did you call me?" Vinnie said.

"I think he called you hook nose," Harry said.

Vinnie glared at Harry. "No shit. Maybe we didn't get our message across the other day. You're lucky that big spook was around to save you."

"Don't talk about John like that," Ronnie said, taking a bite of his donut.

"How about nigger then?"

"Stop it," Ronnie said. He felt the heat start to creep up his neck and into his face.

"Yeah, we weren't bothering you," Paul said.

Harry took a step toward Paul, who skittered backward, then crept forward once Harry turned around.

"He's right," Jack said, sweeping a lock of hair off his forehead.

"Listen, Harding."

Vinnie grabbed for Jack's shirt, but before he could grab hold, Ronnie fired his donut at Vinnie, nailing him square in the forehead. Jack and Paul burst out laughing, Paul's high-pitched laugh carrying over the others'. The donut whacked Vinnie, seemed to hang in midair for a second, and rolled down his shirt, leaving a trail of powdered sugar. He gritted his teeth and let out a steady growl. "You're dead." He pointed at Ronnie, his hand shaking. Before it went any further, Mr. Caldon, the fifth grade teacher, strode in.

"What's going on?"

They all stayed quiet like prisoners trying not to rat.

"Nothing," Jack said.

"Yeah, nothing," Vinnie said.

"That powdered sugar on your melon doesn't look like nothing, Palermo." Mr. Caldon had been a British Commando during World War II, and was the only teacher not afraid of Vinnie.

"It's fine," Vinnie said.

He turned to Ronnie. "And what about you?"

"Everything's okeydoke," Ronnie said.

"Break it up before there's more hullaballoo. Go, get to class." Caldon shooed them away.

"Dead," Vinnie said.

"Move it, Palermo," Mr. Caldon said, nudging Vinnie along.

"Don't touch me," Vinnie said.

Vinnie and his jerky friend left. Paul approached Ronnie, and Ronnie stared at the remains of his donut. He wanted it back, and if no one was around, he would have picked it up. Shame to waste a quality Hostess product.

"That took some guts. Or lack of brains," Jack said.

"What do you mean?" Ronnie asked.

"Winging a powdered donut at Vinnie," Jack said.

"I shouldn't have done that," Ronnie said.

"Actually, it was pretty original. Assault with a deadly baked good."

They actually thought something he did was cool. That had never happened to him before. Usually the other guys in his class called him names and slapped him on the belly in the locker room. But these guys liked him.

"You guys aren't mad?"

"Someone needed to stand up to that prick," Jack said.

"You realize we'll need eyes in the back of our head now," Paul said.

"He'll come after us no matter what. He didn't hurt me bad enough so he's going to try again," Jack said. "You're all right, even though you pulled that tunnel stunt on us."

"Sorry about that."

He almost forgot he had news for them. "I'm going to ask Jessica to the dance," Ronnie said.

"You're nuts," Jack said.

"I told Paul I would. Remember, Paul?"

Paul nodded.

"I'll ask her at lunch," Ronnie said.

Most guys his age would melt at the prospect of asking the prettiest girl in class to the dance, but with Ronnie it was full steam ahead. Bullies and pretty girls be damned.

"You won't do it," Jack said.

"Wanna bet?"

"I'll bet you five bucks," Jack said.

"Deal. Shake."

They shook on it.

"So you guys want to come to my house for a sleepover?" Ronnie asked.

"Sure," Jack said.

"Anything to get me away from the General," Paul said.

"Paul, you're staying with us," Jack said.

"I have to go home sometime."

"What are you guys talking about?"

Jack explained how Paul's dad came home and found them coming up from the basement. And how Paul came to stay at the Harding house.

"Paul can stay as long as he wants. His dad's nuts," Jack said. "No offense."

"It's okay," Paul said, although Ronnie saw the look on his face. Jack's words had cut him.

"We need to get to homeroom," Jack said.

Ronnie followed Jack to homeroom thinking the five bucks was as good as his.

Jack headed to homeroom thinking he was starting to like the new kid. He grew on you, like a fungus. He laughed at the comparison.

Emma brushed past him. "What's so funny?"

Her hair gleamed, tied in a ponytail. She wore a Celtics sweatshirt and jeans, her usual. She looked different to him, glowed more than usual.

"Just thinking about this new kid. Ronnie. You'll meet him soon."

"What's he like?"

"Kind of out there, but he does some cool stuff, too."

She leaned in close to him and he smelled coconut shampoo. His heart sped up. What a fantastic smell.

"You didn't tell anyone what we talked about, right?"

"No. Swear on it." He crossed his heart.

"I knew I could count on you. Are you excited about the dance?"

Like you wouldn't believe, he thought. She sounded nervous, as if he were going to change his mind and reject her. What Jack didn't know (and would find out later in life) was the girls got just as nervous as the boys. At twelve, though, girls could be damn terrifying.

"Yeah, I am."

She smiled, a real hundred-watt job. "We'd better get to our seats."

Vinnie strutted past and threw a wicked look at Jack. "Who's your girlfriend, jackass?"

"Stuff it," Emma said.

"After school," Vinnie said.

Emma looked at Jack, a slightly disappointed look on her face. "Now what did you do?"

"Ronnie beaned him with a powdered donut," Jack said.

"Next time kick him in the nuts. That's what I would do," Emma said.

She strolled to her desk, ponytail bouncing, and Jack thought he might be in love.

* * *

Noon came, and the sixth, seventh, and eighth graders grabbed brown bags from their lockers and stampeded to the cafeteria. Paul grabbed his Dungeons and Dragons lunch box, prompting Larry Leeb to shout, "Nice lunch box, baby-ass!" Paul had no idea what a babyass was, nor did he care. The warrior painted on his lunch box led a life of adventure and danger. The Larry Leebs of the world picked their noses and sniffed their own farts.

He took a seat at the table. Jack, Emma, and Chris joined him. Chris had come in late, oversleeping and arriving halfway through first period. Ronnie was the last to the table, pulling out a chair and making it screech across the tile floor. They dug into lunches, eating peanut butter and jelly sand-wiches, bologna on rye, Ho-Hos, Hi-C juice boxes, and Cheetos. Jack's mom had made Paul a peanut butter sand-wich, the first real-food lunch he'd had in a long time. It beat the shit out of potato chips and pop.

"You guys hear someone else got killed last night?" Paul asked.

"My mom did. She wants me home before dark," Emma said.

"I'm surprised I can even leave the house," Jack said.

"Your mom lets me in while you're gone. She'll let you go out. We need our privacy," Chris said.

"That's rotten," Emma said.

Jack shot Chris the finger.

Paul wasn't going to mention the attack in Jack's garage to Chris. He would snort and dismiss them as idiots. The only way Chris would believe was if he saw it for himself.

The five of them discussed the weather, the ever-growing snow mounds, king of the mountain, and school closing for break. Chris suggested starting a snowball fight with the eighth graders, and they all agreed the punks had it coming.

"My mom says I can have a sleepover. You can all come. Even you, Emma," Ronnie said.

"My mom would pee on herself. She doesn't like me hanging around with you guys."

"We're men, not boys, sweetheart," Chris said. He ripped a bite off his bologna sandwich.

Emma cocked an eyebrow. "Hardly," she said.

"Make something up. Tell your mom you're going to one of the girls' houses," Paul said.

"I'll think about it. When is it?" Emma said.

"Saturday," Ronnie said.

Vinnie, Joe, and Harry cruised past the table like sharks eyeing swimmers. Paul shifted in his seat and kept his gaze on the table, hoping to avoid them. Vinnie kicked the leg on Jack's chair as he passed.

"What's with them?" Chris said.

"We had a little fight this morning," Paul said.

"Ronnie hit the schnoz with a donut," Jack said.

Chris paused in midbite and stared at Ronnie. "Good one. How stupid did he look?"

"Like a number-one asshole," Jack said.

"Sleepover on Saturday then," Ronnie said.

Then all nodded in agreement, even Emma.

"Time for me to get a date for the dance," Ronnie said.

"What are you talking about?" Chris asked.

You didn't dare Ronnie Winter. Paul probably thought he would never ask out the best-looking girl in the seventh grade. *Going to prove him wrong*, Ronnie thought. As he pushed his chair out, the other kids watched him, Chris with sandwich in hand and mouth open.

Jessica was three tables away, sitting with three other girls he didn't recognize. They were almost as pretty as she, but Jessica glowed. Her blond hair was up in pink barrettes and it swished over her shoulder when she moved. She had on a green sweater with a gold butterfly pin above her chest. She looked good. And ready for the Winter man.

* * *

"He's really doing it," Paul said.

"He'll wuss out," Chris said.

"I think he's going to do it," Jack said.

Jack didn't think he would go pussy. Ronnie had a strut about him, like a gunslinger going to stare down the guy in the black hat. It was the same wild-eyed Ronnie who had threatened to smash the flashlight underneath the estate. That Ronnie was a bulldozer ready to roll.

He smoothed a hand through his hair, and a sprig of hairs stood at attention. He smacked into a chair on his way over to Jessica's table and muttered, "Ouch."

"He's going down like the Hindenburg," Paul said.

"What the hell is that, Fussel?"

"A blimp that crashed back in the thirties," Paul said.

"A blimp," Chris said. "Good comparison."

"This ought to be good," Jack said.

"As long as he doesn't fall on her," Chris said.

They watched the would-be Romeo close in on the target.

She ate her sandwich by picking away chunks of bread and placing them in her mouth. Jessica was almost Heather Locklear pretty, on the verge of hot. If he was going to ask someone, why not go for the best-looking babe in the class? The other guys' doubt was all the more reason to go for it.

He approached her. Jessica's head was turned, talking to the girl next to her. Ronnie reached out, took her free hand, and held it in his. He got down on one knee and smacked a kiss on the top of her hand. She turned around.

"What are you doing?" she asked.

Kids at the neighboring tables turned around. Lydia Garden dropped her carton of milk, and it pooled on the floor.

"My lady," he said.

Her nails were painted pink and she wore a gold ring on her index finger. "Do you have a problem?"

"My only problem is I'm crazy for you. Would you come with your fair prince to the Christmas dance?"

He wiggled his eyebrows and that got her to smile. Ronnie glanced over at his friends. They were as still as Michelangelo's David.

"You can let go of my hand," she said.

"Yes, my lady," he said, bowing his head. He let go of Jessica's hand and she drew back.

"You're the new kid, aren't you?"

"Yes," he said.

"What's your name?"

"Ronnie Winter."

"Hi, Ronnie." She smiled at him.

"Hi."

"Are those your friends over there?"

"Yeah. They didn't think I would ask you out," he said.

"You're the only one who asked me out. I think the other boys are afraid of me."

"Will you go with me?"

"I'd love to."

Never in a billion years did he really think she would say yes. He was fat (not husky like Mom claimed) and no Tom Cruise to boot. But like Chris had said, he had stones, and sometimes that got you places when nothing else worked.

"All right!" He pumped his fist in the air.

Her face turned a spectacular shade of pink. "You can stand up now. Everyone's staring."

Once he got to his feet, she took out a pen and wrote her phone number on his hand.

Life was sweet. Hands in pockets, he turned to leave. He didn't see Vinnie and Harry coming up behind him.

CHAPTER 29

"The son of a gun did it," Paul said.

"What do you think of that, bub?" Jack said.

"Nothing." Paul scowled at Jack's use of his pet word. "Shut up. I never thought he'd do it."

Ronnie came back, chest out, head up, the shirt clinging to his meaty chest. Jack looked past Ronnie to see Vinnie crouched over Jessica like a vulture, talking to her. He had one arm around the back of her chair, and she wore a look of disgust on her face. Old hook nose didn't smell like a carnation, as anyone he put in a headlock could have told you.

"You owe me five bucks, Jack," Ronnie said.

"What did she say?" Chris asked.

"We're going. I have to call her."

"Bullshit," Chris said.

Jack wondered about Jessica's answer too, although he didn't want to say so.

"Ask her. I've got her number here." He held up his hand and displayed a phone number written in green ink.

"Emma, you ask her," Paul said.

Chris said, "What's the matter, Paulie, too afraid to tawk to a giwl?"

"Screw off," Paul said.

"I think she really said yes," Emma said.

Whether Emma believed Ronnie or just didn't want to hurt him, Jack didn't know.

"I'll go ask her," Chris said, getting up from the table, unfazed by Vinnie's presence. Vinnie saw Chris coming and stepped back. Chris said something to Jessica and came back shaking his head. The kid who wouldn't shake Ronnie's hand upon first meeting extended his hand, palm out. "Nice going."

Ronnie slapped him five and Chris returned it.

"Told you guys," Ronnie said.

The sight of Vinnie hovering over Jessica troubled Jack. He had a feeling Ronnie's moment of glory might be short-lived.

They sat down and resumed eating, discussing the supposed serial killer lose in Brampton.

Jack glimpsed Vinnie and Harry dragging the twenty-gallon can across the floor like some degenerate garbage collectors. They stopped three feet from Ronnie and before Jack could say anything, they hoisted it over Ronnie's head and dumped it. Banana peels, bread crusts, milk cartons, wrappers, and apple cores spilled on top of Ronnie. Vinnie and Harry tossed the can aside and it rolled until stopping at the wall. Harry burst out laughing, and Vinnie punched him on the arm, a gesture that said *aren't we the fucking coolest?*

Jack and the others stared at Ronnie as if he had just sprouted a third arm. A banana peel rested on his shoulder, and milk dribbled down his forehead. He looked down at his soiled clothes and wiped the sludge off his shirt. For the first time in his young life, Jack hated someone. Raw hate, like he could punch someone again and again, not stopping until they were a bloody mess. Or wanting to see someone hit by a car. Someone like Vinnie.

"You're a rotten piece of shit," Jack said.

"Yeah, Vinnie, you turd," Emma said.

Vinnie ignored them, leaning over Ronnie. "Thought you

were hot shit, asking her to the dance. See if she goes with you now, garbage man."

Ronnie brushed the banana peel from his shoulder and it rolled off. To Jack's surprise, Jessica hurried over to the table. She put a hand on Ronnie's shoulder and gave Vinnie a look that would make a tiger turn and run. "I'm still going to the dance with him, you jerk," she said. "I'm sorry about this, Ronnie." She turned and stomped away.

"Why do you do it?" Emma asked.

"Because I can," Vinnie said.

"Yeah. You want to do something about it?" Harry stepped forward.

Mr. Ruiz, the eighth grade Spanish teacher, flew in and grabbed the moron twins by the arms. Vinnie tore his arm away and Harry laughed. "To the discipline office. Now." Harry and Vinnie turned slowly and left with Mr. Ruiz in tow. Mrs. Grady, all two hundred pounds of her in an emerald dress and pearls, hovered over Ronnie, brushing him off. "I'll write you a pass so you can go clean up. Don't worry about being late for next period. I don't know about that boy. He ought to be expelled," she said.

"Sorry about that, man," Jack said.

"It's okay. I suppose I had it coming," Ronnie said.

"It's not your fault," Emma said.

Ronnie stood up and left the cafeteria, a wounded warrior caked in lunch refuse.

What would Ronnie's mom do when she found out what happened to him? Jack didn't want to know.

The day passed and the final bell rang at three o'clock, causing a rush into the hallway. While Jack and the others sat in class, three more inches fell on Brampton and the wind chill dipped to minus ten. After getting his winter gear on and grabbing some books from his locker, Jack went to the courtyard to wait with his friends for John. Jack had called his mom on the pay phone and told her they were going to Chris's house. Emma left a message for her mom at work that she was going to the library.

The limo pulled up and John stepped out. He had on a red watch cap and matching ski vest. He came around and opened the door, waving at them to hurry and get in the limo. A moment later they pulled away from the curb. Emma looked around, taking in the polished elegance of it all, like something on *Dynasty*.

"And who is the pretty young lady you boys have brought along?"

"This is Emma," Paul said.

"Emma Greer. Nice to meet you," Emma said.

"Same here. My name is John."

They followed a tractor-trailer down Main Street, and it kicked up slush onto the windshield. John hit the wipers and fanned it away. Driving in the bad weather didn't seem to bother him.

"Emma, I don't mind if you come along, but you might find the conversation a little strange."

"If it's about the guy in the tunnel, I know. I can handle it," she said.

"Good. The more of you that know, the better. It'll keep you on your guards, I hope."

"Where's Ronnie?" Jack asked.

"Yeah, don't you always pick him up?" Paul said.

"Serving time."

They must have given Ronnie detention along with Vinnie and Harry.

"He doesn't need to hear about this anyway," John said.

They passed the Stigelmeyer mansion, a Victorian complete with turrets, gables, and a widow's walk. It was the last building on Main Street before leaving Brampton. They drove another ten minutes, passing a barn and field blocked off by a split rail fence. John turned into a driveway and drove up an incline that ended in a parking lot. Emma had been here before to eat.

The Central Diner was a blocky building, purely functional. The walls were white, and the Central Diner sign was done in neat black letters. An awning frame jutted out from the front of the structure, looking lonely and skeletal. She had come here with Mom two years ago on her birthday, and she ate so many pancakes she puked them an hour later. Pancake puking aside, she still liked the food.

The waitress led them to a table in the rear corner of the dining room. Emma wondered what the other people would think when a black man pulled up in a limo with three kids. John didn't seem concerned. He sat smiling, hands folded in front of him. The waitress took their orders. Jack ordered a plate of fries and a shake, while Paul and Emma went for hot fudge sundaes. John ordered coffee and ten minutes later, the waitress brought their order.

"This place will be filling up for dinner soon, so we'll talk quick," John said. "Tell me exactly what happened in the tunnels."

Jack retold the story and even though Emma had heard it already, it still made her shiver.

"And last night in the garage, what happened?" John said.

"We saw it in the window. Then it tried to pull us out of the garage. That's when you showed up," Jack said.

"You didn't tell me about this," Emma said.

"The same thing from the tunnel tried to get me and Paul when we took the garbage out." Jack plucked a French fry from his plate.

"Creepy," Emma said.

"You guys can't tell anyone what I'm about to tell you. Not your parents, the police, your friends, and especially not Ronnie. Got it?"

They all nodded in agreement. Emma wondered what could be so horrible.

Cassie Winter strode through the halls of Brampton Middle School, long skirt flowing as she walked. She drew glances from a few of the male faculty members, furtive glances she could have returned with icy coldness but chose not to. She stopped and asked a man wielding a mop and bucket where the discipline office was located.

"Make a left at the end of this hallway. Third door on the right," he said.

She entered the office to find a woman at a desk. Blond hair cut short, like a man's, doughy face, a pink cardigan. The nameplate on her desk read: NOREEN LEWIS. Cassie assumed she was the secretary, and said, "I was called and told to meet with the dean of discipline. Is he here?"

"He is a she. And I'm her. Noreen Lewis." She rose from the chair and offered her hand.

Cassie shook it. "Cassie Winter."

"I wanted to talk to you about an incident that took place with your son. He's in there." She nodded to indicate another small room off the main office. The door had a frosted glass pane.

"I like to think of that as the holding area." She chuckled. "It used to be a supply closet, but I like to let the students sit in there and think about what they've done before I talk to them."

"Sort of medieval if you ask me."

"Not really," she said.

She didn't like this woman, who Cassie imagined lorded over children like a prison warden and in some corner of her heart took pleasure in doling out punishments. The power of the Reach was tempting, and Cassie considered using it to cloud the woman's mind and make her forget the incident with Ronnie. But she was tired right now and could handle someone like Noreen Lewis without resorting to one of the Powers.

"So can I see my son?"

"Certainly."

Lewis stood up and opened the door. Ronnie came out first, head down and looking as if he expected to be escorted to the firing squad. Another boy followed him. He wore a permanent scowl.

"Vincent, your father couldn't be reached. So we'll have to have our little talk without him. Sit down." She pointed to the three chairs in front of her desk. Then she excused herself, stepped around Cassie, and closed the main office door.

Cassie sat in the chair next to Ronnie's and immediately noticed his clothes. He smelled of rotten food and there were bits of bread and crumbs caked in his hair.

"What on earth happened?"

Ronnie cast a plump finger at the other boy. "He dumped a whole garbage can on me."

She looked at the other boy, who sat slouched in his chair, feet outstretched as if he were lounging on the beach. A bored, disinterested look crossed his face.

"Is this true, Noreen?"

Lewis sat down and crossed her legs. "It is."

"How can you let things like this go on? How did this happen?"

"It appears Vincent didn't like Ronnie talking to one of the girls in the cafeteria. That's when he dumped the garbage on Ronnie."

"My name's Vinnie, Noreen."

"Don't talk to me like that," she said.

"I won't, Noreen."

How could she let him talk to her like that? Cassie wondered.

"Call me Mrs. Lewis."

Vinnie lunged forward, bringing himself up on the edge of his seat. Lewis flinched, and it was very apparent that she was afraid of Vincent, or Vinnie as he apparently liked to be called.

"Two for flinching," he said, smiling.

"We'll deal with your behavior later, Vincent. As I said, Ronnie was talking to one of the girls, asking her to the dance. That's when Vincent dumped the garbage over his head. Some words were exchanged and it was broken up. I met with both boys and told them they would be staying after school today."

"Did Ronnie actually do something wrong?"

"It's my policy to punish both sides. You know how children are. You can never tell who was lying or telling the truth."

The woman was starting to sound like a Supreme Court justice, doling out judgments as if she were on the highest court in the land rather than a modest civil servant. In Cassie's mind, she knew that Ronnie had most likely egged Vincent on in some way, but there was no mention of that by Lewis. "Did Ronnie start anything with this other boy?"

"Yeah, he pissed me off because he's a fat faggot."

"Watch your mouth," Cassie said.

"Watch your mouth," Vinnie said, in a singsong voice.

She sent a blast of psychic energy into his mind, sharp as a pitchfork. He clutched his head and leaned forward, a yelp of pain escaping his lips. "My head," he said.

Lewis looked puzzled and Cassie put her hand on Vinnie's shoulder and said, "Are you okay, Vincent?"

"Ow, my head."

The wave she sent him passed and he probably felt a searing pain from his forehead to the base of his skull before it ended. Maybe that would keep him in line, for it was apparent his parents weren't doing their job. Most likely the boy was trouble from a young age and they never told him no or gave him punishments. As he grew up, his temper most likely became worse and by now he was too big and too far gone to control. It was a shame for any child to wind up like that.

She could do the same to Lewis, or cloud her thinking in any number of ways, but it would be best not to arouse suspicion. A student complaining of a headache was not unusual, but if Cassie did something to disrupt Lewis's thinking, she might remember it. Sometimes they did, and although she had never been found out, it was best not to draw attention to her gifts here.

"Where were we?" Cassie said.

"I'll be giving Ronnie and Vincent detention. They created quite a disturbance in the cafeteria."

"That still doesn't seem fair to me," Cassie said.

"I could suspend them," Lewis said.

"I can see you drive a hard bargain, Noreen. I'd better not push it, right?"

"You don't have to be sarcastic. Punishment has to fit the crime."

"Crime," Cassie said. "What an expression. Let's go, Ronnie." Ronnie and Cassie stood up to leave. She didn't want to hear any more from Noreen Lewis, and if the woman was smart, she would leave Ronnie alone.

"He is quite a bit overweight and I noticed stains on his shirt," Lewis said.

Cassie turned and it took all the willpower she had not to send a bolt like white lightning into the woman's head. It would most likely kill her or render her a drooling invalid, ruining brain function. Not that Noreen Lewis had much to begin with.

"Don't tell me my business," Cassie said.

"And don't tell me mine in my own office."

Cassie grabbed Ronnie by the hand and stormed out of the office.

"Here's what happened," John said. His hands engulfed the coffee mug, making only the lip visible.

Jack ate another fry. They were almost too hot to eat, but the ketchup cooled them. Salty, good, and greasy, the way he liked them.

"The thing you saw is called a Wraith. That's what Cassie calls him."

"The Wraith," Paul said, testing out the word for himself.

"What is it?" Jack asked.

"It used to be a man. Cassie made it." His gaze moved slowly to each of them. "All it wants to do is kill."

All of a sudden Jack's fries didn't taste so good. He set the plate aside, his stomach a mess of knotted worms.

"What do you mean made him?" Paul said.

"Did you guys ever hear of Ronald Winter? You might be too young to remember him."

They all shook their heads.

"He was one of the richest men in America, a billionaire. Made his money in auto parts. About fifteen years ago he met a woman named Cassandra Willis."

"Ronnie's mom," Jack said.

"Right. She literally came out of nowhere. One night Ronald had everyone in the family over for a dinner party. He introduces Cassie and tells everyone they're married. He was twenty years older than her and they didn't like it. His mother stormed out of the place. I remember it. It was at their chalet in Aspen."

"What's a chalet?" Emma asked.

"A fancy ski place," Paul said.

"Ronald's mother took me aside a week later and asked me to dig into Cassie's background. I was his personal assistant and bodyguard, so I guess they trusted me to look after him. I hired a private investigator and he came back with nothing. No birth records, Social Security number, arrest record, nothing. She appeared out of the blue, like I said."

The waitress bopped in, asking with a big smile how everything was. John smiled and said, "Fine." Jack's dad always complained how they waited until you had a mouthful of food to ask how the meal tasted. Jack wanted to open his mouth sometime and show a waitress the food, telling her how good it was.

"I didn't like Cassie. She was after his money. Never treated him well. Gave him the cold shoulder unless she wanted something. Two years after she married him, Ronnie was born. From day one, she adored Ronnie. Things went bad not too long after that. He started seeing other women on the side. You all know what that means?"

"He had other girlfriends," Emma said.

"That's right, Emma. He was seeing a woman named Daisy Flores. I knew about her because he told me everything." John looked down at his coffee cup. "I don't know how, but Cassie found out. I couldn't figure it out then, but I did later on."

"You hired another private investigator?" Paul said.

"No. She can sense things. Read minds. That's why I drove out here." He looked around, as if watching for someone. "I don't feel her right now."

John flagged down the waitress and she came over with the coffeepot. She poured him another cup and he thanked her.

"She healed my ribs. Those are part of her powers," Jack said.

"Yep. She can heal, too. When Ronnie was six, he fell off his bike and busted his wrist. I wanted to take him to the emergency room but she wouldn't let me. She picked him up, took him to her room, and an hour later they came out. His arm was knitted. He said it was still sore, but the bone was in place."

"I would've gotten out of there," Paul said.

"I couldn't leave," John said.

"Why?" Jack asked.

"I'm getting to that part."

CHAPTER 30

The trouble started brewing in the locker room, a sign of things to come. As Chris pulled on his practice jersey, Robbie Munch sauntered past and slammed Chris's locker door shut. It bounced back and hit Chris's exposed belly, leaving a white scratch. He winced and pulled the jersey down.

"Dick lick," Chris said.

"You wish."

"I'm gonna waste you out there, Munch."

"We'll see," Munch said, and sauntered out of the locker room.

The punishment for skipping practice was swift. MacGregor barked at him while he ran ten straight suicide drills. His teammates watched from the bleachers. While the other guys stretched and warmed up, Chris did the six inches drill. By the end of warm-ups, his legs felt like deadwood.

They set up for a passing drill, and he drew Munch as his partner. Munch fired the ball at his head. Chris managed to catch it.

"Knock it off," Chris said.

"Just making sure you can catch."

"You're a douche bag."

He went against Munch, playing center in the scrimmage.

Munch dug his forearms into Chris's lower back or jabbed him in the ribs at every turn. Chris told himself to cool it, because he was already on MacGregor's shit list, and if he did anything else, he might be the first player to ever run a nonstop suicide drill. Taking crap from Munch wasn't an option, either. The other guys were watching, and if Chris didn't do something, they would rag him hard after practice. The pride of sixth grade boys was won and lost on playgrounds and ball fields. Parents always told you to walk away, but it was better to have a bloody lip than wounded pride.

Jason Taylor stole the ball and raced down the court with Munch streaking after him. Taylor lobbed Chris the ball, and as Chris went in for the layup, Munch slammed his hand into the side of Chris's head. Chris hit the floor and rolled.

"Munch! Easy!" MacGregor yelled.

"That's it," Chris said.

As Munch started away, Chris lunged, gripping the legs of Munch's shorts and yanking hard. They slid down his legs, exposing Munch's white butt. A line of brown fuzz ran down the length of his crack, and it was more than Chris ever wanted to see of Robbie Munch, but the humiliation was worth it. MacGregor dropped his clipboard. The other guys stared at first, then started howling. Munch bent over and tried to pull up the shorts, but succeeded in stumbling and hitting the floor. Ass exposed, he wriggled on the floor and got the shorts over his backside.

He got up, scowling at Chris, ready to charge. MacGregor swept in from the bleachers like a bird of prey. He grabbed Munch's jersey.

"Munch. Run a suicide drill. Francis, in the locker room. The rest of you girls run the full-court passing drill we did yesterday."

Chris trotted off the court with MacGregor behind him. Chris entered the locker room and sat on an aluminum bench.

"Look at me," MacGregor said. He slammed the door and it sounded like a rifle shot.

"What?"

"What the hell is wrong with you? Didn't you learn anything the other day from doing six inches all practice?"

"He fouled me."

"Boo fucking hoo. You took a hard foul. It's part of the game, Chris. You don't do that to a guy for fouling you. You want to get him back? Score twenty-five points on his ass." MacGregor paced back and forth in front of the bench. "I don't get you, Chris."

"If I didn't do something, the other guys would call me a pussy."

"They respect you, Chris. They look up to you. Munch is a big mouth, a talker. The other guys think he's a joke. I think he's a joke. He won't even make a high school team, but you're different."

"I know. Just like my dad says, right?" Chris dismissed him with a wave of the hand.

"I've known your dad a long time. He's made a lot of mistakes, but I know he cares about you. You might not see it that way, but he does. Don't you care?" MacGregor stopped pacing, placed his hands on his hips.

"I know you're not the best student. Let's be honest. There's teachers who want you off my team because of your grades. I'm not trying to be a jerk, but it's the truth."

For a moment Chris felt tears welling up. The truth cut deep and hard. He really wasn't going anywhere based on his grades. Even someone like MacGregor could see that.

"I'm suspending you from the team for a week. Maybe you need to get yourself together. Talk to your father, even if it's hard. I'm going to call him tonight and make sure you told him what happened."

MacGregor headed for the door and grabbed the handle. He stopped and turned to Chris. "Anyone else would be off this team. I hope you realize that."

As the door closed, Chris flipped him the bird. Dad was going to be pissed, but he really didn't care at this point. Maybe it was time for him to focus less on sports and more on studying. He sometimes wished he would blow out his knee, or break an ankle. A career-ending injury, as they said in the pros. Then maybe he could work with a tutor, get his grades up. Whatever path he chose, he wanted to leave basketball far behind.

John ordered another cup of coffee, took a sip after making a face. "Hot," he said. "Like I said, she can manipulate minds, get into people's heads. Confuse them. I think her finding out about the girlfriend was a matter of reading her husband's thoughts."

The door to the diner opened and the wind blew inside. A bearded man and a girl of about six stepped in. He sat her on a stool and she spun around, kicking her legs and giggling.

"Someone's happy," John said. "Cassie waited up for him one night. He had a flight coming in from the West Coast. Got in about three in the morning. I was sleeping. My room was upstairs at the time. It was three forty-one on the digital clock."

The numbers on the clock were etched into his head. Some people say they'll never forget where they were when Kennedy got shot, and for John it was the same way with that night. He would never forget the moment he first heard the screams.

"Cassie didn't waste any time with him. Are you sure you can handle this?"

"Sure we can," Jack said.

The other two nodded.

"I heard screaming. I thought it was a woman at first, but there were none in the house. I grabbed my revolver from the nightstand and hurried downstairs."

"What happened?" Paul asked.

"I'm getting there. They were coming from the study. I got down there and looked through the sliding doors." He took a drink of coffee, wishing it were a beer instead.

"She had him pinned to the big cherry table."

"She must be pretty darn strong," Emma said.

"Yep. She bound his hands and feet with phone cord. That woman did some awful things. Burned him with a hot poker from the fireplace. Slashed his face apart. Then she tore his eyes out. After that, she closed her eyes and laid her hands on him. The whole room went dark, even the fire in the fireplace went out. When the lights came back on, he was dead. His face was bone white. She wrapped his face in bandages and dragged him from the room."

He didn't tell them that Cassie wasn't Cassie when she did this. The creature he saw looked like a mutant version of her, and he remembered feeling his sanity start to slide when he saw what she had become.

"What did she do to him?" Paul asked.

"She can heal and she can kill. Just like that. But she made Ronnie's dad into some sort of zombie. The next day I was fixing the garbage disposal and she came up behind me and said, 'I know you saw.' "

"What did you do?" Emma asked.

"Almost crapped in my pants," he said. This drew a chuckle from all of them.

John said, "She took my family away, my wife and son. She says they're locked away somewhere and if I ever went to the cops, she'd kill them."

"Are they still alive?" Jack asked.

"I haven't seen them in ten years. She took me to see them, but I can't remember where it was. She messed up my head so I wouldn't remember."

"I'm never going near that place again," Jack said.

"You have to. You're Ronnie's friend now, and if you stop hanging around with him, you'll make her mad. Act like you never heard this," John said.

It was a lot to lay on a bunch of kids, but he needed to tell them for their own safety. They had to keep hanging with Ronnie, but they needed to be careful, too. If they deserted Ronnie now, they risked Cassie releasing the Wraith on them.

"How are we supposed to hang around with him? What if she tries to kill us?"

"We're doomed," Paul said.

"Just hang out with him. Be his friend and you'll have nothing to worry about," John said.

"Will you ever find your family?" Emma asked.

"I don't know, but it's what keeps me going."

John raised his hand to flag down the waitress.

Paul had just finished drying off with a cushy blue towel when the doorbell rang. He slid on his underwear and the sweat suit Jack had loaned him. The sleeves came down to his fingertips, so he rolled them up to his elbows. He felt sleepy from the hot bath and wanted to hit the cot, but the familiar voice coming from the door drew him away from bed.

Paul cut through the kitchen and found Jack standing in the doorway leading to the back hallway. Jack turned around.

"Your dad's here," Jack said.

"Wonderful."

Paul slid next to Jack and peered down the steps. Mr. Harding stood in the door, the outdoor light spilling on his bald head. Paul's own father stood outside, hair full of snowflakes, pointing a finger at Jack's dad.

"You can't keep him here. It's kidnapping."

"It's nothing like that and you know it," Mr. Harding said.

"Paul, you get out here." Paul's dad stepped forward, and Mr. Harding, a full head shorter, moved forward, blocking the doorway.

"I'll call the cops. He belongs at home."

"Why don't you do that? I'd be glad to tell them how you've been beating Paul."

"Paul, I'm sorry. Why don't you come home?"

That was like a shark encouraging a swimmer to put his leg in the shark's mouth, Paul thought. "I'm staying here."

"Did these two tell you what they did to me? One of them

kicked me in the ass. I'm pretty sure it was your kid, Harding. You always let him get away with shit like that?"

With the snow building in his beard, and the wild look in his eyes, Paul's dad could pass for the abominable snowman.

"I'll talk to Jack about that. Meanwhile, Paul stays here. I'm not sending him home with you."

"Yeah," Paul said.

"You're awful brave standing up there."

"Go home," Mr. Harding said. "Now."

"Fucking hell with all of you." The abominable one slammed his fist into the side of the house and stomped away, kicking up snow as he went.

Mr. Harding shut the door and ascended the steps. He wiped his brow, face flushed.

"You showed his ass," Jack said.

"Watch your mouth."

"You were great, Mr. Harding," Paul said.

Mr. Harding's hands trembled. Apparently fights with bullies didn't upset only kids. Paul had never seen anyone stare down his father like that. The General usually got his way.

"He won't hurt you, Paul. That's a promise."

"Thanks." He gave Mr. Harding a quick hug around the waist and let go.

"What if he sends the cops here?" Jack said.

"We'll cross that bridge when we come to it."

It had been a whirlwind day. Paul and Jack sat in the living room, Jack in the well-worn recliner and Paul on the couch. On the six o'clock news an ambulance crew loaded a sheet-covered body into their rig. It was the Wraith's latest victim, though the police would never know that. They would look for a drifter or some criminal with a violent record. Someone already dead couldn't be traced.

"What do we do?" Paul asked.

"Exactly what John said. We go to his sleepover and hang with him."

"You think she can read our minds right now?" Paul looked around the room, as if she might be hiding behind the couch.

"No, doofus. I'll tell you something though."

"Yeah?"

"We have to protect ourselves."

From the kitchen, water ran and dishes clanked.

"Kill her?" Paul said, in a big whisper.

"I don't know. But remember what John said. She controls the Wraith and it keeps killing. You forget already?"

"Sure, Jack. I almost forgot being dragged to my death by a zombie."

"You know what I meant. I don't want her coming after us, chopping us up like she did to Ronnie's dad."

"So we go to the party at his house. Then what? Do we have to be his friend forever? What happens if we move away someday? Would she come after us?"

"Don't be a dork. I just don't want to wait around to see if every time we have a disagreement with Ronnie she gets pissed. Do you?"

Paul frowned. "No. But we can't kill her."

"We can't tell our parents or the cops, either. They won't believe us." Jack plucked at the hairs on his arm. "Our first step is finding out what makes her tick. We do some exploring around the mansion. Just like in Dungeons and Dragons."

He hoped to appeal to Paul's sense of adventure. "As long as we're in the house, I think we're safe."

"If you say so." Paul shifted on the couch.

"Emma will go with us," Jack said.

"What about too-tall?"

"We'll work on Chris. Maybe he needs to see it for himself."

"But we're not going into the tunnels again, right?" Paul said.

"Nah."

"You're still thinking about going down there, aren't you?"

"We might need to. Not to prove Chris wrong."

"What do you mean?" Paul said. He fidgeted in the chair.

Jack leaned forward. "If we piss his mom off again, she could send it for us. We might need to go after it ourselves."

"We'll go to the cops. They'll know what to do," Paul said.

"Right. A guy with no eyes who's already dead attacked us. But if we got proof . . ."

"How? Ask it to pose for a picture? Not likely, bucko," Paul said.

"We'll think about it."

"I feel sick," Paul said.

"Your dad has a gun if we need it, right?" Jack said.

"It's in his closet."

"Good."

CHAPTER 31

Emma straightened her room, putting away a stack of folded sweatshirts and organizing the assorted deodorant, lip balm, and brushes on the dresser. She rehung the Celtics pennant on her mirror, thinking of the incident with Jacob the other day. Her nerves still crackled, as if tiny sparks might jump from her fingertips. Part of it was the upset of the experience with Jacob, and part of it was the thought of the date with Jack. She felt electric, good one moment and sick the next. It depended on what she thought about.

She slid the dresser drawer closed and the phone rang downstairs. Mom's footsteps echoed up the stairway. "Emma, phone," she said.

Emma went downstairs and her mother held the receiver out.

"Who is it?"

"Jacob."

She wanted to slam the receiver down in his ear right then and there.

"I'm not talking to him," she said.

"Stop it. He's your cousin."

"But, Mom."

"Talk to him."

She took a deep breath and picked up the receiver. "What do *you* want?" Emma said.

Mom walked away.

"Looking forward to coming over," he said.

"I'm not."

"We could listen to more music in your room," Jacob said.

"I'd rather have cockroaches in my room."

"Okay, dyke."

There was a click and then the dial tone came up.

She slammed the receiver into the cradle and it gave a *ding*.

There was no way around it anymore; she had to tell Mom about Jacob. She stormed into the kitchen to find her stirring a mixing bowl with a spoon.

"I need to talk to you right now," Emma said.

"Watch your tone with me."

"Sorry. Can we talk now? Please?"

"Can't it wait? I'm trying to finish the potato pancakes."

"No."

Mom set the bowl down and wiped her hands with a pink dish towel hanging on the cupboard door. "What's on your mind?"

"Jacob."

She leaned back against the counter and folded her arms. "What about him?"

"He's been bothering me."

"Teasing you?"

"Worse."

"What's worse?"

"Bothering."

"Get to the point, Emma."

She felt the familiar heat creep into her cheeks again and wondered if she shouldn't just bolt from the room and deal with Jacob herself. "He touched me."

"How?"

Jesus, she would rather talk about her period and girl parts (as Mom called them) than this. "On my butt and boobs," she said.

"When did he do this?"

"In my room the other day. And last summer at Aunt Sam's."

"Is that the noise I heard up there?" Mom asked.

Emma nodded.

"He was probably just horsing around. Boys like to wrestle and roughhouse."

"He wasn't horsing around. I hang around with boys and they don't do that," Emma said.

"You should know, you're with them enough."

That remark was like a tiny pinprick to the heart.

"You don't believe me."

"Jacob's a shy boy. Awkward. He's never even had a girlfriend." She picked up the bowl again and started stirring. "I'm not sure he's even interested in girls."

"I know one he's interested in."

Mom didn't answer.

"He told me he was going to get me," Emma said. "I kicked him in the balls."

"Watch the language. He said he was calling to see if you had the album he wanted."

"He called me a dyke."

"I'll have Aunt Sam talk to him about that. Is that all?"

She never had time for anything. The two of them used to walk to the park, to Shelby's for banana splits and spend hours taking. Now it was all she could do to get a five-minute conversation out of her mother. It was like talking to a ghost.

"Maybe when he rapes me you'll care."

"Emma Greer. I know you don't like your cousin but he's not a rapist. He's a little strange, but I doubt he's trying to rape you."

"Fine."

Emma turned and stomped up the stairs. Once upstairs, she slammed the door and threw herself on the bed, realizing this was her problem to deal with.

Kempf checked his watch, a Bulova that Jules had given him two Christmases ago. Ramsey's press conference was in forty-five minutes. That left him plenty of time to give an interview and get back to Town Hall.

He sat in an orange booth at Placy's Restaurant, sipping a glass of milk and hoping to calm the fire in his stomach. Perry Como drifted over the speakers, singing a Christmas tune. They all faded together after a while, Como sounding the same as Crosby or Burl Ives.

Kempf checked his watch again. The reporter was running late. The room felt like the devil's sauna. He slid the puffy parka off his shoulders and set it next to him in the booth. A few more minutes and he was walking out of here.

Five minutes later, a skinny college kid approached the table. An army surplus coat hung on his frame and a white scarf adorned his neck.

"Detective Kempf?"

Kempf nodded.

"Jeremy Woods. From the *Observer*."

"Little late."

"Sorry. Weather's nasty."

"Not a problem."

Woods took out a steno notebook and flipped it open. Then he pulled out a pencil and licked the tip of it. That was one thing Kempf never understood. Did licking the pencil make it write better?

"I'm sorry I blew you off the other day. Shit started hitting the fan," Kempf said.

"No problem. So what do you want to tell me?"

The waitress stopped over and Woods ordered a cocoa.

"You ask me whatever you want and I'll tell you. As long as you put a few things in the article for me."

"I'll try."

"No, you will. I'll give you a detailed description of the killer. And where I think he's hiding."

"That's great, but don't the police usually leave out a lot of details so other people don't confess to the crime?"

"This is Brampton. I don't think there's too many wannabe serial killers around here. Besides, people need to know what's happening. I think this guy's on the Steadman Estate and I want to shake it out like a blanket, but Chief Ramsey won't let me."

"Let's start then."

Kempf weaved past the news vans parked outside Town Hall and almost ran over Cindy Bryant from Channel Two News. He parked in the rear lot and made his way to the foyer. Ramsey stood behind a podium, giving that Ken doll hair a last smoothing over. The mayor stood next to him in a blue suit, and next to the mayor was Henry Starch, the county sheriff.

Kempf took his place on Ramsey's left and the chief nodded at him. "Glad you could make it, Tank."

The reporters filed in, and the foyer lit up like a night game at Yankee stadium from all the cameras. Flashes popped and correspondents stepped forward, scribbling into notebooks and practicing looks of concentration. It lasted fifteen minutes. Ramsey mentioned getting two sheriff's cars to patrol in town and assured the good people of Brampton that there was no cause for alarm. Kempf almost swallowed his tongue when he heard that. The deckhands on the *Titanic* probably told doomed passengers the same thing.

Ramsey thanked everyone for coming and as he stepped from the podium, he motioned for Kempf to follow him.

"What did you think?" Ramsey said.

"I was a little surprised when you told people not to be alarmed."

"We don't want a panic."

"You don't think there's already one? I noticed you didn't mention the Steadman Estate."

An incredulous look crossed his face. "Why would I?"

"That's where he was the day I saw him."

"We're not positive he's there," Ramsey said.

"We need to get on that property and tear the place up."

Ramsey exhaled, as if he were dealing with an impatient child. "Wealthy voters don't want the police bothering them. *Comprende?*"

Kempf stared at him, waiting for an explanation.

"I'm thinking of running for county sheriff next year. The owner of the Steadman place could be a big contributor to my campaign. They don't want us showing up there and drawing attention to the place. People gawk at the place as it is."

"You stupid son of a bitch."

"Tank?"

"You would let a murder suspect go loose just so someone can put money in your war chest?"

"Don't overreact." He held his hands up, palms out, as if to placate Kempf. "We've got extra patrols everywhere. The town's not that big. We'll find him."

"I'm going to talk to Cassie Winter again. See if she saw anything."

"Go alone. We don't need a mess of cops showing up there."

I was going alone, you schmuck, Kempf thought.

"Maybe I'll just give her a call and let her know you're coming," Ramsey said.

"You amaze me."

"Just be nice to her. And no more at the Steadman place after this, okay? We'll catch him."

Kempf threw his hands up in disgust and walked away.

It was a long walk home.

To make a bad day worse, Chris's dad never showed up to

get him from practice. He had expected to see the Trans-Am pull up with the radio loud enough to hear through closed windows, but Dad never showed. Snow and ice had nipped at him the entire way home, but he made it without turning into a human Eskimo Pie.

After taking off his coat and boots, he poured milk into a stainless steel pan and set it on the stove. The gas burner came to life with a *poof!* He took a packet of cocoa mix from the cupboard and dumped it in the pan. He needed something to warm his bones after the walk home, and cocoa always fit the bill.

A moment later, the Trans-Am rolled up the driveway. He didn't know whether his father had stopped at practice after Chris left, or if he got held up running errands. Either way, Chris would be able to tell by his father's entrance whether or not he talked to MacGregor. Like the month of March, he could enter as a lion or a lamb.

He stirred up his cocoa and the milk bubbled in the pan. Then he poured it in a mug and sat down at the table. Dad came in, snowflakes covering his shoulders.

"How was practice?"

"Fine."

"Sorry I missed you. Our sales meeting went over. Didn't mind walking, did you?"

"Nah."

Chris sipped his drink. He looked at the blue flower on the mug instead of his dad.

"Something the matter, Chris?"

MacGregor had threatened to call. The warning echoed in Chris's head, and if he didn't tell his father about the fight with Munch, MacGregor would.

"Practice wasn't so good."

"Why not?"

"I got into it with Munch again," Chris said.

"Chris—"

"He was being an idiot. He hit me with a locker door and fouled me hard."

"Haven't learned to ignore him then."

He was waiting for that golden nugget of parental wisdom: it takes a bigger man to walk away.

"No, I haven't."

"What did Coach say?"

"I'm suspended for a week."

"Jesus Christ," he said, barely audible. "I can't deal with this right now. You're going to flush this all down the crapper if you don't straighten up. You're lucky he didn't kick you off the team."

"I don't want to be on the team anymore."

"You're just saying that because you're mad."

"I'm thinking of asking for a tutor and working on my grades," Chris said.

"That's great, but can't you do that and play basketball?"

"The other kids think I'm stupid."

"Well, you're not."

"Then why did I fail two classes? The only reason I eventually passed was that MacGregor talked my teachers into letting me do extra credit."

"He's looking out for you," Dad said.

"Tell him not to."

"It's up to you, I guess."

He walked away, leaving Chris with a lukewarm cup of cocoa.

CHAPTER 32

Cassie's phone rang. She was in the middle of brewing a pot of coffee to sip throughout the day. It had snowed again, and a chill settled into the big house. She picked up the phone on the kitchen wall.

"Mrs. Winter?"

The voice on the end was as smooth as melted chocolate.

"This is?"

"This is Police Chief Samuel Ramsey. How are you?"

Ronnie. It had to be about Ronnie. Did he egg someone's house or spray-paint his initials on a car hood? Or maybe that other boy from the school beat Ronnie bloody.

"Mrs. Winter?"

"Is this regarding my son?"

"No, ma'am."

She closed her eyes, intent on getting a mental image of Samuel Ramsey. A man sitting in an office chair, leaning back, held the phone to his ear. He swiveled left, right, and back again. Then he reached down, scratched his crotch, and did a most peculiar thing: he sniffed his fingers. Amazing the things people did when they thought no one was watching. She took him to be a bit of an ogre, however clean and polished.

"Why are you calling?"

"One of my detectives paid you a visit. George Kempf. Remember him?"

"It was two or three days ago. I think I would," Cassie said.

"Right-o. Do you mind if he comes up again to ask a few questions? It's regarding the murders here in our fair town."

"I figured as much," Cassie said.

"Detective Kempf is bent on proving the killer is hiding out on your property. It's crazy, but that's what he thinks. He's harmless, a bit of a bumbler. I like to make him think he's working hard."

"He won't stay long? And no questioning my son."

"Of course. And I do apologize for the intrusion."

She tapped her red-lacquered nails on the table. "Not a big deal," she said.

"Great. Thank you for your cooperation, Mrs. Winter."

"I look forward to seeing Detective Kempf," she said, and hung up the phone.

Kempf plodded ahead at fifteen miles an hour, the snow pouring down from the white-gray sky. The lake effect machine, as the weathermen liked to call it, showed no signs of letting up. A band of lake effect sat on Brampton and pounded with both fists.

Before he left the station, Ramsey had briefed him on the conversation with Cassie Winter. Kempf was to be polite and tactful. Under no circumstances was he to ask questions about Cassie's son. Ramsey was getting his tit in a wringer over this woman, and it was because she had money. Ramsey made it clear this was to be Kempf's last visit to the estate. Kempf supposed angry rich ladies didn't fork over money for political campaigns, hence Ramsey's lecture.

Cassie greeted him at the mansion's doors. She wore her hair pulled back and a fluffy turtleneck clung nicely to her. Her smile was warm and despite his misgivings, Kempf smiled back. She took him by the arm and led him into the foyer. Inside a tune from *The Nutcracker* came from unseen speakers.

"Do you like the music? I'm trying to get into the Christmas spirit," she said.

"I'm more of a doo-wop fan. No offense."

"None taken."

"Is there somewhere we can sit down and talk?" Kempf asked.

"Certainly."

Kempf stomped the snow off his boots and followed her until they ended up in an enormous room.

"We can sit here in the great room," Cassie said.

A mahogany bar lined one wall, and behind it bottles of liquor sparkled like jewels. A dartboard, pool table, and Foosball table adorned one corner, and the great room even had a chrome jukebox. Kempf bet you could find Frankie Valli or Dion on there without much trouble.

"Can I offer you something?" she said.

"A glass of milk."

She moved behind the bar and Kempf followed, taking a seat on one of the bar stools. She bent over and took out a pint of milk from a minifridge behind the bar. Taking out a beer mug, she poured the milk and slid the mug over to Kempf.

"Some room," Kempf said.

"The Steadmans were fond of entertaining. I guess at one point they had parties every weekend. The Rockefellers were frequent guests."

"Were you related to the Winter of WINCO Industries?"

"He was my husband."

So that's where the money came from, he thought.

"I'm sorry for your loss," he said.

"It was a long time ago. I've moved on since."

He took a sip of milk. On the way up here, he had considered asking some softball questions and leaving after ten minutes. It was what Ramsey wanted him to do. But it stuck in his gut that the killer was on the estate somewhere and he could do nothing. Easy questions wouldn't stop people from dying. He decided to open up with the big guns.

"You know there's been another murder."

"Do you think I'm involved?" She looked amused.

"No, I don't. But I do believe the killer may be hiding on your property. How many acres is it?"

"Around eight hundred."

"That's a lot of room to hide. Not to mention the buildings," Kempf said.

"We went over this before, Detective. I saw nothing. If you're worried about my safety, my assistant, John, keeps a loaded forty-five on him. He's licensed."

Her grip on the edge of the bar tightened. The veins in her hands wriggled.

"These were vicious killings. I don't think there's bigcity homicide cops who see stuff like this. People are panicked, and panicked people do crazy things. Buy guns when they don't know a shotgun from a bazooka, shoot at things in their yard if they hear a noise. You can see my side of it."

She crossed her arms and pouted. "There is no murderer on my property. Has anyone else seen this person? Or is it just you, Detective?"

Kempf rubbed his forehead, just above the eyebrows, trying to massage away tension. "Just me. But you should be careful anyway."

"I'm tired. Are you almost finished?"

He decided to ease up a little. The last thing he wanted was her calling Ramsey to complain.

"I'm sorry, I just want to catch this person. Do you think I could talk to your assistant, John?"

She pulled a phone from under the bar and dialed a number.

"John? Detective Kempf is here and he'd like to ask you a few questions. I'll send him up." She hung up. "It's the houses on the left as you come in. The biggest one is his."

He finished his milk and got up to leave.

"Call me if you need anything." He took out a business card from his pocket and dropped it on the bar.

Kempf walked up the steps to John's house. A porch ran its entire length and on it was a stack of firewood. The storm door rattled in the wind, as did the wreath affixed to the door underneath. It smelled like fresh pine as he approached the door. Kempf knocked and a moment later John answered.

He extended a hand and they shook.

"Come on in."

He led Kempf to a kitchen painted in soft yellows and greens. "Sit down, please."

Kempf pulled out a wrought-iron chair and plunked himself down.

"Get you something?"

"No, thanks."

John took a percolator off the stove and poured himself a mug of steaming coffee. He sat down across from Kempf. "So what brings you here, Detective?"

Kempf unzipped his parka. "Murder. I have reason to believe the perpetrator of two very vicious killings might be hiding on the estate."

"Hmm." He regarded Kempf with a thoughtful gaze over the coffee mug.

"Lots of buildings to hide in. And I saw the guy. He watched me from the woods while I was doing some investigating. Have you seen anyone around the estate?"

He gave Kempf a hard look, as if he was contemplating what to do next. To tell or not to tell perhaps.

"I could talk to you, but not here," John said.

"Why the hell not?"

"I'll explain later. You free in a couple of hours? Say one o'clock?"

"I could be."

"Can you meet me at Rudy's Place?" He got up and set his mug in the sink.

"That's twenty miles from here. In Ashton."

"That's the only way I'll talk. I'll tell you when we get there."

"I guess it's Rudy's then," Kempf said. "But this better be good."

Kempf took a corner booth at Rudy's, the red vinyl squealing underneath as he slid into the seat. The waitress brought him an iced tea and he slid out of the parka. Merle Haggard drifted over the speakers and a lone drinker in a cowboy hat and flannel shirt sat sipping pale beer from a mug. The place smelled of fried fish and beer. Kempf guessed there were two or three fistfights a week at Rudy's Place.

John came in five minutes later. The guy at the bar looked up at him, then went back to nursing his beer.

"You come here often?" Kempf asked.

"Trying to pick me up?"

"You know what I mean. This place isn't exactly around the corner."

"It'll do for our talk. The houses on the estate got some big ears," John said.

"Have you seen anyone or anything that might help me find this prick?"

"No. But you're right about him being on the estate."

You'd better not be jerking my chain, Kempf thought. He didn't drive all the way out to some honky-tonk to have his dick yanked.

"How do you know that?"

"Let's start with Cassie."

John told him how she murdered Ronald Winter after finding out about his mistress and her subsequent inheritance of his billion-dollar fortune. She told the cops he never came home one night, and the investigating officers bought it. They left her alone and Ronald Winter was assumed missing.

"What about the kid? She got pretty ticked when I started asking about him," Kempf said.

"Ronnie's her pride and joy. She wouldn't let anyone harm that child. Would probably kill anyone that tried."

"So she's trying to protect him from talking to the big bad police. Probably trying to cover her own ass. So is she the one doing this?"

"No."

"You're sure."

"Positive."

"You mentioned the estate having ears. What does she have, bugs set up or something?"

John regarded him with a pensive look, as if weighing the consequences of what he was about to say.

"She's the surveillance. You can believe or not believe anything I'm about to tell you, Detective. That's your bag of apples. But she can see into people's heads, know things you don't tell her. She could probably tell you what color drawers you have on."

It made sense. The day in the car when he and Cassie had driven around the estate. He thought he was having a stroke, but it was her inside, poking around his brain like a mechanic under a car's hood. The thought made him a little queasy.

"Can she confuse you, make you forget things?"

"Yeah. I'm pretty sure that's how she got off the hook for murdering Ron."

"She pulled that on me the other day. It felt like someone blew fog into my ear. I can't remember half of our conversation, no matter how hard I try."

"You should stay away."

"Can't do that."

"She might hurt you, or worse."

He wasn't about to be intimidated by some little red-headed woman. "Is it witchcraft?"

"I don't know. She can do other things, though. Heal people. I saw her mend Ronnie's broken arm one time without even touching him."

"Tell me about the killer."

"This is really the cherry on the sundae. It's Ronnie's father."

"How could that be?"

Kempf imagined Ramsey collapsing in a heap of laughter when he told him the killer was one of the walking dead. *That's a good one, Tank, old boy.* He could hear it already.

"Like I said, believe as much or as little as you want. But that's another one of her abilities."

Kempf said, "I don't really know why, but I believe you. Maybe I'm getting soft in the head. Just tell me where to find him."

"In the tunnels under the estate. There's a whole network of them. They're left over from when the estate was a nuthouse."

"Would you mind coming down to the station and telling this to Chief Ramsey? I'd like to get a sworn statement from you. We'll protect you from her if you're worried."

John scratched his cheek, thinking it over. "All right. I'll come down at five o'clock."

Kempf thanked John and they shook hands. They stood up to leave.

"One other thing. Ronnie's been hanging out with some kids he met at school. One's Jack Harding and the other kid's name is Paul. I don't know his last name, but they could tell you some things too," John said.

"Like?"

"They've seen him too. Your suspect."

Kempf took out a small notebook from his shirt pocket and wrote down the name Jack Harding.

Back at the station, Kempf flipped through the white pages until he found the name he wanted: Grady Dowd. Grady had been the head librarian at the Brampton Library from the early fifties until he retired in 1980. He was also the town historian, the foremost expert on everything Brampton.

Kempf dialed and a craggy voice on the other end answered.

"Mr. Dowd, this is Detective George Kempf from the Brampton police. How are you?"

"Fine, I guess. What the hell do you want? I paid my taxes."

Oh, brother. "I need some information on the Steadman property."

"You came to the right place. Are you really a detective? I never heard of no Kempf on the force."

"I am. I need to find out about the tunnels under the property."

"I don't know any Kempf."

"Trust me."

"Suppose you wouldn't make that up. What do you want to know about them?"

"Tell me everything you know about the property, including the tunnels."

A pause, only wheezy breathing on the other end. "I'm only gonna say this once. It's almost time for me to take my pills."

Kempf learned a great deal about the property from Grady Dowd. From 1870 to 1900 it had served as Brampton Sanitarium. Like most mental hospitals, the place had a bad history. Patients were chained to walls, beaten with rubber hoses, and doused in ice-water baths. A patient named Reginald Pike raped and strangled a nurse in the hospital laundry. In 1900 a fire started in the Tanner Building and spread, burning down all six structures on the property. It was suspected that someone set fires in each of the buildings. Twenty-three patients and nine staff members died in the fire.

The tunnels underneath the property linked Tanner, Erlich, and Gretchen Halls to the administration building. They also ran out to a laundry and a staff dormitory. The tunnels were built so staff members could travel between buildings relatively quickly, even in bad weather.

In 1920, Eli Steadman purchased the property from the

state of New York, cleared the remaining ruins, and built a thirty-thousand-square-foot mansion. He built stables, houses for servants, and barns, hoping to do a little farming on the side. He made his fortunes in railroads, but like his father, he was a farmer at heart. Even if the farming was done by hired hands, it was important to Steadman.

In 1925, he commissioned an engineer from the New York Central Railroad to design tracks for the tunnels underneath the property. He wanted something none of the other industry barons of his day ever had. Not Carnegie, Vanderbilt, or even the Rockefellers. A working rail system underneath his estate. Servants and workers could travel from one end of the property to the other in mere minutes. Several storm-cellarlike doors would be built, where workers entered and exited.

Construction of the tracks was hampered by cave-ins, flooding, and quarreling among the workers. Steadman's grand design ended when a worker knocked out a support beam and a roof collapsed, killing three men. The project was abandoned after that, and the tunnels had remained empty since then.

Kempf asked Grady how much tunnel actually ran under the grounds.

"Steadman expanded on them, so maybe a couple miles."

Miles and a million places for someone to hide.

CHAPTER 33

Ramsey strutted down the hallway and flashed past Kempf's office door. Kempf called out to him but the chief either didn't hear him, or was ignoring Kempf. Annoyed, Kempf rose from his chair and poked his head in the hallway.

"Chief!"

Ramsey turned, and Kempf motioned for him to come to the office. The chief seemed quiet, not his usual how-are-you, slap-you-on-the-back self. He had read the article, Kempf was sure of it.

"Want to talk to you about the case."

"Fine."

They entered Kempf's office and took seats at the desk.

"Read the paper today," Ramsey said.

"Lots to keep up with these days."

"What the hell is going on, George? You suspect the killer is on the estate and it should be avoided?" Red splotches crept into Ramsey's cheeks. "We haven't got squat yet, but you've got the balls to go to the paper with this."

"This is the same guy you wanted me to talk to the other day and it wasn't a problem then."

"Things have changed. Another murder, panic. You have a description of the guy in the article. Wearing bandages."

He waved his hands around. "People will think we have a slasher film going on here. A masked murderer who kills in the dark. Way to keep people calm."

"They're already panicked."

"Stay off that property. So help me I'll take your badge if you go back."

Kempf leaned closer to him. "I know what I saw out there and I don't give a shit if you believe me or not. You want to take my badge? Go ahead. I'll still go out there and shoot the fucker myself if I have to."

Ramsey looked stunned.

"And I have a witness who can back all this up. He's coming here to give a statement at five o'clock, so I suggest you stick around."

"What's his name?"

"John Brown. He's Cassie Winter's limo driver. He told me he thinks someone is hiding out in the tunnels under the estate. Grady Dowd confirmed that the tunnels exist, so we should go."

"Dowd's going soft in the head," Ramsey said.

"Stick around until my witness shows up. Whoever killed those two guys is hiding on her property, and I'll bet she knows all about it."

Ramsey rubbed his forehead with his index finger and thumb, working the wrinkles.

"The gauze we found on the college kid's body. It's the same shit on the killer's face."

"Why bandages, George?"

"Disfigured. Burned. Acne scars?"

"Don't be a smart-ass. We need to leave Cassie Winter alone. With her money she could have both our jobs for an appetizer."

Kempf rubbed his eyes. His stomach ached and his temples started to throb. "This wouldn't have anything to do with Cassie Winter being a potential campaign contributor, would it?"

"I'm still a cop."

Then act like one and let me tear that property apart,
Kempf thought.

"Will you at least hear John out?"

"Fine. But after this, no more with Cassie Winter."

He slapped Kempf on the knee, got up, and left the office.

John ascended the porch steps, wondering if his meeting
with Kempf had been a huge mistake. If Cassie found out
what he told the detective, she might do something worse
than her handiwork on Ronald Winter. He had no desire to
wind up as one of the living dead.

The wind blasted, scooping up snow and flinging it. A
few logs for the fire were in order, so he grabbed four off the
woodpile and carrying them in one arm, unlocked the door
with the other. He flipped on the lights and set the logs on
the hearth in front of the fireplace.

A knock came at the door and he opened it to find Cassie
Winter standing in the snow.

"Come in," he said.

She thanked him and walked in the door.

"How about a cup of tea?" she said.

He filled a teakettle with water and put it on the stove to
boil, then took out a mug and tea bag.

"Weather's awful," she said.

"What brings you out here?"

"I wanted to talk to you about Detective Kempf."

"Nice guy."

"Asks too many questions, though."

"Detectives are funny like that."

She passed the table, running her fingers along the maple
top. "What did he want to know?"

"If I'd seen anything. He's pretty sure whoever killed
those two guys is on the property."

"He has no proof."

"But we know better, don't we?"

She sat at the table, folding her leg under her. "I can control it. It's like a trained dog, that's all."

Somehow John didn't believe that.

The water in the kettle began to hiss and John turned off the burner.

"What does the detective know after today?"

"I told him I hadn't seen anything."

"If that's all you told him, why did you have to leave to meet him somewhere?"

They were locked into a dance where one mistake could not only get his toes stepped on, but put him in the grave. And Cassie was leading. "I didn't meet him anywhere. I had to get the oil changed in the limo."

He poured the steaming water in the cup and dropped in the tea bag, bobbing it up and down.

"You didn't tell him anything else while he was here?"

"Nada." He set the mug in front of her.

"I'll control the Wraith. That Kempf is an idiot, but I don't think I'll have much more trouble with him. The chief of police himself called me, and for some reason he doesn't want Kempf coming up here."

"You're sure you can control it? It's tasted blood."

"It's not a vampire," she said. "I can bend its will."

"They'll figure it out sooner or later. I don't think Kempf will let this go, regardless of what his boss says."

"He may be sorry he came up here at all."

"No more killing," John said.

"Do you think I'm that foolish? I'll scare him."

"Like you scared Jack and his friend? It almost killed him and me."

She sipped her tea and looked at him over the cup, probing, trying to see if he told her the truth. It would be nothing for her to slip into his mind and probe, prying out his thoughts and memories to discover what had happened at Rudy's. So far it was only a verbal joust.

"I didn't tell that cop anything if that's what you're wondering."

"You're lying."

With a flick of the wrist, she whipped the tea, cup and all, at him. It burned his chest and he jumped up. He backed up from the table but didn't get far. A thousand needles dug into his skull, sending him to the floor. He gripped his head and rolled on the floor.

Cassie got up and booted him in the gut. "You fucking dirty liar!"

He looked up into the face of a crazy woman. The skin on her face had gone pale and rubbery, as if someone were wearing a Cassie mask. For the second time in his life, he was terrified of her. The first had been the night she killed Ronnie's father, a night when he thought he would wind up buried in a shallow grave behind the house.

"Tell me what happened."

A fresh wave, this time a thousand stinging hornets in his head. He managed a groan.

"John. Tell me. Please. I don't like doing this to you."

"I can't think. Stop."

"Okay, I'll stop."

"I didn't tell him a goddamn thing."

"Why are you doing this to yourself?"

Another blast and he rolled onto his back. Tears streamed down his face. *Jesus, God, please let the pain end*.

She grabbed the kettle from the stove, steam still rising from the spout, and held it over him. "Don't make me do this. Please."

She dumped the boiling water. It splashed over his eyelids and on his nose. He yelped, not expecting that.

"Do I have to keep this up? It's really not pleasant for me, either."

"Okay. No more," he said. "I'll tell you what happened."

* * *

Jack's mother called him to the phone almost as soon as he got his coat off and got in the door. On his way home from school, there had been a snowball fight, with kids from the sixth and seventh grades lining up across the street and winging snowballs at one another. It lasted a good half hour and it was three forty-five by the time Jack got home. That drew an angry scowl from his mother.

Mom handed him the phone.

"Hey, you want to come for dinner?"

"Thought you had detention," Jack said.

"I'm done. So you coming or what?"

"Who else is coming?"

"You, Paul, Chris, and Emma."

"What are we having?"

"Pizza Hut."

There were few things in the world more tempting than Pizza Hut pizza. His defenses were weakened already. The chances of his mother letting him go out for dinner on a school night were slim, but it was worth asking in order to taste Pizza Hut.

"Let me ask." He covered the receiver with his hand and turned to his mother. "Can I go to Ronnie's house for dinner?"

"I've never even met this boy."

"It's Pizza Hut."

"Let me talk to his mother."

That was almost as good as a yes. He reminded her that tomorrow was a half day of school due to the start of Christmas break, and that he had no homework save for reading a chapter in his history book.

"My mom wants to talk to your mom."

"Okay."

Cassie Winter said hello into the phone and asked Jack how he was doing. He said okay and handed the phone over to his mother. Mom said she remembered talking to Cassie the other day, and asked how late the boys would be. Then

she said she guessed it would be fine with only a half day tomorrow.

"You can go."

"Yes!"

Paul came in a moment later, for he had straggled behind.
Jack informed them they were going to Ronnie's and having
pizza for dinner. That brought a smile to Paul's face. Paul
was the only person Jack knew who loved pizza as much as
he did.

His mother handed the phone back to him and Cassie told
him John would come pick them up in the limo in twenty
minutes. The danger of the Wraith and John's stories of it
seemed distant, and Jack was sure they would have nothing
to worry about as long as they stayed in the main house.

All four of them rode in the limo, and they had picked
Chris up last. Jack was shocked to learn that Chris was suspended from the basketball team, and after he stopped laughing about Munch's missing shorts, he asked how Chris's dad
took it.

"Not good. There was no way he was letting me come to
dinner tonight, but after Ronnie's mom talked to him on the
phone, he seemed okay with it. She must be a smooth talker,"
Chris said.

"Yeah," Emma said. "My mom had dinner all ready to go
and I had a Popsicle's chance in hell of her letting me go. But
Mrs. Winter talked to her and she gave in."

Jack had a pretty good idea they had been tricked by Mrs.
Winter, but he didn't say anything. Not only was he looking
forward to eating pizza, but they might get a chance to do
some exploring of the mansion and learn more about Cassie
Winter. Besides, turning down an invitation was not advis-
able. She might view that as an insult to Ronnie, and the last
thing he wanted to do was be the focus of her wrath. They
would go, make nice with Ronnie, and eat free pizza.

He was starting to like the kid despite some of the crap he pulled with Vinnie and the day he had deserted them in the tunnels. It took stones the size of bowling balls to ask the rich girl to the dance, but he had done it with style. Jack never would have had the guts to ask her out. Hell, his insides went to putty when Emma had asked him to go with her. Actually asking a girl would be unthinkable.

They rolled through blowing snow, a silent John steering the limo up the road to the mansion. Paul chewed the tip of his thumb, working the nail. Emma and Chris looked generally spellbound, both of them looking out a window, this their first trip to the estate.

"What do you think?"

"Awesome," Emma said.

"Oh yeah," Chris said.

Cassie greeted them at the door, hugging each one of them and telling Chris how tall and handsome he was.

"Don't let it go to your head, too-tall," Paul said.

She led them to the great room where Ronnie waited, pacing back and forth in front of the bar.

He gave them a broad wave of the hand. "C'mon in, guys. Have a drink. It's on me." He guffawed at his own joke.

A table stood in front of the bar and on it rested a glass bowl filled with ice cubes. Bottles of grape Crush were tucked into the ice, beads of moisture dribbling down their sides.

"Thank you for inviting us," Emma said.

"No problemo," Ronnie said.

Cassie slid into the room behind them and came up behind Chris. She rested her hand on his shoulder and said, "Something's bothering you, isn't it?"

"How did you know?"

"I have a little bit of a gift in that regard. Why don't you tell me about it? Maybe I can help you."

"I don't know if you could."

She took him by the hand and led him to the couch. Chris sat down and Cassie did the same.

"I can help," she said.

"I don't want to talk in front of the guys and Emma," Chris said.

"You're among friends here."

He told her about the problems with Robbie Munch and how he eventually wound up suspended from the basketball team.

"Now his dad's upset with him," Jack said.

"Yeah, he's a real maniac when it comes to sports," Paul said.

"I can make arrangements so that things are better for you. I can fix things, right, Jack?"

He wasn't sure if she meant the healing job she had done on him the other day, so he nodded, hoping he was on the same page with her.

"How would you like to stay here for a while? Away from your father so things can cool down a bit."

Chris said, "It would be nice to get away from him for a while."

"Stay as long as you would like," Cassie said.

"One problem, too-tall," Paul said. "Your dad will never go for that."

"Leave that to me," Cassie said.

"Thanks, Mrs. Winter."

"Cassie," she said.

John entered with an armful of pizza boxes, and for the next half hour they feasted on pan pizza with pepperoni, mushrooms, and onions. John still seemed awfully quiet, nodding at them as he came in and leaving quickly, as if he had something important to do. His normally rich brown skin looked gray. Maybe he was getting the flu.

After the pizza, they played Foosball, darts, pool, and when those became boring, they went into Wrestlemania mode, smashing each other with fake clotheslines and body drops. When they were tired out, all five friends plopped on the couches near the big-screen television. Ronnie offered up a dare.

He said, "When you guys come for the sleepover, I've got a great dare."

"Remember what happened the last time we tried something like that?" Jack said.

"You're not a chicken, are you? We'll go out into the woods and do dares. Like who will go farthest into the trees by themselves. No flashlight. Or who can tell the scariest story."

"We can tell scary stories inside," Emma said.

"Yeah, and there's three feet of snow out there," Paul said.

"Not a good idea, Ronnie," Jack said.

"We'll see."

He got a gleam in his eye that the devil would have envied. Something told Jack they were about to take another ride on the roller coaster that was Ronnie Winter.

John wrapped himself in a blue wool blanket and collapsed onto the couch, his head still singing from the hurt Cassie had put on him. It was all he could do to drag himself to Pizza Hut to get the food for the kids and then drive back to his house. Her interrogation session had left him with a pounding headache. The blood pulsed through the veins in his head, each throb reminding him how close he came to dying.

If Kempf called again, John was to tell him he made the story about the Wraith up and not answer questions. Cassie told him if he talked to the detective again, he would not only never see his wife and son again, but she would flay him alive. The woman was a powerful motivator, you had to give her that.

He was about to drift into sleep when the phone rang.

"Son of a bitch phone." He reached behind his head and picked up the receiver.

"John, It's George Kempf. Where the hell are you?"

"Hmmm?"

"You were supposed to meet me and Chief Ramsey."

"I won't be able to make it," John said.

"Well, you'd better change that. This whole case could be riding on what you told me at Rudy's."

"I didn't tell you anything at Rudy's. And even if I did, I won't repeat it to you."

Silence came from the other end, punctuated by heavy breathing. He sensed Kempf was gathering steam, like a locomotive speeding from the distance.

"What kind of crap are you trying to pull on me? Do you have any idea how this is going to make me look? I promised the chief someone who knew more about the killer. Not to mention that more people might die because of this. What is it again? The Wraith?"

"Don't know what you're talking about. Sorry."

"What's sorry is the bullshit you're giving me. Don't make me have you brought in."

"That's the only way I'll come down. I have to get going."

"Just tell me one thing. Did she put you up to this? She did, didn't she?"

"I have to go, Detective."

He hung up the phone.

It was then he considered leaving the estate for the first time, maybe traveling to Chicago, where his brother lived. Sam would put him up for a little while, and it would put some distance between him and Cassie Winter. He doubted even her powers could reach that far. In his heart he knew his wife and son were gone, most likely murdered in the same way Ronald Winter had been killed. His only hope was that they were at peace somewhere and that their torment had not lasted long.

The only thing keeping him from packing up his bags was Ronnie. In the absence of his own son, Ronnie had filled in nicely, and the boy needed a guiding hand. The other kids who befriended him were a start, but he sensed that their friendship with Ronnie was due more to fear of Cassie than the desire for true companionship. That led to another dilemma. If Jack and his friends slighted Ronnie in the smallest of ways, Cassie could hurt them.

Can't let her hurt those boys, he thought.

So he would stay, not give her any trouble (at least not openly), and keep an eye on the children.

Right now, though, he needed sleep. The inside of his head felt as if it had been lashed with pricker bushes. He closed his eyes and drifted off to sleep.

Kempf slammed the receiver down with such force that the momentum knocked the phone off the side of the desk. It sounded like a gunshot in the small office. Cursing to himself, he bent down and picked up the phone.

"Problem, Tank?"

He was back to being Tank again. Ramsey must have cooled down about the newspaper article. "Phone service is bad."

"When's your witness coming?" He leaned against the door frame, arms crossed.

"He can't make it down today. Not feeling well."

"I see."

Ramsey smirked, and Kempf had the sudden desire to punch him in the mouth and see how many of those perfect teeth he could loosen.

"I'm going to reschedule a meeting with him."

"If you say so. Just remember what I said about the Winter Estate. I promised Cassie we wouldn't pester her. No need to."

"So she's Cassie now. I didn't realize the two of you were on a first-name basis."

"Mrs. Winter. Is that better?"

"I can't just walk away from it. She knows who the killer is and she may be harboring him. I don't know why you think that's so ridiculous. I'll go back up there, and if it means my job or it means suspension, then so be it."

"It's your future, Tank."

With that he walked away.

Kempf had graduated in the middle of his class at the police academy. He was never the fastest one to complete physical drills, or the one to score highest on the tests. There were no commendations in his file, but no reprimands, either. He became an average detective in a small town where, up until recently, there was no crime. But he never gave up, and this case bothered him so that his own stomach seemed to be intent on devouring itself. Despite what Ramsey said, he would not bow out gracefully.

He would go back to the estate again.

CHAPTER 34

Jack pulled out his books, checked his locker mirror, and smoothed his hair with his hand. It was the day of the Christmas dance, and he had to look good, because he would be seeing Emma in a few minutes. He shut his locker and turned around to find Vinnie, Leary, and Harry standing there like trolls.

"Hey, faggot," Vinnie said.

"I've got to get to class."

Vinnie placed a hand against Jack's chest. "I got detention because of your fat friend. You guys are going to pay for that."

"You dumped garbage on him."

"Shut up," Harry chimed in.

"We'll be looking for you at the dance," Vinnie said.

As they walked away, Harry hawked up a wad of phlegm and spat it on the floor at Jack's feet. Jack wrinkled his nose. It was like dealing with a subhuman species disguised as seventh graders.

Chris, Paul, and Emma joined him at his locker a moment later.

"What did the Three Stooges want?" Chris asked.

"They want to beat the crap out of us again," Jack said.

"What do you mean us?" Paul said.

"You, me, and Ronnie. Vinnie's mad because he got detention and he thinks its Ronnie's fault."

"I'll walk home with you guys. They won't bother you if I'm with you," Chris said.

"Thanks, but they said they were going to get us at the dance tonight," Jack said.

"Then we'll stick together and nothing will happen," Emma said.

Chris nodded, affirming her statement.

"Are you really going to stay at Ronnie's house?" Jack asked him.

"I'm thinking about it. Maybe it will make my dad appreciate me a little more than he does. Get him off his sports kick."

"If you do, be careful," Jack said.

"You guys worry too much."

The homeroom bell dinged, and the remaining stragglers in the hallways scattered like roaches caught in a kitchen light.

Kempf had called nine times before John picked up the phone again. He had hung up on Kempf another three times before Kempf could get anything out of him.

"I told you I didn't want to talk," John said.

"I don't have time for bullshit so I won't waste words. Help me find it."

"You're crazy."

"Take me into the tunnels. I'll get a search warrant."

"You'll get us both killed."

Kempf rolled a yellow pencil between his fingers. The receiver was tucked into the crook of his neck.

"It'll kill again. You said so yourself," Kempf said.

"I don't care. I'm getting out of here soon."

"I don't believe that. Ramsey doesn't want me going near that place again. Any ideas why?"

A pause, then John clearing his throat. "She probably has a hold on him."

"I have an obligation to do my job."

"Spare me the hero cop rap. Talk to those boys. They saw it too." Another pause. "I have to go."

The phone clicked, and the dial tone rang.

He needed John to change his mind. John knew the tunnels, and Kempf didn't. Regardless, he would still go after the killer, but having John present would make it easier.

He pulled out a phone book, found the Harding address, and wrote it on a scrap of paper. He did the same with the Fussel address.

At the Fussel house, he slogged through the snow toward the door. Bare wires poked out from where a doorbell had been removed. He rapped on the storm door, and after five minutes, a lumpy bearded guy came to the door.

"What do you want?"

His breath smelled of sour beer.

Kempf flashed his badge. "Detective Kempf, Brampton police."

"So?"

"Are you Mr. Fussel?"

"Yeah."

"I'm looking for your son, Paul."

"He ain't here. You're a cop, right?"

"Last time I checked I was."

"Neighbor kidnapped him. They think I'm beating him. You believe that?"

"I don't know you well enough to say. Where is he staying?"

The man scratched his head and flakes of dandruff tumbled off his scalp. "Hardings' house. Down the street. And I want to file charges against them."

"For?"

"Kidnapping. Like I said."

The guy had been into the bottle and Kempf had no trou-

ble imaging him smacking a kid around. He didn't have time
to deal with this. Let Social Services handle it.

"Bring my son back."

He reached out and patted Kempf on the shoulder, nearly
stumbling out the door.

"I want to ask Paul some questions. Is that okay with
you?"

"Just bring him back to me."

Kempf walked away and underneath the wind, Mr. Fussel
grumbled about kidnapping.

Kempf pushed the Hardings' doorbell. A balding man
who looked like the blueprint for bankers and computer
guys answered the door.

"Can I help you?"

Kempf flashed the badge.

"Detective Kempf. I'd like to ask your son and his friend
a few questions."

"Is Jack in trouble?"

"No. He might have seen something in regard to the murders in town."

"Jack?" He got a faraway look in his eyes. "I'm sorry.
Come in," he said.

Kempf took off his coat and sat at the kitchen table. The
boys came out dressed in button-down shirts and wool dress
slacks.

"Paul's father gave me permission to talk to him."

"That's fine," Mr. Harding said.

The smaller kid looked like he couldn't wait to go to the
bathroom. He shifted his weight from foot to foot. That had
to be Paul. The other kid was taller and regarded Kempf with
a cool gaze.

The boys sat down and Jack's father joined them at the
oval table. A moment later Mrs. Harding buzzed into the
kitchen. Kempf stood up and introduced himself. Her hand-

shake was soft, like squeezing a glove stuffed with cotton batting.

"What's this about?" she said.

Wearily, Kempf explained the purpose of his visit.

"You're not suggesting they're involved, are you?"

"They're not on the list of official suspects."

She took a seat at the table next to Jack and it became apparent he was going to talk to the entire Harding clan.

"Do you guys know John Brown? Cassie's assistant."

They looked sheepishly at each other, then at Kempf.

"He's Ronnie's limo driver," Jack said.

"John tells me you saw something in your garage."

"That's news to me," Mr. Harding said.

"We did," Paul said. "Are we going to jail? 'Cause I'll get killed in juvenile hall."

"You might get the chair," Kempf said.

Paul watched him, perhaps trying to determine if Kempf was serious.

"Can you describe the man you saw for me?"

"He was tall and he had bandages over his face. No eyeballs," Jack said. "And he wore coveralls."

"That's right," Kempf said. He took a look at Jack's mother. She was whiter than copy paper.

"How did you know that?" Paul asked.

"I've seen him too. He's killed two people and will probably try for more unless we catch him."

"Jack, what the hell happened?" Jack's father said.

"We were afraid to tell you."

"Why don't you tell us what happened?" Kempf said, taking out his steno book and pen.

Jack told the story, how he and Paul went out to take care of the trash and they spotted the bandaged man at the window. Apparently they freaked, and John showed up to scare the bandaged man away.

Kempf sensed anger rising from Mr. Harding like lava in a volcano. "Don't be too upset, Mr. Harding. The boys are okay now and they're being a tremendous help."

"You're not going to the dance," Mrs. Harding said.

"What dance?" Kempf said.

"The Christmas dance at school," Paul said.

That explained the dress clothes.

"Mary, you can't stop them from going," Jack's father said.

The woman frowned.

"Please, Mom?"

"All right. But I'm dropping you off and picking you up at the door. And you can't leave the gym for any reason."

"Cool," Jack said.

"Did he say anything to you?" Kempf asked.

"No. He just smelled really bad," Jack said.

"And his skin was cold," Paul said.

"Tell me again what happened after John showed up."

"It grabbed him by the throat and then it left. Ran," Jack said. "And how could he find us with no eyes?"

"That's ridiculous," Mary Harding said.

"I don't think so, Mrs. Harding. I saw it too," Kempf said. "How did you boys meet Ronnie Winter?"

Paul told the story of how they met on the snow hills behind the police station.

"Have you been to the estate?" Kempf asked.

They both nodded.

"I talked to Mrs. Winter and she seemed very protective of Ronnie. What do you guys think?"

"I think she might hurt anyone who tried to hurt Ronnie," Jack said.

"Did you see anything unusual in the house? Any more run-ins with the bandaged man?"

Paul gave Jack a sideways glance, and then opened his mouth as if to say something. He closed it back up. Jack nudged him with an elbow.

Paul leaned over, cupped his hand, and whispered something in Jack's ear. There was a conspiracy afoot.

"We went into the tunnels underneath the house," Jack said.

"Jack Harding!" Mary Harding said.

"Jesus Christ," Jack Harding Sr. said.

"Don't be too upset. Every twelve-year-old boy is a natural Magellan," Kempf said.

"It's just—"

"Mrs. Harding, I realize you're upset. But like I said before, Paul and Jack are okay." Kempf looked at the two boys. "I have a feeling I know what your mother wants to say, so I'll do it for her. Stay off that estate. I'm sure the bandaged man is hiding somewhere on that property. I catch either one of you out there and I will lock you up."

"I guess we're not going to Ronnie's sleepover," Paul said.

"Damn straight," Mary Harding said.

"Double damn straight," Jack Sr. added.

"What happened in the tunnels?"

Paul told them the whole story. Mary Harding looked as if she might fall off her chair.

"I'm a terrible mother, letting them run around like this."

"You are not. Boys get into things. I did it and I'm sure the detective did too," Jack Sr. said.

"Are we in trouble? For not telling the police about this?" Paul said.

"No. You've actually helped me a lot. Mrs. Harding, I'll have a car step up patrols on your street."

"What will the cops do now?" Mr. Harding asked.

"Get a warrant and find him. Thank you all for your time."

He pushed the chair out and stood up to leave.

"How will you catch it? It's not alive," Jack said.

He preferred not to think about that at the moment.

Jack expected fireworks after the detective left, and right now Mom was lighting the fuses on the Roman candles.

"When were you going to tell me about this? Or maybe

you weren't and I was going to have to identify your body at the morgue," she said.

"Mary, you'll scare them worse than they already are if you keep talking like that."

Maybe Dad would save him. He tended to play good cop to Mom's bad cop. The two of them circled around Jack and Paul at the kitchen table, and it felt like an interrogation session, like on *Hill Street Blues*.

"They should be scared. Some maniac running around, almost dragging my son off, and I have no idea it's happening. Don't you know you can tell me anything?" Mom said.

"I was afraid you'd keep me in the house," Jack said.

"We should have gone to the police," Paul said.

"Shut up, doof."

"Not a doof."

"That's enough for tonight. We'll finish this up tomorrow. You two need to finish getting ready for the dance," Dad said.

"Go," Mom said, and they scurried away from the kitchen and headed into Jack's bedroom. They finished putting their ties on in silence. Jack clipped on a red-and-blue-striped tie, and he hated it, but thought Emma might like to see him dressed up. Maybe enough to kiss him.

"What are you smiling about?" Paul said.

"Nothing."

"It was nice of your mom to buy me these clothes."

"Yeah, she's an okay mom."

Mom had gone to Penney's while they were at school and bought dress slacks, a tie, and a crisp dress shirt for Paul. Jack had thought his friend was going to cry when Mom handed him the Penney's bag.

"I wished my dad worried," Paul said.

"What do you mean?"

"They care about you. My parents wouldn't care if I ate a dog shit sandwich for lunch every day."

"I would. Your breath would fucking reek."

"I'm serious. I can't stay here forever."

"You can stay here as long as you want."

Paul had a lousy home situation, was the smallest kid in class, and probably the only one going to the dance without a date. But he was still Jack's best friend, despite all that. Other kids might mock Paul, but they didn't see the good stuff about him.

"You ready?" Paul said.

"Yep. Do you think the police will catch him?"

Paul finished straightening his tie. "No. It could hide anywhere in the tunnels. It's pitch-black down there. How come you didn't tell them about Cassie healing your ribs?"

"Let's forget about it and try to have some fun," Jack said.

"I feel like a dork not having someone to go with."

"You're going with us, aren't you?"

"Yeah," Paul said. "But you're all too damn ugly to kiss."

CHAPTER 35

Emma tied her hair into a ponytail with a lavender rubber band. It matched her dress, which to her surprise hugged her a bit, revealing the start of curves. She slipped on a pair of panty hose for the first time. How did women stand wearing these all day? They were almost as bad as those white tights Mom made her wear.

A knock came at the door and Mom came in carrying a gray jewelry box, the kind rings came in.

"You look beautiful," Mom said.

"I look like a dork."

"You're just not used to being dressed up. Here."

She flipped open the lid on the jewelry box and revealed two white gold hoops. They glimmered in the light from the dresser.

"Your father gave me these. They're real gold, so be careful with them." She ran her finger over one of the earrings.

"What if I lose them?"

"You won't."

"Thanks."

"Aren't you glad I had your ears pierced?"

Emma smiled and nodded. Her mom helped her on with

the earrings. She took a peek in the mirror. Between the gold earrings and the makeup, Emma didn't recognize herself.

"Not too bad," she said. Hopefully Jack would feel the same way.

"Jack's lucky to be taking you to the dance."

She bent down and kissed Emma on the cheek. Downstairs, the doorbell rang.

"He's early," Emma said.

"That's probably Aunt Sam," Mom said.

"What's she doing here? She didn't bring toad face with her, did she?"

"Stop it. Your aunt wanted to see you on the night of your first dance."

"Jeez."

Her mother hurried downstairs.

Emma's stomach tied itself in a knot. She thought of Jacob squeezing her, his rotten breath in her face, his pimples oozing like rotten tomatoes. She almost gagged.

He wouldn't try anything with Mom and Aunt Sam in the room, but what if they went into the kitchen? Before long, Aunt Sam and Jacob would come over, and he might get his chance to do worse things to Emma. She had no desire to see what Jacob was capable of doing.

She glanced at her watch. It was six-fifteen. That left her forty-five minutes before Jack arrived. Enough time to snare a rat in a trap. If Mom didn't want to help her out of the jam with Jacob, then she would do something herself. Time to bait the trap.

Emma heard Aunt Sam chattering away downstairs, asking Mom who the boy was, and what kind of dress Emma was wearing. Emma rummaged through her dresser drawer, clawing through socks and underwear until she found a silver tube of lipstick. She took off the cap and pressed it to her lips, making them good and red. She blotted her lips on a tissue and threw it in the trash can. Then she walked downstairs.

Aunt Sam and Mom sat at the kitchen table sipping wine. Mom sliced a piece of cheese off a hunk of Havarti she had bought at the grocery store the other day. Emma thought it tasted gross but supposed you had to be a grown-up to enjoy foods like that. Aunt Sam sprang from the chair as if it were an ejector seat. She gripped Emma by the shoulders. From the corner of her eye, Emma saw Jacob slouched on the couch in the family room, the remote control in his hand.

"You're a doll, Emma."

"Thanks," Emma said, looking over Aunt Sam's shoulder and watching Jacob.

"Your first dance."

What was with adults? Everything involved marking the passage of time somehow. Maybe when you got older, that's all there was to do. Reflect on how long ago things happened and oh, how time flew.

"You seem a little nervous," Mom said.

"Just wanted to show Jacob another album up in my room."

"Oh?" Mom said.

"Yeah. The album he called me about the other day."

"Right."

Aunt Sam released her grip and Emma entered the living room where Jacob sat watching a *National Geographic* special on lions.

"What do you want?"

"Want to come up to my room?"

"For?"

"I want to show you a new album."

Then it seemed to click with him. She saw it in his eyes. Coming up to her room meant they would be alone.

"Sure."

As they passed through the kitchen, Aunt Sam said, "Have fun."

Jacob followed close and Emma felt his breath on the back of her neck.

"So where's this album?"

"There isn't one," Emma said.

"Then why are we up here?"

"I want to talk to you about what happened the other day," Emma said.

"I still owe you for kicking me in the nuts."

He stepped closer to her. She stood her ground despite the tension that hummed through her muscles.

"I overreacted. My mom told me boys like to rough-house."

"You told your mom? You *are* a stupid little girl."

"Just that you pinned me against the wall. Not about the other stuff you did."

"Oh." He drifted over to her dresser, casually inspecting the items on it. "So, you keep your pussy pads up here or in the bathroom?"

Here he goes again. But it was good he felt confident. She wanted him to start his disgusting little rap again.

"Can I tell you something, Jacob? You have to promise not to tell."

He snorted out a laugh.

"The other day made me sort of curious. About like sex and stuff."

"Bull crap." He picked up her deodorant, worked it around in his hand. She had no problem imagining him sneaking into other girls' rooms and stealing their bras and panties. Lord knew what he might do with them when he was alone.

"No, really. I was scared at first—that's why I kicked you. But maybe we could keep this whole thing between us. You could show me some things."

He looked up at her. "Really?" His voice cracked.

"Why don't you come over here?" she said.

She felt really gross right now, but she needed to provoke him. She reached down and lifted up her dress until the tops of her thighs were exposed.

"Show me yours and I'll show you mine."

She had heard Theresa Gardner telling Shelly Noble in class that she played that game with Brian Barnes in their parents' garage. Why did boys like that kind of stuff?

He approached her, the smell of his body odor almost spicy.

"Why don't you show me yours first? I've never seen one."

His eyes got wide. "I can't believe this is happening," he said.

He undid the wool pants and slid them down, revealing white underwear with yellow stains in the front. *Yuck.* The underwear bulged. She wanted to close her eyes and wish him away.

"Let's lay on your bed," Jacob said.

"Okay."

She moved around him and backed up to the bed until it brushed the back of her knees. He moved in close to her, waddling over with his pants around his ankles. She wrapped her arms around him, barely able to breathe because of his stink, and pulled hard. Throwing herself onto the bed, she held on to Jacob's shirt, bunching the fabric in her fists. The booger fell on top of her. A look of surprise crossed his face. He flattened her on the bed and she sucked in a breath, yelling, "Mom! Mom! Help!"

As if realizing he had been trapped, Jacob struggled to get up, but she dug hard into the shirt, determined to hold him here until Mom came.

"You're in big trouble, ass wipe," she said.

"Let me up or I'll—"

Jacob thrashed and bucked like a bull trying to throw off a rodeo rider.

"Mom!"

Steps thudded on the stairs. Mom appeared over Jacob's shoulder, and behind her, Aunt Sam.

"Get off her!" She grabbed Jacob by the hair and yanked. Emma let go and Jacob stumbled off Emma, crashing into the far wall. Emma cooked up some tears, and she found once the false ones started, the real ones took over.

"What are you doing to her? Pull your pants up," Mom said, and slapped him on the back. It sounded like someone smacking a sack of flour.

"Jacob?" Aunt Sam said.

Jacob pulled his pants up, turning away from the women to fasten them.

Emma got off the bed and Mom grabbed her, hugging hard. She hugged back.

"Did he hurt you?"

"No, Mom."

"You sure, Emmy?" Aunt Sam said.

Mom looked at Jacob, and if looks could kill, the booger would have been stone dead. "You have some real problems, Jacob. I might even call the police about this. Do you have any idea how serious this is? She's a little girl and your cousin on top of it."

"I can't believe this," Aunt Sam said in a soft voice.

Jacob hung his head low, and to Emma's amazement, broke into sobs.

"Let's go, Jacob. Myra, I'm so sorry," Aunt Sam said.

"So am I," Mom said.

"You, in the car. Now," Aunt Sam said. "I'll call you, Myra."

Jacob skulked past her. The trap had worked.

Jack's mother made him call Ronnie and say not to bring the limousine. Jack's dad would drop them off at seven and pick them up at ten o'clock sharp. No being late and no excuses.

Now they sat in the backseat, Jack tugging at his collar. It itched his neck and he wanted nothing more than to unfasten the top button and throw the damn tie out the window.

"You guys nervous?"

"No, Dad. Well, maybe a little," Jack said.

"I'm nervous and I don't even have a date," Paul said.

"Just remember, the girls are just as nervous as the guys. And you can still ask a girl to dance, can't you?"

"No way, Jose," Paul said.

"Just try it. You'd be surprised at the answer sometimes."

Jack's movements around town were limited to going back and forth to school until the police caught the killer. He was amazed his mother didn't pass out when they told Detective Kempf the stories about the killer. All that was in the back of his mind tonight, though. He thought of Emma. How would she wear her hair? What would her dress look like? And would she have perfume on? He had developed an appreciation for the stuff when Ms. Hanretty, the young science teacher with the fiery red hair, started at Brampton. She wore the stuff and it did strange things to Jack.

He was nervous, maybe even terrified, but still he couldn't wait to get to the dance.

"I'm sorry," Mom said. She looked deflated.

"I told you," Emma said.

"You tried to tell me."

"He's a real creep."

"Aunt Sam is going to have to get him help," Mom said.

Mom looked down and smoothed her pants with her hand.

"I wouldn't lie about something like that."

"Jacob's always so quiet. I didn't think he was capable of something like this."

Mom looked up and Emma saw tears forming in her eyes.

"Don't cry, Mom."

"I'm sorry," she said.

She had screwed up bad and she knew it.

"I tricked Jacob into pulling down his pants. That's why I wanted him to come up here, so you could catch him."

"That was very brave. I won't let him anywhere near you, on my life."

"Thanks, Mom."

Mom looked at her watch. "I don't suppose you feel much like going to the dance after what happened."

"I'm not going to let him ruin this for me."

"Then let's fix your makeup. Tears are hell on mascara."

Ten minutes later her makeup was fixed and her cheeks dry. The doorbell rang and Emma opened the door to find Jack and Paul standing on the front stoop. Snowflakes whipped around them.

"Hi," Paul said, giving her a quick wave.

Jack smiled and said, "Ready?"

She stepped out into the cold.

The limo pulled up near the gym doors and John slid around to the passenger side and opened the door. Ronnie stumbled out, followed by Jessica, Chris, and Melanie Peters. They entered the gym, where the others waited for them. Emma said, "Nice wheels."

"Too bad Jack's mommy wouldn't let him ride in the limo," Chris said.

"If you had a brain you'd be dangerous," Jack said.

"Stop arguing and let's go," Emma said.

Red and green streamers hung from the ceiling, and a silver cardboard sign read: CHRISTMAS DANCE 1985. Mrs. Eckerd stood at the punch bowl, spooning out the red stuff into Styrofoam cups and lining them up on the table. There were bowls of pretzels, cheese puffs, and potato chips near the punch. They had the lights down low, giving the gym a cave-like feel.

"Let's get some punch," Ronnie said. "Some for you, my lady?"

Jessica laughed and said yes.

Jack looked around for Vinnie and his crew, but didn't see them anywhere. Expecting Vinnie to come to a dance was like waiting for the pope to show up at a whorehouse. But he was no doubt gunning for them again, and dance or no dance, he would come around to exact revenge. Maybe he and his buddies got lost in the snow (or run over by a plow).

They gathered by the punch bowl. Ronnie stuffed a handful of cheese curls in his mouth, puffing his cheeks out. Melanie Peters said, "Gross." Jessica giggled as if charmed by Ronnie. She seemed like an okay girl so far.

The seventh graders stood in nervous clusters around the gym, the boys playing with their ties and the girls going in their purses every few minutes. It gave them something to do amid the nervous laughter and awkward silences.

The DJ played Duran Duran, The Police, and a Prince song. After Prince, a slow song came up, an old one. Jack thought it was by a band called The Temptations.

Emma leaned over and whispered in his ear, "Let's dance."

Here it goes.

"Okay."

They walked side by side onto the dance floor. Jack faced Emma and slid his arm around her back. They linked hands, and she placed hers on Jack's shoulder. *Don't let her get too close. She'll feel your heartbeat*, he thought. Who said the girls were as nervous as the guys?

They circled around, Jack trying hard not to step on her feet. He looked over at his friends and they pointed and whispered, amazed one of their group had ventured onto the dance floor.

"What did you want to tell me?" Jack said.

"I'm nervous, are you?"

"That's what you wanted to tell me?"

"I took care of Jacob."

"What?"

"I made him do something he didn't want to."

Jack gave her a puzzled look.

"I talked him into coming upstairs with me."

"Are you nuts?" Jack said.

"Let me finish. I set a trap for him."

"Now I'm really confused," Jack said.

"I tricked him into pulling his pants down and pulled him

on top of me. Then I screamed. Mom came upstairs and caught him."

"That was pretty smart of you," Jack said, as they turned. "What happened to him?"

"He's in big trouble."

"Cool. No more Jacob."

He looked at her and became aware of the hand on his shoulder, the presence of it, its solidity. She smelled like flowers, and the light from the ceiling made her hair shine.

"I can always tell you things, Jack. Thanks."

She looked over her shoulder and back at him. Emma leaned toward him and cocked her head. Her lips brushed his and she tasted like strawberries. Jack felt as if he had just taken the first hill on the Comet at Crystal Beach. The room floated around him, as if it were just the two of them. She pulled away, a blush filling her face.

"You're turning red. Are you okay?" she asked.

"I'm great." He would later rewind this moment and play it back hundreds of times in his head.

In his moment of glory, he didn't see Vinnie Palermo slip through the gym doors.

CHAPTER 36

Vinnie Palermo smoldered outside the gymnasium doors.

That fat pussy Winter had gotten him detention. The second Lewis had sentenced Vinnie, he started planning revenge. He had talked Harry into getting his little brother Kenny to help them. Kenny was a wiry little fuck, and meaner than a wolverine.

Vinnie had swiped ten bucks from his mom's purse to pay Kenny for helping, and he got Rudy Vitch to come along, too. Rudy was big enough to handle Francis, and he would fight for no money.

He waited at the gym doors. Kenny, Harry, Joe, and Rudy materialized out of the snow. Next to the other three, Rudy looked like a brontosaurus.

"What you got under your coat, Vin?" Rudy asked.

Vinnie produced an egg carton. "These have been sitting under my bed. We're going to give those little shits an egg bath."

Vitch laughed. Kenny danced back and forth like a boxer waiting to charge out of the corner.

"You guys ready?" Vinnie asked.

They all nodded.

"Hurry up. I'm freezin'," Harry said.

"I'll go in and get Francis to come out first. The other turds will follow him. Rudy, you jump Francis when he comes out. We'll handle the other ones."

Vinnie took an egg from the carton and cradled it in his palm.

"I knew he would kiss a girl first," Paul said. "Who's going out there next?"

Ronnie tugged at Jessica's sleeve. "We are," he said.

"Watch it," Jessica said. They hit the dance floor, leaving Paul, Chris, and Melanie standing at the punch bowl.

"Fussel, why don't you ask someone to dance? Sara and Emily are standing over there by themselves," Chris said.

He pointed to Sara Ray and Emily Stoldt. They stood at the end of the snack table.

"Are you nuts?" Paul said.

"Go on. Ask one of them."

"I need more snacks."

"You're going to dance with someone before we leave," Chris said.

"I wish someone would ask me to dance," Melanie said, scowling at Chris, who didn't notice.

"Yeah." Chris nudged Paul with his elbow. "Dance with Melanie."

Melanie took Paul by the hand. His whole arm tingled and before he could protest, she led him onto the floor. Jack and Emma had broken the ice, and now other kids braved the dance floor. They did the same box-step the others did as The Temptations song came to an end. The DJ put on another slow Motown tune.

"You're not a bad dancer," she said. A smear of punch dotted the corner of her mouth. It made her look cute. It also made him wish he'd asked Melanie to the dance.

"Did Chris tell you to say that?"

"No."

"Honest?"

"Honest, Paul."

They turned and spun under the yellowish light in the gym. The scents of Old Spice and Brut hung in the air. Cologne borrowed from fathers and big brothers. Melanie smiled at him, and he returned it. He could get used to this, dancing with girls.

Someone bumped his arm and jarred him.

Chris dipped the ladle into the punch bowl, lifted it, and let the red fluid dribble into his cup. Something jabbed him in the kidney and he turned, expecting to see Jack or Paul standing behind him. Instead he found Vinnie with one hand tucked inside his denim jacket.

"Hey, Francis."

"Get lost," Chris said.

"You like eggs?"

"Piss off, I said." Chris reached out and shoved him.

Vinnie recoiled and slipped the hand from inside his jacket. He had a white object in his hand and whipped it at Chris, pelting him in the chest. The shell cracked, and cold egg dribbled down his shirt. It stank like sulfur. Vinnie made sure his ammunition was rotten, the prick.

"You want toast with your eggs?" He laughed, a barking sound. Chris started forward and Vinnie darted away, shoving Billy Marino as he went. He flung open the gym door and raced outside. Chris stomped through the crowd, intent on squeezing Vinnie's neck until his eyes popped like grapes. He whizzed past Jack, who said, "Wait!"

He reached the doors with Jack and Paul in tow. Through the glass, Vinnie waited, waving him forward, issuing the challenge. Chris plowed through the doors and the moment he was outside, it felt as if someone dropped a heavy punching bag on his back. It drove him forward and crunched him into the pavement.

* * *

Jack followed Chris out the door. A kid nearly as big as Chris tackled his friend and Chris hit the ground with a smack. The big kid was on top of Chris, shoving Chris's face into the snow. Paul came out, followed by Emma. Harry grabbed Jack and Joe Leary yanked Paul aside. Another smaller kid jumped out from behind a snowbank and kicked snow on Chris. It was Kenny Cross, Harry's little rat of a brother.

"Beat the shit out of them," Vinnie said. "Fatty should be out any second."

As if on cue, Ronnie hit the doors like a Brunswick against a bowling pin. He skidded on the snow and stopped three feet past Jack.

Chris was still on the ground, swinging elbows at the big kid sitting on top of him. The big kid fired rabbit punches into the back of Chris's head, and Kenny Cross kicked him in the ribs. Leary clipped Jack in the ear and spun him around. Harry shoved Paul, and Paul tumbled into a snowbank.

"Can't fight your own battles, can you?" Emma said.

"Shut up," Vinnie said. "Come here, fat boy."

He waved Ronnie on, but Ronnie instead charged forward, wrapping his arms around the big kid's neck and knocking him off balance. Chris threw another elbow and dislodged the kid from his back. As Chris rose, Kenny kicked him again in the ribs.

Ronnie rolled to his feet but before he could turn, Vinnie slammed his knee into his head. Ronnie hit the ground like a box of hammers and Vinnie booted him in the gut. Ronnie moaned and rolled over.

What was with these guys? If they didn't stop, one or all of them were going to take a trip to County Memorial tonight. It was like fighting a miniature version of the Hell's Angels.

Chris lifted his arm and blocked Kenny's boot from striking again. He snapped a jab at Kenny and caught him square on the nose. Kenny reeled away, covering his nose and whimpering. The big kid charged Chris, and Chris wrapped his arms around him. The two of them looked like crazy slow dancers, Chris with the kid in a bear hug, and the kid shifting his shoulders back and forth to break the hold.

Paul wasn't faring much better. He hit the ground and tucked his knees into his chest. He covered his head with his arms, like one of those kids in the nuclear attack films from the fifties. Harry slapped him in the head, saying, "Get up, Fussel."

He was half crouched over Paul, so Emma came up behind him, cocked her leg, and kicked him, planting her toe in Harry's scrotum. Harry grabbed his crotch, howled, and hopped away from Paul, cupping his nuts the whole time. Jack was busy dodging punches from Leary, and he was never so glad for the cavalry to arrive.

Mrs. Eckerd pushed open the door. "Vincent! Joe!"

She hurried down the steps, followed by Mrs. Avino, the eighth grade science teacher.

Vinnie took a look at them. He stomped on Ronnie's outstretched hand and it made a sound like chalk snapping.

"Let's go," he said. Vinnie ran and the other goons followed.

The teachers grabbed Ronnie by the arms and hoisted him up. He looked as steady as someone who had just downed a fifth of whiskey. Blood dribbled down his chin and Mrs. Eckerd cupped her hand under his lip, catching the drops. Chris followed them, his hand pressed against his right side.

"You okay, man?" Jack said.

"I think they busted my ribs, the bastards."

Jack took his friend's arm and wrapped it around his shoulders, allowing Chris to use him as a support. It was like trying to lug a concrete sack around, but he needed to help his buddy.

"Follow me," Mrs. Eckerd said.

She led them to the principal's office and flipped on the lights. They buzzed to life.

Paul, Chris, Emma, Ronnie, and Jack sat in the orange

plastic chairs across from the secretary's desk. Chris leaned back in the chair, hand on his side, eyes closed, and sweat dribbling down his forehead. He had taken the worst of it. Ronnie didn't look much better. He held a balled-up tissue to his lip, now dotted with blood. His eyes were those of a dead fish, glassy and blank.

"Ronnie?" Jack said.

"What time does class start?" Ronnie asked.

"He might have a concussion," Paul said.

Mrs. Eckerd took out a key ring and opened the top drawer of a gray filing cabinet. She took out a white box with a green cross on it and opened it. She took out a piece of gauze and pressed it to Ronnie's lower lip.

"Chris, how is your side?"

"Hurts bad."

"I'm calling the paramedics and your parents. That rotten little shit," she said.

Jack had never heard a teacher swear. That was like being mooned by a priest or given the finger by a librarian. People like that didn't do those things.

Mrs. Eckerd said, "We're having a conference with all the parents, Christmas break or not."

She licked her finger and used it to open a file folder. She dialed a number, spoke with Mrs. Winter, and then called the paramedics.

Five minutes later, two paramedics in pressed white shirts hurried in. One of them knelt in front of Ronnie. He took out a penlight, clicked it, and waved it in Ronnie's eyes. The other guy knelt in front of Chris and pressed a stethoscope to his chest.

"What happened?"

Jack turned to see Ronnie's mom standing in the doorway with a woven purse slung over her shoulder.

"Ronnie."

She swooped down on Ronnie, nudging the paramedic out of the way.

"He has a concussion. We need to get him in for a CT scan."

"This kid's ribs are busted. You're going for a ride," the paramedic in front of Chris said.

They ran out of the room, presumably to bring back a gurney.

"How could you let this happen?" Cassie said.

"Here." Mrs. Eckerd handed Cassie a fresh paper towel. "His lip is bleeding."

"Some of the other boys jumped them, Mrs. Winter."

"You didn't answer my question," Cassie said.

Just don't piss her off, Jack thought.

"It happened very fast," Mrs. Eckerd said.

Cassie pressed the paper towel to Ronnie's bottom lip.

"Mom, my head hurts," he said.

"Who did this?"

Jack said, "Vinnie and his friends."

"The same ones who dumped garbage on you?"

Ronnie nodded.

"Give me names, Jack," Cassie said.

"Vinnie, Joe Leary, Harry Cross, Kenny Cross, and some big kid I never saw before."

He regretted saying that immediately. He liked Vinnie about as much as the stomach flu, but he didn't want to see him hunted down by the Wraith.

"Let's go." She clutched Ronnie's hand and he stood up.

"Mrs. Winter, he needs to go to the hospital."

"I'll take care of it," Cassie said.

She led Ronnie out the door as the paramedics returned carrying a gurney with the wheels folded up.

Jack's dad appeared in the doorway, followed by Mr. Francis. Mrs. Eckerd rounded the counter and intercepted the fathers. "The kids got jumped by some other students," she said. "They need to take Chris to the hospital for his ribs."

"What little son of a bitch did that?" Mr. Francis asked.

"Watch your language, please."

"Was it the Palermo kid?" Jack's dad said.

"We'll need to meet about this next week," Mrs. Eckerd said.

"I should call the cops," Jack's dad said.

It looked like Jack Harding Sr. had his tomahawk out, ready to make war.

"That's up to you, I guess," Mrs. Eckerd said.

The paramedics had Chris on the gurney ready to go.

How the hell did it come to this?

CHAPTER 37

Jack sat in the backseat, listening to the slush and snow hit the underside of the car. He peeked over the seat and looked at the speedometer. The needle stayed at twenty, Dad taking it easy the whole ride home.

"I can just about see with this snow," Dad said.

Jack thought of Chris being wheeled out on the stretcher, the first time he had ever seen something like that. Chris, the strongest out of their group, the one who dragged two of them along when they tried to tackle him in football. He looked shrunken on that stretcher.

"What do you think will happen to Chris?" Paul said.

"He'll be all right," Jack said. He really had no idea but didn't want to worry Paul.

"That Palermo kid's a little bastard," Dad said. He honked the horn at an unseen driver. "Don't tell your mother I swore in front of you."

"What do we do about the sleepover? I'm afraid not to go," Paul said.

"How do I know?"

Right now the party at Ronnie's was about as appealing as a trip to the guillotine. At least that was quick. One sharp cut and off with the noggin, nothing compared to the tortures Cassie might inflict. Or so Jack imagined.

"You always know," Paul said.

"Right now I don't, 'kay?"

"Maybe he'll move away," Paul said.

"Not likely."

They continued home in silence, save for the occasional muttering of "bastard" or "son of a bitch" from his father.

John set the picture of Ray and Maureen in the brown suitcase. He would not see them again, never kiss his wife between the shoulder blades before sleep, never toss his son in the air and catch the boy. And it was all because of that red-haired bitch. Didn't matter now because he was done with her and the whole sick situation.

He placed razor, deodorant, and other essentials on top of his clothes and topped it off with the .45 from the bureau drawer.

It might be nice out West, sitting under a palm tree somewhere and getting lost in the latest Robert Ludlum novel. Anything to get away from Cassie and the slop that passed for weather in this area. She had at least paid him well, and he had a little over a hundred thousand stashed away at First Federal. He would hit the bank, buy a plane ticket, and ride into the California sun. Then try and occupy himself, maybe work as a bodyguard for someone famous and forget about his family best as possible.

He zipped the suitcase up and headed for the closet to fetch his coat. The phone rang.

"Hello?"

"It's Kempf."

"Good-bye," John said.

"You might want to talk to me."

"I've got a plane to catch."

"It happened again," Kempf said.

"Where?"

"Near the old Conrail tracks. Couple of teenagers. We found a bottle of Jack in their car and the boy's head in the backseat."

Suddenly the receiver felt as if it were cast from iron. He wanted to let it slide from his hand and thud to the floor.

"You there?" Kempf said.

"What do you want from me?"

"Help me find it. You know the tunnels."

"You got a warrant?"

"I'll have one soon."

"You really don't plan on arresting it, do you?"

"I'm coming armed to the gills," Kempf said.

"I'm getting off the estate." John cradled the receiver between his neck and shoulder.

"Don't you think it's better if Cassie thinks everything's normal?"

The detective had a point.

"All right. When do you want to do it?"

"She's not listening, is she?"

"She's not here."

They agreed Kempf would meet him tomorrow at the groundskeeper's house, and they would head to the mansion from there. John said good-bye and set the receiver down. He looked at the suitcase as if it were a particularly fine woman he could not have.

"Best unpack."

Kempf thought of the Mossberg twelve-gauge and Kevlar vest sitting in his trunk, and although his suspect didn't carry a gun, he felt better having the supplies. After hanging up with John, he went to the kitchen.

Jules sat hunched over a cup of coffee, an old Jimmy Stewart movie on the black-and-white. Kempf walked in massaging his temples. He could feel the blood pounding through the veins, hear its surges as the headache worsened. He wanted to take a couple of Excedrins and go to sleep.

"You look pretty rough," she said.

"Glad to see you too."

"There's some left over goulash in the fridge."

"Not hungry."

He pulled out a chair and sat down. Kempf reached up and tugged at his tie until it came loose and hung on his chest.

"We're going in there tomorrow," he said.

"I knew you'd find him."

"I don't know what we're getting into here."

"You'll do fine, sweets. You always do."

"We're going to have to kill it, if that's possible."

Kempf gripped the tie and rubbed the material between his thumb and index finger. It made a little shooshing noise.

"You could arrest him for boo-glary," Jules said.

"That was horrible."

"Johnny Carson I'm not." She sipped her tea. "Does numb nuts know what you're doing?"

"He's too busy planning his next PR move. Besides, if he tries to stop me, I'll go to the papers and tell them he tried to hamper my investigation."

He leaned across the table and kissed her on the cheek. "Why did you believe me?"

"I've never known you to lie, George. You're stubborn at times, you snore, and I can't get you to throw out clothes from ten years ago, but you've never lied to me. Why would you make something like that up, anyway?"

"Right. Love you," he said.

She grasped his hand. "You're retiring after this, right?"

"I'll think about it."

"We've got enough. My shop's doing well."

"I'll think about it."

She released his hand and he headed for the bedroom, intent on changing into a T-shirt and jeans.

* * *

Saturday morning came, the big day, and Kempf showered and ate a ham omelet for breakfast. He called Ramsey and told the chief to meet him at the station about nine.

Kempf parked his car out back, jogged up the steps, and strolled down the hall to his office. He opened the frosted-glass door and found Ramsey sitting with his legs crossed, a copy of *Golf Digest* splayed across his lap.

"So you're arresting the gauze man?"

"I have three eyewitnesses who've seen him."

Kempf slipped off his coat, twirled it around, and draped it over his chair.

"You went behind my back," Ramsey said.

"Are you fucking kidding me?"

"I didn't authorize overtime for Stavros today."

"I need some experience going in there," Kempf said.

"You're barking up the wrong tree."

"At least if I'm wrong, we can eliminate someone. But I'm not wrong."

"Mrs. Winter's not involved, George."

"May or may not be, but whoever killed those people is hiding there."

Kempf leaned on the chair with both hands. It felt good to have something solid underneath him, even though he wanted to pick it up and throw it at Ramsey.

Ramsey rolled up his magazine and tucked it under his arm.

"This is a mistake," he said.

"Give it up."

"This could be bad for you."

"That a threat?" Kempf said.

"Take it how you want to."

What the hell went through this guy's head?

"I'll be out of your way anyhow. When this is over, I'm retiring and you can bring that nephew of yours in here."

"Fair enough."

He stood up and stalked out of the room.

Stavros appeared in the doorway and behind him MacKenzie running a hand through his flattop.

"You guys ready?"

They nodded in unison.

Vinnie called Leary at eight and Harry at quarter after, the two of them sounding fuzzy when their moms called them to the phone. A half hour later, they slogged through two feet of snow in the barren lot known as the Weeds. They stopped at the old train station, a brick building with a platform in front that had served as the depot in Brampton from 1880 until 1946. The old farts on the town council voted against tearing it down because Teddy Roosevelt supposedly stopped there on his way to Buffalo one year.

The three of them walked in unison, hands jammed in pockets and chins to their chests to avoid the cold wind that liked to sneak down the front of your shirt.

"We stuck it to Harding and them, didn't we?" Vinnie said.

"Too bad Eckerd showed up," Harry said. "She called my dad and I'm going to get suspended."

"Mine, too. You're brother's a fucking psycho, you know that?" Vinnie said.

"He's gonna get arrested before he's fifteen," Harry said.

Leary said, "I'm cold. Let's stop at the station."

"Mama's boy," Vinnie said.

They stopped and scaled the snow mound in front of the station, crossing the tracks and hopping onto the railroad platform. A shingle blew off in the wind and fluttered away like a wounded sparrow. A sign reading NEW YORK CENTRAL hung from one remaining screw and squeaked as the wind rocked it back and forth.

"Let's go inside for a minute," Leary said.

"You are the world's biggest puss," Vinnie said.

Vinnie shoved aside the piece of plywood standing in for a door, and it clunked onto the platform.

He walked in and sat on one of the benches, where years earlier, anxious rail passengers had awaited steam and later diesel engines to carry them across the country.

"Who brought smokes?" Vinnie said.

Harry reached behind him and pulled out a pack of Chesterfields, the plastic wrapper still in place. He tapped the bottom of the pack with his thumb, unwrapped it, and plucked out three cigarettes. Vinnie took one first, then Leary.

"Stole these from Kenny," Harry said. "Little prick's probably going to kick me in the shins when he sees me."

Harry slid his hand inside his coat and came out with a blue lighter. He flicked it and lit their smokes. Vinnie inhaled and blew out a stream of smoke. He watched it rise up into the rafters, where it curled around an abandoned bird's nest.

"What do we do next, Vin?" Leary asked.

"What are you talking about?"

"Harding and his friends."

"Nothing, dick wad. We'll probably get suspended, so we gotta lay off for a little while."

They smoked down to the filters and Harry flicked his butt at Vinnie, catching him in the cheek.

"Asshole. You almost hit my eye."

"I know," Harry said, laughing.

"Right now," Vinnie said.

Leary said, "Shut up. Listen."

"It's the wind, Joe," Vinnie said.

"I hear footsteps. Crunchy ones."

Vinnie wanted to go at it with Harry, but first he had to listen for footsteps or Leary would whine about it until Vinnie did something.

"It might be Harding and them trying to sneak up on us," Leary said.

"Did your brain fall out your ass the last time you crapped?" Vinnie said. "It ain't them. Let's check it out."

He waved for the two of them to follow him outside.

Outside the station, a line of adult-sized footprints ran from the front of the building to around back. Vinnie stomped ahead until he was standing parallel with the tracks. The other two boys came up behind him.

Leary said, "Too damn cold out here."

What a fucking little girl. Vinnie was three seconds away from popping Leary in the nose.

"What if it's the killer?" Harry said.

Vinnie turned around to say something to Harry. A flash of blue appeared and an arm wrapped around Harry's throat. The guy dragged Harry backward, and Harry kicked the heels of his boots into the snow, the boots leaving tracks. The man lifted Harry off his feet and jerked to the right. Harry's neck snapped and his eyes rolled back in his head and Vinnie wanted to scream. Leary beat him to it. He opened his mouth and screamed like a small child spooked by a Halloween mask.

The guy dropped Harry, and his body landed face-first in the snow.

Vinnie turned and looked across the field next to the station. Maybe a hundred yards to the woods, and he could lose the bandaged freak in there and get to Johnson's creek. From there it was up the bank, over a fence, and on to Main Street. It wouldn't chase him onto Main, would it?

"Run," Vinnie said.

They turned and Vinnie bolted. Each footfall flattened the snow. It was like running through fucking oatmeal. A noise that sounded like "gaaaa!" came from behind, and he knew the bandaged man had Leary. He told himself there were no soft crunching sounds, that the killer wasn't doing horrible things to Leary.

His lungs burned and hot stitches ran through his legs. After twenty yards, he stopped, breath heaving from his chest. Something dug into his shoulder, a jolt that traveled up his neck and down his arm, hot and cold. He looked up into the bandaged face of a freak. It had dug its claws into him and now Vinnie Palermo realized he was going to die.

* * *

Ronnie speared a piece of French toast, slopped it in the syrup, and stuck it in his mouth. It was the last thing he needed, French toast with calorie-laden syrup, but her boy deserved it after the incident at the dance.

He showed no sign of concussion, no glassy eyes, no vomiting or complaints of headaches or blurred vision. If she had taken him to the hospital, they would have stuck him in a tube and taken pictures, kept him in a hospital bed all night. Her brand of medicine worked better, and any emergency room doc who saw it would be left slack-jawed and drooling.

"How are you feeling, hon?"

He sliced off another hunk of French toast. "Good."

"Still want to have your sleepover?"

He nodded.

"But I don't think they'll come," Ronnie said.

"Why?"

"It's my fault they got beat up."

"Those bullies won't ever bother you again," Cassie said. "No more worries, okay? After you finish breakfast, we'll go pick up your friends."

His eyes widened and the glimmer in them nearly melted her heart.

"Hurry up and finish," she said.

"They won't let Paul and Jack come. Jack's mom and dad."

"I'll talk with them."

"Chris is going to miss it, too. He's still in the hospital."

"I can fix that," she said.

Head down, Ronnie dug into the French toast.

CHAPTER 38

Chris lay in the hospital bed with two pillows wedged behind him. He thumbed through a copy of *Sports Illustrated* and skimmed over an article on Refrigerator Perry. He set the magazine on the nightstand, stared at the ceiling for a while. Then he reached for the clicker and ran through the TV stations again, looking for a ball game to watch. All he found were the Smurfs and an Andy Griffith rerun. There weren't even any pretty nurses to look at. He flipped off the TV and rested his head on the pillows. Might as well sleep.

Footsteps came from across the room and he opened his eyes to find Cassie Winter at his bedside.

"Hi," he said.

"I'm sorry I woke you, Chris."

"Nice to meet you."

"The other kids felt bad they couldn't come see you, but maybe you'd like to come to Ronnie's sleepover."

"My ribs are pretty sore. Sorry."

"What if I fixed it so you could go?"

"Are you a doctor?"

She smiled. "I have a very old method that works. Do you trust me?"

He nodded.

"There's a limo waiting outside after I help you."

"The white coats will never let you walk out of here with me. But it'd be cool if you did. I'm bored as hell."

She walked over to the door, ducked her head out, and pulled it back in the room. Then she swung the door shut, the striker clicking in place. She came back to the bed and reached behind his neck. "Did you think about my offer, staying at the house?"

"What are you doing?"

"Untying your gown. You'll have to pull it down a little."

"No way."

"The sheets are covering you."

He let her untie the gown and she pulled it down to just above his belly button. She placed her hands on his rib cage and closed her eyes. He looked out the window at thirty-eight stories of the Marine Midland Building looming over Buffalo.

"Relax, Chris. I'll talk to the doctors, and we'll have you out of here in no time."

CHAPTER 39

The phone rang at nine A.M. and from his bedroom Jack heard his mother speaking, but with whom he didn't know. He and Paul were in the middle of a serious game of Risk, and Paul was getting ready to invade Kamchakta. Crazy name for a country, but Jack had built a stronghold there and was determined to repel Paul's plastic red army.

"Asia will fall within the hour." Paul gave an evil laugh and rubbed his hands together.

"My armies will make toothpicks out of your men's bones."

Paul rolled the die. Jack's mother walked in as Commander Fussel was about to launch his assault on Kamchakta.

"Mrs. Winter is on her way over to pick you up for the party at Ronnie's house."

"I thought we weren't allowed to leave the house."

He had thought they might need to sedate Mom with some pills or a shot after the way she reacted upon their return from the dance last night. She told Jack he wasn't to leave the house until they caught the serial killer and put Vinnie Palermo in juvenile hall. Her little boy was not going to end up as a feature story on the six o'clock news unless he invented a cure for cancer or set a record in the Olympics.

The house suited him and Paul just fine, anyway. The weather was still rotten, and as they played Risk, the wind gusted outside, spraying pellets of hail and snow against the house.

"At first I thought you shouldn't, but Mrs. Winter talked me into it. She assured me you would both be safe at their house."

"I'm not sure I want to go," Jack said.

"Me neither," said Paul.

"Why would you not want to go? She was nice enough to invite you two, so you should go. Now start packing overnight bags. She has a whole day of fun planned for both of you. Get." She clapped her hands together twice and left the room.

Talk about doing a one eighty. Cassie Winter had gone to work on her mind; Jack was sure of that. Why else would she all of a sudden want them to go out when last night the SWAT team could not have busted them out of here?

"What's going on?" Paul said.

"It looks like we're going to a sleepover."

"I'm not going. Not with that thing running around the estate."

"Paul, we have to. She'll probably do bad things to us if we don't. She'll think we don't like Ronnie or something. Let's just go. I'm sure it won't be inside the house, and if he goes into the tunnels, he's on his own this time."

Paul folded his hands and looked down at them. He pursed his lips and twisted his mouth up. "We'll have to take my father's gun."

"Are you nuts? And keep your voice down."

"I'm not going without protection. That thing almost killed you and me. What if it senses us there and comes after us while we're sleeping?"

"If it comes while we're sleeping, we're still screwed."

"You know what I mean."

Going to the fancy house again and making nice with Ronnie was something he could handle, but stealing a gun from Paul's psycho dad was a whole other basket of eggs.

"So we just walk up to your dad and ask him for the gun?"

"Don't be a dweeb. He goes to a war-gamers' club on Saturday mornings and my mom sleeps until one or two. You'd have to set off a bomb to wake her up."

"What the hell is a war-gamers' club?"

Paul rolled his eyes as if embarrassed by the idea. "Him and some other guys who like military stuff get together and play these board games. You can get them in hobby shops. Things like Panzer Attack and D-day and all that crapola. They bet money on who will take over Europe and win the big war."

"That's kind of weird. Grown men playing board games."

"I know, but as long as he's gone I don't care. So do we get the gun or not?"

The idea didn't seem as bad with Paul's dad being out of the house. The idea of holding a real gun frightened him, but it was exciting at the same time. "Do you think bullets would really stop it?"

"I don't know, but it's better than nothing," Paul said.

"We need to hurry, though. The limo will be here soon."

"Your destruction will have to wait," Paul said, pointing at the Risk board.

Jack hoped to return and finish their game if something awful didn't happen to them today. He did not dare say that in front of Paul. His friend actually seemed to have worked up some courage, however foolish, and Jack didn't want to discourage that.

Jack pulled out his old backpack and a duffel bag for Paul to use. They stuffed clothes in the bags, then went into the bathroom and grabbed toothbrushes. Jack didn't have a sleeping bag, but he was sure there were plenty of places to sleep in the mansion.

They entered the kitchen to find his mom working the *New York Times* crossword puzzle with a number-two pencil. She wrote in a word, muttered, "Shit" under her breath, and erased feverishly.

"Is it okay if we wait out in the yard for our ride?"

"Why?"

"We want to have a snowball fight."

"All right. But bundle up good. And don't leave the yard."

Some of Mom's good sense had come back to her. She still wasn't stopping them from going to the sleepover, though.

Once bundled up and outside, Paul and Jack crept along the side of the house and then ran when they reached the end of the driveway. The sidewalk plows had left twin tracks, which Jack was thankful for. If they had not come through, he and Paul were looking at slogging through six inches of fresh snow.

Running down the sidewalk was like being in a valley of snow. The banks rose six feet on either side, piled by plows from the street and snowblowers from the driveways.

Five minutes later, they reached Paul's house. The blue Ford pickup was gone, which meant Paul was right. Mr. Fussel was off plotting the invasion of Europe with his buddies.

"Ready?" Paul said. It came out muffled underneath the scarf covering his mouth.

Jack made a thumbs-up and they started up the driveway.

The General must have cleaned, for the house smelled of ammonia and lemon-scented cleaner. The house was usually a mass of dirty laundry, stacked newspapers, and empty beer bottles. Every once in a while, his father got the urge to clean the entire place, top to bottom. Maybe the stink of dirty dishes and rotten garbage got to him, even in his drunken stupors.

They crept up the stairs and slipped out of their boots but left their coats on at Jack's suggestion. In case they had to make a quick getaway.

In the kitchen a stack of clean dishes stood like a squad of soldiers in the dish drain, and you could actually see the counters. They were normally covered with unwrapped bread, beer cans, and dirty dishes. The dining room rug had fresh vacuum tracks, and the cobwebs that normally occupied the corners were gone. The royal commander really outdid himself this time. If he could do such a cleanup job on himself, maybe Paul would come back here.

"Where's the gun?" Jack asked.

"I think he keeps it in the bedroom."

"What time is he coming home?"

"Probably not until eleven or so. We have time."

They passed the kitchen table, Paul bumping his leg and making the chair squeal on the floor. Jack nudged him. "You're louder than a frigging elephant."

They passed the bathroom, his brother's old room, and then reached his parents' room on the right-hand side. From inside, his mom snored softly. A clock ticked a metronome beat, most likely her two o'clock alarm.

"Are you sure she won't hear us?" Jack said.

"She's like a bear in the winter. Let's go."

The General's cleaning job had not extended into the bedroom. A pile of dirty clothes lay curled up in a filthy heap at the foot of the bed. Dust covered the dresser as well as the television and accompanying stand. Even more distressing was the mirror on the dresser covered in white powder. Paul tried to ignore it, but it kept drawing his attention like a car wreck. His dad's habits were going from bad to worse, and he wondered if that was the shit that made him so violent. The drinking usually just made him stupid and kind of mean, but he sincerely believed his father might have killed them on the day Jack kicked him in the ass. It was the coke.

"Is that cocaine?" Jack asked.

"I think so."

"Wow. I only heard about it on TV."

"Yeah, well, aren't I lucky to have it here in my very own house? Let's find the gun."

His mother rolled over and the bed squeaked. She draped a fleshy arm off the side of the bed, fingers dangling in space. Her brown nightgown had slipped partially off, revealing one massive bone-white shoulder. The beluga whales he had seen at Marine Land didn't look that white.

Paul led the way to the closet and opened the louvered doors, almost wincing as he did so, expecting her to thunder to her feet and catch them. She resumed snoring instead.

The upper shelf contained shoe boxes, a metal lockbox, some old ties, and a half-empty bottle of wine. Paul stood on tiptoes and hooked his fingertips over the top of the shelf. Jack bumped him out of the way and managed to get his hand on top of the shelf, but nothing more.

"I thought I could reach up there. I'm a lot taller than you."

"Do this with your hands," Paul said, showing him.

Jack locked his fingers together, making a cup for Paul to set his foot in. He crouched down and held his intertwined hands at knee level.

Paul placed his foot in Jack's hands and with a grunt Jack boosted him up. Paul wobbled, then grabbed the shelf. He found a can of tennis balls, a trophy from the company softball league, a stack of various romance novels with bare-chested bodybuilder types on the cover, and a pile of *Playboys*. If they had time, he would have suggested he and Jack take a peek at those, but they would have to wait for another time. He nudged the girlie magazines out of the way and found the mother lode.

It was wrapped in a black velvet cloth and next to it rested a box of shells.

"Hurry up. You're not that light," Jack said.

"All right."

He grabbed the box of ammo and the gun. "Okay. Got them."

Jack lowered him down and he unwrapped the gun. It was the color of a Cadillac's bumper and had a walnut handle. They stared at it with a combination of reverence and fear, as if it were an exotic animal with deadly potential.

"Let me see it," Jack said.

Paul handed it to him and he tested its weight in his hand. "Give it back," Paul said. Jack handed it to him.

On the bed his mom moaned, perhaps in the throes of a dream, then rolled over again, twisting the covers around her legs. They had better get moving before either she woke up or the General came home.

They crept out of the bedroom, Paul with the revolver tucked under his arm and Jack with the box of shells. They were in the kitchen when the truck pulled into the driveway and the door opened and shut. There was no mistaking the driver, because the car whooshed into the driveway. The General usually pulled in the driveway like A.J. Foyt on amphetamines and God help you if you happened to be standing in his way.

"Oh, shit. Shit, shit, shit." Paul stamped his foot in frustration.

"Can we beat him to the basement door?"

It took him a second, but he tuned in on Jack's line of thinking: they could hide in the basement, then sneak out after the General came into the house. "If we hurry."

They took off for the back hallway and made it down two steps before the General came in the door, head down and peppered with snowflakes.

Paul stopped and Jack ran into him from behind.

The General looked up in surprise, as if little green men had entered his home rather than his own son. "What are you doing?"

Paul was at a loss for words. His mouth refused to work and he stammered out a long "Uhhhh . . ."

The General's gaze flicked to the gun and then to Paul.

"What in the name of Jesus H. Christ are you doing with that?" He pointed to the gun like a child whose favorite truck was now in the hands of a playground adversary.

"Taking it."

"You have exactly five seconds to give me that gun before I beat your ass into mashed potatoes."

Behind him, Jack chuckled, then broke into a fit of laughter. Paul tried desperately not to laugh, but the floodgates opened and it poured out of him. Within seconds, tears were rolling down his cheeks and his belly hurt. In his twelve years he had never heard the General use that phrase, and it floored him.

"What are you laughing at? I'll tell your father, Jack. And you, you're coming back home whether you want to or not. Now give me that goddamn gun."

He took a step up so that he was on the second stair. Paul backed up, still wiping the tears from his cheeks.

"Paul. I'll beat the shit out of you."

"Do you need all that coke to do it?"

"I don't know what you're talking about. Give me my gun."

"You use a crazy straw with it, Dad? One of those colored ones so you can have fun while you toot?"

"Paul, stop it. He's already mad," Jack said from behind him.

"Yeah. Listen to him." He started to unbuckle his belt.

"You're going to get this across your back," he said, the belt dangling at his side.

"I'm sick of you."

He took the gun from underneath his arm, gripped it with both hands, and pointed it at his father. His hands trembled. "Get out of our way."

"You've lost your mind. I always said you were a little fruit and this proves it. Hand me the gun."

"No."

"Hand me the gun."

"I'll shoot you if you don't move."

"Paul, put the gun down," Jack said.

If he pulled the trigger, what would happen? The beatings would stop and with them the abuse. No more whippings with the extension cord, no more stale beer breath in his face screaming that he was worthless. No more living in fear or being degraded on a daily basis, trying to explain to teachers why you had a bruise on your cheek for the second time this week. It would all end.

But he couldn't do it. It was his father, and a small part of Paul still loved him, bastard or not. There was always the hope he would change and someday ask Paul what he thought, or maybe deliver a compliment, however small. And who was he kidding? He felt bad enough squashing bugs on the sidewalk. Killing a human being was out of the question. But they still had to get out of here with the gun.

"Get out of our way." This time Paul took a step ahead, and to his utter surprise, his father backed up.

"You make me sick," he said, but all the thunder had gone out of his voice.

"Back up," Paul said.

His face had gone a few shades whiter and he backed away, first down one step, then another. Paul kept the gun on him.

"Go out the door," Paul said.

"Take the gun off of him," Jack said.

"Not yet. Back out the door."

"I can't believe you're doing this," the General said.

Still, he reached behind him, opened the door, and backed into the storm. Paul followed down the stairs and stuck his head out the door. "Back off."

To his surprise, his father listened. He half expected the General to charge him, loaded gun or not. He was sure the booze and now the cocaine had made his father loony.

Paul and Jack slipped out the door and backpedaled down the driveway. His father disappeared in the snow like a fading specter.

On the way down the street, Paul tucked the gun into his coat and Jack did the same with the ammo, concealing it in his inner pocket. Jack felt as if his friend had been replaced by an alien. Mousy little Paul, the smallest kid in class, the one who jumped if you said his name too loud. Jack didn't think the kid had something like this in him, and he felt glad for Paul, finally standing up to the bastard. But part of him was a little frightened, too. Would Paul really have shot his father? His own parents had always been so good to him he couldn't imagine doing something like that to them.

When they reached Jack's house, Paul burst into tears.

They stopped running and Jack put his hand on Paul's shoulder. "How's it going?"

"Just great. I almost shot my fucking father. How do you think it's going?"

"I'm just trying to help. That was pretty intense."

"Jesus, I think I'm going to puke."

He bent over and retched. A stream of green vomit dribbled into the snow. Jack turned his head to give the kid some dignity. A small part of him felt ashamed for some reason, though, for not wanting to see his friend puke. If he watched that happen, it might force his own guts up his throat.

Paul wiped his mouth with the back of his hand. "Sorry."

A runner of saliva hung from his lower lip.

"Wipe your mouth again."

"Thanks."

"What if I had shot him, Jack?"

"You didn't."

Snot dribbled from Paul's nose. His bottom lip quivered. "I'm horrible." He sniffed hard.

"You're not horrible, man. You're pissed, and you've got a right to be."

"You don't think I'm a psycho?"

Jack smiled. "Maybe a little, but I always thought that, you dweeb."

"I don't know, Jack. This is pretty fucked up."

"My dad will know what to do."

"I can't go back there, Jack." Paul turned away and wiped his nose with his sleeve. "I hope your dad does know."

The limo pulled into the driveway a moment later. It had a good three inches of snow on its roof and rear window despite the best efforts of the defroster.

John got out first, rounding the car and opening the passenger door. Ronnie bounded out of the backseat, followed by Cassie. She had on a long camel hair coat and wore a red-and-white-striped muffler. She wrapped it around her throat like a World War I flying ace and stepped toward them.

"How's this for weather? Do you have your bags?"

"Hey, guys," Ronnie said, giving them a broad wave of the hand.

"Let's get our bags."

After retrieving the bags from the house and saying good-bye to his mom, Jack got into the limo with Paul. Chris and Emma were waiting inside, Chris with a Cooper hockey bag and Emma with a denim backpack.

"What's a' matter, Harding? You act like you've never seen us before," Chris said.

"I thought you were in the hospital. What about your rib?"

"Ronnie's mom talked to the doctors. And she called my dad."

She was a one-woman surgical team.

Cassie ducked into the limo.

"We can talk about that later," she said. "I hope everybody's ready. I have a ton of snacks for you guys, and you can watch whatever movies you want."

"Wow," Chris said.

Chris seemed the most excited of all of them. Jack and Paul knew better. Emma didn't seem as excited, but she had believed their story about the Wraith, whereas to Chris it was all fantasy. He had nothing to fear from Cassie, so this was all a big adventure to him. If Jack could get Chris alone, he would try to talk sense into him, warn him to be careful around her.

They chugged up Steadman Road, following the fence

bordering the estate. They stopped at the gate and then it whirred open.

They reached the mansion and got out of the limousine. Cassie flipped her scarf back over her shoulder and looked around at the storm.

"Good thing we got here when we did. Looks like the storm's getting worse. But we'll all be safe inside, right?"

They all nodded in agreement. It was only nine o'clock in the morning and already a white curtain of snow obscured the estate to the point where the road was not visible. In the few moments they had been out of the limo, Jack's cheeks had gone raw and he pined for a cup of hot chocolate to relieve the chill.

As if reading his mind, Cassie said, "Let's get inside before we all freeze to death."

They ascended the steps between the stone lions and entered. After John took their coats, they followed Cassie to the great room. Once again, there were tables with bowls of snacks: Doritos, potato chips, plates of chocolate chip cookies, a hot pizza, and a dish full of M&Ms. And all this at nine in the morning.

"There's pop in the fridge behind the bar. Help yourselves."

Ronnie headed for the table and scooped up a handful of M&Ms.

"How can you eat chocolate that early in the morning?" Chris said.

"Like this," he said, and stuffed the whole handful into his mouth.

"Easy, Ronald. You have all day to eat snacks," his mother said.

Jack didn't say anything, but he wondered why Ronnie's mom put out all this food when her son was so heavy. It seemed cruel in a way, giving him access to snacks and feeding the very condition that caused him to be the scorn of so many bullies. If she didn't want him picked on so much, maybe ditch some of the food and encourage the kid to lose a few.

Cassie drifted into the room. "Jack, can I talk to you?"

"Sure."

"Follow me."

They proceeded to the front foyer, where she sat at a small wrought-iron table. "Have a seat."

He pulled the chair out and sat down. "What do you want to talk about?"

"I just want to thank you for all you've done for Ronnie."

There's a big surprise, he thought.

"You're welcome."

"His having friends over, it's wonderful. This is one of the few times."

"That's kind of sad. No offense."

"None taken. He told me what happened at the dance last night. Those other boys are just rotten if you ask me."

"Vinnie's a real ass. I mean jerk. His buddies aren't much better. I think they would have killed us. Ronnie saved one of us this time, you know."

"Oh?"

"He helped Chris when he was down. Bowled right into the kid that had Chris pinned to the ground. It was pretty brave."

It did take guts to go after guys like Vinnie and his gang, but Jack also hoped she would see that her son was becoming self-reliant. He didn't need Jack to protect him. Jack had never applied for that job and he didn't want it anymore. What he did want was to be Ronnie's friend and not his pseudo guardian, risking the wrath of Cassie every time Ronnie got into a scrape.

"Thank you again."

"You're welcome, I guess. They'll probably kick Vinnie out of school for this."

"Would you like that?"

"It would make my school day easier, but he'd probably

still be gunning for us because we got him kicked out of school."

"I don't think you'll have to worry about him anymore."

"What do you mean?" Jack said.

"Best left unanswered, Jack." She patted him on the hand and flashed him a toothy grin.

"What did you do to Vinnie?"

"Nothing he didn't deserve. You're not feeling sorry for him, are you?"

"Hell no. But you didn't, did you?"

"Did I what?"

The big smile faded and he realized he was treading onto the part of the ice where fisherman didn't dare tread. If he wasn't careful, the icy depths awaited him.

"Nothing."

"Those boys won't be bothering you anymore. That's all I'll say, and that's all you need to know."

"Can I go back with the other kids?"

"Of course."

He got up and left the foyer, feeling her gaze on the back of his neck the whole time. Paul had hid the gun in his bag, and for that he was grateful.

They played Foosball, darts, and video games and for a little while Jack forgot about all the problems that went along with knowing Ronnie Winter.

Chris took a break from the Foosball table to get a can of pop from behind the bar, and Jack slipped away. He wanted to ask Chris something.

"What did she do to you?"

"What do you mean?" He took a Pepsi from the fridge and pulled the tab.

"Your ribs. She healed you, didn't she? I saw the way you looked last night and that's what happened, isn't it?"

"She did something. Whatever it was, I feel great."

"Do you believe me and Paul now?"

"Maybe. Maybe not."

Chris was a typical thickheaded jock sometimes. "Just be careful."

They joined the other kids at the Foosball table, where Ronnie was taking on Paul and Emma.

"C'mon, Fussel, he's killing us," Emma said.

"I'm trying."

"Try harder," she said.

Ronnie scored on them and threw his arms in the air. "Yes!"

He took his Dr Pepper off the table and raised it. "I'd like to propose a toast. To the best set of friends anyone could have. Cheers." He chugged it down and burped.

"Gross," Emma said.

"Ronnie, sometimes you're all right," Jack said. And he meant it. Despite all the crap they had been through, it was hard not to like the kid.

Cassie hurried into the room and told them all to stay put. She jogged back out of the great room, muttering under her breath.

"What's going on?" Paul said.

Ronnie shrugged his shoulders.

CHAPTER 40

As the kids had settled in playing Foosball, George Kempf and his backup slogged through the snow, one officer with him in the unmarked and the other two in a squad car. Snow piled in gobs on the windshield and the wipers beat it away as fast as it fell.

They needed to contain the Wraith to the tunnels, which he felt they could do. A second call to the librarian confirmed there were no entrances or exits to the grounds other than through the mansion. If it got loose in a snowstorm, the game was over. You couldn't find a goddamn purple elephant in this snow, let alone a person that didn't want to be found.

He had called John ten minutes ago and asked him to open the gates before they arrived so they wouldn't alert Cassie to their presence there. John had taken care of business, because they rolled right through the open gate.

They pulled up in front of the wide steps and all got out. Stavros had ridden with him and carried a Colt AR-15. The other two carried Mossberg twelve-gauges, like Kempf. They all had sidearms, too. Just in case.

"Listen to me. What I'm about to tell you sounds nutty. You might think I'm crazy or an idiot, but at this point I really don't give a shit. I'm retiring after this little adventure is over. We're looking for a guy in blue coveralls with a face full of gauze bandages. He doesn't have any eyes and he's a fucking zombie. How's that?"

"Zombie?" Stavros said.

"The living dead. I don't even know if these will work on him. Believe what you want but be careful. We're not really going in here to make an arrest, understand?"

He made a point of looking each one of them in the eyes, and when they all nodded at him, he started up the steps.

He rang the bell, thinking the door should have one of those huge iron gates you see guarding castle drawbridges. John opened the door.

"Hello, Detective."

"We have a warrant to make an arrest, John. Can you show us to the tunnels?"

He opened the door and they entered the cathedral-like foyer.

"Some place," Stavros said.

"Admire it later. We've got work to do."

Cassie Winter entered the foyer, a bit out of breath and scowling. "What's this about?"

"We have a warrant for the arrest of the man responsible for four murders in Brampton."

"How can I help?"

That tone changed in a hurry, Kempf thought.

"We think our suspect is hiding in the tunnels under your estate. If you would show us the way so we can start looking for him please."

"Did John tell you?"

"I'm sorry?"

"He did, didn't he? Don't lie to me, Detective."

"He assisted us."

"I see."

In a heartbeat she lunged at John, leaving her feet and seeming to cling to the big man's chest. She cocked her head and got under his chin, biting the neck and exploding his jugular vein in a gush of scarlet fluid. She lowered herself off him and John staggered into a corner, knocking over a table and a pink vase.

"Oh, dear Jesus!" MacKenzie said.

Cassie turned and hissed, her pale skin smeared around the mouth with blood, looking strangely like someone who had smeared beets all over her face.

"You wouldn't stay away," she said.

In an instant, Kempf felt pain in his head he didn't know was possible, and he went to his knees. The shotgun slipped out of his hand. The other officers must have felt the same agony, for they went down, clutching at their heads and shrieking from the pain.

Cassie turned and ran, leaving them writhing on the floor.

It took Jack a moment to realize what he was seeing, Cassie Winter storming into the room with red fluid smeared across her lips and chin, a wild look in her eyes.

"What the hell?" Jack said.

"Go." She was on top of him, grabbing his shirt and pushing him toward the butler's pantry off the great room. "All of you go." There was something in her voice combined with the red stuff on her mouth (was it really blood?) that told him he'd better listen. That meant she had killed someone, or been around someone who had bled like there was no tomorrow. All of a sudden he wanted to go home.

"The rest of you, let's go."

She gave Jack another hard shove and grabbed Emma, dragging her along. Ronnie stood with mouth agape. The can of Dr Pepper fell from his hand and the soda dribbled out onto the floor. He looked at Jack as if Jack had an answer, then at the others before turning to his mother and saying, "Mom, what's going on?"

"Get to the tunnels. Some very bad men are here."

Jack got the feeling he didn't disobey his mother often. This time was no exception, as Ronnie turned and ran into the butler's pantry.

"Come on, guys." He waved them on, oblivious of the red streaks painted on his mother's face.

Ronnie was willing to delve into those dark caverns once again without giving it a second thought. But Jack guessed he didn't know what lurked down there. On the day Ronnie had left them in the dark, Jack doubted if he saw the Wraith or even knew of his existence. He certainly didn't know it was the animated corpse of his dead father.

Jack tried to pull away, but she dug into his arm and her strength was almost machinelike. She did the same to Emma, dragging them both as if they were small dogs on a leash.

Chris and Paul stood by the bar, both of them looking dazed.

"Run!" Jack yelled.

Paul took off first and Chris followed suit, sprinting from the great room.

"They won't last long," Cassie said.

As she said this, a peculiar thing happened. The lights went out in the mansion. But that wasn't entirely correct, for there was a great whooshing sound as if they had been sucked through cracks in the walls. The light was removed, and the entire room grew dim.

"Come out. Come up," Cassie murmured as they reached the butler's pantry.

The refrigerator guarding the entrance to the tunnel rocked as something bumped it. It leaned forward hard, then rocked back. Once. Twice. Then something hit it hard enough to knock it forward so it tipped, the door opening and cans of Pepsi and root beer falling out like paratroopers from a plane. They rolled across the floor and a few burst, showering the cupboards with sticky fluid.

The door banged open and the bandaged face appeared in the opening. The one with the bottomless black eyes usually reserved for nightmares.

Jack and Emma screamed. The Wraith darted past them. Ronnie pressed against the cupboards. "What was that? What was that?" he said.

"Ronald, stay up here," Cassie said. "I have business with Jack and Emma in the tunnels."

The agony in Kempf's head began to subside and he staggered to his feet. His vision was blurred and he felt dizzy, but his head didn't feel as if there were razor blades swimming around inside. John's body lay in the corner, chin to his chest, looking at Kempf as if to say, *I told you this would happen.* Kempf felt sick with guilt and had no idea the bitch would do something like this.

Stavros and the others got up shaking their heads.

Kempf turned to them. "You guys all right?"

They nodded.

"What the fuck was that?" MacKenzie said.

"Some sort of psychic attack is my guess. Let's go find her."

"Did she cut the lights out?" Stavros asked.

"Probably. I have no damn idea how to get into the tunnels."

John was supposed to be their tour guide, but since he was dead, Kempf had to rely on instincts. That wouldn't be easy, given that this place was roughly the size of Versailles. Voices echoed in the distance, and they sounded like kids'. It clicked in his mind that it was probably the Harding kid and his friends, but he couldn't imagine why they'd want to set foot in this place. Especially after being chased by the thing with the bandages on its face. Maybe they didn't have a choice.

"Watch your fire. There's kids running around here."

They started down the main corridor.

Chris and Paul wound their way around to the front door, missing Detective Kempf and the other cops in the expanse of the mansion. Their footsteps echoed on the marble floor, and the large wooden doors loomed in front of them, the gateway to freedom and getting help for their friends.

Paul set the bag down, unzipped it, and fished out the revolver.

"Holy shit! Where did you get that?"

"We stole it from my dad's closet. Me and Jack thought we might need it."

"What's going on, Paul? What was that red stuff on her face?" And as if he answered his own question, Chris slapped a hand over his mouth and pointed at something over Paul's shoulder.

Paul turned and what he saw made him jump back.

John was dead and he saw where the blood on Cassie's mouth had come from. It didn't seem right, the man who had been so kind to them, so friendly, buying them milk shakes and calling them "mister" was dead. And killed in a horrible fashion. Paul wanted to cry. His stomach fluttered and he felt like he might piss his pants.

"We need to get help," Paul said.

Chris opened the front doors and they stepped out between the lions. The limousine was a black smear in the snow and it was at most ten feet away. A curtain of flakes whipped past them and Paul realized finding their way down to the road would be impossible. If they didn't get lost or freeze to death before reaching the road, a passing car would hit them. The drivers couldn't see worth squat, either.

"We're not going anywhere," Paul said.

"This snow's nasty."

"We'll have to call from inside the mansion. I hope the phones aren't out too, bucko."

Chris closed the doors and immediately Paul felt the hairs on his neck prickle. Someone was behind them. Paul turned around. Chris did the same and said, "It *is* real."

The Wraith stood at the end of the main hallway. One of the bandages hung from its face, dangling over the shoulder and reminding Paul of the mummy from one of those old black-and-white movies. The smell of rot and dirt cascaded down the hallway.

"I'm scared, Paulie!"

"That makes two of us."
"Use the gun!"

They ducked under the small doorway, Cassie prodding them along down the steps. She had rummaged in the drawer of the butler's pantry and taken out a flashlight. It lit up the cracked concrete steps and Emma wondered if they wouldn't go ass over tin cups down the steps in the darkness. This whole thing was like a movie being fast-forwarded, everything happening too fast for her to digest. Cassie had shown up at her door and within five minutes had Emma's mother convinced she should go to the party. Emma didn't really want to go, but if the other kids were going (especially Jack), it might be okay.

They reached the bottom of the steps. Cassie came down behind them. She looked even paler in the light of the beam, the blood caked on her pasty face. Emma wondered where the Wraith had gone, and if it would follow them back into the tunnels. The air was cold and stale down here, enough to give you the chills even without a bandaged monster running around.

"Hold my hand. Jack, you hold hers. You do not want to be separated from me down here."

They hurried ahead, Emma almost dragging Jack behind her. She got glimpses of rough stone walls, the occasional rat. They came to several forks and Cassie turned left, right, then left until they came to the end of a tunnel.

"Sit down," she said. The ground felt hard and cold against her butt.

In the cone of the flashlight beam, she saw four thick wooden beams propping up the ceiling. Every few moments, dust dribbled down from the ceiling and with it small pebbles.

"Don't move around too much. You might knock one of the beams loose and bring the whole roof down on your head. I'm going to wait at the head of the tunnel for the detective. Don't make a noise, either."

"Why are you doing this?"

"I wanted to be left alone, Jack. The police wanted things differently. I warned that detective to stay away from me, but he didn't listen. It's unfortunate things had to be this way, but I tried to stop it."

"Did you make it kill those people?" Emma asked.

"No. I can't control it anymore. It kills when it wants to, as much as I hate to admit that. I'm sorry it had to frighten you and Paul, but I felt you needed a warning. Now if you cooperate with me and keep quiet like good kids, you'll go home after this."

"What about Ronnie?"

"He'll be fine. It won't harm him."

"This is too weird," Emma said.

"That's enough."

Emma didn't believe for a second that she would let them go. If that were true, they wouldn't be in the tunnels right now, but going home.

Cassie left them the flashlight, then slipped into the darkness, presumably feeling her way along the wall.

"Jack, I'm scared."

"Hold my hand."

She gripped his hand.

"What do you think she's doing?" Emma asked.

"I think she's going to kill someone else."

"Who do you think she killed?"

"Maybe it was John."

She hated to think of John as dead. He seemed so nice, taking them all to a restaurant and driving them around as if they were movie stars.

"How did she get you to come here?" Jack asked.

"Tricked my mother into letting me go. I didn't really want to, but she looked like she meant business and I remembered what you and Paul said about her, that she could get mean. So I came along." She swallowed. "What do you think will happen?"

"I just don't know," Jack said.

They sat together in the darkness, waiting.

CHAPTER 41

Kempf and the others searched the mansion. They found a billiard room with velvet paintings on the wall, the gleaming stainless steel kitchen, a sunroom full of ferns, and five different bathrooms, all with smooth marble floors and gold fixtures. But no tunnel entrance. There were about a hundred other rooms in this place to search, and the longer it took them, the more time Cassie had to get away. Kempf was about to suggest splitting into two teams when something bowled into him.

He looked down at the kid, pudgy with freckles and a clump of sweaty hair stuck to his forehead. He smelled sweet, like root beer and bubblegum. The kid looked up at him in surprise, then tried to bolt. Kempf grabbed him by the back of his T-shirt and he skidded to a halt.

"Hold on. Where you going?"

His chest heaved and between breaths he said, "What?"

Kempf managed to turn him around and realized he was Cassie Winter's son. The resemblance was slight, but the tint in the reddish brown hair gave it away.

"Where's your mother?"

"I don't know."

"Don't lie to me. This is important."

"Who are you?"

"Detective George Kempf. Do you know how to get into the tunnels?"

"Maybe."

"Yes or no?"

"Yeah."

He tilted the kid's chin up and looked into his blue eyes.

"Listen to me. Ronnie, right?" The kid nodded. "There's someone very dangerous hiding in those tunnels and we have to find him. He killed some people in town. You heard about that on the news, right?"

"Uh-huh."

"We need to find him."

"You're not going to hurt my mom?"

"I promise we won't hurt your mom."

"As long as you promise."

He led them through the maze of corridors and through a room with Foosball tables, a bar, video games, and a projection-screen television. It would be a hell of a room for a party. Too bad it was wasted on someone like Cassie Winter.

"There."

He pointed to a kitchen off the big room and Kempf saw a refrigerator overturned. Cans of Pepsi lay on the floor like wounded soldiers after a battle.

"That's the entrance. Get your mag lights out."

The three officers produced black steel flashlights and turned them on.

"Stay close," Kempf said. "It's going to be darker than a fat lady's asshole down there."

"What do we do with him?" MacKenzie nodded at Ronnie.

"Stay in this room. If you hear anyone coming up the tunnel steps, run and hide. If it's one of us, we'll yell for you and tell you to come out. Okay?"

"Got it."

He stood with his hands in his pockets, watching them.

"Did your friend Jack go into the tunnels?"

"Yep. Him and Emma."

Great. They had a bloodthirsty creature loose along with the serial killer. Trying to find them and not shoot themselves or one of the kids was going to be two steps from impossible. If no innocent bystanders (or hostages) got killed it would make the water-into-wine thing look like a parlor trick.

Paul raised the gun with both hands and aimed for the Wraith's chest, where he guessed the heart was under that dead skin. It started forward, and he could feel it staring at them, penetrating. Even though it had no eyes, the son of a gun was staring at them. He wondered what it saw.

"Shoot it, Fussel!"

He closed his eyes and squeezed the trigger. The metal seemed to bite into the flesh on his finger and the gun boomed like a cannon. It recoiled hard, knocking him back three steps, and Chris caught him before he did a reverse somersault on the marble floor. The shot glanced off the top of the Wraith's shoulder and exploded into the wall in a puff of plaster. The Wraith jerked back as if someone had shoved it but kept up its steady advance toward Paul and Chris.

"We have to go out the door," Paul said.

"Are you crazy?"

"You can't hurt something that's already dead. Open the door. We'll look for another way back into the mansion."

The Wraith raced ahead.

Chris backed up, felt for the doorknob, and twisted it. He pulled on the door, knocked it into himself. He turned around and opened it all the way. Snow lashed into the doorway. They could not stay out very long, for they both wore light shirts and no jackets. The cold would eat them for lunch.

Paul slid through next and slammed the door behind him. They backed down the steps and Chris kept going, smacking into the limousine.

"What if we hide in here?" Chris patted the roof of the limo.

"We'd be trapped. Come on."

Paul followed the front of the house and Chris came after. They ducked low as if this would keep them out of the wind, but it did no good. The twenty-mile-an-hour winds stabbed and poked at them, shoving them backward. Paul heard a faint thump under the wind, and he knew it was the door opening and closing. The Wraith was outside. He wondered how well it could see, and if it was tracking them right now. He had hoped the snow would provide some cover for them, but if it had no eyes, it probably wouldn't be affected by the blinding storm.

Snow crunched behind them.

"Hurry up!" Paul said.

He expected to look around and see a pool of blood on the snow where his friend once stood.

"We can't just sit here," Jack said, after a few long minutes.

"What, then?"

Jack shone the light on the surrounding walls, hoping to find a door or passageway that Steadman's workers had cut out of the rock. He felt around with his hand. The walls were smooth and slick, as if they had broken out in a cold sweat.

"Looking for a door?" Emma said.

"Yeah. Nothing."

He felt the rough wood of the beams holding up the roof. A splinter slipped under his thumb and he pulled it back as if he had been burned. The beams were all that held this section of the tunnel roof up.

"Come on, Emma." He shone the light and felt his way along the wall.

"What if she's waiting there?"

"We'll deal with her."

He felt better thinking that here. When they got to the end of the tunnel, he might feel differently.

"Will you hold my hand?" Emma said.

He extended his hand and she took it. It sent a tiny wave of prickles up his arm.

They came to the junction but Cassie was nowhere to be seen. Water dribbled somewhere far off and a slight breeze blew down the tunnels. He strained his ears to listen but heard nothing, only the drip-drip of water.

"Where do you think she went?" Emma asked.

"Maybe she went back upstairs."

"Which way to the house?"

"Left, I think."

They turned left, Jack shining the light ahead of them.

"It can't be too far. Didn't we turn a couple of times?"

It was so dark when they had raced down here he had trouble remembering the turns. She had pushed them along like cattle through a chute, and all the walls and corridors looked the same to him.

"Jack, what's that? Stop." Emma tugged on his arm and they stopped.

"What?"

"Listen."

A low, purring noise came from up ahead. It sounded as if the purr had been combined with the wheeze of an asthmatic. There were clicks, grunts, and whispers.

"It sounds like a snake," Emma said.

"I don't think there's any big snakes around here."

The noise grew closer, scuttling on the stones. The whispering increased, strange words that sounded like another language.

"I think we should go back," Emma said.

"I think you're right."

They started a retreat down the tunnels.

Kempf took the lead into the tunnels. He had nearly fallen and broken his neck coming down the concrete steps and MacKenzie had snickered behind him. He advised him to keep quiet unless he wanted to be shitting a Dexter wing tip.

The temperature dipped, and the cold began to gnaw at his hands, making it hard to hold the shotgun. He wished for a pair of gloves. Why not just wish for a nice set of thermal underwear, too?

They went a hundred feet into the tunnel and came to a corridor to their right.

"Let's try this way," Kempf said.

He watched the floor, looking for footprints or marks in the dust that would indicate the passage of another person.

"Harris and MacKenzie! Take the tunnel we came down and see where it goes. We'll wait here."

Harris, a big blond kid with a full beard, nodded. The two of them crept into the dark and disappeared around the corner.

"I don't like this," Stavros said. Clear snot trickled into his mustache. He wiped it with the back of his hand.

Kempf said, "The quicker we find him, the quicker we get out of here."

Harris and MacKenzie appeared, their breath visible in white plumes.

"It ends at a wall. Looks like it caved in. There's a big pile of stone," Harris said.

Had the librarian told him about a collapse in the tunnels? It seemed to him there was a story about Steadman's workers dying when the roof fell in on them. That was a hell of a way to go. "Then it's this way."

They reached another junction and had the option of turning right or going straight. How did hospital workers ever find their way around these catacombs without becoming hopelessly lost?

A hissing sound came from up ahead.

"What the piss is that?" Harris said.

"It might be him," Kempf said. "You two move up."

Stavros and Harris flanked him while MacKenzie stayed back.

"Show us your hands and come out." That thing with the

bandaged face was not coming out with its hands up, even if Kempf had a bullhorn.

Another hiss came and with it scraping on the sidewalk. Kempf imagined it in the dark, the dirty bandages stuck to pasty skin, the coveralls stained with blood. Most of all the eyes. Black as a coal mine. In the dark, it wouldn't matter because somehow he knew it could find them. "Come out now!"

His voice echoed down the hallway, and he hoped the kids had heard his shout.

Nothing happened for a moment and he said, "Let's go, there's nothing here."

CHAPTER 42

Paul and Chris turned the corner around the mansion's front wall. Paul's arms were pink and his cheeks stung. His shirt grew more sodden with each step, as did his shoes and pant legs. If they didn't get out of this storm in a hurry, they were dead.

"Maybe we lost it in the snow," Chris said.

"I don't think so."

Paul saw a set of windows up ahead. They extended up the first story of the mansion, three of them in a row. They could break those windows and climb inside. "Head for the windows. We can shoot them out if we have to."

Chris nodded, his arms crossed in front of him. His nose shone red from the cold.

Paul risked a look over his shoulder and saw nothing but blowing snow. He hadn't heard any footsteps in the last few moments. Maybe they did lose the Wraith. Perhaps the snow confused it, and it was wandering off to the wooded part of the estate.

The snow lessened and through the break he saw the far corner of the mansion. The wind still blew hard and fast, but with small gaps in between the gusts. The break lasted a moment, but it was all they needed. Paul looked to his right and saw it speeding toward them. It must have taken a wrong turn, thinking they went farther away from the house and toward the woods. The black eyes looked like two pinpricks in a piece of paper.

"Chris, hurry up! It's coming!"

Ronnie considered staying in the great room for about a second after the police went into the tunnels. If the detective said they wouldn't hurt his mom, he believed them. After all, she hadn't done anything wrong, and he was sure the cops would go home and they could get back to their sleepover. He decided to go look for Paul and Chris. They were probably lost, wandering along hallways.

He had made a sweep of the mansion, including his own room, the study, billiard room, sunroom, and a dozen others. But no sign of Chris and Paul. He reached the front foyer and noticed the draft dancing over his bare arms. The front door was open, and the wind blew hard enough to rattle the oak door on its hinges. Chris and Paul had gone outside, but why?

He turned and saw John's body and knew why. Somebody had killed him, and he thought about the red stuff on his mom's face, but then dismissed the thought. His mother wasn't capable of something like that. Blood dripped from the hole in John's ruined throat, and Ronnie fought the urge to throw up. Instead, he cried, great sobs that racked his chest. Now he had lost two fathers. What a fucking life it was.

He wiped the tears away with the back of his hand. What if the same person who killed John was after Chris and Paul? He ran off toward the west wing of the house and entered the study. Ronnie had already looked for them in this room, but the big windows looked over the expanse of the estate and if they were outside, he might see them.

A few charred logs rested in the fireplace, and the room smelled like smoke. It was dim and he bumped his knee on an end table, cursing the rest of the way across the room. He moved the plum drape aside, looked out, and saw white. A look out the left pane revealed nothing but more snow, and there was nothing straight ahead. He peered out to his right and saw nothing. No, wait. A flash of blue. Paul had on a blue T-shirt, didn't he?

Paul came into view, then Chris. They lumbered through the deep snow, both with their heads down and trying to mow through the snow. Paul looked to his right every few seconds.

Ronnie banged on the window with his palm, but Paul didn't hear him. He pounded ahead through the snow.

"Paul! Paul!" He slapped his palms against the glass. They would never hear him.

This called for more drastic measures. He searched the room and picked up an end table and hauled it over to the window. He set the table down and flung the drape aside. Ronnie picked the table up. He charged forward and thrust it away from his chest as if he were passing a basketball. It smashed through the pane and teetered on the sill. He kicked it three times in rapid succession, forcing it out the window. Careful to avoid the jagged shards, he poked his head out the window. Paul looked up at him as if he had two heads sprouting from his neck.

Chris came up behind him.

"Kick the glass out!" Paul said. "There's someone after us!"

Ronnie didn't wait for an explanation. He kicked at the shards and they tumbled onto the snow.

"I'll boost you up," Chris said.

Paul handed the gun to Ronnie.

"Cool," Ronnie said.

Paul grabbed the windowsill and Chris bear-hugged his legs and lifted him the rest of the way inside. Ronnie and Paul urged Chris on, and he pulled himself halfway up before it grabbed him from behind.

"Who the fuck is that?" Ronnie said. He had never seen anyone so creepy.

Chris pulled, but the bandaged man grabbed his leg. Paul and Ronnie each gripped an arm and pulled, Ronnie propping his leg against the inside wall for leverage. Chris's hold started to slip, and the nail on his index finger tore clean off, like a bottle cap popping. "Ah, that fucking hurts!"

We can't win this one, Ronnie thought.

He grabbed the gun off the windowsill and pointed it at the guy's head.

Ronnie squinted, stuck out his tongue in concentration, and squeezed the trigger. The shot exploded into the guy's jaw, ripping off bandages in blackened strips. Ronnie fell backward. The guy backed up and let go of Chris, who wormed his way inside the room, scrambling over the windowsill. The man drifted back into the snow. The smell of gunpowder and scorched flesh hung in the air.

"Holy shit, my ears are ringing," Paul said.

"Thanks, you guys," Chris said.

"Who is that?" Ronnie said.

"The thing that killed all those people," Paul said. "Let's go before it gets in here."

"Where?" Chris said.

"The tunnels," Chris said. "We have to help Jack and Emma."

"We've got four shots left if we need them. Lead on, Ron," Paul said.

Ronnie liked the idea of being the leader, like Lee Marvin in *The Big Red One*, taking his troops through North Africa and Sicily. "Follow me, boys."

He took off with Chris and Paul behind him.

Kempf stepped forward. The hair on his neck started to prickle. Someone watching, getting close.

That someone lunged out of the gloom and grabbed hold

of Harris. His shotgun boomed in the tunnels, knocking pebbles loose from the ceiling. The thing was grayish white and fast. So fast it pulled Harris into the darkness within seconds. It was as if he got sucked into a black hole, and before the others even got a shot off. What the hell could move that fast? Kempf saw enough of it to know it wasn't the Wraith, but if not the Wraith, then what? He shone his light ahead, but there was only blackness. Clicking noises reverberated down the length of the tunnel. Underneath it were Harris's whimpers. *Jesus, God, don't let me hear that.*

A moment later a shriek like a fire whistle came, a scream so high in pitch it sounded like a woman's. It lasted a moment longer, then trailed off, but he knew he would hear that scream in his nightmares for years. No person should make a sound like that.

He looked at Stavros and MacKenzie, both of them staring as if they had just seen a nine-foot clown appear from the tunnel.

"What was that, Kempf?" Stavros said.

"How in the name of Christ am I supposed to know?"

"We need backup. Hell, let's call the fucking SWAT team in here," Stavros said.

"We can't leave Harris down here," Kempf said. Although judging from that scream, Harris was probably beyond help.

"MacKenzie, go back and radio for help. We'll go look for Harris and whatever the hell took him."

"Yeah, good idea." MacKenzie nodded. He wore his black hair slicked back with gel or mousse or some crap. "Go! It's you and me, Stavros. Look sharp."

This operation was going along just swimmingly. One of his officers was dead and he had a civilian in the house with his throat chewed out. What really disturbed him was the thing that leaped out of the darkness and snatched Harris up as if he were made of paper and feathers. There was something else to deal with besides the Wraith, something he had not planned on. Swimmingly, all right.

They moved ahead, past the corridor to the right.

* * *

Paul, Chris, and Ronnie booked through the house. On the way to the great room, Paul picked up a phone and got what he expected: dead silence. Picking up the phone was worth a long shot, though, and he had thought maybe he could dial 911 and get someone here to save them.

They reached the tunnel entrance and Paul realized they didn't have a flashlight. The tunnel was far too dark to travel without light.

"I'll get a flashlight from my room," Ronnie said.

"You can't go by yourself," Chris said. "Not with that thing running around."

"Come with me then," Ronnie said.

"Let's go."

Ronnie bounded ahead, taking the lead and forcing Chris and Paul to play catch-up. They took the back stairs off the kitchen, the spiral stairs shaking under the weight of three boys in rapid transit. They headed down the hallway, the one with the blue and gold wallpaper that reminded Paul of a Holiday Inn. Every few seconds he looked behind him, expecting to see the Wraith sneaking up, or worse, feel the icy hand on his neck before it jerked him away. But so far they were alone in the mansion.

Ronnie opened the door to his room, hurried to the nightstand, and took out a yellow flashlight.

"This place has everything," Chris said.

Ronnie flicked the flashlight on and off to make sure it worked, then streaked past them yelling, "Death from above!" Paul got the impression this was becoming a huge game for him. He wasn't sure if that was Ronnie's way of dealing with the horrors taking place, or if his boat had finally slipped away from the dock. Either way, it frightened him.

"Wait a second, Ronnie," Chris said.

But Ronnie was juiced up, ready to hit those tunnels again with or without the other two.

"What did you want him to do?" Paul said.

"That thing might be waiting at the bottom of the steps for us. You or me should go first with the gun just in case."

Ronnie hit the steps humming the Green Berets theme song and Paul had the sudden urge to take off one of his socks and stuff it in the kid's mouth. He was going to get them killed if he didn't shut up.

The three of them reached the great room and Chris got a hand on Ronnie's T-shirt and yanked hard, pulling him to the floor. He looked as if he had run into a clothesline.

"Christ, too-tall. Did you leave his head attached?"

Ronnie stood up and brushed off his pants. "What are you doing?"

"We don't know where that guy went. You're gonna give us away if you don't shut up. Try and move more quiet. Okay?"

"Sorry, I just got excited." His face turned as red as his hair.

They crept across the great room, passing the bar, now littered with empty root beer cans. Once in the butler's pantry, Paul reached out an arm and stopped Chris. He handed the gun to Chris.

"What's this for?"

"You're bigger than me and you can fire the gun better. It won't knock you on your butt."

"If you say so, Fussel," Chris said. He lowered the revolver and held it flat against his outer thigh.

"Where do they keep the silverware?" Paul said.

"There, I think." Ronnie pointed to the farthest drawer to the right, near the wounded refrigerator.

Paul opened it and found two butcher knives with black handles.

"What are those for?" Ronnie asked.

"I'm not going down there without a weapon." He started to hand one to Ronnie and then drew it back. "We can trust you with this, right?"

"I'm not gonna stab you or nothing."

Ronnie took the knife and with Chris in the lead, they hunched down and entered the bowels of the mansion.

They descended the steps, Ronnie shining the beam into the dim corridor. Paul held the knife like Norman Bates in the shower scene, ready to plunge it into anything that moved. Ronnie held his out in front of him, like a gang member in a switchblade fight.

A thin coat of slime covered the walls, and it smelled like mold and dust.

They had moved ahead another fifty feet when Chris lurched forward into the darkness and hit the concrete with a smack.

"Are you all right?" Ronnie said.

"I tripped over a log or a rock or something," he said.

"That doesn't make any sense, bucko. Give me the flashlight." Paul took it from Ronnie and pointed it at the ground. It wasn't a log or a rock. A man dressed in blue lay facedown across the tunnel. A black shotgun had fallen to the ground at his side, and the stock was slicked with blood.

"Oh God," Paul said in a barely audible whisper.

"This is more dead bodies than I ever wanted to see in person," Chris said.

"Who is he?" Ronnie asked.

Paul said, "Roll him over, Chris."

"You fucking roll him over, Fussel."

"Why don't we all roll him over?" Ronnie said.

Ah, the voice of reason. And it came from Ronnie. Scary.

The three of them hunkered down, Chris pulling and the other two pushing, until they got him on his back. Paul wished they hadn't rolled him over at all. The face was gone, a mess of red tissue, muscle and skull underneath. It looked like a piece of meat carved by an angry butcher, wet and red and rank. Paul gagged back his breakfast.

"A cop, oh, man, someone killed a cop!" Ronnie said.

"Let's go before I get sick or chicken out," Chris said.

They all stood up and backed away from the body. They were no more than three feet away from it when Paul sensed someone behind him. The hairs on the back of his neck stood up and he whispered to the others, "*It's behind us.*"

CHAPTER 43

They found Harris, or what was left of him. There were two dime-sized puncture holes just below his hairline and two thin streams of blood ran down the center of his face. His cheeks had gouges in them, as did his chest, long strips torn into the shirt and the flesh underneath.

Kempf guessed his abductor took its time ripping the gashes in Harris before delivering the deadly bite to the skull. The sheer brutality of the attack stunned and sickened him. On days like this he wished he'd never put on a badge.

"Kempf, what's going on?" Stavros said. He swept the Colt back and forth in a slow arc, as if it were a talisman to ward off evil spirits.

"There's something else down here and it's not our killer."

If those kids weren't down here, he would beat it the hell out of here and call for backup. Maybe MacKenzie made it out.

"Why don't you yell for the kids?" Stavros said.

"It'll find us if I do."

Jack heard the screams coming down the tunnel and he and Emma hurried away from the junction. He had never heard anything like that before, and the person sounded as if he was in unimaginable agony.

"What do you think happened?" he said.

"Someone's dead. Cassie killed whoever it was."

That didn't surprise him. She had come into the great room with blood on her mouth and a look reserved for savages in old Tarzan movies. She had killed someone and wanted to get away from someone else. Maybe it was the cops that had come to the door and she took one of them out in a geyser of blood.

He thought he glimpsed a softball-sized dot of light pass by, the kind a flashlight might make. Their best bet might be to turn the corner and follow the tunnel and whoever possessed the flashlight. But that horrible scream had forced him back into the tunnel.

"Do you think she'll kill us?" Emma asked.

"How am I supposed to know?"

"You've met her more times than me," she said.

"I don't know."

"Don't lie, Jack."

"When she comes back I think she will."

"Then we should go. Run for it. We've got the light."

It hit him: leave them the light and she could track them if they ran. It was like being third man on a match. Light up and the sniper pops you.

The alternative was to wait for Cassie to return and finish them off.

"Let's get going before she comes back."

Paul whirled around to find the Wraith standing silently on the other side of the police officer's body. For a moment he stared at it, a silent killer. Then it lunged at him, quicker than he would have thought it was able to. He raised the butcher knife and slammed it into the thing's shoulder. It gripped his arm and his flesh seemed to go numb under its touch.

"Shoot it!" Paul said.

Visions of being dragged away and torn apart danced through his mind.

It jerked him forward. He looked around at Chris, who aimed the gun at the Wraith.

"Chris, shoot it!"

Chris waved the gun around, trying to get a shot at it without hitting Paul. "I'll hit you."

He's right. If he fires now, I'm toast, Paul thought.

Paul pulled out the tip of the knife and stabbed again. It was like trying to stab a frozen roast and only the tip penetrated. It had no effect. The Wraith yanked him forward. He dug his feet in, but still it dragged him.

Ronnie charged ahead, wielding his knife like a samurai warrior, jabbing the Wraith in the belly. He only succeeded in putting holes in the blue coveralls. It pulled Paul ahead, almost off his feet.

"Do something!"

Ronnie dropped his knife and wedged himself between Paul and the Wraith. Chris came up from behind and wrapped his arms around Paul's waist, tugging on him.

"Let him go, asshole!" Ronnie said. He pounded on the hand that held Paul.

It let go, and at first Paul didn't know why. Then it grabbed Ronnie by the shirt and pulled him within kissing distance. The putrid bandages were inches from Ronnie's nose, and he said, "Stinks." It cocked its head to one side and raised its hand as if to strike him. It swung at his face. The hand stopped before Ronnie's kisser and it extended a finger and scratched his cheek, leaving it bloody. Then it shoved Paul aside and darted past them.

Ronnie's hand crept up to his cheek. He dabbed the blood with his finger and held it up. "What is that thing?"

"I don't know," Paul said. He realized why the Wraith had let go of him. Ronnie got in the way, and some small part of the Wraith recognized its son. Perhaps the urge to kill had come and then it stopped itself, only scratching Ronnie instead of tearing his throat out. Ronnie Winter had saved them.

"We still have to find Jack and Emma," Chris said.

"Shine the light on the ground," Paul said. He hunkered down and picked up the butcher knife. It made him feel like a questing knight, recovering the blade like that.

"George, we have to find them," Stavros said.

"Damn it." The lives of a few kids were more important than his own, and he had a shotgun to defend himself. They had nothing.

"Jack! Paul!" he yelled, and Stavros did the same.

No answer came.

"Wait," Kempf said, and put his hand on Stavros's chest.

A low clicking came from down the tunnel, growing faster and louder, coming closer. He raised the shotgun and Stavros readied the Colt. It appeared before them, and Kempf fired, the shotgun illuminating the tunnel and tattooing their shadows on the walls. The thing screeched, sliced past him, and pinned Stavros to the wall. He was vaguely aware of warmth running down his leg and he turned to fire at it, but it was too late.

A crunching sound came from the dark. Like tearing gristle from steak. That's what it sounded like. Sucking and ripping sounds came from the darkness and he was afraid to put his light on the scene.

When he did, Stavros was slumped against the wall, head cocked to one side, his eyes glassy and open. The same fate that John had suffered had also befallen Michael Stavros. The thing that did this was gone, also, but he saw a trail of fluid leading down the tunnel and knew he had hit it.

He became aware of his own pant leg growing wet and looked down to see a four-inch gash cut into his leg, just above the knee. A jagged hole remained in his pants and he ripped his pant leg off from the knee down, starting the tear where he had been wounded. He tore it into two strips and wrapped them around the wound. Then he followed the trail down the tunnel, hell-bent on ending this, once and for all.

Jack was about to turn left and bolt down the tunnel when Chris, Ronnie, and Paul ran through like diesel trains. Chris held the revolver, while Paul and Ronnie carried kitchen knives. They looked like a group of wannabe pirates.

"What happened to you guys?" Jack said.

"It chased us outside," Paul said. "It's down here with us."

"How did you get away from it?" Jack asked.

Emma said, "Let's find out later."

"I'll lead the way to victory!" Ronnie said, pumping his fist in the air.

"What's with him?" Emma asked.

"He thinks he's Rambo," Chris said. "Follow me, I've got the gun. Jack, I want you next to me."

Jack stepped up next to Chris.

Something slid into the darkness at the junction, something hissing and leathery. It approached them until it was in his flashlight beam.

The smooth features of her face were still recognizable, and the eyes clear and blue. Her skin was pale gray and two bony lumps had grown above her pointed ears. She grinned at them, revealing a set of fangs a werewolf would envy. It was like someone had crossed a woman with a bat and a large feline. What was she? Jack thought.

She slinked forward, the claws on her feet snicking on the concrete. Malformed, veiny breasts hung from her chest. Things like this were only supposed to exist in horror flicks and fairy tales, not in real life.

All five of the kids backed up, and Jack glanced at Ronnie, wondering if he recognized his mother.

"What is it?" Paul said.

"I'm older than the stars," she hissed. "I've lived for centuries with no one finding out about me. I'm the last of a dead race." She looked at Jack, and the ice-blue eyes seemed to penetrate his guts. "I asked you to watch over Ronnie and you failed me. Now it all comes to an end."

"You're fucking crazy," Jack said.

"Come here, Ronnie," she said in her serpentine voice.

Ronnie backed up. "You're not my mom."

"Come here, sweetheart."

"Ronnie, don't," Jack said.

"Quiet, Jack. You'll die last," the Cassie-thing said.

Ronnie started forward. His eyes were glazed, his mouth slack. Perhaps she was clouding his mind. Jack had an idea.

He ripped the revolver from Chris's hand, threw an arm bar around Ronnie's throat, and put the gun to his head.

"What are you doing?" Chris said.

"Jack!" Emma said.

"Jack?" Ronnie said.

Jack whispered something in his ear. When he grabbed the gun, he had dropped his flashlight, but Paul still had his. "Paul, keep your light on her."

Paul lit up her face. She looked as if she wanted to eat Jack's guts out and have his bones for a second helping.

"Everybody back up," Jack said, and dragged Ronnie with him.

They followed Jack's lead, backing up to the wall, where the rotted timbers held up the ceiling. Chris bumped one of them and pebbles crumbled from the ceiling.

"Let my son go and I'll spare you," she hissed.

"I'll blow his fucking head off."

"Have you lost your mind?" Paul said.

"I know what I'm doing. Start kicking those timbers and get ready to run."

"That will bring the roof in," Emma said.

"Trust me," Jack said. "Come and get him, you bitch! I never liked him anyway."

Chris kicked the beam on the right and dust floated from the ceiling. Emma and Paul booted the support to the left and it groaned and squeaked.

"We're all going to die anyway, right? Let's bring the roof in. Ronnie dies first."

"Let him go," she said.

Jack pressed the barrel into Ronnie's temple. Ronnie said, "Be careful, Jack."

Now marble-sized stones fell from the ceiling and a cloud of dust floated through the chamber. A dry, dusty smell filled the air.

"Come on," Jack said.

"You have no idea how much you're about to suffer," she said.

She charged forward and Jack aimed the revolver at her and squeezed the trigger. His wrist jerked back and he dropped the gun.

Think it might have broken my wrist.

She stumbled, bleeding, but kept coming. Chris kicked his beam one last time, followed by Paul's and Emma's a moment later. He shoved Ronnie ahead and said, "Run!" He fell forward behind Ronnie.

Cassie lunged at him, but Chris came from behind and grabbed her, throwing her off balance and into the chamber. A rock the size of a bowling ball hit her in the head. Paul and Emma ran from the chamber as if it were on fire. Chris and Jack followed as the roof came in, pouring tons of stone on Cassie. Stone grated, the wood split with a crack, and a cloud rivaling ash from Vesuvius blew down the tunnel.

They all hacked and spat out dust. Jack felt as if he had swallowed half the Sahara and chased it with a dirt cocktail. He looked up at the ceiling, relieved that the rest of it held. Only the small end of the tunnel, the chamber portion, had been held up by the timbers.

Jack picked up his flashlight. He shone it in the chamber. A pile of splintered wood and rock stood seven feet high. Cassie's arm stuck out and the clawed hand twitched once and was still. He felt pity for the strange creature, so driven by the love of her son, yet so horrible underneath and capable of tremendous brutality. She had loved Ronnie, Jack was sure of that. But what was she and were did she come from?

He supposed the answer would stay buried under the rock.

Ronnie came up beside him and in a small voice said, "Was that really my mom?"

Jack didn't want to answer that one. Instead he put his arm around Ronnie and gave him a squeeze. "Let's get out of here."